MAYDAY!

Bursting out of the clouds, Rowan saw the three warships below. The next bank of cloud was rushing to meet him—then suddenly he was gasping for breath, staring through his prop, which was revolving more and more slowly...

The stark realization hit him: half his port wing was gone completely, and he was crashing. There was no sky or cloud anymore, just sea. He smelled burning and felt his left boot filling with blood.

Dear God, I'm hit! He released the canopy and gasped for breath in the bitter air as the sea rushed up to meet him. . . .

DOUGLAS REEMAN

WINGED ESCORT

A JOVE BOOK
PUBLISHED BY G.P. PUTNAM'S SONS
DISTRIBUTED BY JOVE PUBLICATIONS, INC.

To John Gellender
and
to members of the Fleet Air Arm past and present

This Jove book contains the complete
text of the original hardcover edition.
It has been completely reset in a typeface
designed for easy reading, and was printed
from new film.

WINGED ESCORT

A Jove Book / published by arrangement with
G. P. Putnam's Sons

PRINTING HISTORY
G. P. Putnam's Sons edition published 1975

Five previous paperback printings
Jove edition / September 1982
Second printing / March 1984

ISBN: 0-515-07634-1

Jove books are published by The Berkley Publishing Group,
200 Madison Avenue, New York, N.Y. 10016.
The words "A JOVE BOOK" and the "J" with sunburst
are trademarks belonging to Jove Publications, Inc.

PRINTED IN THE UNITED STATES OF AMERICA

Contents

He raised his fist and grinned,
I knew the sign.
Last one down sets up the pints.
And then they ran, those round black holes.
From near the tail. A perfect line
Of perforations straight to him.
The forward jerk, the smile transfixed.
That's when he wept, I watched him go,
A gentle roll, a twisting spiral trailing smoke.

They're all gone now, it's in the past.
It doesn't fill my mind except on days like this
And sometimes in the lonely night.
I wonder why they went?
They must have gone for something
Mustn't they?
They can't have gone for nowt!

Extract from: *I Watched Him Go* by Shaw Taylor

I

A Fresh Start

LIEUTENANT TIM ROWAN stood on the side of Gladstone Dock and studied the overhanging bulk of the aircraft carrier with something like apprehension.

Behind and around him the air was filled with all the usual noises, creaking gantrys, a clatter of dockside machinery, and the sloshing footsteps of workers and sailors alike as they bustled through a steady drizzle.

It was mid-July 1943, but this was Liverpool, where it always seemed to rain a great deal, and where war had left too deep a mark for people to think much of past summers.

Tim Rowan was twenty-six, but at this particular moment felt older, less sure of himself. It was often like this when you returned from leave, no matter how short the break, how elusive the ability to relax.

He ran his gaze critically along the newly painted ship's side from the high stem up across her flight deck, past the small, boxlike bridge, the 'island', and aft to where some oilskinned seamen were hosing down wood shavings from emptied crates.

She was not a *proper* aircraft carrier. Not by any stretch of the imagination. But then the war had gone on for so long that people were able to believe almost anything. Like his parents who slept every night beneath the frail stairs of their house in Surrey. Like the unending intake of naval recruits who accepted a one-time holiday camp as a training base, merely because of its flag and its uniforms, and the fact that they *believed* it.

Old paddle-steamers which had once plied between Southampton and the Isle of Wight with cheerful holidaymakers were now accepted as minesweepers or patrol vessels.

He walked slowly along the carrier's side towards a brow. On the deck stood a solitary lifebuoy on a varnished stand. Even the ship's name, H.M.S. *Growler*, sounded as if someone at the Admiralty had had to think of it in a hurry. Like the ship.

For *Growler* had been thrown together without much concern for style or beauty. With several others she had begun life in an American shipyard to become, it was thought, a freighter. Fate, and the desperate need for air cover over the battered and butchered Atlantic convoys, had decided otherwise.

To help plug the breach left by the losses of more gracious carriers early in the war, the conversion from freighter to warship had started. Now, with her flight deck and her blunt, uncompromising lines, there was little left of *Growler*'s original design.

Rowan watched the comings and goings of dockyard men and naval personnel up and down the two steep brows. It was a strange, unnerving feeling. As if he were an onlooker. As if none of these preoccupied-looking men could see him. He shivered inside his raincoat. *As if he were dead.*

He had been in the *Growler*, now officially classed as an escort carrier, for three months. Before that he had been in a heavy fleet carrier in the Mediterranean. And before that . . . He shook himself from his thoughts, shutting out the jumbled pictures which had made up his life since the outbreak of war.

Places and faces always stood out more than the ships. Norway, the burning ships, the exhausted retreating troops. The Mediterranean and Greece, Crete and beleaguered Malta. It was always an uphill fight. The faces rarely left him. Broad smiles to hide taut nerves. The expressions becoming set and grim, like strangers, as one by one the aircraft had rolled snarling along a carrier's deck, then off towards an horizon. He could barely recall the names of some of them, especially those who had not come back.

In H.M.S. *Growler* he had discovered an unexpected change. He was no longer a unit in a trained team. From the losses, and the growing requirements in every theatre of war, he had emerged a veteran. It was still hard to grasp. He did not *want* to accept it. It lessened the odds on living, they said.

They had done two big convoys in the North Atlantic, in the 'Gap', as it was termed, that vast seven hundred miles spread of mid-ocean between longitudes thirty and forty degrees west where land-based aircraft could not operate to any purpose from British or American fields. It was for the Gap, and similar areas, which had caused *Growler* and her consorts to be born.

After working up the new ship's company, learning each other's jobs and flying-on her two brood of aircraft, *Growler* had gone to show her paces in earnest.

An Atlantic convoy, eastbound or westbound, was something to make even the most hardened sailor take notice. Line upon patient line. Tired, rusty freighters, tall, proud grain ships, their histories as varied as the flags they flew against a common enemy. Two enemies, if you counted the Atlantic.

And from the air each convoy was even more inspiring. Soundless and terribly vulnerable when viewed through a racing prop, or a tear in the clouds.

When a ship was suddenly torpedoed it merely seemed to fall away, slowly and gracefully, while the space she had left closed up immediately and her companions of many days sailed on without stopping. Only amongst the lithe, angry escorts was there movement and hate. You could almost feel it from the sky.

Lieutenant Tim Rowan of the Royal Naval Volunteer Reserve, aged twenty-six, had seen it many times. For he was a fighter pilot.

During the last convoy an escorting corvette had hit a mine, a 'drifter', and had gone down in seconds. Had she seen and avoided the mine, *Growler* would most likely have taken her place, as she was close astern of the little escort. But the explosion had given the hull a good shaking, and after completing her patrols *Growler* had come into Liverpool, the headquarters of Western Approaches, for a quick lick of paint and an inspection to ensure her shaft was in no way damaged. For if she fought as a warship, *Growler*'s lower hull was still that of a freighter. One shaft, one propeller. It was something

3

to think about in a screaming Force Twelve in the Atlantic. Also something she had in common with her overworked aircraft, Rowan thought grimly. One prop between you and the deep blue sea.

He made up his mind and strode towards the brow, from the top of which the quartermaster and gangway sentry had been watching him curiously for some minutes.

Like starting for the first time. Anywhere. A new job. Beginning school. There would be different faces to adjust to, fresh jokes, more irritations and small things which had not bothered you at the beginning.

It was bad luck, everyone had said. He paused, one hand resting on the brow, his senses suddenly very alert and taut. Like wires.

On that last convoy a submarine had been reported on the surface by one of *Growler*'s hardy, two-winged Swordfish aircraft. She had been trailing oil and had not dived when sighted. It meant that the U-boat had probably been damaged in an earlier fight. She could even have been mauled by one of the convoy's own escorts.

Six Swordfish had been flown-off instantly, their crews grinning and giving the usual 'thumbs up' at the prospect of doing something definite instead of the endless round of patrols.

The plane which had given the sighting report had fallen silent. It had no doubt gone too near to the U-boat's ack-ack for safety. In thirty minutes after the scramble a blustery gale had lashed into the convoy with unexpected fury.

As dusk had closed around the plodding lines of ships Rowan had stood with his companions on one of the walkways which ran along either side of the flight deck, and despite the wind and bitter rain had waited and watched the blurred horizon. Only when the sea and sky had merged in black shadow did he go below. None of the Swordfish had returned. Lost, out of fuel, blinded by the storm, they had been unable to find their carrier.

Rowan sighed again. Yes, there would be quite a few new faces.

4

He hurried up towards the side party, raising his hand to the peak of his cap as his feet touched the steel deck. He shivered slightly. That was the trouble with *Growler*. She was all steel, with not much room for personal comfort. He glanced up. Except the flight deck, which unlike any carrier he had served in, was made of Oregon pine. It helped to ease the vessel's tophamper apparently. God help them if it caught fire.

He saw the O.O.D. watching him. New face number one.

The officer, a harassed-looking sub-lieutenant, asked irritably, 'Name, please?' He was already scanning his lists on the little desk, oblivious to the sentry's grin, the quartermaster's warning frown.

Rowan stripped off his crumpled raincoat.

'Tim Rowan. I belong here.'

'Well, I can't be expected to—'

The O.O.D's gaze darted rapidly from the pilot's wings stitched above the two wavy stripes on Rowan's left sleeve to the blue and white ribbon on his breast.

'I—I'm sorry.'

Rowan regarded him calmly. 'Not to worry. But take it easy, Sub, or some of the fliers aboard here will have you for breakfast.'

He walked into the bowels of the ship, feeling it surrounding him, swallowing him whole. He smiled. *Jonah is back*.

As usual, and despite the ship being in harbour, there was an air of purpose and activity in the great hangar, the huge expanse of steel, smells and din which ran beneath the flight deck. A few fitters and riggers were stooping and crawling with powerful lights around some of the tethered aircraft at the far end.

Any stranger or novice would think it so crowded with wings, jutting engines and propellers that nothing could ever be shifted to one of the two powerful lifts. And yet to Rowan it was only partly occupied. The Swordfish replacements would fly-on once the ship was at sea. Break them in the hard way.

5

He stood quite still, his eyes adjusting to the harsh inspection lamps, the strange shadows which loomed against the tall sides of the hangar deck.

A little apart from the other aircraft stood his own fighter. For a moment more he was able to forget what had passed, could ignore the smells of hot oil, the sharper tang of dope, like a girl's nail polish, as he studied his other, private world.

It was strange how she seemed to be watching him. Waiting for him. Rowan always thought of his fighter as she. Despite the fact she was labelled R for Roger in the squadron, and had his special name, Jonah, painted brightly on the engine cowling, her sex had never been in doubt.

He walked towards the smooth outline very slowly. R for Roger was a Seafire, and to almost anyone but the men who serviced or flew them, Seafires were the Navy's reflection of the land-based Spitfire. Fast, graceful, deadly, they looked totally out of place on an escort carrier's deck.

Rowan touched the starboard wing. It felt like ice under his fingers. He toyed with the idea of climbing up into the cockpit, but discarded it. He would wait until the right time, not push his luck. Besides, any watching mechanic might think he had at last gone round the bend. It happened often enough.

He made his way towards a companion ladder, past glaring red warnings about the dangers of smoking, of leaking fuel, of naked lights, everything. He sniffed out of habit. Unlike an airfield, a carrier was the one place you did *not* smell petrol. If you did it meant trouble, for when she was fully operational, her own and her aircrafts' tanks topped up with fuel, *Growler* was a floating bomb.

On the deck below it was unusually quiet. At sea, or when the bulk of the ship's company returned from home or local leave, it would be bedlam again. Including her Fleet Air Arm personnel, *Growler* carried some five hundred souls within her echoing, vibrating hull.

He walked past the vacant cabins with their heavy fireproof curtains. Only the captain and a few privileged officers had doors, which was a pity. After a patrol you needed as much privacy as possible to put your thoughts in order again.

He wondered how the captain liked his command. He had only met him a few times in the three months aboard. Working-up a new command was tough on everybody from commanding officer to stoker. But the captain carried the can if things went wrong.

There were varied views amongst the ship's company about *Growler*. On the whole, her advantages outweighed her faults. British ratings hated sharing their messes with those of other branches, but here, telegraphists and stokers, seamen and riggers, enjoyed one vast gleaming cafeteria, where the main galley served over four hundred meals three times a day, in hurricane or calm.

They also had a fine laundry, which all but some of the older hands accepted as better than dhobying clothes in a borrowed bucket, even if it was a Yankee custom.

The showers were good for everyone, but had been the one thing to make the captain show some sign of irritation. He had wanted a bath.

In the U.S. dockyard where the ship had been finally fitted out before being handed over to the Royal Navy the captain had asked that a bath should be fitted in his own quarters. The Americans had been helpful, understanding and considerate. But no bath. Escort carriers, like most American ships, had showers. It said so on the plan. The captain had given in gracefully, for the moment.

Rowan pushed aside the curtain of his own cabin and switched on the lights. Even now, in harbour, he could hear muted mutterings in the pipes across the deckhead, beneath his feet, everywhere. As if the ship was in constant conversation with another planet.

He looked at the three bunks. One would soon be occupied by his friend Bill Ellis, another Seafire pilot. The other would have a new owner.

Rowan glanced up at a brighter rectangle of paintwork above the third bunk where some thoughtful steward had removed one of Dick's lovely pin-ups. Poor old Dick had been in one of the Swordfish which had bought it in mid-Atlantic. It must be a terrible feeling. Flying on and on into nothing. Watching the gauges drop. Knowing that no one would see you go. Except your crew.

Rowan threw his cap on the bunk and ruffled his dark brown hair. That was the best of a fighter. You were on your own. Nobody to watch your doubts, your despair. You shared it only with the aircraft.

A tannoy squeaked in another passageway and announced harshly, 'D'you hear there! D'you hear there! The film show in the canteen tonight will be *Waggons West*. Duty part of the watch will muster at 2015 and rig cinema.' A pause, and then as an afterthought, 'Men under punishment to muster on the hangar deck.'

Rowan switched on the tap of a small bulkhead basin and waited for the usual vibrations and spitting drips to give way to piping-hot water. He was still thinking about something he had seen and heard in London. As he had waited for a train to begin the first leg of the journey back to Liverpool.

It had not been raining in London, in fact, the sky had been clear and ice-blue.

He had noticed that some would-be passengers, several of them servicemen, were shading their eyes to watch some tiny vapour trails high above the bomb-scarred city. So high, so fragile had they looked from the station that they had hung almost motionless on their blue field.

Then he had heard it. Just briefly. The *tap-tap-tap-tap* of machine guns, almost lost in the noises around him, distant and impartial.

One of the onlookers had shouted, 'Got the bugger! See the bastard drop!'

Rowan had looked at them and then back to the sky. *See the bastard drop*. The man had spoken of the plane. Perhaps that was what made them different. They were the aircraft, good or bad, according to country, like the men who would be fighting in the cowboy film in the canteen tonight.

Perhaps that unknown onlooker had the right idea, Rowan thought. Better not to see your enemy's face, recognise him as a living person like you.

Rowan had seen it twice. The head jerking round in the cockpit to see him for the first time. The second German had even dragged off his goggles as if unable to accept that it was

8

his and not somebody else's turn to die. *See the bastard drop*.

'Nice to have you back, sir.'

Ede, one of the stewards, was peering in at him.

'Good run ashore?'

Rowan threw off his jacket and loosened his tie.

'Fair.'

He thought of the leave. Night was the best part. Their house was on the edge of Oxshott Woods. Every night he had lain on his bed below the window, despite all his mother's pleas for him to join her and his father under the stairs.

Each night had been the same. He had heard the wind hissing through the great trees, like surf on shingle. Like the unspoiled dream when you saw the girl walking towards you through the same surf. The perfect girl.

But the rest had been strained. Wherever he went people had asked him about the war, without wanting an answer. Not that he would have known how to reply to their questions, which had varied from Russia to the anticipated Second Front, from clothes rationing to bombing.

Some attitudes had confused and vaguely angered him. The war had gone badly for a long while. In the Navy alone many fine ships had gone to the bottom, while on land the army had had limited success and too much stalemate.

But this year, 1943, there was already a fresh mood. The Germans had been driven out of North Africa, Field Marshal Rommel's magic had been broken. Only this month, the Allies had followed it up with that first vital step with landings all along the coasts of Sicily. It would be Italy next, and then . . .

Perhaps he should have gone with Bill Ellis to London. Not tell their parents or friends where they were going. As Bill had urged, 'Live a bit, Tim. Just in case.'

In the same bedroom which he had grown up from schoolboy to naval lieutenant, with not much in between, Rowan had thought of Bill's words as he had listened to the wind across Oxshott Woods, and to old Simon's unsteady breathing beside him on the bed. Simon, once a big black dog, now rather grey and almost blind, had never left him. It had been like being the schoolboy again.

9

But then life got harder to fathom, he thought. He recalled the people in the village pub, and then thought of that special Seafire on the deck somewhere above his head. *Why me?*

He looked at himself in the misty glass by the basin. Dark, unruly hair, with level brown eyes which seemed to watch him like a newcomer. Tall, slim, and very ordinary, he decided.

Ede said helpfully, 'Like a cuppa, sir? The rush'll be on in a jiffy.'

Rowan turned and looked at him, his sadness falling away as he replied, 'A cuppa would be just fine.'

The steward winked. 'Never fails, sir.' He bustled away, whistling to himself.

In the pantry at the end of the long passageway, and which adjoined the great tin box of *Growler*'s wardroom, Ede found Petty Officer Grist, his lord and master, busily counting wardroom cutlery.

'Lost something, P.O.?' Ede kept his face averted as he reached for a clean teapot. He knew damn well that the petty officer steward occasionally stole some of the better pieces of cutlery to pass to his oppo in the engineroom, an artificer who had a good racket going for him. He carved and welded forks and spoons into nice little brooches of anchors and aircraft before selling them to the sailors for their girl friends.

Grist looked at him suspiciously. 'Just checkin'.' He saw the teapot. 'One of 'em's back aboard then?'

'Mr Rowan.' Ede swilled hot water round the pot. 'Nice bloke. For an officer.'

Grist nodded. ' 'E 'ad a rough time a year or so back. I was in the same ship. 'Is plane caught fire. 'E came down in the drink. Bad do, it was.'

Ede frowned, remembering how Rowan moved his shoulders sometimes. The way he sat for long periods in his cabin. Saying nothing. Staring into space.

Grist bared his teeth in a grim smile. 'Tell you somethin' to cheer your Mr Rowan up, I *don't* bloody think. We are shippin' an admiral aboard for the next trip, so you'll 'ave to watch it, my boy.'

Ede looked at the cutlery. *So will you, mate*. He said,

'That's good. They never send admirals anywhere dangerous!'

In his spacious day cabin Captain Bruce Buchan sat in a red leather armchair and waited for his steward to close the door behind him. The chair was almost the only article he had brought with him when he had assumed command of *Growler*, and it gave him some small pleasure when he noticed how its homely polished glow was always at odds with the plain paintwork and steel furniture around him.

Across a small table from him his wife was stirring a cup of tea, her eyes lost in thought.

Buchan had turned forty, and was prematurely grey, so that as he sat very upright in his red chair, his thickset body clothed in his best uniform, he had the appearance of an old master mariner of earlier days.

He often thought about his age. Others he knew who had entered the Navy as tender twelve-year-olds just before that other war seemed to carry their age better. Some were very senior, one a full admiral. Others, because of misfortune, or because of being out of the Service for some while between the wars, were holding down exciting appointments in various parts of the world. It was no consolation to realise that quite a few were dead, too.

His wife said quietly, 'Off again then, Bruce.'

Buchan regarded her tenderly. She had aged more than she should since he had last seen her.

He said, 'I've got a good bunch, Ellen. Most of 'em are pretty green, but I've had a lot worse.'

She dropped her eyes. 'And better.'

He stared. It was unusual for her to show such bitterness. Perhaps she blamed him?

He saw her glance up at the picture on the opposite bulkhead. The *Camilla*, a light cruiser, at full speed. His last command before *Growler*. Even in the photograph you could easily see the commodore's broad pendant standing out like a sheet of metal as she tore through the water. *Commodore of Destroyers*.

Buchan heard himself say wearily, 'Things may have

changed, dear.' He did not really believe it.

His commodore had been Lionel Chadwick, a ball of fire, as everyone agreed. They had been together at Dartmouth, competitors in regattas and reviews in almost every port and naval base you could think of. Not friends ever. But the Royal Navy was a family, and ships and men always crossed one another's paths repeatedly. Never far away.

He looked at the closed signal log on his desk. His petty officer was a very neat man. Everything in its place, peace or war.

He had received the lengthy signal a week ago. Orders, instructions about new personnel, and of course the bit about receiving the flag of a rear admiral to assume overall control of a new Air Support Group. Two escort carriers, sloops, everything.

It should have been a proud moment, especially for one such as Buchan who had been forced to quit the Navy during the depression and find his living away from the one calling he understood.

But Rear Admiral Lionel Chadwick, C.B. and D.S.O., would never allow it to rest. Buchan could see his face at the court of enquiry as if it were yesterday instead of eighteen months ago. Fresh and clear-eyed, *a ball of fire*.

He could even hear his crisp voice, see the line of grave-faced officers along the table with its baize cloth.

Little phrases stood out in his mind like gunfire. *Did his best. Under the circumstances could not carry the blame. However.* That last word, *however*, buried all the rest.

The loss of the *Camilla*, the severe damage to the ship with which she had collided, the deaths of several seamen were not laid directly at Buchan's door. But Chadwick's evidence, his *however*, made certain that he would never rise to higher command.

The months which had passed had been a nightmare. A meaningless office job in a minesweeping depot, something he knew nothing about. Command of a small training base for salvage teams. There his instructors had known far more than he, and had probably regarded him as one more misfit, left behind by a war for which he had never been prepared.

And then out of the blue had come *Growler*. He had, it appeared, some friends left at the Admiralty who had not forgotten him after all. It was typical of Buchan not to accept that he had been appointed because he knew his job, and there were too few of his sort for far too many appointments.

It had been like starting again. Over to America to see his ship being completed. A lively, exciting America after the dull ritual of nightly air raids, shortages and an enemy which stood just a few miles across the English Channel.

The ship might be ugly, difficult to handle in confined spaces because of her single screw and vast hull which took any sort of wind like a sail, but she was alive, and *needed*.

Buchan was 'old navy' through and through, but he was intelligent enough to realise that he had to accept a compromise. The young, untidy hostilities-only officers and ratings who flew and maintained the ship's aircraft were like nothing he had known before. Youthful and scruffy they might be, but he had been proud to watch them taking off around the clock to patrol the crawling convoys. *As regular as a good bus service*, his chief engineer had remarked.

His wife said huskily, 'That man will never give you any peace.'

Buchan smiled sadly. She never referred to Chadwick by name.

She added, 'It was not your fault, Bruce. It was proved at the enquiry. But for that man it would never—'

He stood up. 'I was in command. It was my decision. Maybe it was the wrong one. Sometimes I'm not sure any more.'

He heard an order being piped over the tannoy. The squeal of a winch somewhere on the flight deck. The carpet under his brightly polished shoes gave a little tremble. One of the Chief's generators. Part of the chain. His ship.

Buchan glanced at the brass clock. Edgar Jolly, the commander, would be along soon. To discuss arrangements for tomorrow. Sailing orders. Anything else which might cross his mind. He quite liked Jolly, his second in command. Dark, handsome, eager. It was to be hoped that having an admiral aboard would not affect him too much. He frowned. Better tell him to inspect the quarters which were being allocated and repainted for the new arrival.

Admirals, even junior ones, took up a lot of room with their fads and fancies.

She said, 'I'd better leave now, Bruce,' She always knew.

'Yes, dear.' He watched her. Her uncertainty. The acceptance that she could not share this part of him. 'I'll be home soon. You see.'

She laid her head on his chest and he held her against him. She felt rather frail, but had that fresh smell of flowers. What he remembered when he had first met her at Cowes. A young lieutenant. A pretty girl in a blue dress and big floppy hat.

'Take care, Bruce.'

There was a discreet tap at the door. It was over.

The staff car hissed along a stretch of shining road, the windscreen wipers barely able to cope with the steady rain.

Rear Admiral Lionel Chadwick pressed his foot harder on the accelerator pedal and ignored the stiff anxiety of the marine driver beside him. He loved anything fast which he could control. Cars, horses, yachts, planes. He grinned as a man on a bicycle swerved away and almost fell into a ditch. And of course women.

His little party of aides had gone on ahead, which suited him very well. Only Godsal, his elegant flag lieutenant, was with him, trying to appear relaxed in the back seat while his admiral drove north to Liverpool like a man possessed.

It was difficult for Chadwick to describe his own feelings. Elation, excitement, even a sense of mischief perhaps. It was like part of a great game. If you survived each move, you planned the next, and so on. Only the timid stood fast, or went under.

He grinned again. *Poor old Bruce Buchan. I'll bet he choked when he saw the signal.*

One of Chadwick's friends, and he had a great many, had suggested he was making a mistake in accepting his new appointment so readily. Something at the Admiralty would be vacant shortly. Chadwick had the sort of friends who knew such things, who could decide if they wanted to accept or refuse jobs. Who understood 'the game'.

But Chadwick had laughed at him. Behind a desk? Signing stupid signals and memoranda about clothing issue to Wren cooks? Not bloody likely!

He glanced briefly at the wings on his sleeve. He had not flown a naval aircraft for many years, although he had owned a private one since he was in his twenties. He might get a chance to show some of his new command a thing or two.

He stamped on the brakes and said briskly, 'I'll get out. Take over.'

Chadwick stood beside the car letting the drizzle fall across his upturned face and immaculate uniform. He was quite tall, but had the broad shoulders of an athlete which made him appear heavier than he was. His dark hair was brushed straight back, not a strand out of place. He had long side-burns which by comparison were almost white against his tanned skin. A woman in Plymouth had commented on them one night.

'Easier to see in the dark,' he had said as he had reached for the bedside lamp.

Godsal, the flag lieutenant, was watching him through the wet glass. His admiral never seemed to tire. Was never short of ideas on almost everything. Sometimes he got impatient and snapped, 'Oh *you* sort it out, man! God help you if you foul it up!'

He studied Chadwick's upturned face, the wide mouth and steady grey eyes. If only half the things he had heard about him were true, he would have to be on his toes.

A friend had said, 'Stick with him and you'll really get somewhere. But he'll work the arse off you if he can.'

The nearside door slammed and the marine driver let in the clutch very smoothly, breathing out as he did so.

Chadwick grinned at him. 'I'll bet *that* got you going, eh?'

'Yes, sir.' The marine kept his eyes on the road. He liked his job driving a staff car. If he told the admiral what he really thought, he would not hold the job more than ten seconds.

Chadwick knew exactly what the man was thinking and grinned more broadly. That's what they all needed to fight and win a war. A damn good jolt.

He thought of his new appointment, an Air Support Group, an excellent idea already being bogged down by conventional, suburban thinking.

He leaned back and closed his eyes. He would change all that.

2

Replacements

THE *Growler*'s Ready Room was on the gallery deck, as was every other department vital to the running of the ship and her aircraft. It was the big, cheerless space where the pilots, observers and air gunners sat around in the slingback seats which were supposed to relax you while you waited for the signal. The order to 'scramble'.

Apart from a desk, a couple of blackboards and a locked cabinet, there was little to betray its importance. To the officers who sat or lounged in it this morning, chatting and smoking, flipping through magazines and newspapers, items such as the gramophone and dartboard were of far greater importance.

Rowan had his fingers laced behind his head as he stared up at the deckhead. It was the forenoon, and in the steel box it was already like a Turkish bath. He had slept badly on his first night back. Not because of his dreams, but also because of his friend, Bill Ellis. He had returned aboard late. Noisily drunk, and persistently apologetic about it as he had reeled about the cabin trying to free himself of his trousers and cannoning into the unyielding metal furniture. That had brought more anger and curses. From Bill, and from those in adjoining cabins who had threatened to 'fill him in' if he did not pipe down.

Rowan twisted his head and looked at his friend. Ellis was huge and blond, like a great bear. A rugby forward of some renown before joining the Navy, he was a good man to have beside you in an argument. When he was in his full flying gear it was surprising that he could move in the cockpit of his beloved Seafire.

Rowan smiled. Despite his power and size, Ellis was a gentle type for most of the time. He was sitting back in his chair, wearing his dark glasses, which most pilots donned before going out on to an unlit deck at night. Except that this was a bright July forenoon, *Growler* was still in Gladstone Dock, and Ellis's mouth had fallen wide open. He was sleeping off his leave while there was still time.

He shifted his glance to the others. All of them he knew. Some over the weeks. A few on and off for several years. One of the latter was Lieutenant Dymock Kitto. He had flown a lot before the war. Stunt pilot, trips round the bay at a quid a time, part-time mercenary in China. He had got plenty into his life. Very swarthy, with a cleft chin which was like blue steel within an hour of shaving.

Ian Cameron, another R.N.V.R. lieutenant, sat thumbing through a catalogue of something or other. He was a first-class fighter pilot, and had shot down a big Focke-Wulf and two German seaplanes in one month. Thin as a stick, with a drawling accent of a music hall marquis. His crew called him 'Lord Algy', but in fact he had been in his father's furniture business.

Apart from those three, the squadron commander and himself, the rest were competent, apparently keen, but as yet unchallenged.

He looked at the latest to join the ship, just after the first convoy. Two sub-lieutenants, Mariot and Creswell. Very, very young, with that smooth freshness which always made them appear vulnerable.

Andy Miller, the squadron commander, strode through from the Air Operations Room, and before he could close the door Rowan heard the usual hum of plots and static from receivers as the round-the-clock watch went on.

Lieutenant Commander Miller, 'Dusty' to his friends, was a square man. He had a jutting black beard, and when he was wearing his flying helmet looked like the devil himself. But he was very professional, even though he had been a market gardener prior to the war.

'Hello, Tim.' He waved his hands as Rowan made to rise. 'Just looking in to see if all my yokels are present and—' he paused and glanced scornfully at the lounging figures, 'and *correct*, I was going to say.'

Most of the men around him were in their usual assortment of dress. Grey flannel trousers, battledress blouses or old monkey jackets with the gold lace almost black and crumbling with wear. Battered caps or woollen, home-made efforts, anything went in the Ready Room.

Rowan asked, 'When are we sailing, sir?'

Miller shrugged. 'Tomorrow. It *was* tomorrow yesterday, if you catch my meaning.'

Rowan grinned. He liked Miller. He had done it all. Chased the battleship *Bismarck*, and had been shot down twice. He had flown raids over Taranto, North Africa, just about everywhere that a carrier could take him.

Miller added, 'The admiral's aboard. Slipped in with barely a whisper. The commander told me that he liked it that way. Tries to catch people on the hop.'

Rowan considered the idea of an admiral on board his own ship. Did it mean, as some thought, that *Growler* was going to some dull billet? Or would it imply that something special was being hatched?

'Anyway.' Miller looked at the watch on his thick wrist. 'He's coming here to speak with all of you shortly. That's why you're here instead of wandering up and down the walkways shooting lines at each other.' He sounded irritated. 'I hate speeches.' He held the watch to his ear as he always did.

Even the watch had a story. Miller had been shot down over the channel and had dropped into the sea almost alongside the German pilot he had himself brought down. The German had been in a bad way. Bleeding and dying in his little rubber dinghy as Miller had swum to join him and await rescue.

For three hours he had done all he could to ease the other pilot's last moments on earth. The man had been delirious for much of the time and had called out a woman's name. Wife, girlfriend, sister, who could say?

Even as an air/sea rescue launch had ploughed towards them the German had died. But in his final minutes he had realised that Miller had tried to help him, and had dragged off his watch, thrusting it at him with a fierce desperation which

19

had just as swiftly frozen the eagerness on his face like a mask.

Miller was looking at the watch now. 'It's got his name on the back. I may go and hand it over to somebody one day.'

Bill Ellis said without opening his eyes, 'Like bloody hell you will! You'll be after the poor bastard's widow, more likely!' His mouth split into a grin. *'Sir.'*

Miller grunted. 'Oaf!' He walked to the door. 'He'll be here in about five minutes.'

Ellis dragged off his dark glasses and rubbed his eyes. 'Who? *God?*'

'The admiral.' Rowan felt for his pipe but decided against it. The air in the Ready Room was foul and quite unmoving.

'Oh.' Ellis was unimpressed. 'I'll bet he's an old dear with an ear trumpet and two gorgeous Wrens to push him round the flight deck in his bath chair!'

The door banged open and Lieutenant Commander Eric Villiers, *Growler*'s Commander (Flying), peered in at them.

Just as Commander Jolly was responsible to the captain for the state of the ship and her efficiency, so was Villiers responsible for the flying and air maintenance personnel.

Rowan had served under him before. Villiers had been a senior pilot while he had been as green as grass. He had been everyone's idea of an ace, confident, level-eyed, efficient. Yet with that touch of recklessness which had singled him out as a leader.

Rowan watched him gravely. In the years between something had gone badly wrong for Villiers. His eyes were dull and his shoulders looked stooped. Everyone knew Villiers had crashed in the sea near Tobruk and had been taken prisoner. For a whole year he had been out of circulation, and then one night in the North Sea a patrolling Asdic trawler had challenged a Danish fishing boat. It had been crewed by members of the Resistance, and after unloading their passengers, several escaped prisoners of war, they had returned to Denmark to risk their lives all over again. One of the exhausted passengers had been Villiers.

He snapped, 'Stand by, all of you.'

There was a shuffling of feet and scraping of chairs, and

then Rear Admiral Chadwick appeared in the entrance.

Rowan studied him curiously. Chadwick was much younger than he had expected, but then he had only seen a few senior officers, and at a distance. This one looked very alert, extremely sharp. He smiled. No bath chair.

At his back the captain and Commander Jolly kept a discreet distance.

'Sit down, gentlemen.' Chadwick placed his beautiful cap with its double line of oak leaves around the peak, squarely on the desk. 'I won't keep you long.'

He took a few paces towards them and halted. He almost shone against the dull paint, the scribbled notes on the blackboards.

'I am getting to meet each section in turn. With the captain's *permission*,' he turned and shot Buchan a broad smile, 'I will meet the ship's other officers in the wardroom later, and the new squadron officers, the *replacements*, when they fly-on at sea. Some of you will have heard the rumour, the "buzz",' again the ready smile, 'that we are all part of a new Air Support Group. This is true. What you will not be told outside of this command is that it is going to be the *best of its kind*.'

One arm shot out, a finger pointing at the youngest pilot, Sub-Lieutenant Frank Creswell. The arm was quite rigid, the one inch of white shirt, the gleaming stripes of gold, one thick, one thin, above it, like part of a perfect machine.

'How old are *you*?'

Creswell lurched to his feet, blushing wildly, a copy of *Men Only* falling from his battledress blouse and bringing a spread of chuckles all around him.

'N-nineteen, sir.' Creswell looked as if he wanted to vanish.

'Well.' Chadwick seemed satisfied. 'Sit down again.' He looked slowly round the room. 'When I was his age I was also flying a machine of sorts.' He tapped the wings on his sleeve. 'I was too late to fight in the Great War, but I flew just about every kind of sortie and patrol before I quit that side of the Service and went on a staff course.' He let the words sink in. 'I learned to do every side of an officer's duties. I don't give a tinker's damn if you're an engineer or paymaster, pilot or bloody marine, I expect every one of you to be first and foremost a *naval officer*!'

His voice had become very loud, or to Rowan it appeared so. Perhaps it was because of this metal box of a room, and the fact that every man present seemed to be holding his breath in front of this compelling admiral.

'I am not blaming you, or any member of this ship's company. Not yet. But I intend that this new group, *my* group, is going to be of real use in the war, not just one more idea that is going to go off half-cock because some bonehead at the top doesn't know what to do with it.'

Rowan could sense the tension around him, the resentment, the hostility.

Chadwick added sharply, 'In the first year or so of this war, I suspect that more British servicemen were killed because of stupid leadership than by anything the enemy could do to them.' He had their full attention now. 'Ships and men are not always lost by bad luck, they are thrown away by incompetence or plain ignorance. Capital ships sent inshore without air cover cost us command of the sea in Malaya and Singapore when we most needed it. It cost us an army, fine ships.' He dropped his grey eyes for the first time. 'And one *hell* of a lot of honour.'

He glanced at the bulkhead clock. 'I expect you to make mistakes. Once. Only rear admirals are allowed to make more than that.' Nobody laughed. 'But in the end we will have something to show for it. And God help you if you foul it up.' He smiled calmly. 'I just wanted to have a look at you. To make my number. Thank you, gentlemen.' He made as if to leave as once again they all rose to their feet.

'One more thing and then I'll not mention it again. When you are waiting to fly, to fight if need be, you can dress as you please. In port, and on all other occasions, I want you to dress like members of the Service.' He paused, balanced on his toes as if to fight off their obvious anger.

He added softly, 'When you see your admiral walking the bridge with his arse hanging out of his trousers and a day's growth on his chin, you can do likewise!'

Creswell's youthful face opened into a great smile, and some of the others laughed, caught out completely by Chadwick's bluntness.

Rowan watched, not wanting to miss a second. What sort of man was this? An actor? A gifted leader? He looked at the captain, but his features gave nothing away. They were like stone.

The admiral turned about and removed his cap from the desk all in one economical movement. Then the door was closed, the visitors gone, and for a moment they all stood as before, as if under some kind of spell.

Kitto rubbed his blue chin furiously. 'Well, I'll go to the top of our stairs!' He looked at Rowan and Ellis. 'What sort of a Napoleon have we got now?'

His voice broke the silence, and the room swelled with confused and noisy conversation.

Cameron drawled, 'He has a *point*, of course.'

Kitto glared at him. 'Pipe down, Algy. I've come a *long* way, taken too many short cuts, to be talked down to like a kid on his first day at school!'

Ellis watched Rowan, his eyes questioning. 'You're very quiet, Tim.'

'I'm not sure about him.' Rowan wondered at his own feelings. Uncertainty. Apprehension perhaps. 'You go on for months on end. Flying, worrying, playing the fool.' He saw some of the newer pilots moving in to listen. 'You don't think much about the pattern.' He smiled awkwardly. 'The *war*.'

Ellis nodded. 'All separate bits and pieces, you mean.'

'Something like that. Perhaps our new admiral is a sign of the times. A fresh mind to put right earlier mistakes.'

Rolston, a tall, gangling lieutenant known for his short temper, said, 'He'll have us in cocked hats and frock coats if we let him! Stupid bugger!'

Cameron eyed him mildly. 'It'd make a change.'

Ellis touched Rowan's arm. 'Let's go on deck.' He gestured to the noisy throng around him. 'This is no use.'

Together they wandered along the starboard walkway, hands in pockets, watching the continuous activity of men and vehicles on the dockside.

It was strange. Rowan thought, to look out over Liverpool, to feel so detached even though the ship was motionless. The gaunt overhead railway and the grey roofs of the houses and sheds were below the level of the flight deck. Bombed buildings, puddles left by the night's rain. It was a dismal place.

Ellis said, 'I'm not sorry to be going out again. I don't much care where.'

Rowan glanced at him. He sounded unusually serious.

Ellis added, 'In London it was like another existence. I met this girl. A Czech who works with her people at their embassy. Some bloody fool I knew in Devonport introduced us at a party. *A pushover*, he said.' He gave a great sigh. 'And we think *we've* got troubles.'

Rowan leaned on a stanchion. 'Nice girl?'

'She knows London better than I do.' Ellis was thinking aloud. 'Took me to restaurants and a club where her own people go. It was all so—' he searched for the right words, 'different, so bloody sad. Here they are in Britain, fighting alongside us, their own country occupied by the Krauts, and God alone knows what is happening to their friends and families. Yet they can still put on a cheerful front. Make you welcome *in your own country*.'

Rowan tried to shake him out of it. '*Did* you win her over?'

Ellis nodded. 'She won me. Utterly. She's got a husband somewhere. Doesn't even know if he's still alive. Christ, what a bloody mess it all is!'

He looked at Rowan's grave profile. 'What about you? Good leave?'

'Not really.' It was easy to be frank with him.

Ellis slapped his shoulder. 'We're a right pair. Next time we'll—'

'Yes.' Rowan fell in step beside him. 'Next time.'

Captain Buchan tucked his cap under his arm and stepped into the freshly-painted quarters which the admiral had occupied. They had been built into the carrier's structure for just such a purpose, or to be used as an additional operations area should the ship be used at some later date as a command vessel. They looked spartan, unlived in, even by *Growler*'s standards.

Chadwick looked up from his new desk. 'Yes?'

Buchan saw Godsal, the flag lieutenant, writing in a large file by an open scuttle, and at another table Lieutenant Commander James, the Operations Officer, was initialling a whole list of neatly typed signals.

Buchan said formally, 'Ready to get under way in about half an hour, sir.'

Chadwick nodded, his features very composed. 'Good. Fine.' He looked at the others. 'A Scotch, I think.'

Godsal opened a cabinet and started to fumble with some glasses as Chadwick asked, 'Satisfied with everything, Bruce?'

Buchan stared at him, caught out by the use of his first name. He had been with the admiral almost continuously since he had slipped aboard. *Since yesterday.* It felt ten times as long. But their conversation had been entirely confined to matters relating to the ship, the group, the state of readiness, anything but personal. Chadwick had been like a whirlwind. He had spoken to the ship's officers, all of them, from the executive ones to the engine-room staff and the paymaster's branch. Whenever he had met a seaman, or any other rating during his fast-moving tours throughout the ship, Chadwick had snapped, 'What's your name? What do *you* do?' Buchan did not know how his company had reacted to this sort of brisk informality, but it had certainly left its mark.

He replied, 'I think so, sir.'

'Good.' Chadwick reached out, taking a glass from his aide. Knowing it was there. Expecting it. 'Well, she's your baby, as our Transatlantic friends would say.' He tossed back the glass. 'Down the hatch.' He slid the glass across the desk towards Godsal and the decanter. 'By the way, what time do we rendezvous with our other carrier?'

James, the Operations Officer, said quickly, 'Eighteen hundred, sir. *Hustler* is also flying-on some replacements.'

'Hmm.' Chadwick swirled the whisky round his glass. 'Have you informed the escort commander of all the problems?'

'Of course, sir.'

James dropped his eyes as Chadwick snapped, 'Of course *nothing*! Take nothing for granted, right?'

James glanced unhappily at Buchan. 'Right, sir.'

Chadwick sighed. 'Perhaps you gentlemen would continue your work in the office. My secretary has a few details to clear before the postman nips ashore.' He gave a slow smile as they downed their drinks and hurried away.

Alone with Buchan he said, 'Got to watch 'em. Especially James. About as much idea of convoy protection as my aunt.'

Buchan said quietly, 'I've always found him very helpful, sir.'

'Really?' Chadwick eyed him coolly. 'We shall see.'

Buchan could feel the old anger returning like a wound throbbing in his chest. Chadwick sitting there, relaxed, watching him, mocking him.

He said, 'He's been the Ops Officer since I took command, sir. I think I know him pretty well.'

Chadwick gestured to a chair. 'Sit down.' He slopped two generous measures of whisky into the glasses. 'Now listen. I want, no I *demand* loyalty of all my officers. Likewise I do not expect them to love me. Not all the time.' He held the glass to a shaft of watery sunlight from a scuttle. 'And I do not wish to be treated as a complete cretin.'

'Sir?'

'I have been aboard for twenty-four hours. Not much, I agree. In that time I have found several weaknesses, a few things which together we can put right.' He placed the glass on the desk. 'Did you know, for instance, that your Commander (Flying), er, Villiers, has had treatment for mental trouble?'

'I heard he had a bad time as a prisoner of war, sir.'

Chadwick ignored him. 'And James, the Operations Officer of whom you think so highly, did you know he had a German wife?'

Buchan swallowed hard. 'Well, as it happens, sir, no, I did not, but—'

'But you did not think it mattered, eh?' Chadwick stood up, his dark hair almost brushing a deckhead fan. 'Believe me, everything matters if you want to stay alive, to *win*.'

Outside the cabin a tug hooted mournfully, and on one of the walkways somebody was dragging a length of mooring wire.

Buchan found that he too was on his feet. 'I realise that. I also know there's a *way* of winning.'

Chadwick picked up a pair of brand-new binoculars and walked to a scuttle.

'Like cricket, you mean?'

'Look, sir, it's not my fault we're in the same ship.'

Chadwick trained his glasses on a Wren officer who had come out of a nearby dock building to look up at the carrier.

'Nice legs,' he said absently. Then. 'No, it's mine. I knew about this new group ages ago. I *asked* for you to be appointed.'

Buchan stared at him, his one prop already falling away. 'You?'

'Correct. I don't like amateurs. I also dislike yes-men. I think you are neither. Remember, you have served under me before, I know a *lot* about you.' He turned, his eyes hidden in shadow. 'Do your job, and we'll get along fine.' A telephone buzzed in the outer office. 'That will be Commander Jolly, I expect. I told him to put calls through to you here.'

Buchan felt the deck quivering gently, and pictured Laird, the Commander (E), far below his feet in his shining, roaring domain of pumps and machinery, and his one great propeller shaft. The ship was almost ready to cut her ties with the land, and yet Chadwick seemed to hold him like a trap.

He was being manipulated, just like the last time. The reliable subordinate when things went well. The scapegoat if they did not.

Chadwick urged gently, 'Forget the past. I have. It can serve neither of us. Our responsibility is to the ship and the group. It is a weapon, not a way of life. Results are more

27

important than ideals. In war you get no thanks for being a brave loser.'

'Is that all, sir?' Buchan barely recognised his own voice.

'I think so. I will come up once we are clear of the Bar lightship. Let me know when our escort are on station.'

When Buchan had left he returned to the scuttle, but the Wren officer had disappeared.

The hull was shaking more urgently now, and he could hear the rasp of orders across the tannoy, the bustle of a ship about to leave harbour.

A small steam engine was puffing down a dockside railway line, and cloth-capped workers were already moving towards the bollards and sagging mooring wires in response to an important-looking man in a bowler hat.

Dundas, his personal chief steward, slid into the cabin and replaced the decanter in its cabinet.

'Going to the bridge, sir?'

He was a severe-faced man, like an old-time executioner, Chadwick thought. But he was an excellent servant, and after the war he would try and hold on to him. Ford, the butler at Chadwick's country house, was old and almost past it. Dundas might make a good replacement.

'I think so.'

Dundas handed him a gleaming white scarf which he wrapped negligently around his throat. Then he put two tablets and a glass of water on the table. The scarf would present the right effect. The tablets would take away the smell of whisky.

Chadwick smiled. Oh yes, Dundas knew his requirements very well indeed.

Rowan climbed the last few steps to the upper bridge and paused to get his breath. He wished now he had done more walking and less brooding on his leave.

In the hours it had taken for *Growler* to work free of the port area and then head purposefully out to sea the weather had changed considerably. There was a lot of low cloud, and he could tell without consulting the met. officer that the wind was getting up, too. He stared up at the bright new flag which streamed from *Growler*'s steel lattice mast. Red cross on white ground, with a red ball in top and bottom cantons. It must be an impressive feeling to be an admiral, he thought.

He always liked visiting the bridge. Like the rest of the ship it lacked grace. A rectangular tower which contained the charthouse, the helmsmen, the signal platform. Above it, apart from the stubby mast, was the radar lantern, a searchlight, and little else. *Growler* had no funnel like her big consorts, but a large vent on either side of the hull which did the work just as well, if less artistically.

He saw Commander (Flying) at his station on one wing of the bridge, shoulders hunched, his cap pulled hard down over his eyes.

The captain was sitting on his high steel chair, which was welded to the deck where he could keep an eye on everyone.

Rowan peered over the glass screen and down at the flight deck. It looked huge, like a great planked field. But at four hundred and a few odd feet long it was half the size of a big carrier. From the air it was minute. As Ellis had once commented when they had started, *it's like trying to land a bedstead on a postage stamp!*

He saw the Deck Landing Control Officer in his bright orange smock talking with some of his men. 'Bats', as he was called, would be doubly vital today with the new aircraft arriving.

The walkways were filled with the handling parties, the firefighting teams, and he could see Minchin, the senior doctor, watching with the others. Just in case.

How grey the Irish Sea looked, with endless thousands of tiny white horses stretching out and away towards the horizon. Ahead, and on either quarter, an escort of three sloops were keeping their allotted stations. All veterans of Western Approaches, their low hulls were streaked with rust as evidence of long months on convoy duty.

Far astern there was the fatter silhouette of the rescue tug. They had thought of everything.

Villiers turned and looked at him. 'Ah, there you are, Tim.'

Villiers always liked a pilot with him whenever possible.

Anyone who was not on stand-by was expected to put in an appearance, to observe the other side of the coin. As an understudy perhaps.

The tannoy squeaked and intoned, 'Hands to flying stations! Stand by to receive aircraft!'

The captain turned in his chair. He was muffled in a duffle coat, a thick scarf round his neck. He looked like a rock.

Villiers nodded. 'Ready, sir.'

Buchan gave what might have been a smile. 'Make the signal to escort commander.' He ignored the bustle on the platform, the bright bundles of bunting breaking out stiffly to the wind.

'Starboard fifteen.'

Through the voicepipe came the coxswain's acknowledgement. 'Starboard fifteen, sir. Fifteen of starboard wheel on.'

Rowan watched fascinated as the forward end of the flight deck started to swing very slowly into the wind. The escorting sloops were turning in unison, as if held to the carrier by invisible strings.

'Midships.' Buchan was off his chair as lightly as a cat, his eyes to a gyro repeater. '*Steady.* Steer two-eight-zero.'

He was taking no chances this time, Rowan thought. He could tell from the expression on the navigating officer's face that *he* had been expecting to complete the alteration of course as usual.

The coxswain's voice again. 'Course two-eight-zero, sir. One-one-zero revolutions.'

'Aircraft, starboard quarter, sir!'

A dozen pairs of binoculars rose as one, and from the sponsons along either side of the hull beneath the flight deck *Growler*'s batteries of Oerlikons and Bofors cannon swivelled towards the sky, as if to sniff out any danger.

'Six Swordfish torpedo bombers!' The officer of the watch gave a grin. 'Poor old Stringbags. All over the place in this wind.'

Rowan looked at his back, hating him, yet knowing that the comment was natural enough.

He stared astern, his eyes watering as he tried to follow the little black dots against the racing clouds.

A lamp clattered busily from the signal platform, and from the bridge superstructure a Very light rose lazily to port and burst like a bright green pear.

'How does it look, eh?'

Rowan turned and then stiffened. It was Rear Admiral Chadwick.

'I can see the first of them, sir.' It angered him that he was almost tongue-tied.

Chadwick handed him his own powerful glasses. 'Use these, then tell me what's happening.' He was smiling. Very relaxed.

Rowan raised the glasses and found the leading Swordfish. The first three were already wheeling into a wide arc, losing height, making their run-in. He could feel the sweat on his spine like ice water. As if he were up there instead of here on this great island of metal.

Arrester wires up across the flight deck. Crash barriers in place. The handling parties were no longer lounging and bored, but along the walkways like athletes waiting for the gun.

Easy, easy. The first Swordfish had grown larger in those few seconds. He saw her racing propeller, her straddled wheels, strangely wide without the familiar torpedo slung in between.

Chadwick asked. 'Is he doing it well, d'you think?' He could have been discussing a bowler at some local cricket match.

Rowan felt his stomach muscles bunch as the Swordfish roared throatily down across the aft end of the flight deck and skidded on the wet planking, the arrester wire jerking out beneath it, taking the strain, controlling and braking it. Bats stood alone and windswept giving the signal to cut the engine as the men swarmed from the walkways to wheel the aircraft to a safe area beyond the crash barriers.

Rowan exclaimed. 'Bloody good.' He flushed. 'Sorry, sir.'

Chadwick was studying him. 'Rowan, isn't it? Seafire pilot. Home in Surrey, right?'

Rowan stared. 'Well, yes, sir.'

31

'Good.' Chadwick added, 'Keep the glasses for the moment. Drop them in on my steward whenever you like.' He strode towards the bridge officers.

'Nice day for it, eh?'

Rowan watched the other Swordfish landing on with dignified precision. Soon the helmeted heads and goggles would emerge as people. Friends, some of them.

'*Hello*, Foxtrot, *Hello*, Foxtrot, *this is* Eagle Five. *Request emergency landing!*' The sudden interruption from the R/T repeater at the rear of the bridge broke the earlier calm like an explosion.

Villiers snatched up his handset as Buchan snapped. 'Tell him affirmative. All other aircraft to keep clear until this one's down.'

Rowan felt the admiral at his side again but did not turn or speak. He was watching the Swordfish which had just called *Growler*'s code name. It was already side-slipping away from those still circling, and even above the roar of fans and the wind around the 'island' he could hear the fractured, intermittent roar of the plane's engine.

The pilot was levelling off, almost in direct line with the carrier's deck, and losing height fast.

Without taking his eyes from it, Rowan could sense the deck parties moving towards the stern, the crimson fire appliances already jutting from either beam.

Oh God. Oh God. He's not going to make it.

Rowan watched the plane's prop feather and suddenly stop. The Swordfish dipped steeply and almost reached the flight deck. But a break wave lifted *Growler*'s hull just a few extra feet, so that the aircraft's wheels hit the curved rounddown of the deck's overhang. It slewed violently from side to side, a lower wing tearing adrift before it toppled like a broken bird and disappeared over the side.

The tannoy rasped, *'Release float!'*

But *Growler* was moving at fifteen knots, and as the raft splashed over the side Rowan saw that the broken aircraft was already well astern and half submerged.

Captain Buchan called harshly. 'Signal the escort. We will alter course to—'

They all turned as Chadwick said flatly, 'Belay, that. Signal the *tug* to retrieve survivors. I want the remaining Swordfish flown-on without any more delay.'

Buchan clenched his fists. 'But, sir, the tug will take twenty minutes or more.'

Chadwick shaded his eyes to look for the other aircraft which were circling above one of the escorts.

'Think about it, Captain.' He did not raise his voice. 'Imagine yourself as a brand-new pilot, sitting up there, waiting to land on this Woolworth carrier. You've just seen a friend ditch, maybe die. It won't help you to be kept waiting while we all play at being bloody Nurse Cavell, will it?' The last words came out like a whip.

The captain looked at the navigating officer and said heavily, 'Carry on.' To Villiers he added, 'Fly-on remaining aircraft.'

The other Swordfish landed without mishap.

Then Buchan said, 'Signal escort to resume course and speed to rendezvous with *Hustler*.'

Villiers saluted. 'Fall out flying stations, sir?' He looked ashen.

'Signal from tug *Cornelian*, sir.' The chief yeoman watched his officers warily. 'One survivor. Pilot and air gunner went down with plane.'

Buchan nodded. 'Acknowledge.'

Villiers muttered brokenly, 'Thank God one of them is safe.'

Chadwick brushed past him on his way to the ladder. 'But we have lost *a complete aircraft*. When we get that survivor aboard I'll expect a full report. I want combatant crews, not *survivors*!' He left the bridge.

Villiers was still staring at the empty ladder. 'Oh, you bastard! *You bloody bastard!*'

Buchan rapped sharply. 'That will do. Go and greet the new squadron commander. I'll see him as soon as we're on course again.' He studied Villiers' face. 'I *know*. But keep it bottled up.'

Rowan made his way down a series of ladders, past lookouts and gun crews, signalmen and messengers, his mind

33

grappling with what had happened. Two men had just died. In a flash. Every time you scrambled an aircraft you expected to be killed. But not like that. He felt the deck tilt as *Growler* leaned heavily on her new course, more flags breaking out from her yards. As far as the ship was concerned, those two unknown men did not even count.

Ellis was shaking hands with a Swordfish pilot but broke away when he saw Rowan.

'All right, Tim?'

'I just discovered something.' He looked astern at the long curving wake, the tug's smudge of smoke. 'When you ditch from now on, you're on your own.' He walked away, hands in pockets.

He had reached the gallery deck before he realised he was still carrying the admiral's glasses. He stood and looked at them. Remembering Chadwick's composure.

The tannoy boomed, 'Starboard watch to Defence Stations. Able Seaman Robinson report to the Master-at-Arms at the double.'

It never stopped, no matter what.

He heard Ellis behind him. He was worried for him.

Ellis asked casually, 'Okay, Tim?'

He met his gaze and smiled. 'Why not? Nothing lasts forever.'

3

The Old Enemy

FROM mid-July and for three backbreaking weeks Rear
Admiral Chadwick kept his newly-formed group working-up
and going through every manoeuvre he could invent. From
the Irish Sea to the Outer Hebrides, close together or spread
across the sea like a line of armoured knights, the group
learned the behaviour of each other's ships and abilities, and,
after a few near-collisions when steaming full speed at night,
their faults and failings as well.

They fuelled at sea, they flew-off and landed-on aircraft
almost round the clock. Fire drill, abandon-ship exercises,
officers and key ratings changing jobs without more than a
minute's notice, it was, as *Growler*'s coxswain remarked,
'Like living in a bleeding madhouse!'

For Rowan the sudden and unexpected pressures of training a new team all over again had proved to be a benefit. In his
heart he had been dreading the strain of facing it. The last
seconds before take-off, the aching stomach muscles as the
plane gathered speed, the world compressed into a single
shaft of engine and power, until with something like surprise
you realised you were off and away, the carrier losing personality and size, a painted model on the sea, her escorts like a
child's toy fussing around her.

In the Irish Sea the R.A.F. had loaned Chadwick a couple
of fat-bellied Wellington bombers to act as marauding Focke-
Wulf Condors. Chadwick, it seemed, could charm or drag
favours from anyone.

But as Kitto had mentioned after one such exercise, 'Just
so long as the new lads don't think a Jerry Condor is going to
be so obliging when they meet one!'

For Rowan it had summed it all up. It was not flying which

had troubled him. Despite all the dreams, the memories and the doubts, it had been the thought of *fighting* again. Of seeing an enemy, right there in the sights, or you in his.

The group, now consisting of the twin escort carriers, six sloops and an ocean-going rescue tug, returned to Liverpool to replenish stores and make good any last minute flaws. An additional Swordfish was found from somewhere, and a new pilot and air gunner posted aboard. The observer of the one which had crashed, a pale-faced midshipman, had been kept busy after the accident. He had said very little to anyone, and fortunately Villiers had had him running errands on his flying bridge.

Beyond the tight world of *Growler*'s hull the war followed its own course. Sicily had been completely taken by the Allies, and the Italians were doing all they could to surrender and turn their backs on their German partners. On the Russian Front the German armies were fighting hard to hold on to old positions against tremendous pressure. Daily, thousands were killed or crippled, and the war of supply and demand became even more important. U-boats preyed in packs on the Atlantic convoys, M.T.Bs and German E-boats fought it out nightly in the Channel and North Sea across the smaller but no less vital supply routes.

The Americans were locked with the Japanese in the Pacific, and throughout Europe and the Balkans the partisans and Resistance watched the skies and the lonely beaches for their own weapons and the resources sent at no small risk to strike at the occupying power where it would do the most damage.

No home leave was granted to the group when it returned to Liverpool. Something was brewing, said the latest buzz. There was a good chance of the Pacific. Of the Mediterranean. Of India. Anywhere.

Apart from a few anxious officers and ratings allowed ashore on compassionate grounds, homes bombed, next of kin killed or badly injured, the ships' companies waited and stirred the speculation.

The newly arrived Swordfish crews contained the usual mixture of seasoned and very amateur members. There were two Dutch pilots, which made a nice change, and one New Zealander. There was an observer who knew all about growing orchids. 'A very useful asset,' Bats had observed dryly. And there was a pilot who had been an actor of sorts.

Chadwick had gone to London, according to his steward. Several people had murmured, 'Let's hope he stays there!'

A few days later Chadwick returned aboard, looking strangely human in a tweed suit, and the following morning the group put to sea.

Then, and only then, was the news released. None of the buzzes was right. They listened to the captain's unemotional voice over the various speakers throughout the ship. On the hangar deck, strangely hushed as fitters and riggers paused by their aircraft to hear his words. In the canteen and throughout the offices and stores, the parachute packing room and sick-bay, wardroom and messdeck alike.

The group would be making a rendezvous off Iceland.

The captain need not have said anything further for the old hands, and Rowan guessed he must have been thinking along those lines as he continued, 'It will be a very important convoy to North Russia. Tanks, munitions, aircraft, fuel, everything.'

Rowan sat staring at the opposite bulkhead, oblivious to all the others in the wardroom. *Russia*. It was like a nightmare returning.

The captain continued evenly, 'It is essential for our Russian allies to make all the headway they can before the next winter sets in and the whole front becomes ice-bound again. The German general staff are fully aware of the time limit and the importance of the next few months. They are short of fuel, they will do everything to hold the front in stalemate, regardless of human losses, until the winter comes to their aid. I'm certain that everyone in this group is well aware of the trust placed in our protection.' There was the merest pause, as if the captain was trying to think of the right ending, then, 'Thank you.'

The tannoy speakers faded, and like characters in *Sleeping Beauty* the five hundred human beings throughout *Growler*'s complex hull came back to life.

37

Kitto said dully, 'Russia. *Jesus!*'

'But it'll be better at *this* time of the year, surely?' Cotter, the newly joined New Zealander, looked from face to face.

Rolston turned on him, his eyes angry. 'Grow up, can't you?'

Ellis said calmly, 'Take it off your back, Nick!' He smiled at Cotter. 'It's warmer, that's all. But there's hardly any darkness, and the ice barrier will be as far north as Bear Island. So it'll mean a long, long haul. We'll be nearer to Spitsbergen than Norway before we turn and run south for Uncle Joe Stalin's homeland.'

Rolston interrupted harshly, 'By which time Jerry will have plenty of opportunity to get ready. To throw the bloody lot at us!'

Cotter sat down, his tanned face set in a frown. 'I see.'

No you don't. Rowan watched him. Seeing himself a few years ago. There had been miseries like Rolston aboard his first ship, too. But they sometimes made sense. This convoy would be much as he had described. Long, empty days, with the ships steering north and further still. Watching for the Focke-Wulfs, praying that they could be shot out of the sky before they could flash their sighting reports to Group North in Norway, to the U-boats and the big cruisers, and even capital ships like *Tirpitz* and *Scharnhorst* which were said to lurk amongst the fjords.

He watched the stewards laying the tables for lunch, heard the sound of a crooner coming from the intercom. *We're going to get lit up when the lights go on in London* . . .

Van Roijen, one of the Dutch pilots, settled down in a chair beside him. He was a big man, not unlike Ellis.

'You've done one of these Russian things, I think, eh?'

Rowan came out of his thoughts. 'A couple. A year or so back.'

'Back?'

'Sorry. I mean, ago.' He turned to look at the man, thinking of Ellis's Czech girl, of all the others who had no country, no news of home.

He smiled. 'I'm Tim Rowan.'

'And I am named Peter.' The Dutchman dragged out a

wallet. 'And this is my wife and my little son.'

He looked up as a steward said, 'Commander (Flying) wants you on the hangar deck, sir.'

Van Roijen stood up and nodded. 'I go now. But I will come back and we talk some more. Too damn right, eh?'

The other Dutchman, Jan de Boer, tiny by comparison, sat in the empty chair.

He said simply, 'Peter is a good man. My friend.' He did not look at Rowan. 'Be easy with him and his little pictures. He has no wife. No little boy. Some traitor told the Germans he had come to England to continue the fight.' He shrugged. 'They reacted the only way they know.'

Rowan stared at him, thinking of the wind in Oxshott Woods. The old dog by his side.

'Not *both* of them?'

'Yes. They were taken away by the S.S. Peter still hopes. But for his sake and theirs I pray they are dead.'

He laid one hand on Rowan's arm. 'I know what you are thinking, but do not reproach yourself. Your freedom from the Germans is our only hope now.' He looked away, his voice harsh. 'So we will get this convoy to the Russians and to anyone else who can lift a rifle or use a knife. The rules are broken now. When I see the enemy I feel only hate.'

The deck lifted unsteadily, and along the tables the crockery began to rattle in unison.

Rowan sat back and tried to relax. *Growler* was feeling the first big rollers. The Atlantic again. Nothing changed.

A shadow fell across the chair and Lieutenant Commander Miller stood looking down at them, his devil's beard jutting aggressively.

'All pilots will be required in the Ops Room after lunch, so don't eat too much and fall asleep, right?' He nodded at the Dutchman. 'Settled in?'

'Thank you, yes.' De Boer eyed the squadron commander thoughtfully. 'This operations officer,' he hesitated and then continued bluntly, 'I have heard he is married to a German.'

Miller replied, 'Perhaps.' He glanced questioningly at Rowan.

'*So?*'

The Dutchman stood up and stretched. 'I was merely curious, sir.' He walked away.

Rowan said. 'I didn't know about that.'

'Does it concern us, then?' Miller glared at him. 'Don't tell me *you're* going round the twist as well!'

Rowan grinned and watched Miller's square shape bustle out of the door. His talk with the Dutchman and Miller's sudden anger had in some strange way steadied him. He looked at Ellis.

'Let's go and eat, Bill. May be the last well cooked meal we get for a while.'

Ellis caught his mood. 'What, spam and chips? A really *fine* lunch for a naval officer, I must say.'

Rowan peered through a salt-misted scuttle. How dull the sea looked, like rough pewter. It was funny, he thought. When he looked back at his childhood he could never remember a summer when it was not sunshine and blue sea.

Ellis groaned. 'And I was only kidding!' He gestured towards the stewards. 'But it really *is* bloody spam again!'

The dream progressed much as usual. Dark sea, with only the necklace of surf to make a moving pattern against the perfect sand. And there was the girl, very pale against what must be the night sky at the top of the beach. Walking slowly and steadily towards him without getting any closer. It was always the same.

Rowan awoke with a gasp, his throat like dust as he tried to collect his wits.

He was in the Ready Room, but instead of dozing in one of the comfortable chairs he was sitting bolt upright, his dream gone as the tannoy barked, 'Duty air crews report to Air Staff Officer immediately!' He was on his feet, seizing his helmet and jacket and already through the door as the speaker continued, 'Range a strike of two Swordfish and one Seafire on flight deck immediately. Hands to flying stations! Stand by to fly-off aircraft!'

Bells jangled in other parts of the hull, and he heard a stampede of feet along the nearest walkway. He had been on the bridge that morning and knew vaguely where the group was. Steering approximately north-west and standing well out into the North Atlantic, with the little islands of Barra and South Uist hidden somewhere to starboard.

He pushed through the figures in the Operations Room and saw Broderick, the A.S.O., mentally ticking off the breathless arrivals.

He frowned impatiently as Villiers, and James, the Operations Officer, came through the opposite door, and then said, 'We've had a signal. An eastbound convoy has been having a spot of bother with a U-boat pack.' He raised a pointer to his great coloured wall-chart. Sinkings and convoy routes, minefields and known U-boat areas. It was a panorama of war.

'It's about here.' The pointer rested on a little numbered flag. The convoy was almost home. *Almost* by comparison with all the hundreds of miles they had come to reach this far. The Air Staff Officer added, 'Approximately one hundred miles to the nor'-west of us. They have a good escort,' he paused as the observer of one of the Swordfish scribbled a few notes on his pad, 'and are coping as well as can be expected. But the Admiralty reports two or more U-boats in direct line ahead of their route. The convoy's commodore dares not make another big alteration of course. Too many of the German pack still at his heels, and a Liberator is on way to rendezvous and do what it can.' He looked meaningly at Rowan. 'The convoy had no air cover of its own.'

Villiers looked at Rowan too, his eyes very bright. 'Right, Tim? You fit for it?'

Rowan felt his lips frozen in a grin. 'Piece of cake.'

Lieutenant Commander Rathbone, who commanded the Swordfish squadron, snapped, 'I'll lead.' He nodded to van Roijen. 'You take Number Two.'

That was it. Nothing to it.

Rowan tugged his leather helmet over his unruly hair and zipped up his flying jacket as he hurried through the door. He did not see anyone or distinguish a single voice. His mind was blurred. Like the dream.

And yet in that short while since he had jumped from his chair in the Ready Room this small fragment of war had gone into operation.

Commander (Flying) was already dashing for the bridge where he would find the captain giving orders to the engine room. Bats and the handling parties were assembled along the flight deck. Signals jerked up to the yards, and *Growler* tilted a grey shoulder into the sea as she altered course and headed into the wind, two escorts moving up watchfully on either beam.

The wind along the flight deck was cold after the quarters below. Or perhaps he was imagining it. He ran, half bowed, towards the three aircraft at the after end of the wooden deck.

He saw a fitter giving him a white grin and a thumbs-up as he clambered up and over the cockpit, seeing the name, Jonah, in a red glare, the men bending near the tail, a petty officer, hair standing upright in the wind, a check list in one greasy hand.

Rowan felt the canopy snapped into place, felt the wind cut off as he ran his eyes over the neat dashboard and adjusted his microphone across his mouth. The air was full of static and inhuman voices.

He leaned back and tightened his harness and eased the awkward parachute like a cushion. It was taking far too long. He peered at the dashboard clock. In fact, it had taken exactly thirteen minutes since the order to range aircraft.

He rubbed an oily smudge off his perspex canopy and peered to port. He could see the other carrier at a different angle, to show the speed with which *Growler* had altered course.

Rowan saw the leading Swordfish already rolling forward, K for King, that would be Rathbone. He was not leaving this to a new pilot. He saw the twin wings swaying and dipping as the plane trundled along, the black helmeted heads of the observer and gunner just showing above the big rear cockpit. Bats made a brief signal to the bridge and seconds later the Affirmative broke out from *Growler*'s yard. The leading Swordfish let out a great roar and gathered speed along the centre line, puffing out blue smoke and making a bright diamond light from its exhaust as it tore towards the bows and then off, tilting steeply as it turned to starboard.

The second Swordfish was already following, the Dutchman's arm waving above his head to someone as he brought the plane on to the white centre line.

Rowan took a deep breath, watched for the stab of an Aldis lamp and then opened the throttle slowly and firmly, hearing the great throaty roar of the Rolls Royce Merlin engine as it responded instantly. Because of the big engine immediately in front of the cockpit Rowan could not see the centre of the flight deck and had to weave the plane evenly from side to side as it started to roll towards the bows. It was all in his mind and he went through the motions without conscious thought. He could not take too long taxiing without dangerously overheating the engine. He prepared to kick the rudder when the usual swing developed. Ease the stick forward. A bead of sweat ran down under his goggles. *Not too much, you idiot! Or you'll have the prop ploughing up the deck!* He opened the throttle wider, seeing the island sliding past the starboard side, the pale blurs of faces on the signal platform. Stick back. *Easy, for Christ's sake!* He felt the plane shiver, and when he turned his head he saw the rear admiral's bright flag waving below him like a church steeple. He was off.

He retracted the wheels and then pulled the stick back, his left hand gripping the throttle with unusual tightness.

There were the two Swordfish, seemingly unmoving against the clouds. He adjusted his mouthpiece.

'Hello, *Leader*, this is *Jonah*. Do you read me?'

'Yes, I read you.' Rathbone did not waste words apparently. 'Take station.'

Rowan relaxed slightly and listened to the Merlin's whistling roar as he began to climb towards the cloud bank, his mind only partly involved with the course to steer, the right boost. He was thinking of the hundred miles ahead. The same back again. If the weather closed in it might be hard to find the carrier. Impossible.

He thought too of the U-boats which were supposed to be across the convoy's path. If they could sink just one, or even cripple it, he knew the loss of all three aircraft and crews

43

would be worth it. As Ellis had remarked when the idea was put to him, 'Sounds fine and dandy from down here, chum!'

The wings quivered as the Seafire sliced through the cloud and up into bright sunshine. He levelled off, smiling as he peered out at the foaming clouds beneath him. It never failed to fascinate him. The Swordfish would keep at their most economical level below. His job was to protect them from something faster and better armed than they were, which covered almost everything, he thought.

He checked the instruments more slowly and then pressed his right thumb firmly on the firing button on the joystick. Just a short burst from the two twenty millimetre cannon and four machine guns. The whole plane vibrated as if it enjoyed it. Rowan frowned and looked in the mirror above his cockpit. Remembering when he had pressed a button once before and nothing had happened. He shivered.

He unclipped his mouthpiece and leaned back as far as he could. He could feel the sun on his face through the perspex, the sudden warmth running through his body like a drug. He felt elated, as if he wanted to put the Seafire into a steep climb or point her down through the clouds. He grinned, peering to starboard and port, through occasional gaps in the cloud to the sea, thirteen thousand feet below. How grey it was.

The two Swordfish could not manage more than a hundred and thirty miles an hour with their full load of depth charges. It was criminal to keep throttled back for their benefit. He weaved from side to side, feeling Jonah answering his messages, purring and roaring without hesitation.

He thought of the people on the railway station who had watched the dog-fight. Jonah would look like that from the ground.

He glanced at his clock. Twenty minutes. He adjusted his goggles and studied a cloud directly across his path. It rose up from the rest like a great frothy glacier, glittering and solid.

Rowan twisted his head sharply as the two Swordfish rose sedately through the clouds about half a mile to starboard.

'Hello, *Jonah*. This is *Leader*. Do you read me?'

Rowan tipped his wings in reply. It saved time.

'Submarine on the surface dead ahead! They've not seen us. Attacking *now*!'

Rowan gripped the stick with his right hand, the other resting on the throttle. The Dutchman knew about flying. He saw the other Swordfish tilt steeply to fall in line behind Rathbone's K for King.

Rowan watched the two aircraft dip into the clouds, swallowed up, smothered. Then he too was in the great towering one, seeing the broken streamers of it like steam through the racing, four-bladed prop.

He pushed the stick forward and kept his eyes on the compass as he turned slightly before continuing in a steep dive.

Patches of dull grey came through the thinning cloud, several little wavecrests, tiny on the Atlantic's vast spread, and then as he roared clear of the cover he saw the submarine.

It was a darker grey. A pencil-like shape which could have passed unnoticed but for her arrowhead of bow wave, the frothing wash around her casing.

Rowan levelled off, seeing several things happening at once. The Swordfish flying purposefully towards the submarine's port quarter, the sudden flash of automatic fire from the conning tower, and the fact that the German was not attempting to dive.

He tried to think clearly. It could be damaged. No. It would not remain here with the convoy and escorts so near. He peered towards the dull horizon. Haze, or was that funnel smoke from some elderly freighter in the convoy?

He heard Rathbone's voice on the R/T. 'Tally-ho!'

Rowan banked steeply to watch the U-boat's length blotted out by the attacking Swordfish. He stiffened, seeing the air come alive with leaping green tracer. There were tons of it. Ripping towards the slow-moving plane in a bright, lethal cone. The U-boat had some multi-barrelled cannon on her bandstand abaft the conning tower. What the hell was happening? He saw a depth charge detach itself and plummet towards the sea. Seconds later a great leaping column of water burst up from the surface, but the charge had fallen well short.

As Rathbone twisted and weaved his plane clear, Rowan imagined he could see the tracers passing through it, tossing it about like a bit of waste-paper in a wind.

He bit his lip. The Dutchman was going in. He thought of his little photographs, the smiling woman and little boy.

No, we will not do this by the book. He opened the throttle and turned firmly towards the U-boat, watching it growing and lengthening across the racing propeller as he dived straight for it.

Funny, nobody had said anything about this sort of gun mounting. He gritted his teeth as a smaller machine gun hurled a spray of tracer in his direction. He was well out of range, but they had seen him. The German commander was probably wishing now that he had dived. They only had to damage his boat to keep him out of the fight.

He waited, gripping the joystick, his thumb on the button, his eyes almost watering as he stared at the target which was now reaching out on either side of him like a great, slime-coloured whale. *Here comes the bloody tracer*. He held his breath. Five hundred yards. Three hundred. He pressed the button and watched his own tracer ripping down, churning the sea into a seething pattern of white feathers and then cutting diagonally across the U-boat in a torrent of fire.

He pulled back the stick, throwing the Seafire violently on its side as he swung away, the Merlin labouring as he twisted to avoid the green bars of tracer.

Something made the pad behind his head jerk painfully, and he saw two holes appear in the port wing. He banked again, pulling Jonah round in a tight turn just in time to see the Dutchman's depth charge explode almost alongside the U-boat's hull.

His head-on attack must have caught the German gun crew out completely. Van Roijen had kept flying in as before and had done what he had come to do.

The surfaced U-boat was reeling in a great oval pattern of broken water, like soap suds. The charge would not sink her, but the next one might.

Rathbone called, 'Am attacking *now*!'

As he swept past Rowan, some five hundred feet below

him, he saw the long rents in the fuselage and wings, and also that the air gunner had fallen back into the cockpit, his arm still caught around his gun.

The Swordfish carried two charges each instead of their customary torpedoes or bombs. Rathbone was flying dangerously low towards his target, the green tracer reaching towards him, crossing his path like a glittering mesh. But not every gun was firing, and the one on the conning tower was pointing at the sea. Rowan's attack must have raked the bridge as well.

There was a bright explosion and the Swordfish seemed to split apart in mid-air, the fragments making great splashes in every direction.

Rowan pushed the stick forward, seeing the multi-barrelled gun swivelling round, following him as he tore into another attack.

He shut his mind to the scattered remains which patterned the sea like shavings. The U-boat had a weak spot. He gunned the engine and roared down almost to sea-level, the shockwave from wings and prop ripping the choppy water like some invisible speedboat.

Round and still further round, with the port wing-tip barely inches from the sea. The U-boat looked huge now, and as he straightened up and eased the stick very slightly he saw the submarine end on towards him, the multi-barrel mounting masked and impotent behind the conning tower.

He heard the Dutchman's voice on the intercom, crackling but wild, as he yelled, 'What you do, Tim? You going to land on the bloody thing?'

Rowan did not trust his voice to speak. He had never been able to at times like this. Not like Bill and some of the others. Like Rathbone.

And then he was right there, the conning tower with some white faces above it, and a flapping wet pendant from the periscope standards. He saw it all in the smallest part of a second. The open hatch. A body sprawled below the machine gun. And then with a great, deafening roar he was cutting down towards her stern, every gun hammering like mad things. Two cannon and four machine guns, even like this within the proper spread of fire, were more than enough. He felt his spine tingle and throb as he pulled away, half expecting to feel the tracer ripping after him.

By the time he had managed to regain control of himself the Dutchman had dropped his charge. It exploded level with the conning tower and must have caved in one of the ballast tanks. Even as he watched Rowan saw the periscopes start to tilt over.

He said quietly, 'Well done. Bloody well done.'

The Swordfish turned again and dropped two smoke markers near the floundering U-boat. Then it circled the drifting fragments astern of the U-boat and the men who were already releasing rubber dinghies and crowding out of the conning tower and hatch like bewildered insects.

Rowan circled round well above the little drama. A quaint-looking Swordfish searching for any sign of life from Rathbone's plane. A cable or so clear, the U-boat starting to settle down, her crew laid bare and impotent.

He watched them grimly and recalled the other Dutch pilot's words. *When I see the enemy I feel only hate*. These Germans were fortunate he was not here today. Rowan had no doubt what he would have done. He rubbed the firing button with his thumb. And why not? Where was the point of letting an enemy who had probably killed hundreds of unarmed merchant seamen go free?

He sighed and held the mouthpiece to his face. 'We will return to base.' There were no survivors. He had known it. 'That was a fine job of work, Peter.'

Rowan peered at the compass and at the sky. Once again. He had made it. *Once again*.

He snapped down the catch. 'Hello, *Foxtrot*, hello *Foxtrot*. This is *Jonah*. One U-boat destroyed.'

He broke off with a sigh. There was no response, and he guessed that he was either out of range of *Growler*'s R/T or, more likely, a bit of flak had put his set out of action.

Rowan waited for the Dutchman to pick up the course back towards their carrier and then climbed again towards the sun.

In due course three homes would be getting telegrams. *Killed in action*. Commander (Flying) or maybe the captain would write to their families. But they did not really know any of them. There had been no time.

He dragged out a handkerchief and blew his nose. Funny how it always made it behave like that after a fight.

Then he saw *Growler* and her escorts, and further off still the other carrier.

He saw the flash of a signal, and pictured the hasty preparations, the grim looks when they realised that one aircraft was missing.

Round past the nearest sloop, the *Turnstone*, and banking steeply as if to follow *Growler*'s long, curving wake.

The usual juggling to change hands on the stick while you lower the undercarriage with your right hand. Flaps down. A careful, steady approach, the tiny aircraft carrier now yawning wide like a broad steel cliff. There were some seamen waving from the isolated gun mounting on the quarterdeck.

Nice and easy. He saw the arrester wires as he crossed the turn-down above the quarterdeck, felt the sudden pressure of his harness as *Growler* took hold of one of her own.

Men were running towards him from either side, while others still watched for the slowly-circling Swordfish.

He slid open the canopy, sucking in salt air like a man saved from drowning.

Bill was hurrying from the walkway as the engine died away in a great trembling sigh. Rowan dropped to the deck and heard his friend say, 'Welcome back, Tim.'

'Thanks.' He watched a petty officer who was following the handling party as they manhandled Jonah to safety beyond the crash barrier. He was pointing at two holes. They must have missed Rowan's body by less than six inches. He added huskily, 'I'm luckier than I thought.'

4

Disagreement

BY the time Rear Admiral Chadwick's Air Support Group had reached its anchorage at Akureyri on the north coast of Iceland it was apparent that most of the convoy was ready to sail.

It had been gathering for some weeks, and even the men of the escorts, whose past optimism had been blunted by the savage opposition along the routes to Russia, were impressed. This was no make-do collection of ships of varied ages and tonnage, where the faster ones would be kept at a snail's crawl because of the more elderly members of the convoy. Thirty-five in all, and only two or three more than ten years old, they gave a meaning to the importance placed on their safe arrival at Murmansk and Archangel.

Shore leave for the *Growler*'s company was minimal, and as Bill Ellis commented, 'Just as well. All those lovely girls, and no chance of laying a finger on 'em. It's enough to make a bloke ill.'

It was strange about the hostility of the Icelandic townsfolk. Did they look on British and American servicemen in the same way as the people of occupied Europe saw the Germans? It baffled Rowan, but did not trouble him much.

Whatever happened, Iceland would look just fine on the return trip, he thought.

August was drawing to a close when the final preparations were approved. There were many comings and goings amongst captains of escorts, senior officers of the merchantmen, base staff, and all the other desk-bound people from headquarters in Reykjavik who made this vast, complicated mass of ships and men into a single, controllable force.

The weather was unusually calm, with hardly a breath of wind to build up the familiar swells along the Denmark Strait. Every day was long, bright and wearing for the nerves. The ships, the aircraft, the guns and machinery were as good and ready as they ever could be. The waiting was as usual worse than the doing.

On the last day of the month Captain Buchan assembled all of *Growler*'s officers in the wardroom. The moment had apparently arrived.

Buchan held himself very upright while he waited for everybody to find a seat or something to lean against.

He began in his resonant tone, 'The convoy will weigh tonight and complete assembly during the forenoon tomorrow.'

He smiled briefly at the big sigh which came from almost everyone.

'I know, gentlemen. Not a moment too soon.'

He nodded to James, the Operations Officer, who waiting like a conjuror's assistant beside the pantry hatch, unrolled a large coloured chart.

Rowan studied it, his mouth very dry. He had seen it, or similar ones, many times. The Denmark Strait, then north-east to Jan Mayen Island, further still, up and away towards the summer ice-edge and Bear Island, that lonely, dismal outpost between North Cape and Spitsbergen. Dotted arcs to mark the extent of Allied air cover from Iceland and Scotland. A much larger one to indicate the reach from the German airfields along the Norwegian coast. Anchorages, minefields, areas which were especially dangerous because of enemy destroyer bases or bigger units which lay hidden in their deep fjords. Altogether it looked like a blueprint for war itself.

Rowan glanced at Cotter, the young New Zealander. There was no sign of uncertainty or doubt. More like excitement. A boy in a toyshop before Christmas.

Buchan walked slowly to the chart, his shoes squeaking on the deck.

'Thirty-five ships, gentlemen. They will have an escort of an A.A. cruiser, ten destroyers and eight minesweepers.' He brushed his fingers lightly across the chart. 'Units of the Home Fleet will carry out a constant sweep to the north of the convoy. Two battleships with suitable escort, and perhaps another carrier.' He faced them gravely. 'So you can see how strongly everyone feels about this.'

Rowan bit his lip. All told, the spread of warships would equal the merchantmen. Cotter would probably think it disproportionate and unnecessary. Rowan knew, and had seen otherwise.

Buchan said, 'Our group will be on call at all times. The admiral will use the two carriers as he thinks fit or is directed to meet each eventuality as it arises.'

Rowan pictured the aircraft taking off round the clock. With almost endless daylight, it would soon become automatic, and some of the newer hands might become bored. Careless.

'The enemy will be aware of our convoy, although I hope he does not know *everything* about us yet.' He smiled. 'But we must be ready to give him a bloody nose before he can rally a big force to delay us.' The smile faded. 'This convoy will *not* scatter. No matter what.'

Rowan watched him, wondering if he was referring to the bitterly remembered convoy, P.Q.17, which had been ordered to scatter because of a misunderstanding, and in consequence had been decimated.

Buchan asked, 'Anyone want to put a question?' He tried to bring back the smile, but he looked strained and tired, despite his neat uniform and freshly shaved chin.

Lieutenant Ian Cameron stood up and drawled, 'Might I ask what the convoy is carrying, sir?'

Buchan regarded him calmly. 'Everything. Tanks, aircraft, munitions, weapons. Even a railway engine or two, I understand.'

Someone called, 'Sit down, Algy, you'll be able to come home by train if the worst happens!' Everyone laughed. It helped to snap the tension.

The captain seemed glad of the interruption, and said curtly, 'The group will slip and proceed at six tomorrow morning. Flying stations from the moment we rendezvous with the convoy.' He looked at the deck. 'After that—' He shrugged. 'We shall take it as it comes.'

Jan de Boer whispered, 'We *give* it too, eh? Too damn right, we do!'

The captain left the wardroom, the chart was rolled and carried back to the Operations Room, and the bar was opened within five minutes of Buchan's departure.

Rowan saw Kitto pushing between the crowd, his blue chin set as he made towards him.

He asked, 'All right, Dymock?' He watched the other man's grim expression. 'You look like a wet Sunday.'

Kitto showed his teeth. 'I've just been told. I'm taking over the Seafire squadron. Getting a half stripe to boot.'

Rowan smiled. 'I'm glad for you.'

Kitto hurried on. His promotion seemed to embarrass him. 'Dusty Miller has been told to take over the Swordfish boys. The admiral seems to think they'll be more important on this convoy than fighters.' He scowled. 'I've got news for him!'

Rowan thought about it, seeing the Swordfish torpedo bomber bursting apart under the onslaught of the U-boat's multiple cannon fire. Lieutenant Commander Rathbone was dead. One more pilot killed in action. But not so to the admiral. Rathbone should be here now. Leading his Swordfish. And of course, Miller was the obvious choice. He had flown just about everything, and he was known and respected. He studied Kitto. And if they had to have a change, then he too was the best they had. All his experience before the war as a mercenary, a stunt pilot, and his ability to make a plane keep in the air when there was very little of it in one piece, made him a first-class leader.

Kitto grinned at him. 'You've not understood, have you, Tim?' The grin widened. 'You are now my senior pilot, so how about that, eh?'

Rowan stared. Of course. He should have realised. He examined his thoughts. Pleasure? Pride? His stomach muscles contracted. There was nothing but a sense of shock.

Kitto added quietly, 'It's been coming, Tim. You must have known. A lot of good blokes have bought it, but you've always kept your head.' He punched his arm. 'Just as well.

You'll probably have to keep *my* back in one piece now!'

Rowan nodded. He wanted to be in his cabin. Alone on the flight deck. Anywhere but here. But a piano had started, and some of the officers had begun *Bless 'em all*. His inner feelings would affect nothing. It was the night before sailing. He glanced round the faces, the voices washing over him like rain. Some of them would never know another carefree night in harbour. He sensed something like panic.

Kitto gripped his arm. 'Come on, Tim. Bill's coming over to us.' He tightened his hold. 'One more time, eh?'

Rowan nodded, unable to speak. He had seen it on Kitto's face when he had come to tell him his news. But he had not recognised it. This sort of promotion was because of one thing only. The other rungs on the ladder above you were suddenly empty.

Everyone knew about it. In stations around the British Isles it was taken for granted. Here for breakfast. Dead by tea-time. He had often heard the R.A.F. pilots joking about it. They *had* to joke about it. He forced himself to smile and face the packed bodies around the piano.

'Of course. It's only a game. I heard the admiral say so.'

The admiral's quarters were as crowded as the wardroom. The whole place was filled with visitors. Mostly captains of other ships, officers from the base, and a good sprinkling of R.A.F. and American uniforms to make up the balance.

Buchan paused between two panting stewards who were carrying enough glasses to serve a regiment, and tried to catch the admiral's attention.

Chadwick saw him and raised an eyebrow.

Buchan had to shout. 'Can I have a word, sir?'

The admiral smiled. 'Won't it keep, Bruce?' He took a glass from his solemn steward. It looked like champagne. 'It may be a while before the next party!'

Buchan stood firm. 'I've a lot to do, sir.'

'Very well.'

The admiral led him to the small office which opened off his personal quarters, nodding and smiling to his guests.

With the door closed the party seemed muffled. Unreal.

Buchan said, 'I've been studying your special orders, sir.'

'Oh?' Chadwick looked at himself in a bulkhead mirror. 'What is that supposed to mean?'

'At all the briefings nothing was said about independent action by our group.' Buchan kept his eyes on the admiral's broad shoulders, willing him to turn.

Chadwick replied dryly, 'It's *meant* to be secret, Bruce.'

'Up to a point, sir.' He tried to find the right words, seeing the contempt in his wife's eyes whenever Chadwick was mentioned. *That man*. 'We're an Air Support Group. We can't exist as a completely separate unit. It's not practical.'

Chadwick turned and regarded him calmly. 'Neither is buggery. But quite a lot of it goes on, I believe.'

He seemed to sense that Buchan was unmoved.

'It's a theory I have.' He examined his hands. 'I saw some chaps at the Admiralty and the War Room.' His steely eyes lifted slowly to Buchan's face. 'Quite *important* chaps, actually. They seemed to agree with my ideas.' He continued without emotion, 'I have believed for some time that our support groups are being misused. Just added to the weight, so to speak. But it's not enough. Nor ever was.'

'According to your orders, sir,' Buchan spoke carefully, trying to examine each word before it left his mouth, 'we will supply air cover to the convoy.' He swallowed hard. 'But if *another* target presents itself, we will act with total independence.' He shook his head. 'It won't work, sir. It can't.'

Chadwick gave a sad smile. 'They said that in Western Approaches until Max Horton took over. And until captains like Walker proved with sheer guts and skill you could go after the enemy and kill *him* for a bloody change. Instead of leaving the poor, plodding convoy bleeding itself over thousands of miles of ocean and taking everything that Jerry could hurl at it!' His voice was sharper. 'Like this convoy. *Our* convoy. I'll bet they know to a pound of margarine in Berlin what we're carrying. Every enemy agent in Iceland will have had plenty of time to count the ships, gauge their value. What they can't discover they can guess, just as you would under similar circumstances.'

'I still don't see what—' He got no further.

'Well listen then. I'm not going to see this convoy cut in half, bashed to bloody hell all the way to the Kola Inlet. When Jerry shows his nose we'll go after him. It's something new. We won't just wait to be picked off by U-boats and Focke-Wulfs, or pounded by the *Scharnhorst* or *Tirpitz*.'

He turned and watched Buchan in the mirror.

'The admiral commanding the screening force will do his part. The commodore of the convoy will do his. Do I have to add the rest?'

Buchan looked away. He felt old. Beaten.

'I understand.'

'Good man.' The steely eyes were still watching him. 'So come and have a few gins. Anything you like. Let Commander Jolly take the strain for a bit.' He added calmly, 'I'm sure he's more than eager to prove his value.'

'Thank you, sir, but no.' Buchan felt better. That last remark had done it. Set one against the other. What Chadwick had done aboard his last ship, the *Camilla*. 'I really do have a lot of loose ends to clear up.'

Chadwick guided him through the door, back into the noise and smoke.

'Suit yourself, Bruce.' He patted his elbow. 'Can't have things getting on top of my captain, can I?'

He was still chuckling as Buchan strode blindly out of the opposite door.

Rowan settled himself more stiffly in the cockpit and watched *Growler*'s oblong flight deck level off through his racing propeller.

It was ridiculous, he told himself, the Seafire which responded so willingly to every demand was exactly like his own. But he was flying Miller's plane while Jonah was having final touches done to her repairs. The U-boat's flak had hit nothing vital, but up here, in the vast open wastes of sea, the mechanics took nothing for granted. Miller's fighter was about the same age as his own. Had probably come from the same factory, the same workers. And yet, despite all his reasoning, it *felt* different.

He saw the stab of light from *Growler*'s flying bridge, the tiny dots on her walkways becoming real people as he dipped carefully towards her stern. The sea looked oily and very cold, and as he glanced quickly at an escorting sloop he noticed she was showing more of her bilge than usual. Rolling steeply beam to beam. The sea was getting up perhaps? He made himself relax and loosened his grip on the stick, checking yet again to make sure all the gear was down, the undercarriage locked.

Why then had this patrol been recalled half an hour early?

He thought of the great convoy as he had just seen it, some thirty miles north-east of the group. Four long lines of ships, the commodore leading the starboard column in a big cargo liner which had seen more leisurely days on the Australian run before the war. In the rear had been the dazzle-painted anti-aircraft cruiser. She was very like the one in the picture he had seen in the captain's day cabin.

The destroyers had looked very impressive too, sweeping ahead and on either quarter of the convoy. And further still the sturdy minesweepers and Asdic trawlers, the latter mostly ex-whalers, had kept the sea's face in constant movement. But the combined wakes of the merchantmen had been the most impressive. They had stretched astern and away on either quarter like deep, glassy furrows. The whole convoy was doing nearly eighteen knots. A bit different from the eight and ten knot efforts he had seen.

He tensed as the wheels hit the deck and the arrester wire snared the Seafire with casual dexterity. Two other fighters were already being trundled towards a lift, and as a startling contrast he saw some off-watch seamen doing P.T. under the guidance of Lieutenant Faulconer, *Growler*'s gunnery officer, known to be a real keep-fit merchant.

The Merlin engine shuddered into silence, and as he slid back the canopy Rowan felt the bite of the air across his eyes and nose. Much colder already. The convoy and its spread of escorts had reached the no-man's-land to the north-east of Jan Mayen Island. Beyond the reach of land-based aircraft, Allied or German, it made the convoy's own carrier patrols all the more necessary. U-boats took this dangerous area as their own. Their killing ground.

The next Seafire, Bill Ellis's, was already plunging towards the round-down, the prop making an icy circle, the wheels spread apart like claws preparing to seize hold of the ship.

Petty Officer Thorpe, the senior rating of Rowan's crew, yelled above the throaty roar of engines, 'Yours won't be ready for a couple of days, sir!'

Rowan nodded. 'Blast!' He patted the petty officer's filthy sleeve. 'Do what you can.'

As he ducked through a screen door below the island, feeling the moisture and warm air from within the hull crowding around him, he found Kitto, hands in pockets, watching the aircraft landing-on with professional interest.

He said, 'Sorry about the recall, Tim. There's a flap on. All air crews to muster in the Ready Room in fifteen minutes.' He breathed out slowly, his eyes very still, as the last fighter from the patrol landed-on with a loud screech of rubber. It was Creswell, the youngest pilot, and Kitto said savagely, 'He'll have to keep his mind on his job, that one!' He turned on his heel. 'Let's go.'

The best seats in the Ready Room were already taken when they arrived. Rowan glanced at the huddle below the wall-charts. They were all there, too. Commander (Flying) looking more strained than ever. Bats, his cheeks red from his hurried run from the flight deck. The Air Engineer Officer, the Operations Officer with his coloured chart, Broderick, the A.S.O., and no less important, Lieutenant Hector Syms, R.N.V.R., the Met. Officer. This was Syms' first real operation with the group. The previous met. officer had had a complete breakdown after the Swordfish bombers had failed to find the carrier in the Atlantic. It had been a freak storm, everyone had said. *One of those things*. But a lot of the pilots had watched him just the same. Wondering if he could have warned the patrol, could have known about the oncoming squall if he had really tried. If next time it might be their turn.

Syms was a mild little man with the globe-like head and round pale eyes of a scholar. It was said he had been a schoolmaster. Others, less charitable, alleged he foretold the weather by using two sets of seaweed. One for fighters. One for torpedo bombers.

Dusty Miller stood up and glared as young Creswell scurried into the room.

Then to Villiers he reported, 'All present, sir.'

The door from the Operations Room opened and Rear Admiral Chadwick stepped over the coaming. He wore a gleaming white scarf above his jacket, and his face shone with apparent good health.

He nodded to Villiers and said, 'Take no notice of me. I'll just sit in and listen, eh?'

Bill Ellis whispered, 'Which is guaranteed to make poor old Villiers relax, of course!'

Villiers cleared his throat and stared at the upturned faces.

'I've called you here—' He looked at Broderick, but he was watching the admiral. 'The fact is—' He did not know how to begin.

James, the Operations Officer, said abruptly, 'We have received reports that the Germans are moving heavy surface units to northern bases on the Norwegian coast.'

He looked quickly at the admiral. Rowan thought it was like the expression of a rabbit mesmerised by a falcon.

'Two cruisers were reported as being in Trondheim. *Now* they're supposed to be in Narvik.' He pointed one finger at the chart. 'Several other ships have moved as far north as Tromso. A sort of leap-frog operation. No apparent patrols or exercises in between.'

Villiers nodded. 'So it looks as if they are preparing some kind of attacking force for later on, when we head for longitude twenty-five east.' He hurried on as if afraid of losing the thread now that he had started. 'The convoy will be past Bear Island by then and within reach of enemy air attacks. It also means that his surface units will have air cover.'

They all looked round as Chadwick said smoothly, 'Also, it is the best point for them to tackle us from North Cape. The neck of the sack, so to speak.' He was not smiling. 'Is that *all*?'

Villiers stared at him. 'Well, sir, you've seen the reports and the operational stand-by for the Home Fleet's shadowing force. It's more or less what we anticipated.'

'I see.' Chadwick pushed himself from the door and removed his cap. Beside the chart he turned and ran his eyes over the assembled officers. 'It *is* what we expected. But war is like a pair of scales. A game of poker. What helps one, hinders another. Move to move, brain to brain.'

There was complete silence in the Ready Room, and the distant sounds of sea against the hull, the muffled clatter of machinery from the hangar deck were like parts of another existence.

Chadwick nodded slowly. 'Group North will naturally put their best surface ships into positions where they can reach our convoy.' He touched the chart with his strong fingers, his cufflink glittering in the strange glare, like molten copper. 'What Commander (Flying) *failed* to mention was that there is a damn great oil tanker heading north also. She is steaming only at night because of the R.A.F. But once clear of our bombers' range she'll crack it on a bit to get her cargo after the warships where it'll be needed.' He waited, watching their expressions, their varying degrees of understanding. 'The enemy will be moving aircraft, too. I told you when I took command that the Germans need fuel more than men. Group North would never risk a big tanker at this particular time unless they intended to act in depth against our convoy!' He smiled lazily. 'It all sounds rather grim. However, this is a move, part of the game.' He shot Villiers a quick glance. 'Which *should* have been examined, taken apart and then re-examined in context with the enemy's other movements.'

Broderick, the Air Staff officer, said quickly. 'By gathering his main units in the north, and all the extra air cover they will require, you mean there'll be a gap left in his defences, sir?' He bobbed his head as if to emphasise that he was the only one who understood Chadwick's comments.

The admiral smiled. 'Quite so.'

Villiers said, 'But if the R.A.F. can't get at the tanker—' He swung away from the chart, his face pale. 'You'll not send our aircraft, sir?'

Chadwick flicked something off one sleeve. 'We will still be between the convoy and any surface threat. An attack at first light, low down to avoid German R.D.F. It would only need a couple of planes. That tanker is probably snug and sound during full daylight.' He glanced calmly at the chart. 'Trondheim, Bodo, then Narvik perhaps. Or through the Lofotens and straight up to Altenfjord. One thing about the Germans, they may be damn good at their job, but their one weakness is their total lack of originality.' He smiled cheerfully. 'Yes, Villiers. This is the kind of eventuality I discussed in London. Why this information was transmitted to the admiral commanding the Home Fleet units.' He beamed. 'And to *me*.'

He paused, allowing the babble of voices to ebb and flow around the crowded room like echoes.

James said suddenly, 'I think it has a fair chance, sir.' He looked at Villiers, as if surprised by his own words. 'But our Swordfish will have a hard time getting away.' He faced Chadwick, as if expecting him to disperse his fears.

Chadwick said nothing but, 'We shall have to see.'

'It's all decided then?' Villiers watched him, his eyes deep in shadow. He looked ill.

'Not entirely.' Chadwick saw Rowan and held his eyes with his before passing on around the room. 'The Admiralty, the Intelligence chaps, and of course our friends in the Norwegian Resistance, have all been briefed.'

James exclaimed, 'But the Germans will get to know more and more about us, sir!'

Chadwick replied coldly, 'Well perhaps you know more about Germans than most of us.' He turned away from James's shocked face. 'But our convoy is of tremendous importance. Keep that in mind, gentlemen. This tanker could be only one move, but a damaging blow at the enemy all the same. The convoy will be attacked, no matter what we do or say. The Germans have no choice, any more than we do. So one deed cancels out the other. It is up to us to find what we can along the way to lessen the impact when it comes.'

Villiers asked huskily, 'Is that all, sir?'

'It is.' Chadwick picked up his cap. 'I think I'll go and join Guns's P.T. class. The air is a bit stuffy here.'

Villiers waited for the admiral to shut the door and then said quietly, 'That sums it up. Today was the first I heard of it. The admiral intends to separate our two carriers. Leave *Hustler* and half the escorts with the screen and move *Growler* stage by stage towards the Norwegian coast.' He looked at them wretchedly. 'I shall ask for volunteers, of course.'

James said, 'The admiral just told me. The crews are already selected. *He* will let you know when he's good and ready.'

Rowan thought of the admiral's eyes. That brief moment. *Selected.* His glance had told him that, if nothing else.

As he had listened to the counter-play beneath the chart he had seen more than Villiers' despair and James's anger at Chadwick's words. It was the same old argument. If every one of *Growler*'s planes were shot down, and the carrier herself sunk or badly damaged, it would still be worth it.

'*God,*' he spoke aloud, unaware of Ellis's sudden concern, 'I never counted on this!'

A telegraphist came from the Operations Room and handed a signal pad to James. He read it and said, 'Two U-boats reported to the east of the convoy.' He looked at Villiers. 'Here we go.'

Villiers straightened his stooped shoulders. 'Duty crews report to the A.S.O. when you dismiss.' He added, 'Not to worry. Something may turn up.'

Above the gently swaying carrier the sky had changed yet again. Painted in long copper brushstrokes from horizon to horizon, it looked at odds with the keen bite of the air.

Around the two stubby carriers the sloops dipped and lifted across the undulating water, their decks shining as the spray burst across their stems and angled guns.

Far away across the port bow, and just visible on the hard horizon line, the nearest convoy escort showed herself like a flaw on the sea's edge. A tiny dot circled above the escort, and as Rowan watched from a walkway, his cheeks stinging in the air, he knew it was the A.A. cruiser's ancient Walrus seaplane, a Shagbat as they were affectionately known throughout the Navy.

Just the thing for keeping an eye open for surfaced U-boats. As helpless as a blind baby against anything which flew.

And beyond that, he wondered, were the great Goliaths of the Home Fleet really there? Waiting to dash down and defend the convoy at an hour's notice? There were too many maybes for comfort.

Something bobbed out below the bridge structure, and he turned to watch Lieutenant Syms as he paid out his large orange balloon. He made a few half-hearted attempts with it and then withdrew it.

Rowan called, 'What do you think?'

Syms looked down at him, his eyes opaque. 'Not sure.' He hesitated. 'But I've been thinking about it since this morning. We could hit some fog.'

Rowan turned away. Fog. That really would put the tin-lid on it.

Syms stared after him. 'I might be mistaken of course.' He looked up at the masthead, Chadwick's flag whipping out to the breeze. 'On the other hand . . .'

His thoughts and doubts were scattered to the wind as the next two Swordfish rumbled along the deck towards the bows, their engines snarling as they received the signal to take off.

Another patrol. Syms shook his head and retreated within the island.

Rowan watched them lift and then circle away towards the distant convoy, and from his steel chair on the bridge Captain Buchan followed them with his binoculars.

Bray, the Navigating Officer, who was in charge of the watch, said absently, 'Funny when you think about it, sir. A merchant ship's hull, a carrier's top, and a whole gaggle of seamen and fliers mixed up inside her, I don't know. It doesn't seem right.'

Lieutenant John Bray was an R.N.R. officer who had served in oil tankers as a second mate until the war. He still did not know if the Old Man liked him or not. Some regular officers loathed the reservists. Especially those who had been on the beach between the wars, like Buchan.

Buchan did not turn in his chair but said, 'Bring her back on course again, Pilot. *Hustler* will be flying-off the next patrol.'

Bray grinned at his back. He hadn't heard a bloody word he'd said.

He crossed to the voicepipe. 'Port ten.'

Buchan felt the steel arms of his chair pressing into his ribs as Bray conned the ship round again to her original course.

It all seemed to be going well enough, so why was he so uneasy? Weather reports were fair. The two battleships were at sea with their escorting destroyers. Do them good to do a bit of sea-time instead of swinging round their buoys in Scapa, he thought. It was unfair, and he knew it. A few months ago, when he had been pining out his life in one of those awful shore establishments, he'd have given his right arm for anything which floated. Even a boom-defence ship at Scapa Flow would have seemed like heaven.

He ran his gloved hand along the rough metal plates below the glass screen.

Poor *Growler*. She was not at all beautiful. He had heard Bray's remarks and had been surprised at his own immediate resentment. She was his ship and nobody, not even Chadwick, he smiled, *that man*, would put her in senseless jeopardy.

A bosun's mate called, 'From W/T, sir. Two U-boats to the east of the convoy.'

'Very good.'

He kept his gaze on the horizon as it sloped back and forth as if trying to tip the ships over the edge.

He heard Bray shuffling his leather sea boots and softened his heart towards him. Bray was a bit of a bore sometimes when he went on about the good old days of the Merchant Service. But once, in the Atlantic, they had seen a convoy savagely mauled, and one old freighter left to capsize and sink, while her consorts of a long passage had steamed away, closing their ranks. He had turned to Bray to ask him about the freighter. She had looked so old. So very forlorn as she had lifted her outdated stern and solitary screw towards the smoke and the sky. Buchan had been shocked to see that

65

Bray had removed his cap and had been staring at the sinking wreck as if unable to take his eyes from her.

Bray had said brokenly, 'My first ship. Poor old girl.'

The words of a simple sailor, he thought. But how they summed up the whole bloody war.

He said, 'What you were just saying about *Growler*, Pilot.' He heard Bray's feet stop shuffling. 'She'll do me.'

Bray grinned. 'Me too, sir.' He moved to the gyro repeater. 'She's a bit like me, I suppose. Half and half.'

Buchan stiffened in his chair as he heard the far-off crump, crump of exploding depth charges. Miles away. The convoy escort commander was on the ball. The Swordfish would be there now to add their weight if the U-boats showed themselves.

Bray said, 'This'll mean another big alteration of course, I suppose, sir.'

'We'll know soon enough. The submarines might know nothing about the convoy. The destroyers could drive them deep before they find out.'

Bray sighed. He thought of the hundreds of miles to go before they dropped anchor again. Nothing seemed to bother the Old Man. Which was just as well, he decided.

5

Hand Picked

FOR four days the convoy steamed steadily north and north-east, keeping to the same high speed, staying in its regular formation, until it seemed as if nothing could or would ever change.

The early U-boat scare had almost been forgotten, and to Rowan, and most of the others who lived, slept and worked within *Growler*'s sturdy hull, time and distance had grown out of all proportion.

Only when he had visited the Operations Room or had chatted with Bray, the Navigating Officer, had he kept a sense of real understanding. Of the one and a half thousand miles astern of the convoy, of the fact that the jutting horn of Spitsbergen, which still lay a thousand miles beyond the bows, was the nearest land, and that when they passed it they were only halfway to their destination. It made him edgy and irritable, which was alien to his nature, and he was helpless to forestall sudden bursts of temper, which even Bill's prevailing good humour failed to quench.

It was the complete emptiness of each dragging day which made it harder to take. The long, eye-searing days weaving over the rigid lines of merchantmen. The strain of the eerie dusk and the shadows on the sea's face which became packs of motionless submarines. He had sighted some gleaming teeth of drifting ice, and huge patterns of sea birds floating unconcerned over a patch of water, only flapping away as the intruding aircraft had roared overhead, and then alighting again to continue their ritual. Resting, or waiting for unwary fish, nobody seemed to know.

The incoming W/T messages continued to mark their progress far beyond the Arctic Circle. The routine ones told

Syms about changing fronts and varying pressures. Elsewhere they were having rain and sunshine, sleet and drought. Around the convoy, the weather remained the same. *Faceless*.

The news of the war was cautious. The Allies had completely taken Sicily, and the Italians were busy trying to surrender everything to them and turn their backs on their German partners. If the Germans were depressed about it, their own broadcasts gave little hint. *Growler*'s W/T often picked up their radio programmes from Norway and further afield. Stirring military music, marching songs, and one alarming item in English which had proclaimed that H.M.S. *Growler* had been sunk with all hands. Only when the newsreader had gone on to describe the carrier's destruction in the Mediterranean had the company relaxed.

A week after leaving Iceland the convoy made a rendezvous with two large fleet oilers, and the overworked escorts took on more fuel with barely a break in their daily routine.

The organisation was certainly impressive and accurately timed. Rowan had had plenty of opportunity to study the thirty-five merchant ships. It was a wonder they could retain such a good speed. He had never seen such overloaded ships. Every foot of deck space was crammed with tall wooden crates, folded aircraft, tanks and armoured vehicles of every make and size. Had this been a winter run to North Russia it would have been very different, he thought. They would have had to cut their deck cargoes by half, or turn turtle at the first coating of ice with its frightening topweight which could cripple even the largest ships.

He often flew quite low across the convoy, seeing upturned faces and waving hands. It took guts to be a merchant sailor. You were always the target. With nothing to hit back with but a few pop-guns.

Rowan's father had been in the army in that other war, and had often told him about the Russian Revolution, and the effect it had made on the eventual uneasy peace with a new Germany. It was strange to think of them as allies, especially as they had been so ready and eager to sign a peace treaty with Hitler when it had suited them.

And now, all those ships, tanks and boxes of equipment would soon be on the Russian Front. He hoped that the cost of getting them there would not be forgotten as quickly as his father's efforts had been.

On the eighth and ninth days the convoy lost some ground in a wide alteration of course away from an alleged U-boat sighting report. True or false was anyone's guess, but the possible lengthening of the voyage could only add to the tension as well.

The next day it was announced that the Allies had invaded Italy. A week or so back there would have been a party to celebrate the first real foothold in Europe. But it was so sudden, so remote, that it made many of the men in the convoy feel more cut off than ever.

In the Ready Room, drowsing and chatting over coffee, cigarettes and pipes, Bill Ellis said, 'I'll bet it'll be roses all the way to Rome for those lucky sods. I wish to God we were there instead of up here.' He laughed at his own frustration. 'Wherever *here* is!'

Villiers walked through the room on his way to the bridge, shoulders hunched, his face expressionless.

Ellis stood up. 'Any idea what's happening, sir?'

Villiers paused, dragging his mind to the present. 'Intelligence seem to think that Jerry knows what we're up to. But because of the escort and covering force he intends to wait for the grand slam.' He gave what might be a shudder. 'But I don't know, Bill. The bastards must have something up their sleeves.'

Rowan had been half-listening and half-watching the two youngest pilots, Creswell and Cotter, the New Zealander. They were playing noughts and crosses, their faces totally absorbed.

He asked abruptly, 'What about our *special role*, sir?'

The other two looked down at him.

Villiers replied, 'Talk, I should think. If the Intelligence people are right, I believe it'll be a battle between the heavy ships. The rest will be so much arithmetic.'

Lieutenant Commander James came out of his Operations Room.

He nodded to Villiers. 'Conference on the bridge. The admiral is calling for blood.' He gave a weary smile. 'Somebody has stolen his champagne, I expect.'

Rowan watched them leave and said, 'They're both scared to death of the admiral, Bill.'

Ellis sat down heavily. 'If we ever get to their exalted positions, I expect we'll show the same symptoms, my lad.'

Rowan realised he must have fallen asleep in the chair. He woke up with a start as a coffee mug rolled from a table and shattered on the deck.

Ellis said, 'We're turning.'

He stood up and hurried to a scuttle. It was caked with salt outside and heavy with condensation within.

He said tersely, '*Growler*'s turned to starboard.'

The pilots dropped their magazines and letters and joined him, straddling their legs as the carrier tilted with unexpected force, her decks vibrating to a surge of engine revolutions.

Rowan watched a blurred escort standing away from the carrier, the intermittent blink of a signal lamp and a sudden bright hoist of flags at her yard.

The deck righted itself again, and Cotter said, 'Well, that bit of dazzling excitement is over for another day!'

Several of them laughed.

Ellis was unbuttoning his battledress and scrambling inside his fleece-lined leather waistcoat. It was a strange garment which Ellis always claimed he had won from a French major at cards. He dragged out a little oilskin bag and produced a pocket compass.

He said quietly, 'South-east.' He closed it with a snap and looked at Rowan. 'Villiers was wrong. We're leaving the bloody convoy.'

The next batch of stand-by pilots entered the Ready Room, but the relieved ones stayed put.

Villiers and James came back together and paused uncertainly by the door as they were met by the watching faces, moulded together in an unasked question.

Villiers said, '*Hustler* is closing the convoy. She is taking two sloops and the tug.' He glanced at James as if for

70

confirmation. 'We are steering towards Norway with the remainder of our escort.'

Lieutenant Rolston snapped angrily, 'I think we can be trusted not to swim ashore and tell the enemy, sir!'

James shot him a warning glance, but Villiers replied calmly, 'I know. But I have no further information to give at this moment.'

James said, 'And if you speak like that again, Rolston, I'll have you in front of the captain, got it?'

Rolston glared at him. 'Aye, *aye*, sir.'

Ellis said, 'I think I'll go and eat. It helps me at moments of great crisis.'

James added in a more level voice, 'No, Bill. You and Tim will report to the bridge.' He looked round the room. 'And you, Creswell. Jump about. The admiral's up there.'

The three officers reached the bridge and were hurried to the chartroom. It was unusually crowded, and misty with heat.

Rear Admiral Chadwick was standing across the vibrating chart table, arms folded, his long side-burns like silver in the deckhead lights. The captain, navigating officer and Broderick, the Air Staff Officer, were grouped around the brightly lit rectangle like actors waiting for a prompt.

Chadwick glanced up and nodded. 'Good.' He looked at Rowan, isolating him from the rest. 'Sleeping better?'

Rowan felt the others staring at him. He answered uncertainly, 'Well, yes, sir.'

Chadwick gave a brief smile. 'Fine. You've been looking a bit fraught lately. I keep an eye on my people, y'know.'

He turned to Bray. 'Well, Pilot?'

Bray cleared his throat. The atmosphere was very tense, and Rowan guessed there had been some sort of argument before they had arrived.

The navigating officer rested his brass dividers on the chart. 'This is our present position. We are now steering approximately south-east. In four days we will be here, provided—'

Chadwick interrupted impatiently, '*Provided*, well, that's

always a good beginning!' He looked at the three pilots. 'A lot depends on our intelligence and sighting reports.' He glanced at Buchan. 'And the behavior of our little force. But with any sort of luck I intend to launch a hit-and-run attack on that big tanker. It seems she's had a spot of trouble. An accident or sabotage, we don't know. But she will be delayed. It will give us time.'

Buchan spoke for the first time. 'You'll be expected to fly as an escort for three Swordfish. Knock out the tanker at her anchorage and come straight back.' He sounded as if the words were strangling him.

Chadwick ignored him. 'You, Rowan, will be in command.'

Rowan wanted to moisten his lips. 'Yes, sir.'

Surprisingly, Chadwick grinned, his wide mouth almost touching his side-burns.

'Is that all you've got to say?'

Rowan moved closer to the chart, seeing Bray's neat calculations, the final pencilled cross off the Norwegian coast. At a very rough guess it was about one hundred miles from the land. A Swordfish had a range of just over five hundred miles, A Seafire a good bit less. It would not allow much time for sightseeing.

'It could be anywhere, sir.'

Broderick said in his flat voice, 'Don't worry. We'll fill in the details. I've got drawings and some photographs in my intelligence files.'

Ellis glanced at Rowan and then at the admiral. 'If we pull it off, sir. What then?'

Chadwick eyed him calmly. 'What then? Back to the job, of course. We will rejoin the convoy with all haste and be ready for the final free-for-all. It will be quite a detour. It will also mean we'll be on our own for several days. But the C. in C. has approved. *Our* yardarm's clear.' It sounded as if nothing could go wrong.

Broderick faltered between Chadwick and Buchan. 'Then if that's all, sir?'

The admiral frowned. 'For the moment. Keep it amongst

yourselves. I don't want a whole lot of gossip. These officers and the Swordfish crews will be kept off the patrol roster *unless*,' he shot a quick glance at the captain, 'we are overwhelmed by the whole Luftwaffe.'

Broderick kept his face stiff. 'Carry on, gentlemen.'

As they made to leave the chartroom Godsal, the urbane flag lieutenant, said, 'Not you.' He smiled at Rowan. 'The admiral wishes you to wait in his quarters.'

Rowan stared at Ellis. He had not even realised that Godsal had been there. Perhaps that was the most important thing in a flag lieutenant. Be invisible until needed.

The three pilots stood together in the steel passageway abaft the chartroom.

Ellis said, 'Watch your step, Tim.' He scratched his head. 'Still, you are now our boss. That must be good, eh?'

They heard raised voices in the chartroom, and Buchan saying hotly, 'That was unfair, sir, speaking like that in front of my subordinates!'

The door opened and closed and Bray strode past on his way to the forebridge. He looked at Rowan and grimaced. *'Jesus,'* he said.

Rowan found his way to Chadwick's quarters, feeling the ship shaking and pitching to the additional revolutions. The sloops would be glad, he thought. Instead of rolling along as slow escorts for once.

Dundas, the admiral's steward, took his cap. 'Have a pew, sir. He'll not be long.' He could have been a manservant in some grand house, a thousand miles from the sea and the war.

Chadwick entered the day cabin and hurled his cap at Dundas.

'Sit down.' He glanced at himself in a mirror and seemed satisfied. 'I'll not waste your time.' He looked for Dundas. 'I'll have some sherry.' He studied Rowan for the first time. 'You can have what you like now that you're off the duty roster.'

'Sherry will do fine, sir.'

'Good.' Chadwick sounded distant. 'Can't bear lack of decision.' Then he smiled. 'Now. About our little raid . . .'

73

Rowan sipped the sherry, watching Chadwick the whole time. Here, in this spartan place, he felt untidy and awkward in Chadwick's company.

Chadwick continued, 'Van Roijen will be the senior Swordfish pilot. Seems very competent.' He chuckled. 'For a foreigner.'

Rowan hid his surprise. He was to lead the fighters, and the Dutchman would control the torpedo attack. Not Miller or Kitto.

Chadwick said slowly, 'I know what you're thinking.' He came to some sort of decision. 'You are a good pilot. I've been told so, and I've watched you myself. I like what I see. But if you're thinking I've given you command of the attack because you're the best thing on two feet, you can forget it.' He grinned at Rowan's expression. 'You're good. Not the best.'

He stood up and moved restlessly across the cabin, the glass held in front of him like a talisman.

'I think Jerry will do all he can to bash the convoy. If and when he makes his big stand, I'll need every fully experienced leader I've got. This raid of ours could make a difference to things. But then again it might fail. You might not get back.'

Rowan wanted to finish the sherry, to move his limbs, anything, but Chadwick's level, matter of fact tone held him rigid in his seat.

He pulled no punches. Gave no hint of optimism, even of survival. How different from Villiers. He could not help making the comparison. Villiers seemed to take every pilot's life as part of his own before each patrol or exercise.

Chadwick said, 'I've studied your record. You did not begin in the Fleet Air Arm.' It was a statement. 'You started in destroyers. East-coast escort duties.'

'Yes, sir.' It all came flooding back. The elderly, First World War destroyer, the routine and deadly business of coastal convoys. Bombers, E-Boat Alley, it seemed a hundred years ago.

'I got fed up with convoys, sir. They were asking for

volunteers for flying training. I think I'd have volunteered for anything to get off convoy duty.' He grinned. 'As soon as I could fly, I went straight back to doing just that.'

Chadwick watched him, seeing his change of mood. The youth emerging as he smiled, from behind the grave, set expression he usually wore.

'Yes. And you obtained a watchkeeping certificate while you were in destroyers.' He nodded slowly. 'Bit of each. Flier *and* sailor. You'll need both for this job. To get the attack going. To get 'em back to the ship afterwards.'

Afterwards. Rowan said, 'I'll do my best, sir.' It sounded inadequate.

'Yes.' Chadwick looked away. 'This is how it's done. Routine never won a war.'

There was a tap on the door and Godsal looked in at them, his face blank. It was over.

Chadwick said, 'Learn all you can in the next few days. Landmarks. Channels between the islands. That sort of thing. If we can get you to the jump-off position without raising an alarm, you will have surprise on your side.' He held Rowan's gaze. 'But not much else, I'm afraid.' He nodded. 'We'll have another yarn sometime.'

Rowan walked out into the passageway, dazed with the ease and speed of Chadwick's appraisal. He had been given a job, cut down to size, and handed very small hope of getting back alive, all in a few minutes.

He found Ellis and van Roijen waiting for him in their cabin.

He said quietly, 'Pep talk. I don't know whether to admire him or hate his guts.'

Van Roijen beamed. 'It will be fine, Tim. What is it you say? A piece of cake!'

The six air crews sat in the Ready Room, not looking at each other, their breathing reduced almost to the gentle throb of *Growler*'s main engine.

The lights were dimmed to ease the strain on their eyes. It was like sitting and waiting for the world to end, Rowan thought. His emotions were in turmoil, so that he was surprised to find that his hands and feet were quite still, his breathing slow and regular.

He let his eyes move around the others. Six aircraft. Twelve men. Ready to move. *Expendable*.

Bill Ellis, legs out-thrust, eyes closed, his blond hair ruffling slightly from a deckhead fan.

Creswell, his face even more youthful in the orange glow.

The Swordfish crews, pilots, observers, and air gunners. It was odd to realise that Troup, the ex-actor, had an orchid grower as his observer. And young Cotter had come from the opposite end of the world to meet this moment.

True to Bray's calculations, *Growler* had arrived at the pencilled cross, some one hundred nautical miles north-west of the Lofoten Islands. They had not sighted a single ship or aircraft since they had left the convoy, and with their four rust-streaked escorts they had had the Arctic to themselves.

From the babble of W/T signals it seemed that the convoy had been stalked twice by U-boats. No ships had been sunk or damaged, and the escorts had not reported any kills. A probing exercise perhaps. *Flexing muscles*. Either way, the enemy knew about the convoy, its strength and its value. The destination was obvious. Over the last days Rowan had often thought about the thirty-five ships steaming in their long, straight lines. Not crews or human beings. Just the ships. Unflinching. Unstoppable.

The door opened and Lieutenant Commander Miller walked below the one central light.

He said quietly, 'Time to go, lads.' He smiled, his devil's beard jutting above his leather jacket.

They all stood, picking up their helmets and goggles, mentally stripping and readjusting their minds. The plans and charts, Broderick's sketches of islands and landmarks were now real and stark.

Rowan walked with him towards the passageway. How quiet the ship was. She had been at action stations for four hours. Every gun manned, all air crews mustered and ready just in case the enemy knew about Chadwick's private war.

They had been briefed and briefed again, until their minds

had refused to accept another titbit of information. *There was a ship at anchor close inshore of an island. It had to be sunk.*

Miller said, 'If you can't hit the bloody thing, forget it and come back.' He sounded grim. 'There'll be other targets.'

Out on to the flight deck, empty but for the six aircraft. Below in the hangar deck the rest of *Growler*'s planes and crews waited and listened.

Rowan shivered and tightened the scarf around his neck. He had never got used to this strange copper light. But it was five in the morning, and the wind across his face was quite raw.

He saw Petty Officer Thorpe crouching by the aircraft. He looked towards him and gave a brief wave. He would know what Rowan was thinking.

Just a few hours ago he had said worriedly, 'You could have had Jonah tomorrow, sir. But in all honesty I can't let you take her on a caper like this one. Not after the hammering she had.'

Chitty, the Air Engineer Officer, had confirmed it. 'You'll have to be content with Dusty Miller's.' He had tried to dispel Rowan's apprehension. 'Good as gold.'

He was right of course. This stupid preference, this superstition and folk-lore were absurd. Things were bad enough without . . . He stopped his racing thoughts as the first Swordfish roared into life.

Miller shouted, 'Give van Roijen his head, Tim. You just watch for fighters and flak.'

Rowan nodded, feeling his pockets, adjusting his leather helmet. He could see it in his mind as if he were there. The low, sleeping hump of an island, the swirling water and the long, boxlike hull of the tanker. He tried to remember all the other details. The Germans had plenty of fighters at Tromso and Bardufoss. There were probably some local fields as well.

He looked at the shadowy figures around the aircraft and on the nearest walkway. Some were friends. All were part of him. It was dangerous to think that in twenty minutes he would be over the target.

He dragged on his gloves and strode quickly to the waiting

Seafire, and climbed into the cockpit with barely another glance. *When you started to think of what you were leaving behind.* Again he had to check himself.

Rowan slammed the canopy over his head and settled himself on his parachute, his hands and eyes moving over the instruments, checking, trusting nothing.

How loud the Merlin sounded as he tightened his harness and eased the throttle very slightly.

He watched the darting flames from the Swordfish exhausts, the shaded blink of a lamp from the bridge. He saw the twin wings of van Roijen's plane like black lines against the strange sky, the sudden tilt as it began to move forward, the others pivoting clumsily to follow. He could just make out the pencil-like shape of a torpedo slung below the nearest plane. That would be young Cotter's.

He turned his head to look for Bill's plane, seeing only a wingtip shivering violently as its engine shattered the dawn air. In his mirror he could see the third fighter more clearly. Creswell's cockpit hidden by the uplifted nose and racing prop.

A crackling voice said into his earphones, 'All Swordfish airborne. Stand by, *Jonah*.'

Rowan gripped the stick and tried not to think about his real Jonah, down there in a corner of the hangar deck. Like a patient in a hospital. On the sidelines.

The lamp blinked again and he opened the throttle with slow deliberation. It was always a difficult time, with so much to see and do that it was rarely possible to contemplate what would happen if the plane stalled as it left the deck and plunged over the bows. *Growler* would not even notice.

He felt the cockpit quivering violently as he swung the Seafire to one side, searching for the white centre line, oblivious to the pale faces and scarlet fire-fighting gear, yet noting it all the same.

A voice crackled 'Good luck' in his ears, but he forgot everything but the final moments of take-off.

He saw the sea rushing beneath him, like black silk, touched here and there by metallic reflections. He swallowed hard, checking his compass, the undercarriage light, the boost, as with a joyful roar he lifted higher and higher from the carrier.

He said after a few moments, 'This is *Jonah*. Take station on me.'

R/T would be unused from now on, until the fun-and-games started. It was dangerous even to test the guns. There could be a patrol boat below, an outgoing U-boat.

He smiled despite his taut nerves. If they had any sort of sense they would all be asleep.

He felt as if he were flying at ten times his usual speed, the sea flashing beneath him in an unending panorama, broken occasionally by small white-horses or darker patches of deep troughs.

Rowan checked either quarter, seeing Bill and Creswell spread out like the other two prongs of a deadly trident.

He wondered what van Roijen and his companions were doing. Slower, and flying even lower than the three fighters, they were quite invisible.

Something small and dark and ringed with white spray leapt out of the gloom. A fishing boat by the look of it. Rowan felt sweat under his helmet. He should have seen it much earlier. He saw the single mast and tiny wheelhouse vanish beneath him, half expecting to feel the flak slamming into the Seafire's belly. Just a fishing boat. But he should have seen it. It could have been anything.

It was getting much brighter already. He could see the camouflage paint on the port wing, the red and blue roundel at the end of it. And there, through the throbbing prop, the low-lying hump of land.

He checked his instruments, his mind taking one thing at a time. He was at two thousand feet. He moved the stick gently, knowing the others were watching him, waiting to follow. Fifteen hundred. A thousand.

Another boat was end-on across the starboard bow, and he thought he saw smoke rising from it. But not flak. Either its engine or an early breakfast. He grinned, feeling his jaw ache with the effort.

Then all at once the land was right there underneath, hills, tiny streams and barren looking crags leaping towards him as he swept across the island from west to east. Two little houses, like white cubes, a tiny, fast moving dot. A dog probably.

A wide arrowhead of glittering water to starboard, and more houses far beyond. That would be Svolvaer.

He pulled the aircraft to port in a wide turn, losing height, his eyes straining across a smoother patch of sheltered water. There was the little church, the one he had memorised from the files.

He stared, his thumb on the firing button, his brain unwilling to accept that the anchorage was empty.

There was a puff of smoke to starboard and he felt a shell exploding, well clear, unreal.

He snapped on his microphone. 'This is *Jonah*. We'll steer north.'

He heard Bill reply just as tersely, 'Roger.'

Rowan was sweating badly. This was no good at all. The islands seemed to be all round him, and there was more flak rising from the top of a bald hill. A line of scarlet jewels, lifting so slowly and then whipping past the fighter with the speed of light.

He pushed up his goggles and wiped his eyes with his glove. Ten more minutes. *No longer*. He saw the three Swordfish for the first time, flying in line ahead between two islands. Very slow and sedate, as if they were seeking a place to perch.

More flak. This time it was from a battery inland. He saw the dirty brown explosions like cotton wool against the sky, catching the first real sunlight above a small village.

All hell would be breaking loose now. Phones ringing. Pilots and ack-ack crews leaping out of bed. Serve 'em right, he thought vaguely.

He thrust the stick forward and watched the water dashing to meet him as a tall headland screened the shellbursts and the torpedo bombers from view.

And there she is. Larger than he had expected, making just a small wash as she turned slightly towards the main channel.

He shouted, 'Tanker dead ahead! I'm attacking!'

Unblinking he watched the rounded poop and squat bridge

80

structure blocking his way, a flag hanging limp above her taffrail. Some men were tearing a canvas canopy from a machine gun mounting abaft her single funnel.

He riveted his full attention on the sight, his hand almost numb while he controlled stick and firing button in one unit.

She was full to the gills with fuel. Beyond the bridge he could see the small shadow her hull was making on the water. She was so deep-laden he could almost feel the frantic efforts of her captain to take her closer inshore.

He pressed the button, feeling the wings jerk violently while he watched the tracers smoking towards the stern and the limp flag. With a great roar he was climbing diagonally across the ship, seeing his shadow on the water being joined, first by that of Bill's Seafire and then young Creswell's. He levelled off, taking precious seconds to watch the tracers raking across the hull. The machine guns pointed at the sky, the canvas cover still in place. One body lay nearby, of the others there was no sign.

He heard van Roijen's thick voice, 'Hello, *Jonah*! *I see her!* Am attacking now, by God!'

Rowan tried to imagine the scene below. For days the tanker's captain had been moving and hiding. Dodging the R.A.F., keeping close inshore to avoid submarine attack. Then, when he was moving into safe waters, and at a time of day when few felt at their best, enemy fighters had appeared. Where from, how many, no longer mattered. They were attacking his ship, while he and his men were standing on one giant bomb.

'Close on me!'

Rowan tore his eyes from the tanker and the moth-like wings of the first Swordfish as it flew straight down the channel towards her.

Flak interlaced between two islands, but it was haphazard, blind.

All caution was gone now. He heard the Swordfish pilots yelling to one another, van Roijen's great bellow as he took his plane even lower, so that it seemed to be straddling its racing reflection on the swirling current.

There was a brief white splash as the torpedo hit the water.

Rowan wiped his face, tilting over to watch, holding his breath. But the torpedo ran true. It did not porpoise and break its back as so many did when the moment came.

As the Swordfish lifted away he saw the rear gunner pouring a long burst across the tanker's steel deck.

Here was the next one. That was Troup. What a perfect name for an actor. He tore his eyes away, veering from side to side as some bright tracer floated past him. Some shellbursts, too. From between two islands, so there was probably an anchored warship here. The tanker's escort maybe.

He saw a vivid flash, and imagined he could hear the torpedo explode as it struck the tanker's hull just forward of her bridge. Spray and smoke erupted skyward, and he saw Troup's plane fly directly through it, reeling violently as it was caught in the shock-wave.

The second torpedo also struck home, and with it came the biggest explosion so far. When the smoke drifted to the nearest island the whole of the tanker's foredeck was belching flames, the catwalk and forward mast pitching down into a great, glowing crater.

The ship's wake was curving, the wash dropping away, as a boat was swayed out from some derricks, and several splashes showed that rafts were being jettisoned. The crew were abandoning her.

Creswell's frantic voice seemed to scrape the inside of his skull.

'Fighters! Twelve o'clock high!'

Then Bill's voice, harsh and angry. 'You bloody fool! You should have seen them!'

Rowan said, 'This is *Jonah*. Break off the attack.'

Van Roijen sounded far away, almost drowned in static. 'Roger.' A pause. 'Pull away, damn you!'

His last comment was addressed to the third Swordfish. It was circling round the blazing tanker, and Cotter obviously intended to fire his torpedo, having been driven from his original attempt by the explosion and great gouts of burning fuel.

'Tallyho!' That was Cotter. He was yelling aloud, his

voice that of a jubilant schoolboy.

Rowan forgot Cotter as he opened the throttle and went into a steep climb. He had seen the German fighters coming out of the pale sunlight. Two of them, with another one just lifting over the nearest island.

Bill was right. Creswell should have done his job and watched over his leader. Now it was all too late. The thing to do was to wing one of them and then get away after the Swordfish.

A shadow flashed across his sight and he hurled the Seafire into a steep turn, the other plane's silhouette twisting away and then starting another climb. Rowan tried to steady his breathing, to stop himself from peering into his mirror. It was an ME 109, with yellow stripes on its wings, inboard from the stark black crosses.

He pressed the button and swore as the tracers fanned harmlessly above the German's tail.

Round again, the cannon and machine guns hammering while the other pilot tried to shake him off.

Thoughts scurried through his mind, while his eyes, hands and feet moved in oiled unison. The German pilot was handling his machine as if going through the training manual. He was probably brand new, sent to Norway to get in some training before going to the Eastern Front.

He pressed the button again and saw the shells ripping across the black crosses, the tell-tale plume of smoke twisting and writhing as the Messerschmitt went plunging out of control.

Rowan sucked in his breath, willing the man to bale out. But he did not, and he knew he must have been hit in the last burst.

He levelled off, his eyes watering as he swept round into the sun's path.

He heard the muffled rattle of machine guns, and twisted his head to see Bill and another ME 109 tearing across the empty sky, through a pall of smoke which must have reached this far from the torpedoed tanker.

'Hello, *Jonah*!' It was Creswell. 'Derek's under attack!'

Rowan did not bother to acknowledge, but put the Seafire into a steep dive, the engine's note rising to a whistling whine.

He called, 'Hello, Derek, this is *Jonah*. Drop that bloody fish and get the hell out of it!'

From a corner of his eye he saw the first ME 109 explode on a hillside, and the shadow of Bill's plane as he roared above, all guns firing as he went after his quarry.

Creswell was close on Rowan's tail now, his lesson learned.

Cotter shouted, *'Here we go!'*

Rowan gritted his teeth as the low-flying ME 109 swept round the jutting headland to meet the Swordfish almost head-on. It was finished before Cotter even knew what was happening.

The darting tongues of flame from the German's guns, the familiar sight of fragments hurled across the water, and then the Swordfish drove on to explode against the sinking tanker in a great ball of orange fire.

Bill's ME 109 was trailing smoke, and without stopping for more was already heading towards the mainland.

Creswell was almost sobbing. 'Let me go for him!'

'Denied! Return to base!' Rowan peered at his clock, his eyes stinging with sweat. They had been far too long already.

Creswell was saying, 'He killed Derek!'

Bill called, 'Shut your mouth and do as you're told!'

The two Seafires swam out like sharks and formed up on Rowan's quarter.

Van Roijen called, 'Returning to base. Over and out.'

The islands vanished under the curved wings, and ahead stretched the great desert of empty, glittering water.

Compass, clock, height and fuel. He found that he wanted to blow his nose.

Beneath him the two Swordfish, unhampered by their torpedoes, were working up to their full speed of one hundred and thirty plus, and he could see van Roijen's red scarf whipping over his cockpit like a banner on a field of battle.

Three young men dead in exchange for a shipload of

desperately needed fuel. It made sense, he thought bitterly. It had to.

He craned his head round, the sun following him in his mirror. *Watch for the Hun who comes out of the sun.* And they were not home and dry yet. Not by a long shot.

6

News from Home

THE return of the small attacking force to *Growler*'s deck was
as wild as it was moving. As the handling parties swarmed
from the walkways to take charge of the aircraft Rowan could
only stare at the waving arms, the grins and excited faces on
every side.

Even the loss of the New Zealander's Swordfish failed to
break the obvious delight in their achievement. All the delays
and preparations, the endless patrols and the ceaseless work
on aircraft and machinery now seemed worthwhile.

Rowan waited below the island as Bill hurried towards
him, dragging off his helmet and Mae West and taking great
gulps of air.

Rowan felt the ache leaving his body, and said, 'Not one
bloody German all the way.'

Funnily enough, he had thought very little of enemy pursuit on the run back to the carrier. *Fog*. He kept remembering
Syms' doleful expression, and his feeling that fog was about.
But the sea had been bright and clear as he had tacked back
and forth across the tails of the slow-moving Swordfish.

He looked up, seeing the smoke from the engineroom
vents drifting abeam as the carrier started to heel round on a
new course.

Bill took a wrinkled apple from his pocket and rubbed it
slowly on his jacket. 'Heading north. Getting the hell out of
it. Just the job.'

Rowan watched his friend, wondering if there was fear or
uncertainty behind his homely face. He thought of his own
feelings when he had at last sighted the fat carrier and her four
escorts across the horizon like small fragments of land.

It had been something akin to love. The realisation that it
had been more than his own life at stake. Every minute while

he and the others had winged towards the target, and then started their return, *Growler*'s company, and those of her escorts, from admiral to junior stoker, had been waiting, almost motionless, for their reappearance. Not knowing if they had found the German tanker, or if they had all been shot down before they had even made a landfall. Knowing their own complete vulnerability.

He had been unable to resist doing a R.A.F. style victory roll above the carrier's deck, perhaps to share his true feelings with them.

From the air, with her splayed-out masts and aerials poking from either beam, the carrier had all the looks of a portly beetle. But at that moment she had seemed beautiful.

A bosun's mate said, 'You're wanted on the bridge.' He could not resist adding, 'Bloody well done, sir!'

Rowan noticed Bill's face and turned to see a petty officer who was standing by the arrester wires. He was wiping his hands with a lump of waste, but his eyes were towards the horizon. It was the P.O. who was in charge of Derek Cotter's crew. Keyed up like everyone else. Now he had nothing to do, no share in what had happened to the three young men who had died in a fireball.

He began to climb to the upper bridge, his limbs heavy and without feeling. It could easily have been Petty Officer Thorpe down there, waiting for the aircraft which would never return.

He found Chadwick pacing across the gratings, his face deep in thought. He saw Rowan and nodded briskly.

'Damn good show. Better than I expected.' He glanced at Villiers. '*Told* you, eh?'

Villiers looked at Rowan. 'I'm glad you managed it, Tim.'

Rowan tried to recall what he had reported on R/T while he had waited permission to land-on.

Chadwick said, 'Tanker destroyed, and one fighter shot down.'

Rowan looked at him. 'And Lieutenant Ellis's Messerschmitt was almost certainly a kill, sir.'

'We shall see.' Chadwick watched a steward struggling

across the bridge with a jug of tea. 'God, this *is* living.'

Rowan noticed the violent shaking of the bridge structure for the first time.

Villiers said quietly, 'The Chief's pulled out all the stops. We're heading north to Bear Island.'

Rowan tried to clear his mind, to rid himself from the darting shadow of the attacking fighter, his smoking tracers ripping across the enemy's wings.

He asked, 'But surely that will draw any pursuit straight to the convoy?'

Chadwick watched him over the rim of his mug. 'Doesn't matter any more. There's been a heavy U-boat attack.'

Rowan tried to discover some dismay on Chadwick's face.

The admiral added, 'Don't worry. Not on the convoy. It was on the heavy support group from the Home Fleet.'

Villiers shook his head and waved a mug of tea away. 'Fourteen U-boats. Strung out like pickets. They sank a destroyer and crippled a cruiser. Almost the worst part was that they managed to score a hit on the fleet carrier. She's gone back to Scapa with some of the destroyers. She should make it all right if they leave her alone.'

Chadwick said angrily, 'Bugger *their* problems! It makes our support vital from now on. Thank God *Hustler*'s with the convoy.' He forced himself to speak more calmly. 'The sinking of your tanker will start the Germans thinking a bit. And it proves my point. Sooner or later the Germans will start hitting the escorts first and *then* carving up the convoys.'

Rowan glanced through the open screen door at Buchan sitting on his steel chair, as if he were welded to the ship with it.

Chadwick snapped, 'Must go to the Ops Room and check a few points.' To Villiers he added, 'You, too.'

And to Rowan he merely said, 'Did well. I'll see it's noted.'

As he vanished down a bridge ladder Bray called, 'The captain would like to see you, Tim.'

Rowan walked into the bridge, seeing the quiet routine and order which seemed to flow from Captain Buchan.

'Thank you for waiting, sir.' He felt uncertain beside Buchan. All the years, the ships, the experience, even if he had been on the beach for a time. It was something which awed him.

Buchan said quietly, 'I'm glad you were lucky.' For once he seemed at a loss. 'Pity about young Cotter, but . . .'

He stood up violently and faced Rowan.

'I'm sorry to be the one to tell you. We had a signal from Admiralty just after you took off. There was a raid last night.' He was watching Rowan's face, his eyes like slate. 'Your home was hit. There were no survivors.'

Rowan stared at him, his mind stunned. The house. The wind across Oxshott Woods. His parents. Everything.

Buchan added quietly, 'God, I hate doing this. I've done it too much already. But to you especially. And at this moment in time.'

Rowan wiped his mouth with his hand. 'I'm glad you told me, sir.' He did not know why he had said it.

Buchan replied, 'Thank you for that. And if there's anything I can do. Anything, you understand?'

'Yes.' He could feel his chest shaking, the tears running down his face. But all he could do was stand there. 'Yes.'

Bray said urgently, 'The admiral's coming back, sir.'

Buchan nodded. 'Take this officer through your chartroom and down the starboard ladder. Get him to his cabin, and then report to me.'

Commander Jolly had entered by the opposite door and turned away as Rowan and the navigating officer walked past.

Then he said quietly. 'You learn to live with it. But you never get used to it.'

Buchan looked at him. 'True, Edgar.' Jolly had been his second in command since he had been given *Growler*. It was the first time he could recall his showing the slightest hint of compassion for anyone.

Chadwick strode amongst them. 'I've just heard about Lieutenant Rowan. Whose damn-fool idea was it to tell him about his parents?' He did not wait for an answer. 'It won't bring them back to life. It would have waited until we touched land again.' He walked to the clear-view screens. 'It's coming into the Operations Room now. Strong surface force has left Tromso. U-boats are already closing the convoy, and I expect they've got every recce plane and bomber from here to blazes ready for the signal from Group North.' He faced them grimly. 'And when that happens I want all our people on top line. I also want them alive, not being knocked down out of the sky because they were thinking of homes and families, *right*?'

He swung round as Bray re-entered the bridge. 'Check your calculations again, Pilot.' He looked at Buchan. 'And tell the engineroom to give us more revs. This is an escort carrier, not a bloody banana boat!' He stormed out of the bridge.

Jolly breathed out slowly. 'Well, now.'

The captain groped for his pipe, and then picked up the engineroom handset. He could see the knuckles on his beefy fist standing out pale as he gripped the handset with all his might. *Bloody banana boat, was she? He would show him.* He forced himself to think of his wife. *That man.*

Buchan was calm again. 'Oh, Chief? This is the captain.'

'Hands to flying stations! Stand by to fly-off aircraft!'

Rowan pushed his way into the Ready Room, half-listening to the mounting roar of engines, the throbbing din thrusting down through decks and cabins as a new strike of torpedo bombers prepared to take off.

It had been like that for twenty-four hours. While *Growler* pounded her way northwards towards the rendezvous at Bear Island, and the W/T collected an endless pile of signals about sightings of U-boats and heavy surface ships which had vanished from their Norwegian bases.

Rowan shivered despite his fleece-lined jacket and Mae West, and the press of figures all about him. He had been like it for two days. Since the raid, the news about his parents. Like being ill, or recovering from a terrible hangover. It was the only way he could describe his feelings. The doc had called it shock. Too much strain on top of all he had been doing for months. What did he expect, for God's sake? For pilots to go on leave whenever . . . He shivered again. Even that train of thought was instantly snapped. There was nowhere to go on leave. He remembered what Bill had said after the last one. Now he would never lie in bed with old Simon at his side, listening to the night wind. He hoped that none of them had suffered. He felt the returning pain behind his eyes and tried to hold it back.

The doc had been right of course. It was shock. But what was the use of knowing about it?

Broderick looked over the assembled air crews. 'Good. I'll fill you in on a few items.'

He seemed very calm, his training as Air Staff Officer pushing whatever he felt inwardly aside.

'The convoy has been attacked again. One escort has been put down, and it's generally believed that a U-boat was destroyed, too. *Hustler*'s flying patrols are all over the convoy and well ahead of it, so that the U-boats will be forced to run deep for much of the time. More to the point, none of the merchantmen has been hit.'

Some of the pilots shuffled their boots and stared at the coloured charts. Others were listening to the noise from the flight deck as the last of the Swordfish roared away, the sound swallowed up within seconds.

Broderick added, 'With luck we will be in close contact with the convoy tomorrow. It is a critical time for the commodore. U-boats ahead and possibly shadowing and trying to find a gap in his screen. And surface ships heading to intercept his last run towards the south. He has to keep in touch with the support group, but be prepared to make violent changes of course if and when Jerry can pin him down with a definite sighting.'

Cameron, 'Lord Algy', muttered, 'Here we go. *Focke-Wulf Blues!*'

Broderick had very keen ears. 'Right, Algy, if a Focke-Wulf or two gets to sniffing distance the convoy will really be in trouble. With the fleet carrier knocked out of the fight,' he was ticking off the flaws in their armour, 'the support group will have to share *Hustler*'s air cover with the convoy's commodore. And to catch a Focke-Wulf you need plenty of fighters.' He glanced at the operations officer. 'Does that sum it up, Cyril?'

James had been staring at one of the charts. 'Yes. There's only one solution now. We must fly fighters direct to *Hustler*.'

There was complete silence, so that the sounds of creaking steel, the occasional boom of water along the hull seemed extra loud and close.

Dymock Kitto, his newly added half-stripe shining between the original faded lace on his shoulder straps stepped up beside the desk, his chin blue in the harsh light.

'We'll be leaving just two fighters aboard *Growler*.' His voice was quite level, as if the task of flying to a Seafire's extreme range and finding the other carrier before the fuel ran out was mere routine. 'I'll take Red Flight.' He looked at Rowan. 'You'll have Blue.'

They all looked at each other. Then Kitto added, 'Andy Miller will have to take up his old role again and defend the ship while we're away.' He glanced at Mariot, a junior pilot who had joined the ship with Creswell. 'You, too. The rest will fly-off in half an hour. Get your gear together and check with Ops and the Met. Office.' He did not ask if anyone had any questions. There was not much point.

Rowan stood looking at the charts. He pictured the tiny aircraft hopping from carrier to carrier like flies. That great span of sea. Suppose they did run out of fuel? Or *Hustler* was torpedoed before they got there?

It reminded him of a cartoon he had seen on his last leave. A deep-sea diver standing in a wreck, and a message coming down to him from the salvage vessel above. *Don't bother to come up, Fred, we've just been torpedoed!* It had made him smile, and he could feel his mouth trying to respond again.

He turned and saw Bill watching him. He said, 'Sorry I've been such a bastard lately. You know how it is.'

Bill smiled gravely, 'You've been fine. Forget about it.'

Kitto called, 'Just a word, Tim.' He waited for Rowan to join him. 'We might spot a Focke-Wulf en route to *Hustler*. Use your discretion and keep one eye on your fuel gauge. My flight will be leading yours by some twenty minutes, so we'll be able to cover quite a bit of water between us.' He grinned. 'That would please the admiral, eh?'

Rowan nodded. There was about as much likelihood of two aircraft meeting by accident up here as landing on the moon. But there was always the *chance* and you had to be ready. The great Focke-Wulf Condor was slow by comparison with a fighter, but she packed a punch which was not to be taken lightly.

Across the sea routes of the Atlantic, Biscay and the Arctic the big Condors had proved their worth time and time again. They would pounce on a convoy and keep lazily circling it until relieved by another Condor, or until the U-boat packs were homed to the kill.

The little aircraft carriers had made their work less easy, but they had the whole sea to hunt in, and a range of nearly four thousand miles to do it.

He recalled with deadly clarity the time he had met a Condor. It had not been so far from here, but it had been winter, the sea below like black glass. That particular convoy had been savagely attacked by both U-boats and then mountainous seas. Two freighters had been lost without trace, their crews drowned during the night. Seven other ships had been sunk by torpedo attack before the foul weather had enabled the commodore to shake off the pack.

Rowan had been aboard a fighter-catapult ship, a bastardised merchantman with a solitary Hurricane fighter on a catapult. Once airborne, there was no place to land. You just had to ditch, and pray that somebody pulled you out before you froze solid. If the long-suffering British public had known how flimsy were the convoy's defences they would probably have cracked long ago.

But that one, expendable Hurricane was worth more than all the corvettes, depth charges and trained seamen in the convoy, once the commodore had shaken off the U-boats.

And on their seventh day at sea an escort had sighted a Focke-Wulf Condor.

After that it had all seemed to happen in a split second. The violent pressure as the fighter had been hurled from its catapult in a rain squall, the lines of merchantmen sliding away beneath him, as if they were steaming downhill. The rain had been their only chance. If the Condor had already sighted the convoy and had wirelessed its position to base, the detour, the fight for survival had all been in vain.

And then, just as suddenly, he had found the big German plane. Diagonally above him and filling the sky.

He watched the vapour coming back from his racing engine, knowing the rain was getting worse, and that each second was paring away his chances of finding the convoy again. In those flashing moments he had seen his whole life. He had been twenty-four then, and had wanted very much to go on living. It had seemed empty, unfair, and had filled him with an unreasoning bitterness which had pushed all caution aside.

He had flown straight for the Condor, unable to believe they had not seen him. But who would expect a fighter in the Arctic when there was no carrier for a thousand miles? He had pressed the button, and had almost flown headlong into the bomber's port wing with stunned surprise. His guns had not fired.

Tracers had come within a few feet of his prop as the Condor's gunners had come out of their trance. He had felt the aircraft jerk violently, and had seen oil splash across his perspex screen.

He had become very calm and had pressed the button again. That time every machine gun had fired. He had made one diving attack across the Condor's massive tail, seeing his tracers ripping home, killing the rear gunner, and feeling at the same time that the Hurricane was already falling out of control.

Almost the worst part had been that he remembered nothing more. He had not been able to release his parachute and be dragged from the cockpit, of that he was certain. The Hurricane was starting to burn, and there had been a lot of choking smoke, and somebody yelling. Then he had remembered nothing until hands had dragged him into a ship's whaler and somebody had started to cut his smouldering leather jacket from his back.

The rest of the convoy had reached the Kola Inlet intact. It had seemed unlikely that Rowan's brief skirmish had destroyed the Condor, but he must certainly have knocked out the radio.

No U-boats came, and somewhere at a Norwegian base a German pilot was probably still pondering on the solitary Hurricane in the Arctic.

He sat down and filled his pipe. Trying not to think about his parents. Knowing that if he survived this convoy he would have to go to the house.

Bill sat beside him. 'I know how you feel. I'm not fancying this flight much, but I'd rather be doing *something*.'

Rowan looked at him. 'It'll be all right, I expect. Tea and buns all round. It'll be a home from home.'

The tannoy crackled again. 'Range Red Flight at after end of flight deck immediately.'

Rowan tried not to think about it. At least he had Jonah again. That was something. Better to be with friends.

He nodded to Cameron and Creswell. 'Let's get ready. Our turn soon. I'll check the recognition signals. I'd hate to be shot down by our own blokes!'

They nodded, hiding their true feelings, as he was from them. He turned as a rating wrote their names on the board with the blue top.

Rowan, Ellis, Cameron and Creswell. They could be sponged off in seconds.

The whistling snarl of Seafire engines told him that Kitto and his bunch were already taking off. For once he did not want to watch. He would shake hands when he reached *Hustler*. Or not, as the case might be.

He thought of Buchan on his chair, solid reliable. Villiers on his flying bridge, haunted and tortured by whatever had changed him to half the man he had once been. James with his charts and purring plot tables. Was he worrying about his German wife at home? How she felt in a food queue, after an air raid, when her fellow countrymen had killed some of her neighbours?

He thought of the man he had shot down over the Lofoten Islands. Was it really just a few days and hours ago? A telegram would have reached his home, too. *Killed in action*.

His parents would be wondering about who had done it, just as Andy Miller pondered over the watch a German pilot had given him.

The hands of the bulkhead clock must have jumped forward. Rowan stood up and felt his pockets. His razor and toothbrush. Tobacco pouch and spare pipe. He touched the folded letter inside his inner pocket. It was the last he had had from home. His mother had written, *Don't worry about us, dear. Just take care of yourself.*

You were not supposed to carry personal letters. But what the hell. He snatched his helmet from the chair and held the goggles up to the deckhead light. It was all he had left.

A bell jangled, and he felt the urgent tremble of the nearest hangar lift.

Time to go. *Just take care of yourself.*

He looked at his companions and felt strangely moved.

'Let's get the show on the road.'

The tannoy pursued them. 'Stand by to fly-off aircraft.'

Bill did his usual act. A little mincing step and one large hand in the air. 'I'll do no such thing, *you brute*.'

It was always funny.

Cameron said, 'I knew you were bent, Bill.'

Outside the air was keen, the sky bare but for a few arrows of cloud. The sea beyond the carrier's side was furrowed with dark shadows, regular and even, the long lines of troughs rolling towards the five ships, lifting them with indifference before undulating towards the opposite horizon.

Three Swordfish were circling overhead. The returning patrol. The others were off somewhere searching for signs of a U-boat. On this harsh sea, standing as she did like a block of flats, *Growler* presented a perfect target.

Petty Officer Thorpe touched his arm, his grimy face worried. 'A mate of mine is in *Hustler*, sir. Petty Officer Denny. He'll look after you. Just mention me.'

Rowan smiled. It made him realise that he was leaving more than just the ship.

'I will.'

They stood in the keen air looking at the Seafire as it was manhandled into position, its nose towards the sky. Jonah.

Bats hurried past, dragging on his helmet. He grinned. 'Mount up!'

Three hundred empty miles. Tea and buns at the end of it.

He sighed and pulled himself into the cockpit.

'This is *Blue Leader*. Ready for take-off.'

'Stand by.'

The Affirmative broke from *Growler*'s yard and the nearest sloop moved even closer. Just in case someone ditched.

The engine roared and shook into life. *Check every damn thing.*

There was the light.

Here we go.

Rowan wriggled his toes inside his fleece-lined boots and peered carefully from side to side. The four Seafires were flying in loose formation at eighteen thousand feet. It was not the most economical height, but under the circumstances vision and the ability to spot the convoy's screen and the carrier might prove more important. If things went badly, it could be vital.

They had been airborne for twenty minutes, and it was still a surprise to Rowan that the sea and sky could change so quickly and so much in this unfriendly place. The sky was duller now, and towards the horizon it was like bronze.

He bit his lip. The sea's edge was blurred. He removed his goggles and examined them. Then he checked his course and speed and replaced them. The horizon was still misty.

He stared across his quarter towards Bill. He could see him quite clearly, his mouth opening and closing as if he were champing gum. In fact he was singing, his oxygen mask jerking up and down like a goatee beard.

Whenever he stopped thinking about his instruments and the other aircraft his mind kept returning to his parents. Things he had taken for granted. Their attitudes, which he had so often regarded as routine, became clearer, like a gun-sight.

His mother would ask her husband, *'Had a good day, dear?'*

His father would reply without hesitation, *'Much as usual, my love.'*

Perhaps that had been their strength. *Routine*. So that even their affection for each other had become unshakeable, untouched by things out of the ordinary.

And now they were dead.

He blinked as his cockpit was suddenly enveloped in tattered cloud.

'Hello, *Blue Leader*.' It was Bill. 'I can see a ship.' He chuckled. 'Fine time to take a cruise!'

Rowan lifted one hand, and then craned over to look for the ship. He saw her, just below the horizon, white and buff, with tiny glittering lights along her hull, despite the brightness of day. A poor, bloody neutral, he thought. Swedish, most likely. There were precious few neutrals left, and it was harder for them to stay out of the line of fire.

Better take a look, he thought. It would give them a fright if nothing else.

Even the ship was wrong. Blurred and indistinct. He pushed Syms' globe-head from his thoughts, his uncertain gloom about fog.

He said, 'Line astern.' He saw Creswell in his mirror, waggling his wings. 'We'll keep together.'

He heard Bill croon, 'Take me to your arms again!'

More patches of cloud now, all bunched up and lumpy, much lower. He checked his altimeter. Probably no more than ten thousand feet.

He held his breath, not daring to blink. A harder shadow had shown itself for mere seconds amongst the clouds. A few more minutes, less even, and they might have missed it. It was a big aircraft, and he had no doubt it was steering directly for the lonely merchantman. Interest, boredom, it did not matter now.

He snapped, *'Condor! Going down!'*

Then he put the Seafire into a steep dive, knowing the rest were following close astern.

The cloud became more congested until he was flying right through it, his jaw aching as he strained every muscle to keep

99

his fullest concentration. The clouds shivered and parted like ripped curtains as he held the fighter in a power dive. Down, down, it would be any second.

He gripped the stick harder and switched the gun button to 'Fire'. He'd not get caught out a second time.

With the plane swaying violently he swept out into the bronze light, barely able to accept that the other aircraft was really there. Just as he had pictured it. The perfect position. He was still well above the big Focke-Wulf's port quarter, and every small detail stood out like items in a recognition manual.

Three hundred yards. He held the German in his sights, hardly able to breathe. A split second and he pressed the button, raking the other plane with a long burst along the port wing, over the top and on towards the stem. The Focke-Wulf's upper rear gunner was swinging towards him, metal and perspex flying in bright fragments as the deadly hail of bullets and cannon shells turned his little pod into horror.

The bomber tilted steeply, falling away like a huge, gaunt crucifix.

Rowan pulled out of his dive, seeing a pale splash of colour far below, knowing it was the neutral ship. The spectator.

He saw Bill's Seafire diving steeply across the Condor's full span, hammering a four-second burst into the body and perhaps the cockpit as well.

He was yelling, 'Got him! Got the bugger!'

Smoke belched slowly and then more thickly from the Condor's tail, and it started to go into a shallow dive. The pilot would try to ditch near to the ship. He had a good chance, and therefore a last-minute opportunity to get his signal off to base. Fighters meant a carrier. The rest would be easy.

Rowan levelled off and brought Jonah round in a tight turn, the Merlin labouring as he lifted the nose to gain more height.

He heard Creswell cry, *'Tallyho!'*

Rowan fumbled with his switch and shouted, *'Break off, Frank!'* He saw the Seafire dropping out of the sky like a dart, guns blazing, as Creswell fanned towards the bomber's shattered gun mounting and then swept down and beneath its oil-streaked belly.

'*Oh, Jesus!*' Rowan pressed his button, pouring a long burst into the Condor's full length from stern to stem.

He heard the loud clatter of the German's heavy machine guns. In his eager excitement Creswell must have forgotten about the gunner in the Condor's belly. He must have seen it like a whaler of old sighting the huge and helpless catch, only to be destroyed himself by the giant tail.

The Seafire reeled away, rolling almost on to its back as the German staggered and then began a violent plunge towards the sea.

Rowan levelled off behind Creswell. 'This is *Blue Leader. Do you read me?*' He hesitated, his heart heavy, as the other fighter reeled to one side and then straightened up again. 'This is *Jonah*.' He kept his voice unhurried, even gentle. 'Do you read me, Frank?'

He saw the others taking station on him, and some parachutes floating towards the sea like tiny pieces of fluff. He noticed too that the ship was end-on. Hurrying away or towards the crashing Condor, he did not know.

Then he heard Creswell's voice. 'Hello, *Jonah*, I read you.'

Rowan wiped his face. Small and jerky, the pain as near as if Creswell was right here in the cockpit.

Creswell added, 'I made a cock of that. Sorry. Never thought—' He coughed.

Rowan glanced abeam and saw the Condor hit the sea and explode, but it no longer mattered.

He concentrated on the solitary Seafire ahead of him.

'What about your instruments, Frank?'

'All right, *Jonah*. I—I think.' In a sharper tone, which revealed the true loneliness of terror, he said, 'I'm bleeding! All over the place! *Oh, dear God!*'

Rowan said, 'You lead, Bill. Algy, you take tail-end Charlie.'

He took the Seafire slowly and carefully until he was flying abeam and level with Creswell's. He was close enough to see the big holes, the shining wetness which was most likely a fuel leak. He also saw Creswell, his head lolling forward and trying to turn towards him.

Rowan said carefully, 'Continue as before, Frank. Don't bother about instruments. Just watch old Bill and follow him.' He raised his voice. *'Frank!'* He had seen the nose drop, had known Creswell had all but blacked out.

'Keep talking. Watch Bill's plane, and *talk*. Anything.' He found he was pleading.

Creswell answered brokenly, 'Never saw that bloody gunner. But I remember an instructor who said once—'

Rowan called sharply, 'Said what, Frank?' He tried again. 'What did he say?'

Creswell replied, 'My girl's gone and married a pongo. A bloody soldier, can you imagine?'

'My father was a soldier.'

Rowan blinked and darted a glance at his instruments. They were at thirteen thousand feet. Please God, they should sight something soon. Or would they all fly to the north, making conversation, and falling one by one like slaughtered birds as their fuel gave out?

Saving Creswell's life was suddenly the most important thing in the world. He hardly knew anything about him. He was young, fresh-faced, and should have had no worries. And now he was trying to obey orders. He was probably dying, flying into oblivion, and all he could think of was that his girl had married a soldier.

When he looked again he saw dark haze on the horizon, slightly to port.

Bill called hoarsely, 'Bear Island, if I'm any judge.'

Creswell said vaguely, 'Fuel's low. Must have winged me badly.' He groaned. 'Oh, Christ, it hurts like hell.'

Rowan said, 'Hold on, Frank. We mustn't break up the gang now.' It sounded stupid, but it was all he had to offer. 'Think of the next leave. Bill will find you a girl.'

'Hello, *Jonah*.' Bill cut in. 'Ships dead ahead.' Then in a voice which almost broke, 'And *two Swordfish*, at three o'clock low. *Oh, you dear old Stringbags! I love you!*'

Rowan snapped down his catch. 'Hello, *Lapwing*, this is *Blue Leader*.' His mind was spinning, and yet he had still remembered *Hustler*'s call sign. 'Request permission to land-on immediately.' He pounded the throttle with his fist. 'Answer, damn you! *For Christ's sake, answer!*'

The voice when it came was very faint and dry. 'Hello, *Blue Leader*. Affirmative.'

Rowan tilted slightly and sought out the escorts carrier's blunt outline, beyond which was a great spread of shipping. She was levelling up on her new course, ready to receive them. Kitto must have arrived shortly before and got everyone on top line. He felt his eyes stinging. *Bless 'em all*.

'Can't hold her!' It was Creswell. 'I'll not make it!'

Rowan saw the prop of Creswell's plane become blurred and uneven, and then stop completely.

He said urgently, 'I'll follow you down.' He changed his switch again. 'I've got a pilot ditching.' He tried to sound calm, knowing that one break in his voice would finish Creswell, like slamming a door.

'Message understood.'

Rowan fixed his attention on the punctured Seafire as it went into a steep dive.

'Get ready, Frank!'

For a moment longer he thought he was too late. Then he saw a slight movement in the cockpit, the yellow scarf which Creswell always wore waving into the air like a flag. Except that it was more red than yellow now.

Then he was plucked from the cockpit as the parachute tore him from the seafire like a cork from a bottle.

Rowan dived steeply, circling and watching. Creswell tried to wave and then hung limp in the harness, drifting rapidly downwind.

'This is *Lapwing. Land-on immediately*.'

Rowan watched the parachute, seeing one of the escorting sloops tearing to meet it, a bow wave rising on either side if any evidence was needed of their efforts to reach Creswell.

He said. 'This is *Jonah*. Lead the way, Bill.'

Bill too sounded preoccupied. 'Going down.' He was able to ignore the usual qualms of landing, the fact they had found the carrier. The parachute was all that counted.

Rowan flew around the ships, seeing the two patrolling

Swordfish, a boat shoving off from the sloop's side and pulling towards the parachute as Creswell hit the water.

It was like watching himself, Rowan thought.

He sighed. He could do nothing more. He straightened up and watched the *Hustler* taking on personality as she grew larger through his prop. An exact twin of *Growler* to the last rivet. And yet completely different. Only a sailor would understand that, he thought.

He held his breath, watching the turn-down, the apparent roll of the carrier's deck in a cross-swell, before making his decision. Strangely enough, it was the best landing he could remember.

Kitto was waiting for him.

'Well done, Tim. The sloop's just signalled that Creswell is alive. They'll ferry him across at once so that the surgeon can have a look at him. The captain is fuming mad at you for taking so long to land-on. But I think he's glad to see us all the same.' He studied Rowan's tired face. 'You met a Focke-Wulf then?'

Funny. He had not even mentioned it. 'Shot it down.' Just like that.

Kitto touched his arm and turned as Ellis and Cameron hurried to the island. 'Commander (Flying) will want to meet you right away, as will the Old Man.' He smiled gravely as the three pilots shook hands.

Bill said, 'Poor Frank.'

Lord Algy looked at the sloop as it edged nearer to the carrier. 'Those bloody jerries will all be safe and snug aboard that ship by now. Swedish stewardesses and lashings of booze.'

Bill grinned, but his eyes remained sad. 'Yeh, shame, isn't it.'

Two hours and ten minutes after landing aboard H.M.S. *Hustler* a fog closed in around the convoy, completely hiding every ship from her consort.

Rowan lay in a borrowed bunk, his fingers interlaced behind his head, listening to the rattle of pipes and machinery, the inexplicable noises above and around him.

It had been a very close thing.

7

Gesture

THE fog which closed over the convoy and its support group only lasted one day, but in that time several important things happened. Not least was the fact that the merchantmen had become scattered, and their hard-worked escorts had risked collision and worse to try and hold them in a manageable formation.

Aboard *Hustler* the sweat and effort amongst the convoy were vague and distant. Occasionally, when Rowan took a turn around the flight deck, or paced the walkways, he heard the muffled bleat of a ship's siren, the immediate whooping retort from a searching destroyer. Both of the support group's remaining sloops were always in sight, if only blurred out-lines, like ghost ships. Their watchkeeping officers must have had the worst job of all. Fearing to get too close to *Hustler*'s towering bulk, and equally so of losing her in a thicker patch of fog.

As a sub-lieutenant in an escort destroyer, Rowan had known it at close hand. Dense, unmoving fog in the North Sea, with a convoy scattered and invisible all around him. Then above the starboard guardrail, high up, like two great eyes, he had seen the twin anchors of a troopship. But for the captain's nerve, and an immediate response from the engineroom, the ex-liner would have cut the elderly destroyer in half, with the ease of a hot knife through butter.

There was nothing much to do but wait for the fog to lift. The air crews lounged around, talking and reading old magazines. The ship's company went about their affairs, content to leave the worry to the bridge and the lookouts.

The other unsettling thing was the complete absence of news about the large German warships. They had not returned to their Norwegian bases, so they had to be some-where. *Hustler*'s met. officer was certain there was no fog along the Norwegian coast-line, so the Germans were prob-ably staying at sea from choice, the convoy still high on their list of objectives.

When the fog glided slowly away from the scattered ships Rowan noticed that the sea's motion immediately began to get worse, the troughs closer together, their steep sides crumbling occasionally into crests.

The carrier responded badly, swaying and dipping as she kept station on her two sloops, her flight deck sometimes dropping as much as thirty feet, with spray pattering across the gun sponsons like tropical rain.

Nobody had been allowed to visit Creswell in the sickbay. *Hustler*'s P.M.O. had said briefly that he had removed some steel splinters from his side and thigh. It was 'early days'. Doctors always said things like that. But Creswell had been lucky in one respect. Had the sloop which rescued him taken longer to ferry him over to the carrier, the fog would have prevented the transfer altogether. The sloop in question, the little *Brambling* which had first tasted salt water before anyone had ever heard of Adolf Hitler, carried no doctor. Creswell would almost certainly have died there and then.

Kitto had remarked bitterly, 'The young idiot. He was probably brooding about his friend Derek Cotter. When you begin to think like that in the middle of a fight you're halfway to disaster. You win with skill, not revenge.'

Rowan was re-reading his mother's letter when a message came for him to report to the bridge.

Hustler's commanding officer was waiting for him with his Commander (Flying) and two Swordfish pilots.

Rowan did not know Captain Arthur Turpin very well, but what he did know, he disliked. He was a haughty-faced man, with a great beak of a nose which completely dominated his features.

Like Buchan, he had spent some years outside the Navy, but there was no other similarity. Where Buchan presented an impression of stolid dependability, Turpin gave off an air of permanent irritation and ill humour.

He turned to Rowan and snapped, 'It's taken you long enough!'

Rowan replied, 'I'm sorry, sir.'

Turpin seemed disappointed, as if he had been expecting an argument. He had a reputation for goading temporary officers, *damned amateurs*, as he called them.

'Well.' Turpin tucked his hands into his jacket pockets, his thumbs poking forward like horns. 'It's all going as I expected.'

Rowan waited, seeing a warning on the face of the Commander (Flying).

'We've just had a signal from Admiralty. A German battle cruiser, probably *Scharnhorst*, is to the north-east of us. She slipped out of her fjord to do gunnery exercises, or so everybody thought. Our agents, or whatever they call themselves, were so damn sure that it had nothing to do with the big movement of cruisers towards North Cape that they failed to report it in time.'

Commander (Flying) said, 'In all fairness, sir—'

'I am speaking.' Turpin turned his back to him. 'The Home Fleet shadowing force is going to search for the battle-cruiser, while *we* will have to try and hold the convoy together until,' he eyed Rowan coldly, 'our admiral arrives with *Growler*. There is going to be merry hell to pay over this. One escort carrier, *mine*, to do the whole damn job. The convoy commodore will be unable and unwilling to spare any of his escorts for us. So here we are, two sloops and a bloody tug, and we're expected to protect all of them from U-boat attack.'

Hustler's commander cleared his throat cautiously. 'What about the German cruisers, sir?'

Turpin glared at him. 'A trick. If they existed, they are probably on their way back to Norway by now.'

There was a stiff silence until Rowan asked, 'Is the weather forecast any help, sir?'

But Turpin walked to a clear-view screen, merely saying over his shoulder, 'Tell him.'

The Commander (Flying) said evenly, 'It's bad for us, but not bad enough to hinder submarine attack.' There was an apology in his eyes. 'We will fly-off two patrols of Seafires, ahead and to the south-east of the convoy.' He dropped his voice. 'When the U-boats move in closer we'll need all our Swordfish boys for depth-charging, so you see—'

Turpin said flatly, 'Let's get started.' He was standing with his feet wide apart, determined not to hold on as the ship tilted heavily to one side.

The commander added, 'We will fly-off two Swordfish for our local patrol. That should do it.'

A handset buzzed in its case, like a trapped bee.

A lieutenant turned to the captain. 'From W/T, sir. Seven U-boats believed to be in our vicinity.'

Turpin grunted. 'That all? They must be slipping.'

Rowan followed the others down to the Operations Room, his mind empty. It was impossible to know what was happening. There seemed to be too many people making decisions on the sparse facts which the Admiralty and Intelligence services managed to sift from their various sources. So perhaps Turpin was right about the differing sighting reports. It was not unknown for independent groups to send in signals about the same ship or group of vessels, so that it eventually seemed as if a whole fleet was at sea. But he could not bring himself to accept Turpin's angry dismissal. It was obvious he was furious with Chadwick for leaving him without full support, yet at the same time could be pleased to be in a position of unexpected power.

He heard the usual clatter of lifts and equipment as the aircraft were taken to the flight deck, the orderly bustle of preparations.

The Operations Officer gave him and the other pilots their instructions. Rowan would take the south-easterly sector, a second Seafire would overlap in twenty minutes' time.

Rowan said, 'I expect *Growler* will be joining us before dark, sir.'

The other man shrugged, his eyes on his chart. 'She's late. I shall fly-off another fighter soon to look for her. She's either had a breakdown or been delayed.'

The Met. Officer said, 'Or sunk.'

'We'd have heard by now.' The Operations Officer

sounded tired. 'It would be just like Rear Admiral Chadwick to go off on some little scheme all of his own.'

Rowan thought of the depleted force of aircraft still aboard *Growler* and of Chadwick's outward indifference to his own superiors. If Turpin was right, he could be in for a sharp fall. Even with the sanction of a senior officer, if Chadwick's attack on the oil tanker was holding him back when his ship was most needed, *his* head would be on the block. As the Admiralty always said in such cases. *Use your discretion.* Which meant that the man on the spot carried the can when things went wrong.

He steadied himself against a bulkhead as he adjusted his jacket and boots and pulled on his flying helmet. The deck was lurching badly, and he had to hold a rail to keep his balance as he made his way to the flight deck.

It was colder, and the sea had broken into a turmoil of torn whitecaps and deep, angry-looking troughs. The carrier was already steaming into the wind, her attendant sloops on either bow, the fat tug *Cornelian* following astern, giving off far too much greasy smoke. As usual.

The petty officer recommended by Thorpe shouted above the roar of engines, 'She's all ready for you, sir! Sweet as a nut!'

A tannoy speaker barked, 'Get a move on down there! I've not got all day!'

The petty officer winked. 'The Old Man's a bit humpty, sir.'

Rowan nodded and waved to Bill Ellis who was standing on a walkway, his fair hair whipping in the wind.

'He's not the only one.'

The take-off was a bad one, and in the final split-second, as *Hustler*'s bows plunged heavily into a yawning trough, Rowan thought it was the last he would make. The engine coughed and whined, the cockpit dropping several feet below the flight deck before he managed to bring everything under control. In that fragment of time he saw the waves rearing up to meet him, imagined he could hear their triumphant hiss as they tried to pull him down and smother him.

Buffeted by the wind, he climbed slowly and headed away

from the carrier. When he circled once to get his bearings he saw the convoy far off below the iron-hard horizon, in long lines again, but still much too far apart for comfort. He saw some of the big fleet destroyers pushing past the heavy merchantmen. Tribal Class from their lean outlines and uneven funnels, he thought. That was the best of being half-airman, half-sailor. It kept your mind off other things. He levelled out at thirteen thousand feet and began a methodical search.

He could picture the carrier which was falling and dwindling behind him. Flying-off the two Swordfish to cover the actual convoy, and preparing to send a second fighter at a faster speed to sweep ahead of those precious ships.

He wondered if Turpin would ask for one of *Growler*'s pilots to be sent instead of his own. It was just as if he was working off his anger against Chadwick through his pilots. The fact that they had flown almost to their range limit to find his ship, and had shot down a Condor in the process, seemed to have had no effect on him at all.

Rowan thought of Creswell and his voice on the intercom. He had lost a lot of blood, but if the fragments had all been taken from his body he should be all right. He was young, with all the tough resilience which war seemed to create. Just so long as he was not burned. He recalled his own time in hospital, seeing the pitiful creatures hobbling about the wards. No faces at all, some of them. Just shining masks with eyes like stones.

He turned his head and moved the stick automatically. He had seen something, without recognising it. He steered towards the sun, his eyes watering in the metallic glare.

There it was again. Not just another broken wavecrest, or a shadow. He steadied the Seafire and darted a quick glance at the altimeter. He was at eight thousand now. He must take another look.

He circled warily, seeing his shadow crossing the instruments as he flew past the sun. He groped for his binoculars, using them to push up his goggles as he searched for the convoy. It was all but invisible, just a smoke haze and one dark shape. A wing escort probably. The carrier was at a different angle, separated from the convoy by a great spread of angry, broken water.

He tilted Jonah very carefully, listening to the Merlin's confident whine, looking for the intruder. He swallowed hard. A small feather of smoke from the sea itself, a plume of spray around it.

It was a submarine, submerged, but with her schnorkel raised to suck air down to her diesels as she recharged her batteries for the final approach. Her attack on the convoy.

He pulled up and away into a steep climb. The submarine's O.O.W. had not seen him. The forthcoming attack was probably pushing all else from his mind. The U-boat had doubtless been homed on to the merchantmen for days, while others gathered nearby for the killing. The Allies had had much more success with their U-boat sinkings this year than ever before. Better equipment, air cover, and above all radar had shifted the balance for the first time. The U-boat commanders had lost none of their skill or courage, but casualties had pared away the quality of their crews.

That German officer down there, standing in his wildly rolling hull, his mind dazed by the pounding diesels and his constant efforts to keep the boat from plunging out of control in the big waves, was more concerned with his job than a tiny speck in the sky.

Rowan levelled off above some clouds and tried his transmitter.

'Hello, *Lapwing*. This is *Jonah*.' He wondered if there was another submarine below him. 'Do you read me? Over.'

The reply was muffled, fractured in static. 'Yes, *Jonah*. Over.'

There were some other words in between which could have been anything.

'There is a U-boat.' He spoke slowly and with great care. 'About seven miles to the south-east of you, steering north.' He flicked over the switch.

'Wait.'

He smiled gravely. *Wait*. Up the ladder of authority. Ops Room to bridge. To Captain Arthur Turpin. *A bit humpty*.

At times like this he could see Turpin in a better light. Up here you made your decisions, lived or died by them. Just you. Thinking. Watching. Expecting.

Turpin had a lot more to consider. If he ordered Rowan to drop a smoke float the German would doubtless see it, lower his schnorkel and run deep on his electric motors. But Rowan could not hope to keep flying round and round to guide the patrolling Swordfish with their depth charges to the exact position without being spotted himself.

'Hello, *Jonah*. This is *Lapwing*. Are you receiving me? Over.'

A decision had been reached in five minutes. Less.

'Roger.'

'Extend your patrol. We will engage.'

Rowan began to climb again, watching the altimeter, listening to the big engine, thinking of Turpin. With that wide gap between him and the convoy he would have to send his two sloops. Working as a pair, with the Asdic sets sweeping before them like blind men's sticks, they would be able to detect the U-boat if they cracked on speed. He looked at his watch. It would take them about twenty minutes. He trained his binoculars over the cockpit and waited for a gap in the cloud.

He saw the two sloops end-on, cutting through the big waves with abandon, throwing up spray and digging their narrow sterns deep into the water as they worked up to full speed. He was too high to see if the U-boat was still just below the surface.

Turpin would wait a little longer to allow the sloops to make contact and then start flying-off his Swordfish. The German commander would soon have all hell round his ears.

Regretfully Rowan headed further towards the south-east, turning his back on the silent drama below.

Something glinted momentarily, low down and far away to port, and for an instant he thought it was sunlight on a ship's bridge. He stared, fascinated. It was an aircraft. Very small and seemingly motionless against the great moving panorama of broken water.

Growler must be near after all. Flying-off a patrol to try and contact the group. Whoever the luckless pilot was, he was well off course, and if he remained at that height would even be sighted by the U-boat, or one of her consorts.

He toyed with the idea of turning back and reporting his discovery to Turpin. Knowing that *Growler* was nearby might make him change his tactics, close ranks and wait for the U-boat to force home an attack.

But the thought re-crossed his mind that the other pilot might be lost. He made his own decision.

He began a shallow dive, watching the clouds skudding beneath him, layer by layer, running before the wind. He twisted his head from side to side, looking for the other plane. It was not where it should have been. It must have ditched.

He craned forward and saw it quite suddenly. It was a small aircraft, very slender, with protruding floats like skis beneath each wing. He pulled the stick and then levelled off amongst the clouds while he tried to work it out.

So far from land. A seaplane, probably an Arado 196. The realisation came to him as if he had heard someone's voice. They did not have to fly from land bases. They could be carried by large warships.

He watched it flitting across the sea. It could not be flying at more than a thousand feet. The sun was glinting on its long, boxlike cockpit, and he tried to remember how many were in its crew, what weapons it carried.

He put the nose down, aiming straight for the seaplane, his ear recording the sounds, his mind lingering on the fact that the parent ship must be fairly close.

The seaplane tilted steeply to starboard and changed course by ninety degrees.

He's seen me. No matter. Too late now.

He saw the crosses on the wings, the tiny heads bobbing beneath the perspex. Two men.

He pulled out of the dive and held the seaplane just below him before firing a four-second burst.

The seaplane pilot was no amateur. He zigzagged from side to side even as pieces flew from his starboard wing, and almost stalled as he pulled away to allow Rowan to over-shoot.

Rowan tried his transmitter but got nothing but squeaks

and clicks. Out of range. He wondered what had happened to the U-boat, marvelled that he could even think about it as he turned in a steep arc to try another attack. There were two men out there, and both knew they did not stand a chance.

He closed to four hundred yards and fired a long burst right above the seaplane, the bright tracer reflecting on the cockpit like fireworks.

Why had he done it?

He saw the German waggle his wings and begin to descend towards the sea. When he landed on those waves the Arado would almost certainly break up and the two Germans be drowned. So why hadn't he made it quick and killed them himself?

He circled the airplane, seeing its floats glance off the first big wave, stagger and then dip steeply into a trough. The tail came up towards him, and he saw the sea breaking over the long cockpit. The prop feathered and stopped, and he watched as the little plane lifted and rolled over the tossing water like a fallen leaf. He roared low above it and released a smoke marker, again knowing it was useless. But the two Germans would know. And he would know.

Rowan headed back towards the convoy, realising it was darker and the clouds were more menacing.

He tried his transmitter yet again. This time he got an acknowledgement.

Between ear-shattering blasts of static he explained about the seaplane, its original course and position in relation to the convoy. They would be able to work it out from their own intelligence reports, he thought. The Arado's maximum range, what sort of ships carried them, all the statistics which were hoarded like gems. He did not say that he had failed to destroy the aircraft.

He saw snowy columns of water shooting skywards and a whole confusion of ships' wakes and exploding depth charges. Amidst all the fierce-looking waves they lacked their usual menace, but to anyone on the receiving end it would seem as bad as ever. And there were two Swordfish, flying very slowly and almost diagonally in a strong crosswind as they added their depth charges to the display.

'Hello, *Jonah*. This is *Lapwing*. Return to base. Over.'

He checked the compass and his gauges. Turpin was probably eager to hear about the seaplane from him directly.

He flew low over the two sloops, watching their churning wakes burst upwards again as another pattern was rolled off their quarterdecks and fired from either beam.

Then he saw the *Hustler* on his starboard bow, her side very clearly outlined by leaping spray as she edged round in a quarter sea. A light was blinking towards him, and he began to concentrate on his approach. She was about four miles away and wallowing heavily. It would need a very careful, last-minute decision.

He realised he was humming aloud. Perhaps he always did and had not noticed before.

'This is *Jonah*. Permission to land-on.'

To his surprise, the voice replied, 'Negative.'

Then he saw another Seafire coming in to port and slightly below him. He tried to see its markings, but the visibility was too poor.

An emergency landing. He levelled off, his mind chilled as he watched the other pilot making his run-in.

He was near enough to see the water boiling under the carrier's blunt stern as she lifted and crashed down in the troughs. Her deck was shining dully, soaked with falling spray, despite the height from the sea.

He was following the other Seafire, and would pass over the ship's length and begin another turn round. Wait his chance.

Almost there. The Seafire's wheels were down, as were the flaps. He could imagine the pilot changing hands, gauging the deck's rise and fall. As Kitto often said, like putting your last hand of poker on the table.

Rowan heard the voice in his headphones very loud and sharp. 'Stand off! Torpedo running to starboard!'

It all seemed to happen in a second, and yet lasted forever. The carrier heeling violently, twisting like an armoured mammoth as she turned towards her danger.

Rowan could see no torpedo, but saw the Seafire hesitate and then make a final attempt to land. Instead it struck the deck at an angle, one wheel collapsing even as the ship continued to swing.

Rowan went into a dive, looking for a sign of the submarine which had fired, yet unable to tear his eyes from the Seafire as it ploughed along the deck, breaking up, and skidding finally into the base of the island, its tail in the air, its prop smashed into the planking.

A Swordfish flew past, dropping two charges, and Rowan looked again, expecting to see a tell-tale column of water burst alongside *Hustler* to show that a torpedo had found its mark.

A destroyer had appeared from somewhere, charging through the waves like a plough, smoke streaming from her funnels as her guns swung round towards the broken water.

More depth charges, and then a great, dirty stain which seemed to flatten the waves in a spreading pattern of filth.

The destoyer let go another salvo of charges, and this time there was no doubt. Like a shining finger, the U-boat's pointed stern lifted above the oil slick, as if making one last effort to surface. Shells burst around her, and one scored a direct hit by her hydroplanes. She dived immediately, taking her crew to the bottom, to the worst death of all.

Rowan acknowledged his new orders and began his approach. He felt ice-cold, without fear or feelings of any kind.

As he prepared to land-on he saw only the other pilot in his mind, as if he was watching himself, so that he almost expected to hear one more frantic call to stay clear. *Too late*.

He watched the deck lifting towards him, the sea frothing around the carrier's screw. As it began to dip once more he went in, feeling the shock of his wheels, the insistent pressure of the arrester wire. He cut the engine and threw open the cockpit, pushing away hands which tried to help him as he half climbed, half stumbled to the deck.

He ran past the busy seamen and the fire parties with their extinguishers and hoses, pushing through the overalled figures until he had reached the upended fighter.

The doctor and his sick berth attendants were already

116

there, but they had to wait while some stokers cut away the cockpit.

Rowan made himself look at the pilot's face. He was hanging in his harness, his head to one side. The crash had probably broken his neck.

There was some blood running under his goggles, and his eyes were wide open, even angry.

Rowan turned away. He had seen the pilot once or twice, but he was nobody he knew.

He paused by a screen door, oblivious to the spray on his face, the bitter wind which moaned through the bridge structure and lattice mast.

When he glanced at the crashed Seafire he saw them lifting the pilot clear. His boots were sticking out under the arms of the stokers, and one jerked up and down as he was carried towards the forward lift.

Rowan tore off his helmet and wiped his face with spray. It was not right for a man to look like that in death. It had no dignity.

He reached the bridge without seeing a foot of the way.

Captain Turpin was sitting in a steel chair. One like Buchan's.

Rowan did not wait for him to speak. He said harshly, 'It wasn't a ruse, sir. There may be a battle-cruiser to the north-east, but there's something else bloody big coming our way.'

Turpin watched him, his eyes cold. 'Is that the way you usually speak to your superior officers?'

Rowan eyed him calmly. 'Not usually, sir.'

The Commander (Flying) said, 'It was definitely a *little* seaplane, not a Heinkel 115?'

Rowan looked past him, through the squeaking clear-view screens.

'I'm sure. I put it down. It might have been around for some time, but I doubt it. I didn't see any sign of the ship.'

A lieutenant said, 'Operations have been in contact with *Growler*, sir. She's rejoining the group tonight.' He kept his voice hushed, his eyes on Rowan.

'I see.' Turpin walked to one side of the bridge, his body angled to the deck. Then he said, 'You can carry on.'

Rowan turned on his heel and left the bridge. He could not face the questions in the wardroom and went instead to the hangar deck. He was just in time to see Jonah being trundled to her place where a team of mechanics waited like surgeons with their lamps and instruments.

To the petty officer he said abruptly, 'Could you get me a mug of something, please?' His legs felt as if they would collapse under him. 'Anything.'

'Certainly.'

The man hurried away and returned almost immediately with a chipped and steaming mug of tea. He watched Rowan as he sipped it and said, 'Don't let on, sir, or I'll get busted.'

Rowan realised that a third of the mug was neat rum.

He smiled. 'Thanks.'

The man wiped his greasy hands on a rag. 'I saw the tin-fish. Streaked right down the port side, it did. Missed the old cow by no more than twenty feet at a guess.'

Rowan considered it. The U-boat's commander had been that confident. He had fired just one torpedo, saving the rest for the convoy, the real prize. He had known that *Hustler*'s little escorts were after one of his consorts, that there was nothing else between him and a good angle-shot.

So he knew too that something heavier was on the way. A ship which could sink a crippled carrier in seconds. His confidence had destroyed him instead.

A lift rattled into life and the crashed fighter was lowered slowly into the hangar deck. Men hurried towards it to check that the deck party had done its bit and there was no fire risk.

The petty officer said quietly, 'That was Mr Maynard's. Nice young chap. Twenty last week.' He studied Rowan's face. 'Still, I suppose the Old Man had to choose. It was him or all the rest of us. But still . . .' He did not finish it.

The tannoy bellowed, *'D'you hear there! Range a strike of two Swordfish at the after end of the flight deck at the hurry! Stand by to fly-off aircraft!'*

Rowan went to his borrowed cabin and found Bill waiting for him.

118

They sat side by side on a bunk, and Bill said suddenly, 'You know something? I think the Jerries are going to wipe out this convoy.'

Rowan looked at him. It was not like Bill at all.

He said, 'Then we'll have to stop 'em, right?'

Bill grinned. 'It seems as if we're the only ones who can, eh?' He leaned back on the bunk. 'How do you feel, Tim?'

Rowan considered it. He felt calmer. It must be the rum.

'Sometimes I think I'm going out of my mind. Just now on the bridge I was bloody rude to the captain. I couldn't help it. And I put that seaplane down in the drink when I should have done it properly and killed the bastards. We're not playing cricket,' he faced his friend, 'or rugby either, for that matter. And yet we go on pretending, posturing. It makes me sick.'

Lord Algy peered in at them. 'Frank's sitting up and taking some nourishment. How say we pay him a visit? I've fixed it with the doc.'

They stood up, glad to be freed from confidences, from themselves.

Far above their heads the deck vibrated and trembled to the beat of engines as the next patrol trundled along the slippery planking to take their chances beyond the convoy.

8

Separation

ROWAN sat at a wardroom table and watched the stewards handing out the morning offering. An arm came over his shoulder and withdrew. He studied his plate. Two tinned sausages and an uneven circle of powdered egg, the whole sliding in a puddle of grease.

A steward on the opposite side of the table saw his face and grinned. 'It's war, sir.'

Rowan looked across the other table and saw the way the ship was sloping away from him. The sea had risen further overnight. He had heard that the convoy had cracked on more speed, so there was a faint chance that with the worsening sea they might lose the U-boats for another day.

He tried to think clearly, shut out the creak and shudder of the hull and superstructure, the half-hearted conversation of the few officers who were free to take breakfast at this civilised time. The signal from Admiralty had suggested there were seven U-boats nearby. One was a definite kill. A second, the one he had reported, may have been damaged by the sloops. That left five. It didn't sound bad for a Russian convoy.

Five submarines. He broke them down in his mind, trying to imagine them and their crews. Each boat carried about sixty men, so right now, as he sat staring at his rapidly congealing breakfast, there were some three hundred Germans out there in the Arctic, waiting to have a go at the ships.

He smiled bitterly. Round the bend. He must be.

Bill Ellis thumped down beside him and groaned as the ship slid heavily into a deep trough.

'Christ, I hope there's no flying today, mate!'

Rowan nodded, thinking of Creswell down in the *Hustler*'s sickbay. He wondered why the builders had put the medical section right up forward. To anyone in real pain, the rise and plunge of the carrier's bows would be no help at all. But young Frank Creswell seemed bright enough. Maybe that was why they never let you see a friend immediately after a crash or a bad injury. It protected the visitor, just as it gave the injured man time to recover his guard.

He had been very pale, and somehow older. They had stayed with him beside the bunk, keeping their talk silly and light.

But Creswell had said suddenly, 'We're slowing down, why?'

They had all looked at each other, Rowan, Bill and Lord Algy, at a loss for words when they were really needed.

The tannoy had been muffled. 'Attention on the upper deck, face aft and salute.'

A pause, and then the steady increase in engine revolutions again.

Creswell had said in a small voice, 'They just buried someone, didn't they?'

Rowan pushed his plate away and reached for some toast. At least the bread was always good in these American-built carriers.

He found himself thinking of the miles they had steamed overnight. That pilot with the angry eyes and broken neck was way, way astern now, hundreds of fathoms deep.

He came out of his brooding as the wardroom tannoy squeaked into life.

It brought a chorus of angry protests and curses, and shouts of 'Switch that bloody thing off!'

Then, 'This is the captain speaking.'

Bill said, 'No wonder they couldn't shut it off. Like trying to silence God!'

Turpin said, 'This morning I received an important signal from the Admiralty.'

In the brief pause Rowan thought of the millions of messages which filled the air at every second of every day. One had brought news of his parents' deaths.

'It informed me that our shadowing force from the Home Fleet engaged heavy enemy units during the night, one of which was probably the battle-cruiser *Scharnhorst*. The engagement was carried out at extreme range, and severe damage inflicted on the German ships. Our own force received some damage and casualties, but no vessel was lost.'

He paused, and Rowan thought there should have been cheering in the distance. It was always like that on the films.

The captain's unemotional voice continued, 'I have been instructed to take steps to avoid meeting with those same units, and the admiral commanding the Home Fleet will do all in his power to head off any such attempt by the enemy to pursue another attack.'

Several of the officers banged the tables with their knives and forks, and one said, 'I should jolly well think so!'

Turpin had not finished. 'I have been in contact with the commodore of the convoy, and he is of my opinion. That we should alter course now and make a more southerly approach to our destination. As *Growler* did *not* rejoin us as expected, I have no alternative but to act independently. That is all.'

The murmur of speculation came back as the tannoy went dead.

Bill Ellis said, 'Maybe he's right. It seems daft to take a wide detour when the real enemy is being pinned down by the big boys. I'll bet it was some show, Tim. All the guns firing over miles of sea, with neither side being able to see more than a shadow of each other.'

Rowan had spoken to the pilot who had been sent to make contact with *Growler*. She had been steaming right on course, with the four sloops strung around her like watchful terriers. The interchange of signals had been brief. *Rear Admiral Chadwick was rejoining the group*. But he had not, and Turpin had decided not to wait for him.

Bill ran his fingers through his hair and yawned. 'We'll soon know what's what. Turpin'll scramble a few kites, and if the way is clear he'll give the signal to alter course.'

Rowan tried not to think of *Growler* being out of it. It was bad to get too attached to a ship in wartime. Yet the little carrier had come to mean a lot to him, and he belonged with her, not with Turpin.

It would be a feather in Turpin's cap when he anchored with the convoy under the Russian shore batteries. Maybe it was wrong to dwell on personalities. The convoy safe, a swift victory over an attacking German battle-cruiser and her consorts would be just what the public wanted to read and hear in war-grey Britain.

Another lieutenant had heard Bill's comments and said, 'Lucky if we could fly-off the Met. Officer's balloon in this gale!'

Bill looked up as Rowan made to leave the table. 'What's wrong?'

Rowan shrugged vaguely. 'All this. What we just heard. It's not adding up right. And what about the seaplane? I didn't imagine it.'

'I expect the Old Man thinks he's in the clear now.' He sounded worried. 'I should drop it, Tim.'

Rowan knew the others near him had stopped eating and talking to stare at him. He knew he was being ridiculous. *Yours not to reason why*.

He said abruptly, 'I'm going to the Ops Room.'

The other lieutenant asked quietly, 'Your pal all right?'

Bill rubbed his chin. 'He's fine. Been pushing it a bit for some time. He had some bad news from home, too.'

The lieutenant said, 'Oh.' Then, 'Pass the jam, old son.'

Bill smiled sadly. The unwritten code. Fill the gaps. Move on. Don't speak of other people's troubles. Usually you had plenty of your own.

Rowan reached the Operations Room and found it unusually busy. Plots ticked and murmured, and from every side came the hum of electricity, the discreet tick of morse and an occasional tinny voice over an intercom.

The Operations Officer looked at him wearily. 'You're not on stand-by, are you?'

'No, sir.' He felt stupid now that he was here. 'I was thinking about the captain's announcement.' He shrugged, almost lost. 'It's all too glib, too simple.'

'And you came up here just to tell me that?'

'What's bothering you?' It was Commander (Flying) who had appeared around a glass screen.

'He says that we're being hoodwinked in some way.' The Operations Officer sounded dangerously calm. 'The commodore, the Home Fleet, Intelligence and the Admiralty all think we're halfway home and dry, but he knows differently!'

Rowan said hotly, 'I'm not a complete fool, sir, just because I've got two wavy stripes on my sleeve and didn't serve in the China Station in nineteen hundred and seven.'

'That'll do.' Commander (Flying) stepped between them. 'Both of you.'

He looked at Rowan, seeing the strain, the fatigue of unbroken sea duty.

He said very quietly, 'You think the Jerries are *letting* us make each move, that it's all planned to go just as it is?'

Rowan nodded. 'I do, sir. I've been on this run before. The Germans have never let us get a convoy this far without a real hard thrust at it.' He pointed to the tall glass screen where the convoy's position and various other information had been chalked for easy plotting. 'If the enemy had used some cruisers to make an attack from the north-east, the Home Fleet ships would have stayed put, kept the screen intact, in case a bigger unit was out.'

The Operations Officer admitted, 'That's true. We know *Tirpitz* is in her fjord, and that *Scharnhorst* is about the biggest unit they have in these waters.' He sounded less sceptical.

Commander (Flying) said, 'So they make a push with the really heavy ships and all the while are pushing other units from the south.' He nodded slowly. 'Could be. It all hinges on that damned seaplane. Without it, the parent ship may have turned for base.' He beckoned to a communications rating. 'Put me through to the captain.' He winked at his friend. 'He's going to love this.'

Turpin remained quite silent until the Commander (Flying) had put his point of view. Rowan heard Turpin's voice very briefly, a sharp, angry sound in the handset.

The commander put it down very carefully, as if it were cut-glass.

'The captain says that the A.A. cruiser had already flown-off her Walrus at *his* suggestion. A short patrol will be made, and then the Walrus will return and be hoisted aboard the cruiser. The convoy will alter course as directed in one hour *precisely*. No further exchange of signals is contemplated at this stage.' He smiled. 'That's it.'

They turned as Dymock Kitto stepped under the bright deckhead lights.

'I'd like permission to fly-off a fighter patrol, sir. Right now. I've known Lieutenant Rowan for a long time, and I trust his judgement.' He eyed the Operations Officer calmly. 'And as I am now equal in rank to you, sir, I can add that although I am a "temporary gentleman" too, I have probably flown more hours than any pilot in the entire Navy.'

To everyone's relief the Ops Officer grinned. 'Mostly on our side, I trust?' He became brisk again. 'The Old Man'll not allow a full flight. I'll suggest one Seafire.' He frowned. 'Not you, Kitto. You are supposed to be in charge of *Growler*'s unruly mob.'

Rowan said, 'I'll fetch my gear.' He glanced at Kitto. 'Okay?'

Kitto lifted his head as if to listen to the wind, his blue chin shining in the glare. 'No heroics then.'

As he hurried to the cabin Rowan heard the pipe on the tannoy for one fighter to be prepared for take-off. So Turpin had agreed. He struggled into his leather jacket. Probably suggested he should be the pilot.

Back at the Ready Room he found Bill and the stand-by pilots protesting to the Commander (Flying).

The latter merely said, 'This is not a routine flight.' He caught an ashtray as it slid from the desk. 'Nor will it be a comfortable one.' He nodded to Rowan. 'I'll give you the details now. Then you have fifty minutes. Not a second more, so let's hop about.'

It was a strange sensation to realise that Jonah was alone on the glistening flight deck. Figures crowded around the Sea-fire as if paying homage for the last flight ever. Even the weird light, purple streaks between the racing clouds, the endless, tumbling mass of wavecrests looked vaguely unreal. The light made the crests dirty yellow, and the air was like stinging, cold sand.

The petty officer helped him into the cockpit and strapped him in with extra care, his eyes watering as the wind moaned through the lattice mast and above the bridge.

He shouted, 'The skipper's taken over the con himself, sir.' He reached in to help plug the headphones in position. 'So you should be all right.' He patted the cockpit and then slammed it shut. His lips mouthed 'good luck' as he ducked away, and the prop swung stiffly and then burst into life.

The Affirmative was hoisted, the flag already in ribbons. Rowan hoped the yeoman had several spares.

The light blinked and Jonah started to weave forward, delicately, as if to avoid the puddles on the wooden deck.

Forward gently. Tail up. He felt the usual chill sweat as he pictured the blades slicing into the deck. *Easy now.*

The familiar panorama slid past. The coloured overalls, Bats and his crew. A solitary seaman by the island carrying a bucket, frozen as he realised he had emerged at the wrong moment.

He watched the straight edge of the deck dashing to meet him, the sensation of driving an uncontrollable, brakeless car over a cliff, and then with a thunderous roar he was off.

It took several minutes to work his way round the carrier, to compensate for a buffeting wind which seemed determined to hurl him back on board.

But it had been a good take-off, which when he saw the carrier's violent motion below his starboard wing was hard to believe. He hummed quietly. Each showing the other what he could do. Turpin coming off his high-horse to prove that he could handle the awkward *Hustler* better than anyone else. He smiled tightly. *And me?*

Before he turned and headed towards the south he took a long look at the distant convoy. The Ops Room had told him that a cruiser had joined it from the Home Fleet force, and he could just make out her splash of dazzle-paint beyond the more slender silhouette of the A.A. ship.

He banked away, putting it astern like a moving picture.

Poor old Walrus. How could a man who had designed anything as beautiful as a Spitfire have been capable of dreaming up something like the ungainly Shagbat? The only comfort an amphibian's crew had was that they could land on water. But in these seas it would be rough going. He thought of the Arado and wondered if the Germans had been picked up.

Carefully and methodically he began a sweep of the horizon. It was misty with spray and blown rain, but good enough.

The voice in his headphones said, 'Hello, *Jonah*, this is *Lapwing*. Any signs of Walrus?'

Rowan flicked his switch. 'Negative.'

He imagined Turpin saying, 'Waste of time. Bloody amateurs.'

He was running into patches of cloud now, and could feel the wind buffeting him like an invisible giant. He started to climb, checking his compass repeatedly. It was so easy to be carried away. He smiled to himself. *Literally*. With no land in reach, it was prudent to take navigation very seriously.

Twelve thousand feet, the engine behaving perfectly. He tried to relax, but it seemed to be getting harder every day.

When he thought of going on leave he thought of home. Of that first visit he would have to make. The sympathy. The strange curiosity you saw in people's eyes when something bad had happened.

He tensed. Through a narrow ravine in the clouds he saw a dab of colour. He put the nose down carefully and switched on the firing button. This time it might not be a helpless Arado.

But as the cloud fanned away from the prop he saw the A.A. cruiser's Walrus far below him, barely appearing to move against the ranks of wavecrests. He peered down at it, wondering how he would like to be given such a job. Maximum speed one hundred and thirty-five . . . He gasped aloud as the nearest cloud erupted in a great vivid flash. For a split second he imagined that while he had been watching the flying boat two other planes had been stalking him and had collided inside the cloud. Then he saw the drifting ball of dirty smoke, and as he flew past the cloud's massive over-hang he saw the ships. They were off the port bow. He saw more bursts, felt the Seafire rock dangerously as one shell exploded right astern, but he concentrated on the ships. Three of them. One was big, and although end-on, showed her bridge and powerful armament, her high bow wave as she thrust purposefully towards the north.

The others were destroyers, large, probably *Karl Galster* class. He had met them before in these waters.

More flak exploded across his path and he swerved to port, losing and then regaining height in a great bound to throw the gunnery officers off balance. They were not using pop-guns either, he realised. Some of the big ship's secondary arma-ment by the punch of it. *Crump . . . Crump . . .*

He turned away, losing height rapidly as he plunged down towards the Walrus which hardly seemed to have moved. As he got closer he saw it had been hit by flak, and there were several large gashes on both upper and lower wings. But the one prop, the 'pusher', was still going strong, and he saw the blink of an Aldis lamp to show they had seen him.

He levelled off, searching in his mirror and overhead, just to be sure, before flying directly past the flying boat. He could see two of its crew, but of the others there was no sign.

Rowan wondered if the carrier was in R/T range and switched on his transmitter. He knew instantly that it was quite dead. That big burst of flak must have shaken some-thing loose. He groped for his signal lamp and flashed a brief signal to the Walrus. *Returning to base.* Their wireless had most likely been done in as well.

He started to climb again, watching the strange light recrossing his smeared screen. No time to lose. The big German warship would need a lot of stopping. He began to estimate the speed and distance of those three ships.

Keep your head. He looked around for more cloud cover and climbed towards it. Turpin would have to be convinced. He would want to know exactly what he was up against.

When he burst out of the clouds the second time he saw the three warships angled away on the starboard bow. They were all going flat-out by the look of them. He steadied his binoculars, seeing the gun turrets swinging round, the long barrels lifting towards him. He was well out of range of the anti-aircraft guns, but not of those massive weapons. He made up his mind. She was big all right, probably the *Hipper*. He saw the next bank of cloud rushing to meet him.

Rowan did not recall feeling or seeing anything. It was more of a sensation than a crude shock. One second he was watching the bulging cloud, and the next he was gasping for breath, as if his lungs were on fire, and his ears felt like twin probes of pain.

He could only stare at the picture through his prop. It was not rigid and firm, but was starting to revolve, slowly, and then more rapidly.

He wanted to cry out, to move, but he could only stare. There was no sky or cloud any more, just the sea. The frosted surface was breaking up, into great white patches, then into rollers, now into individual waves.

The stark realisation reached him. The big warship had fired her main armament. A rough estimate across his path. He was crashing. Half the port wing had gone completely. His hands started to move, fumbling at first and then with frantic desperation as he smelt burning and realised for the first time that the inside of his left boot was sodden.

Dear God. He released the cockpit and gasped for breath as the bitter air drove the mounting panic aside like an overwhelming tide-race. *Crashing. Baling out. Mayday. God help me.*

He was upside down, hanging, then dropping, kicking and hitting out like a drowning man. He felt the savage jerk of the harness, the sudden pain in his leg helping to steady him again as the chute opened above him, suspending him, and letting him sail with the wind, his lips and eyes almost frozen.

He twisted in the harness, sobbing with pain, as he heard an intermittent coughing roar. Then he saw Jonah. She was almost down, spiralling and leaving a trail of smoke until she hit the sea. He heard nothing, and when he wiped his eyes again even the smoke had vanished.

Rowan peered down between his feet. One boot was bright

red. He retched and tasted vomit in his throat. He felt his Mae West, his fingers all thumbs. He heard more shellbursts and wondered why the Germans were wasting ammunition. *Unless* . . .

He waited for the chute to swing crazily with the wind and then saw the flash of gunfire. The Germans were far away. It had taken Jonah longer to die than he had realised. He felt the pain and anger welling inside him like fire. *Poor Jonah.*

He watched incredulously as the Walrus appeared beneath him and porpoised violently across two large waves. It was an insane dream. There was somebody standing in the bows, poking through a little round hole and waving at him. He looked like half a man. A mascot perched on the Walrus's nose. It made him laugh. He could not stop laughing until he hit the water with a tremendous splash, the chute dragging him through the pounding crests like a piece of driftwood.

Rowan was losing consciousness fast. He could hear the grating roar of the Walrus's engine, somebody yelling. *Crazy fools. The Jerry gunners would get them. They'd not be able to take off anyway. Crazy, wonderful fools.*

It was over at last. He was dead.

He opened his eyes, feeling something burning his lips. Terror lurked just seconds away, and then he grappled with the understanding that he was not dead. Nor was he in the water. He was in the Walrus's boxlike belly, and he could see the waves through great rents in the side, but the sea was below. He tried to understand. *They were airborne.*

He realised that someone was crawling towards him. It was a young man with very blue eyes. He had to yell above the pounding roar of the engine. 'All right, chum?' He patted his leg. 'I've got a dressing on the wound, but it's best left for a doctor.'

Rowan tried to speak but nothing came. Another figure was sitting in a small seat below the pilot. He was jerking to the violent motion, and Rowan saw he had one arm torn off, and there was blood everywhere. They had gone through enough already, yet they had risked everything to land on the sea for a man they probably thought was past saving anyway.

The man with the blue eyes stumbled forward and touched

131

the pilot on the shoulder. He shouted, 'He's all right, Jim! Caught one in his leg, but I think he'll be okay!'

The pilot was not wearing a helmet, and had his headphones fastened over a battered peaked cap.

Rowan heard him reply, 'Must have been the brandy you poured into him! Glad it wasn't wasted!'

Rowan lay back against the vibrating frames, knowing there was another dead man somewhere, wondering why he had felt nothing of the rescue or the take-off. Maybe he had died but had somehow come back.

He moved and felt his flying gear squelching with water. His watch had gone. And the pain was getting worse.

'Get the Aldis! There's the bloody convoy!' The pilot was laughing. 'Oh, you beauties!'

The other man was pointing the lamp through the port side as the Walrus gave a steep tilt and began to descend.

'Shall I tell them about the Jerries?'

The pilot turned to stare at him. 'Not bloody likely! Wait till they've picked us up!'

It was the first time Rowan had seen his face. There was a rough eye-patch jammed under his cap and dried blood on his cheek. He should get the Victoria Cross for what he had done.

The other one was crawling aft again. He shouted, 'Get ready, chum! When we hit the sea, we *hit*!'

Through a gash in the side Rowan saw something solid rushing past. It was a big freighter, the sea lifting and curling along her side apparently without effort. He watched it, fascinated. Then the Walrus struck the water, and the pain took away the last of his reserve.

When Tim Rowan opened his eyes again he had to adjust to a completely new set of sounds and smells. He was instantly aware of a feeling of warmth and safety. He was in a white-painted cot, and beneath the stiff sheets he was naked, his wounded leg encased in some firm, heavy dressing which by itself seemed to keep all pain at a distance. He moved his head very carefully, afraid the agony would return.

Then came the other awareness. The motion was different. It was the regular, restless plunging movement of a destroyer. He watched the other cots swaying in unison, they were all empty, the bright, clinical perfection of a warship's sickbay.

He listened to the roar of fans, the confident vibration of the destroyer's engines. He was obviously under some kind of drug, and it was hard to keep his eyelids from closing.

A voice said cheerfully, 'Now then, sir, we don't want no peepin'!' It was a sick berth attendant, his jacket pocket full of pencils for some reason or other.

Rowan asked huskily. 'What ship?'

The S.B.A. answered automatically. ' '*Ard*ship, sir.' He chuckled. 'The *Pathan*, Tribal Class destroyer, and the skipper's monniker is Commander Nash. *Now* will you go back to kip, sir?'

He saw the look in Rowan's eyes and added more gently, 'I'm sorry about your friends, sir. Just think you was lucky. It's all you *can* think.'

Rowan felt he was going mad. He asked very slowly. 'What happened? Please *tell me*.'

The S.B.A. leaned over the cot and dabbed Rowan's forehead.

'Don't you remember *nothin'*, sir?'

Rowan shook his head. Even that was a terrible effort.

The man sighed. 'We was on the starboard wing of the convoy when your plane was sighted. Cap'n (D) ordered us to stand-by 'case you broke up like. A freighter spread oil ahead of us, an' the skipper decides to chance it an' lower the sea-boat. There was some sort of argument with your pilot. He wanted to get some bodies off, but the commodore an' Cap'n (D) ordered 'im to abandon and let the Walrus adrift. While all this was goin' on the boat's crew got you passed across.' He looked away. 'After that, nobody seems to know what 'appened. Jimmy the One reckons it might have been a flare explodin', or some kind of electrical fault, anyway—'

Rowan reached out and gripped his wrist. 'Were both the men killed? Is that what you're saying?'

The S.B.A. watched him uneasily. 'Like I said, you was lucky, sir.'

133

Rowan tried to struggle up but the man restrained him easily.

He gasped, 'How long have I been here?'

' 'Bout two hours after the doc 'ad seen to you, sir. Bein' one of the big Tribals we carries a doc.'

'Get him for me.' Rowan saw the man's expression changing. *In a second he'll put me right under.* He said urgently, 'I was not a member of that crew. They picked me up.'

'Then 'o th' 'ell?' The man reached over and snatched a handset. 'Doctor, sir? This 'ere is Wilkins. That flier is wantin' to speak to you.' He nodded to the telephone. 'That's what I told 'im, sir.'

Rowan said as loudly as he could, 'Tell him . . . I was shot down by . . . a heavy cruiser.' He saw his words hitting home like fists. 'P-probably the *Hipper*. Just you tell him *that*, for God's sake.'

At that moment the alarm bells shrilled throughout the ship like mad things, and above it all the tannoy bellowed, *'Action stations! Action stations!'*

There was a muffled explosion overlapped by a second before the bells had stopped their clamour, and some paint flakes floated down across the cot.

The S.B.A. replaced the handset. 'I think we've got company, sir.'

The curtain across the door was wrenched aside. It was obviously the destroyer's captain. A tough-looking commander with a dirty brown sweater beneath his reefer, and long leather sea boots.

He said, 'A cruiser you say? That must be her now. Anything else?'

A seaman in a steel helmet hovered in the passageway.

'Captain, sir. First lieutenant wants to speak to you, please.'

'Wait.' He looked at Rowan.

'Two destroyers. Big ones.' He watched the captain's mind working. At any moment he would be taking his ship into action. He was needed on his bridge, and needed to be there. But he had come here all the same. To be certain. To glean what information there was which might help. Even to discover the reliability of it from Rowan's face and manner.

When Rowan had blurted out all he could remember the captain nodded. 'Good. Thanks. At least there are no more surprises.'

He strode down the passageway, calling for the yeoman of signals as he went in the same level, unhurried voice.

'Now, sir.' The S.B.A. stood looking at him. 'Some 'ow I'm goin' to get you dressed in somethin' warm.'

Outside the little sickbay bells rang, ammunition hoists clattered up and down and men stood to their weapons and waited.

From his bridge Commander Nash watched his information being flashed to the commodore and the senior officer of the escort.

He said, 'Make a signal to the flat-top, Yeo. Tell her we've picked up one of her chaps. His name's Rowan.'

He turned, watching the twin columns of bright water far away to starboard. The big cruiser was out of sight, out of range. She was employing a few frightening tactics in the hope the merchantmen would scatter. Then the U-boats would pick them off at leisure.

The navigating officer watched his captain filling and lighting his pipe.

He said, 'Funny *Hustler* didn't report a plane missing, sir? I'd have thought her captain would be worried.'

Nash looked at him through the match flame. *Not if you knew Turpin as I do.* 'Didn't see any point probably.'

He turned as a signalman handed him a pad. He read it slowly and then nodded.

'Yeoman!'

The petty officer lowered his glasses. 'Sir?'

The captain gave a small smile. He had known the yeoman of signals a long time.

'Hoist battle ensigns, if you please.'

Into the Fire

THE sickbay door banged open and a lieutenant, with scarlet between his wavy stripes, hurried to a small cabinet, jammed some things into his pockets and made to leave again.

The S.B.A. asked, 'What's 'appening, sir?'

Rowan watched the confusion on the young doctor's face. Could barely have qualified before entering the Navy. Probably his first ship, too.

The doctor glanced at them, his eyes anxious. 'Nothing much.' He swayed against a cot as the destroyer pitched and shook violently. 'Cracking on more speed. The other destroyers are with us.' He rubbed his eyes. *'I must think.'*

The S.B.A. had managed to get Rowan into a heavy submariner's sweater and some trousers. He had had to slit one of the legs because of the heavy dressings. The efforts had worn out both of them, but the doctor's obvious fear helped to revive them.

The S.B.A. said, 'You'd better go to the wardroom, sir. My mate's got it ready to lay out casualties. They'll be expectin' you.'

The doctor blinked rapidly. 'Yes. I will.' He tried to smile at Rowan, but it made him look worse. 'You'll be fine. Just stay here and—'

More explosions rumbled against the hull, like distant thunder, and he hurried away without another word.

The S.B.A. said under his breath, 'Poor little bugger. Fair enough at takin' a splinter out of a kid's finger. 'E'll be bloody useless when the bits an' pieces start to fly about.' He picked up his Red Cross satchel. 'I'm off then.' He grinned. 'You stay 'ere, like the man says.' Then he too was gone.

Rowan lay back on the cot, feeling his ribs while he

listened to the sea and the engines. When the S.B.A. had got him sitting against the cot's side, and had struggled to get him into the sweater, he had realised that his body was a mass of raw bruises. Some where the parachute harness had jerked his shoulders. A great livid one on his ribs where he had hit Jonah's cockpit, or had been thrown over when the Walrus had landed. He looked as if he had been in a brawl.

He thought back slowly. But there was nothing there. Just vague pictures without time or proper connection between them. But he could recall exactly the pilot who had been blinded in one eye. His companion, and the taste of brandy on his lips. Jonah spiralling down. His last-second refusal to accept he was really crashing. *Going into the drink*.

Rowan felt the returning despair and anger. But for Turpin's arrogant stupidity *Hustler* would have flown-off a full patrol. Then, no matter what had happened, one at least would have got back with the warning. He heard the intermittent boom of gunfire. What a bloody foul-up.

He thought of Bill, wishing he were here. What had he once said about war? The effort to remember was painful. But to Rowan it was very necessary if he was to hold on.

He nodded. Bill had said that war was *a series of disasters welded together by insanity*. That was it.

The *Pathan* lifted and then plunged into a deep trough, making the racks of bottles and jars rattle in protest. Rowan tried to stand, holding onto a stanchion for safety. Naked but for a borrowed sweater and somebody's trousers. In this place he did not own one single thing.

Above the sickbay desk, where in more normal times sailors queued to prepare themselves for runs ashore, or to face the doctor afterwards, there was a mirror. Rowan studied himself as he would a complete stranger. It was odd, he thought. Above the white sweater his face looked younger. The tousled hair and dark brown eyes could have been out of an old school photograph. He peered around him. *Robinson Crusoe*. He had gone into the drink, and barely remembered it. He had been rescued, and had lost that, too. Now he was in a different ship altogether, and could recall nothing. He grimaced, dragging himself hand over hand along the cot. If he was to catch another packet he would have to prepare. He saw some battered sandals under a table and thrust his bare foot into one of them. Not much for a survival kit, he decided.

Another explosion made him hold on more tightly. That was much nearer. He heard the clatter of a gun mounting, the sudden bark of the destroyer's own armament. *Crash-crash. Crash-crash.* Two pairs. He made himself think it out. They were shooting their two forward mountings. He thought of the captain's face and wondered how he could have imagined otherwise.

The commodore would keep the old anti-aircraft cruiser and the smaller escorts. The cruiser from the Home Fleet and all the big destroyers would turn towards the Germans. They would try to hold that big cruiser off until the shadowing force arrived. *Like the U.S. Cavalry.* He swore aloud, furious with himself for being unable to control his haphazard thoughts. It was like madness.

The sickbay shook again to gunfire, and after that it did not stop for more than a few minutes at a time.

I must get out of here.

He heard heavier guns firing, the sudden swoosh of shells passing directly overhead. The cruiser was having a go now.

He opened the door and peered along the narrow passageway. At the far end were two ratings with axes and fire-fighting gear. Some of the damage control team. They did not even glance at him as he lurched between them, using the handrail above one of them to hop past. Their faces were frozen in concentration.

Rowan saw another steel door, the clips shut, a seaman standing beside it with a telephone to his ear. At action stations he would no more open that door than make a bacon sandwich.

The next salvo from the enemy was perfectly timed, it had to be, for the violence of the explosions told Rowan it was a straddle. Despite hearing the short, abbreviated whistle, he was unprepared for the tremendous force of the detonations. They seemed to lift the hull and shake it bodily before dropping it again, slewing it round so that the passageway rattled and bucked until he thought it would split open. As it swayed upright again he heard the racing screws as before, the irregular bang of gunfire.

But there was a difference. The telephone was dangling from its lead, the seaman lay on his back staring at the deckhead, and there was a red smear down the steel plates, beginning where two holes had been punched through by splinters.

He stooped over the man but he was dead. Rowan noticed that he had a cigarette already rolled for smoking tucked inside his jumper. *For when it was over.*

Without further hesitation Rowan knocked off the clips and pulled back the door. For a long moment he clung to it, staring at the towering bank of broken sea which surged back from the bows, at the dense, choking smoke, and at the buckled devastation along the *Pathan*'s deck. He was on the starboard side, and could see half of the ship's motor boat trailing from its davits. Bright gashes glinted through burned paintwork, and there were two bodies sprawled below an Oerlikon gun. The long steel barrel had been sheared off. Like a carrot.

He staggered and hopped past the after funnel. It too was punctured by splinters. There was smoke everywhere, and he guessed the destroyers were laying a screen to protect the cruiser.

Whooooosh—Bang. The salvo ploughed into the sea and threw up four towering columns of spray. Water deluged over the ship, hurling one of the bodies through the buckled davits and into the sea like a rag.

He struggled on, past another gun mounting, where the crew, like members of some strange order in their anti-flash hoods, watched him blankly, until one yelled, 'Where you goin', mate? You'll catch cold out 'ere!'

The two gunnery ratings grinned at each other as if it was a tremendous joke.

Rowan reached a bridge ladder and clung to it, sucking in air and the stench of cordite while he gathered his strength. It was icy cold, but he was burning all over. Had he been naked he would not have cared. He saw the streaming battle ensigns, so bright against the scudding clouds, and wanted to cheer. Or cry.

Up and up, past another Oerlikon, its helmeted seaman peering through his sights at the greasy smoke.

'Here, take my hand, sir.' A signalman was holding him, while an astonished sub-lieutenant stared as if he had just come out of the tomb.

The captain was on the gratings, his glasses trained over the screen. The navigating officer crouched over his gyro-repeater, and around the bridge messengers, lookouts and a bosun's mate waited at voicepipes and handsets like clumsily-made waxworks.

More great crashes.

The captain remarked, 'Over. They've shifted target to *Kirkwall*.' He added, 'Tell Chief to make more smoke.' To the navigating officer he said, 'Alter course, Pilot.'

'Starboard ten.' The lieutenant saw Rowan and smiled. 'Good God!'

The captain turned. 'You might as well stay as you've come this far.' He waited as a seaman helped Rowan to the bridge chair. 'The cruiser *Kirkwall* is doing well.' He seemed very calm. 'She's hit the enemy twice, and we are going in with torpedoes.'

His eyes glowed red and orange, and the intercom at the rear of the bridge snapped, '*Kirkwall*'s been hit. Just abaft the bridge.'

Rowan peered over the screen and saw something sticking out of the water like an upended submarine. It was the stern of a destroyer.

The captain said sharply, 'Captain (D). He caught a full salvo.'

There were several small figures splashing wildly around the upended wreck, one of them waved his arms as the destroyer raced past. Rowan saw him swept aside by the bow wave. Buried under a wall of water.

'All tubes at the ready, sir.'

'Very well.' The captain thrust his unlit pipe into his pocket. 'I hope to God you're right about there being only two escorts with the big chap.'

Rowan winced as more heavy shells exploded off the port bow. Tons of water cascaded over the forecastle, and splinters whined and cracked against the hull like grape-shot.

Around the bridge the voicepipes kept up their clamour.

Two men killed down aft. X-gun out of action. Four casualties in boiler room.

When the smoke billowed upwards in the wind Rowan saw the cruiser. She was steaming between the destroyers, her guns high-angled as she fired again and again at the German. Rowan still could not see the enemy, and his eyes watered too much anyway. He stared instead at the cruiser. He could even forget the ear-shattering roar of gunfire, the insane chatter of orders and requests which came from every side, as he watched the *Kirkwall* steaming in to close the range.

Everyone aboard must know they had no chance at all. Six-inch guns against the massive German battery and those great steel plates. But if the destroyers were going to get close enough to loose their torpedoes she had to make a diversion.

He heard someone say brokenly, 'Oh, see that one! *Jesus!*'

A bright, fiery ball burst up from the cruiser's forecastle, shooting smoke and fragments into the air. They were still falling after the cruiser had passed the spot and was still charging towards her enemy.

The captain said, 'Soon now.' He trained his glasses. 'If we can get just *one* hit on the bastard!'

'Captain, sir! *Pitt* has been straddled!'

Rowan stared above the heads of the lookouts, seeing the destroyer on *Kirkwall*'s port beam slewing round in a welter of spray and pressurized steam. As the smoke screen cleared slightly he saw that twenty feet of her bows had gone and the force of her charge was doing the rest, ripping her apart as she drove forward into the waves.

She began to capsize immediately, her screws still turning like those on a toy boat, as the stern lifted through the smoke.

The yeoman shouted, 'Signal from *Kirkwall*, sir. *Have flooding in engineroom. Must reduce speed immediately. Good luck.*'

'Acknowledge.'

The captain still had his glasses trained on the sinking

destroyer. He gave no hint in his voice of what the signal really meant. That, with the captain of the flotilla dead, the cruiser out of the fight, he was now in overall command of the attack.

Then he looked at Rowan. 'Might need you yet.' He turned towards the bows again.

'And if you *can't* hit her, sir?'

'Then I'll ram the bastard.' He said over his shoulder, 'Tell the torpedo gunner to stand by. He is, of course, but he likes to be spoken to occasionally.'

Rowan watched the simple joke make its way to the grubby faces near him.

He felt something touching his leg, and when he looked down he saw one of the signalmen adjusting his dressing.

The youth said anxiously, 'It's bleeding again, sir.'

Rowan made to reply when the whole world exploded.

Someone was trying to lift him, and when he wiped his streaming eyes with his sweater he realised it was the yeoman.

'Can you look after yourself, sir?' The man's face was cut and bleeding. 'It's a god-awful mess here!'

Rowan struggled across the gratings, coughing out smoke as he groped his way to the forepart of the bridge again. There was broken glass, splintered woodwork and fragments everywhere.

He saw smoke billowing above the port side of the bridge, and knew at least one shell must have exploded inboard. The shock had flung him from the captain's chair and halfway across the open bridge, yet he could feel nothing.

As his proper hearing returned he heard men yelling and calling for help, and further aft someone screaming like a tortured animal.

The mast was gone, and the bridge upperworks, including the radar and gunnery director, had been completely wrecked.

As he pulled himself up the side of the chair he saw the captain lurch to his feet, his eyes everywhere as he tried to sense the hurt to his ship.

The navigating officer had been practically cut in half, and most of the men at the rear of the bridge were either dead or badly wounded.

The captain staggered to the compass and then looked at Rowan. He did not ask if he could cope, he merely snapped, 'Take over from Pilot. Bring her round to one-seven-zero.' He knocked off the cap of a voicepipe. 'Report damage, Number One. Send a stretcher party up here, chop-chop.'

Rowan leaned over his voicepipe. 'Wheelhouse!'

He heard somebody coughing violently, then, 'Wheel-house, sir! Able Seamen Lewis on the wheel!' He sounded close to breaking.

'How is it down there?'

A pause. 'Cox'n and two of the lads are dead. The pilot's done in an' Mr Prince is bleedin' terrible. I think 'is leg's 'alf off.'

Rowan knew nothing of these people, but guessed the wretched Mr Prince was probably the midshipman.

He watched the gyro-repeater ticking remorselessly round. Guns were hammering from every angle, and above the shattered remnants of the screen he could see the dull, hazed silhouette of the German heavy cruiser. From the air she had looked formidable enough. But now, angled across the horizon like a chunk of rock, she was awesome. He watched her guns flash, counted the seconds, and then winced as the falling shells exploded somewhere astern.

He had to win the confidence of the man on the wheel. It must be terrible for him. In semi-darkness behind steel shutters, his friends mangled and dying around him.

Rowan said firmly, 'Starboard ten.'

'Ten of starboard wheel on, sir.'

Rowan clung to the compass, feeling the pain again, his limbs quivering uncontrollably as if he had a fever.

'Midships. Steady.'

He saw the captain glance at him before he was away again at the opposite corner of the bridge, his voice rapping out orders to the new faces which had arrived amongst the chaos.

Rowan waited, willing the helmsman to acknowledge. It was a miracle that the ship was still responding to screws and rudder.

'Steer one-seven-zero.' He drew a deep breath. 'That was well done, Lewis.'

He saw bodies being hauled away by the busy figures below him, covered by oilskins, bits of bunting, anything to hide the horror of their last seconds on earth.

Another destroyer was in difficulties now. Rowan was just in time to see her bracketed by more heavy shells, her foremast and forward funnel ripped away as if by a great gale. Lines of jagged holes appeared along her side, and he could tell by her wild alteration of course that her steering had been shot away.

The captain said hoarsely, 'Three of us left.'

'Chief wants to speak with you, sir.' A bosun's mate thrust the handset towards him, but his eyes were watching the German ship, fascinated. Like a rabbit mesmerised by a fox.

'Yes, Chief.' They all ducked as shells screamed above the bridge. 'I can't help it. You must keep her moving at full revs.' He looked at Rowan, his eyes angry. 'If that big ship gets past us it will be the end of the convoy. *We* don't matter any more.' He slammed down the handset.

Rowan turned away. Even the captain knew they were not going to stop the enemy. Three destroyers, and the *Pathan* was only able to fire with Y-gun mounting, and that would only bear when the destroyer veered away to avoid a fresh fall of shells.

But the four torpedo tubes were trained outboard, as they were on the other destroyers. *Just one good hit*. It was like expecting the sea to dry up.

The convoy was barely visible now. What with the drifting banks of smoke and the falling shells it was not surprising. The merchantmen, so precious, so well guarded over the many days since they had left Iceland, were hurrying away from those murderous guns as fast as they could. A handful of small escorts, *Hustler* and her two sloops, a rescue tug and the elderly A.A. cruiser. If the Home Fleet support did not arrive within the hour the rescue tug would be the only useful one afloat.

As if to mock his reeling thoughts, the yeoman called, 'W/T report that the Home Fleet force is still engaging heavy

German units, sir. No extra support will arrive before dawn tomorrow at the earliest.'

The captain looked past him. He had known it from the beginning.

How well the enemy had played it. Move and counter move, just as Chadwick had said war should and must be waged. Poor *Growler* had probably gone to the bottom already.

A great explosion battered the ship to one side, men and loose gear cascading across the decks and from gun mountings like so much flotsam.

'Direct hit on the quarterdeck, sir.'

Men were shouting at each other, calling names, some must have gone mad in the belching smoke and fire which made a swirling, angry cone high above the ship.

Rowan felt the effect immediately. The speed began to fall away, and as the ship ploughed across a line of jagged crests he sensed the motion dragging at the narrow hull like an arrester wire.

The captain said, 'Tell the Gunner (T) to prepare to fire. Extreme range, but we're losing way. No more time left. Make a signal to the others.'

Rowan could see it all. With the resistance broken the Germans would hurry after the convoy, and either scatter it with long-range bombardment or destroy it at leisure. Like fish in a barrel. The badly mauled *Kirkwall* would stand no chance at all. One of the German destroyers would finish her.

He turned his head as a lookout started to yell something. He was almost afraid to look. Fearful that something even worse was about to happen.

'Look, sir!' The rating was almost incoherent. *'Aircraft! Starboard bow!* God Almighty! They're bloody Swordfish!'

The yeoman exclaimed hoarsely, *'Hustler*'s skipper has quit the convoy. He's decided to give us a hand!'

Rowan hopped to the gratings and clung to a rail, oblivious of the broken glass, the trail of blood he was leaving on the splintered woodwork.

The captain saw his face and held out some binoculars without a word.

Rowan steadied the glasses against the ship's unsteady rise and fall, almost blind with shock and disbelief. His eyes kept misting over, and it took precious seconds before he could find the approaching aircraft.

Then he said huskily, 'Nine Swordfish, sir. But not from *Hustler*. Wrong bearing.'

He could barely hide his emotion as he watched the torpedo bombers in three tight arrowheads as they sailed unhurriedly towards the enemy. Just feet above the wavetops, three by three. He could even recognise the squadron insignia, the polar bear holding a torpedo in its paws like a lance.

So intent had the German guns crews been on their methodical bombardment that they had not seen the aircraft's slow approach from the other horizon. But surprise gave way to vicious response from all three ships as they opened fire with every automatic weapon which would bear.

The whole sky above and around the twin-winged planes was soon pockmarked with exploding cannon shells, while in gathering strength across their path grew a criss-cross of glittering tracers which made such a mesh that Rowan imagined nothing could survive in it.

One Swordfish exploded and cartwheeled away into the sea. Another swerved, a wing torn off, and it too plunged down and disintegrated. The other seven flew on. They ignored the destroyers which were altering course to protect their great consort, ignored their murderous fire-power, the inferno of tracer which even as they watched caught another Swordfish and set it ablaze.

The captain yelled, 'Tell the Chief to give me a few more revs and never mind the bloody damage! This is our chance, *our only chance*!'

Lights blinked from the other destroyers, and Rowan could feel the sudden wild excitement, the desperate eagerness around him, where just before there had been only defeat.

A fourth Swordfish exploded in the air and scattered burning pieces for a hundred yards. *Five left*. Very small now, very alone as they pushed on towards their target.

Rowan cursed as he tried to hold the glasses steady, feeling the battered ship beneath him stir, rally to the clang of the

147

telegraphs and the hoarse shout of commands.

He watched the second Swordfish, saw the green and yellow stripes on its cowling and knew it was Andy Miller leading the attack, could picture him sitting forward in the cockpit, his devil's beard poking towards the enemy, showing the way.

Another Swordfish was losing height, then hit the water and blew up with its own torpedo.

The leading plane released its torpedo, but it was too soon, or it hit a bank of waves, Rowan could not tell. He saw it break its back, and as the Swordfish lifted and tried to pull away it took a burst of cannonfire from nose to tail, hurling it over and down within feet of the ship's side.

'Tubes ready, sir!'

'Harda-port! Midships! *Steady!*' The captain leaned his elbows on the screen, his glasses unwavering. *'Fire!'*

Rowan heard the measured thuds as the four torpedoes left the tubes.

'All torpedoes running, sir!'

Rowan held his breath as he watched Andy Miller's Swordfish touched with little droplets of fire and then begin to sway from side to side like a wounded bird.

Pathan's last challenge had been forgotten, and even the captain ran to the other side of his bridge to watch the Swordfish, as with smoke gathering and streaming from its tail it continued to head for the cruiser. The Germans were shooting with everything, but the Swordfish seemed to have a charmed life. The torpedo dropped and was lost in the welter of spray, and as somebody raised a solitary cheer, Miller's plane burst into flames and then fell, lost from view behind one of the destroyers.

The German captain had decided to take avoiding action. By so doing he exposed his full broadside to the destroyer's own torpedoes.

One by one, three hit her massive hull, hurling huge waterspouts as high as her scarlet ensign.

One more torpedo hit her right aft, on the opposite side. Andy Miller had done what he set out to do.

The surviving Swordfish had already turned and were

heading away to the south again. Their torpedoes had either gone astray or misfired, but the enemy had had more than enough. The two big destroyers were keeping close to their flagship, and even though it was unlikely the damage would be fatal, she would have a hard struggle to reach Norway if the weather got worse.

Commander Nash was saying, 'Make a signal, Yeoman. Discontinue the action and retire under smoke screen. We will rejoin the convoy.' He took out his pipe and looked at Rowan. 'That was the bravest thing I have ever seen.' He added simply, 'Anybody who worries about a victory should have seen that.' He waited, watching Rowan's pale face. 'Did you know all of them?'

Rowan laid down the glasses. Now, that German pilot's family would never get the watch which Andy Miller always wore.

'All of them. Some better than others. Andy Miller could fly anything. Above all else, he was a fine man.'

He sat down heavily as the same S.B.A. started to re-tie the dressing on his leg.

The *Pathan*'s first lieutenant strode on to the bridge and looked around before asking, 'Where's Pilot, sir?'

The captain gestured towards a body half hidden under an oilskin. He looked desperately tired. Then he pointed to Rowan who was still sitting in his smoke-stained sweater and split trousers watching the smoke pall where it had all happened.

'He took over, Number One. A pilot as a Pilot. He did damn well, too.'

The first lieutenant glanced at his battered ship, the broken guns which pointed impotently to the sky, at the dead, and those who were just beginning to realise they were still alive.

'I think they all did, sir.'

Rowan accepted a duffel coat which somebody had found for him.

He did not leave the bridge for the rest of the day, despite the pleas of the S.B.A. and the suggestions of the harassed doctor. He remained in the captain's chair, drinking endless cups of tea and soup, watching the ship and her defenders putting themselves to rights as best they could. And remembering the nine underpowered Swordfish.

By dusk they had rejoined the convoy, and as signals of congratulation and sympathy rippled up and down those same rigid lines of ships a further diamond-bright light flashed a recognition signal.

H.M.S. *Growler* was back with her brood. Then and only then did Rowan go below.

10

Price of Victory

CAPTAIN BRUCE BUCHAN leaned out over the side of the flying bridge and waited warily while the rescue tug *Cornelian* nudged alongside. Both vessels were moving at reduced speed, but as he watched the bandaged figures, inert shapes strapped in stretchers, and others who were still able to fend for themselves, he seemed to feel every jarring impact against the hull.

It was very early in the morning, and the sea was smoother than for some days, with just the long, undulating swells to make the manoeuvre difficult.

But the tug's skipper knew his business, and as the wounded were ferried up and through one of *Growler*'s entry ports Buchan found some satisfaction with the speed it was accomplished.

Beyond the carrier the long lines of merchantmen stretched away to the southern horizon. The depleted escorts were carefully placed ahead and on the wings, and the anti-aircraft cruiser had moved up to the centre of the formation where her multiple weapons could give maximum cover. On *Growler*'s starboard beam, about half a mile away, was the *Hustler*, some aircraft warming-up on her flight deck, coughing out blue vapour in the crisp morning air.

Buchan felt tired, worn out with the strain of getting back to the convoy. They had been forced to stop completely when the Chief reported trouble in the solitary shaft. The bearings could take a lot, but the way they had forced the ship through all sorts of weather had had its effect in the end.

And while his ship had rolled and pitched heavily, her screw still, her decks filled with watchful, listening men, Buchan had thought about the convoy, of the battle being reported by the Admiralty far away to the north-east. Great armoured giants locked in combat, while the convoy sailed on, hoping for the best, denied full support when they had needed it most.

Rear Admiral Chadwick had ordered a Seafire to be flown-off as soon as it was light to report back if the pilot sighted anything. The aircraft had returned with the startling news that there was a big German cruiser and two destroyers between them and the convoy.

Buchan, and probably others, had expected Chadwick to show alarm, or at least the realisation that he had delayed too long away from his group.

Instead the admiral had snapped, 'Just as I envisaged from the start. The Germans have played this one well, but perhaps too thoroughly even for them.' He had looked at his officers and added calmly, 'We will launch a full torpedo strike right away. See to it, Villiers. Tell the squadron commander I want all-out effort. This is what we've been waiting for.'

Again Buchan recalled the long and anxious wait, searching the clouded sky, listening for the throbbing beat of engines. The sight of just two Swordfish flying towards the carrier had been almost heart-breaking for many of the men. And one of the survivors had made a crash-landing when its undercarriage had collapsed. Two of its crew had also been wounded.

And now here were the rest of those who had been snatched from all kinds of death being lifted and swayed up in tackles from the wallowing tug alongside. Some were from the destroyers which had been sunk in the fight, and others who were too badly wounded to be left in the cramped quarters of an escort's sickbay. *Growler* carried the senior doctor. And maybe Chadwick had other reasons for ordering the transfer.

Two destroyers, including Captain (D)'s, had been sunk by gunfire. The third had gone down only after her company had worked throughout the night to keep her afloat. But to no avail.

And amongst those listless figures was also Lieutenant Timothy Rowan.

The navigating officer asked, 'Do you think we've seen the last of Jerry on this trip, sir?' He too looked lined with strain.

The yeoman shouted, 'From *Cornelian*, sir. *Ready to cast off*.'

Buchan said heavily, 'Very well, Yeo. Tell him thanks.'

He was glad of the interruption. Glad to be released from Lieutenant Bray's question. He had been answering questions and solving problems without sleep for forty-eight hours.

The commander appeared on the bridge, a megaphone under his arm.

'All done, sir. Doc's got them below, and I've detailed off a working party for him, and as many more as he needs.'

Jolly waited respectfully, his cheeks flushed from the salt air.

'Good.'

Buchan looked at his chair. Dismissing its invitation. He would fall asleep if he sat for an instant.

'Go down and speak to the fitter ones, Edgar, as soon as Doc says it's all right. I'll come myself when I'm sure what's happening.'

Jolly took a mug of tea from a bosun's mate. 'The destroyers were bloody good apparently. Held the big Jerry off just long enough.'

'Long enough for Lieutenant Commander Miller and his men to reach the target.' Buchan opened and shut his hands with sudden anger. 'By God, if only we'd been there from the start.'

A steel door opened and slammed, and Chadwick walked on to the bridge. He returned their salutes and then stepped on to a grating to watch the tug falling away, belching smoke, her crew gathering up ropes and fenders, drinking tea, glad to be on their own again.

Buchan watched him narrowly, hating him, afraid of what he might say.

Chadwick was freshly shaved, and beneath his oak-leaved cap his silver-grey sideburns were perfectly matched.

He said over his shoulder, 'I've been in the Ops Room and

passed my signals to the commodore and the new senior officer of the escort. He's Commander Nash of the *Pathan*. Laid on quite a show to all accounts. His ship's a bit of a potmess after the battering she took, but he's the man for me. A goer. A fighter.'

He turned and studied Buchan.

'You look pretty rough. Why don't you get your head down for a few hours. Commander Jolly can take over, eh?'

Buchan stared at him, his eyes stinging. 'I can manage, thank you.'

'Fine.' Chadwick watched him. 'Splendid.'

Without shifting his gaze he added, 'I'm ordering *Hustler* to carry out permanent patrols from now on. We will fly-on our fighters which Captain Turpin *borrowed* as soon as the convoy takes up its new course.' He snapped his fingers. *'Pilot?'*

Bray jerked upright. 'Ten hundred, sir.'

Buchan asked, 'Are we getting any more support, sir?'

'I gather so. Two cruisers and a couple of long-range escorts are joining towards noon. Our Russian friends are ready to send every anti-submarine vessel and plane out to meet us to make the Jerries run deep and keep out of our way.' He grinned. 'All the way. Just like we promised.'

Buchan said thickly, 'What about the cost, sir? Did you read those figures, too?' He knew Jolly was giving him a warning frown, that the O.O.W. had moved away so as not to be involved.

Chadwick eyed him calmly. 'Three crack destroyers sunk. Our cruiser knocked out. *Kirkwall*'s been ordered to make her own passage to Iceland, by the way. Nine aircraft shot down, including the Walrus and our own Seafire. *All involved in a single battle*, a vital part of a pattern.' He pressed his strong fingers together. 'Our job is to protect the convoy, not to force a battle with the German Fleet.' His grey eyes were cold, like the sea. 'Look ahead. Every merchant ship is still there.' He turned to Jolly. 'I've seen it on their faces in the Ops Room. The Swordfish crews meant a lot in this ship, I don't have to be told. But if that cruiser had got to the convoy, nothing, but nothing would have saved it. *Pathan*'s guts, and the efforts of all the rest would have been just so much blood spilled for damn all!' He looked away. 'Seven Swordfish were shot down. Twenty-one brave men died. But the cruiser was snared, and by driving her round with a torpedo we gave that big bastard to the destroyers *on a plate*!'

The O.O.W. called nervously, 'Resuming original revolutions, sir.'

It almost broke the spell. Jolly put down his speaking trumpet and moved to a door.

The admiral asked casually, 'Where are you off to?'

Jolly sounded uncomfortable. 'Thought I'd look in on the wounded, sir. Later, when they've settled in.'

Chadwick adjusted his beautiful cap and studied his reflection in a clear-view screen.

'When you're in a car accident you need a brandy, *double-quick*, Commander, not a month afterwards!' He looked at the bridge at large. 'And since nobody can be spared for the job, I shall go myself, *now*.'

Minchin, *Growler*'s P.M.O., glanced quickly through the scrawled docket which Rowan had brought with him from *Pathan*'s young doctor. He was a grave-faced man, and like many of his trade, outwardly callous.

He said, 'You were lucky again.' He signalled to one of his busy S.B.A.s. 'I'll have the wound re-dressed, then get you shipped to your own cabin.' He looked around at the over-crowded sickbay, the bandaged figures, his white-coated team of assistants. 'Can't spare the space down here.' He gave a cool smile. 'Another few inches to the right and you'd have some metal where *Pathan*'s doc could *not* have extracted it.'

Rowan listened to a man sobbing behind him. The whole area seemed full of pain.

'Was it flak?'

The doctor shook his head, his eyes already on the next stretcher.

'Bits of your own plane apparently.'

A sort of hush felt its way through the cots and stooping figures.

The P.M.O. said softly, 'God Almighty, it's the man himself.'

Chadwick strode down the centre of the cots, his cap under one arm, his face set in a mask of composed gravity. A few paces behind, Dundas, his steward, followed with a large cardboard box.

'I'm sorry, sir, I wasn't expecting a visit. We're in a bit of a mess here.'

Chadwick eyed the doctor gravely for a few seconds. Around him, and from the tiers of white cots, the less badly injured men were craning their heads, propping themselves on their elbows to see what was happening.

Chadwick replied, 'I won't disturb you. You've got plenty to do.' He turned, his voice carrying easily to the other bulkhead. 'And these brave fellows don't want a damn pep talk from *me*.'

His humility caught the doctor off balance. 'I don't mean to imply—'

Chadwick raised his hand, brushing the apology aside. 'But I could not stay away. Could not restrain myself from coming to tell them how proud, how very honoured I am to have them with me.' He stared round the silent faces. 'They told me we had a long way to go. That the Germans still held the upper hand in these waters.' He cleared his throat. 'With men like these I could take the whole bloody world. And I'll tell them *that* when we get home!'

Rowan watched, fascinated, as several of the injured men started to clap and grin at the impeccable admiral. Most were unable to use their hands because of bandages and worse, but their pleasure at his words was obvious.

Chadwick walked slowly towards the door adding, 'My steward has plenty of cigarettes and chocolate for you, lads. I'll be back when we're out of danger.' He hesitated beside a bunk and looked down at a young seaman.

Rowan had seen him carried up from the tug. He could not have been more than eighteen, and appeared younger. He was barely conscious, and his eyes were little more than slits. Rowan knew from the coloured label tied to his cot that he was due for immediate surgery, an amputation.

The admiral touched the boy's shoulder and said, 'You can't hear me. But God be with you.' He strode away, the curtain swishing across behind him.

Rowan did not know what to think. *Actor? Fraud?* Or was Chadwick genuine in his grief, his sympathy with these few survivors?

An S.B.A. said gruffly, 'Your turn, sir.'

Later as Rowan lay in his own bunk again, his leg throbbing hotly in its new dressings, he wondered what would happen to Chadwick.

He listened to the roar of engines, ebbing and fading as the *Growler*'s Seafires returned to their proper base, the varying vibrations of the hull and the mattress under his body as the ship changed course yet again.

It seemed an age before Bill Ellis came down to the cabin.

He sat on a stool beside the bunk and said quietly, 'Hello, Tim. You gave us quite a turn, you know.' His eyes moved along the blanket. 'Oughtn't you to be in the sickbay?'

Rowan moved his wounded leg slightly to reassure him. 'I'm okay. They got the bits out. Poor Jonah, I didn't—'

Bill interrupted. 'Leave it for now, Tim. Try and rest. When we got that signal from *Pathan* to say you were picked up, it was like a bloody holiday. We thought you'd gone into the drink, and that bastard Turpin did nothing to inform the other ships about you.'

Rowan asked, 'Have you spoken to our lads aboard *Growler* yet?'

'Some.' Bill looked at him steadily. 'I guessed you'd ask.' He sighed heavily. 'You saw it all of course, the old Stringbags going in for the attack on the cruiser. It must have been something.' He looked at the deck. 'Most of them bought it. Andy Miller, Ron Kirby and Dutchy—'

Rowan gripped his wrist. 'Which one?'

'Little Dutchy. De Boer. Peter van Roijen got back and then had his undercarriage collapse. But he's all right.'

Rowan closed his eyes, remembering each face with difficulty. As it had looked across the breakfast table, or dozing in the Ready Room. Drinking in a pub, or playing some energetic game on the flight deck. Pilots, observers, air gunners. Twenty-one of them wiped out in fifteen minutes.

He said at length, 'It'll mean an entirely rebuilt squadron when we get back.' He forced a smile. 'Looks as if you were wrong about the convoy.'

Bill shrugged. 'We'll see. Ops told me we should be safe in port in three days at the outside. But we're in range of Banak airfield in the north of Norway. The big ships have had a go, and the U-boats seem to have had a few knocks, too. I'll bet the air will be full of planes tomorrow.' He looked unusually grim. 'Perhaps we can even the score a bit.'

Rowan was getting drowsy again. 'It's good to be back.'

Bill watched him sadly. 'In this old cow?' He smiled. 'I suppose.'

Rowan nodded. 'The admiral was in the sickbay. He spoke to the destroyers' wounded survivors.'

'So I heard. From Villiers. I think he's halfway round the bend because of all this. He was spouting something about lives being thrown away to cover Chadwick's mistake, his misjudgement of the enemy's movements.' He looked at Rowan. 'I know. He was a great chap. *Once*. But whatever happened when he was in the bag has knocked him for six. I wish they'd find him a shore job. He makes me nervous.'

Feet moved in the passageway and then the curtain was drawn aside. Bill lurched to his feet as the admiral stepped into the small cabin.

Chadwick nodded. 'Relax, er, Ellis, isn't it?' He looked at the bunk. 'Didn't have a chance to speak with you, Rowan. I'll not disturb you. Just wanted you to know that I'm very pleased with the way you handled things. A seaplane added to your score, and then the sighting of the cruiser. You did splendidly. Properly backed-up, you might have saved a few more lives as well.' He did not elaborate but said, 'Anyway, I shall see that you get some recognition. Time some of your sort were given some sea room, eh?' He chuckled. 'We're not home and dry yet. But I'm optimistic. Anything I can arrange for you?'

Rowan said carefully, 'If the enemy have a real go at us, sir, I'd like to do something. I never realised it was so hard to stay still and watch it all happening.'

'Don't worry.' Chadwick grinned. 'If and when we get a big attack I'll get every man in the air who can still use his eyes and brain!' He swung round as a telegraphist appeared in the door. *'Yes?'*

The telegraphist held out a pad, his hand shaking slightly.

'From Operations, sir. As you requested.'

'Yes.' Chadwick's grey eyes skimmed along the pencilled wording. 'Thank you. Tell the bridge I'm coming up.' To Rowan he said, 'Visibility's not so hot. More clouds about. It'll make an air attack harder to hold off.' He was thinking aloud. 'I'd better get things moving. God help everyone if they foul this one up, eh?'

Bill stood aside as the admiral left the cabin. He murmured, 'I could smell the brandy. Lucky chap. I'll bet he needs it right now, too. I'd not have his job for a bloody peerage!'

He smiled. Rowan was fast asleep. He walked out quietly, drawing the curtain and switching off the light. He saw the big Dutchman walking towards him, his face set in a frown.

Van Roijen asked, 'Tim okay?'

Bill nodded. 'He's pretty well drugged. It'll do him good, he's had a rough time.'

Van Roijen nodded. 'You take walk with me, yes? I can't go and sit in the bloody wardroom. All those empty chairs. Not yet anyway.'

Bill said, 'Twice round the deck.' He grinned. 'Get some of that fat off!'

When they reached the starboard walkway the change in the sky was very apparent. More cloud at several levels, and only occasional patches of sky still visible.

The ships were in firm formation, shining dully in the grey light, and aboard the nearest sloop Bill could see the duffel-coated seamen at work with tackles and hoists, taking up extra magazines and clips of shells for the short-range anti-aircraft guns.

It was funny how you never thought of the things you had

achieved. The dangers you had avoided. But only of the next one ahead, and the one after that.

Growler's tannoy boomed. 'All anti-aircraft weapon crews will exercise in half an hour.' As an afterthought the quartermaster added, 'Senior hands of messes to muster for rum.'

Van Roijen rubbed his hands. 'The British! I wonder you did not issue the rum *first*!'

It was barely dawn when *Growler*'s company went to action stations. There was no alarm, but Chadwick was taking no chances. Breakfast was issued an hour earlier than usual, and the captain broadcast to the whole ship what might be expected to happen.

The gap was narrowing, the time for the Germans' final attempt to destroy the convoy was running out. Every turn of the screws took the ships closer to their goal and brought the additional sea and air cover from the Russians nearer.

Chadwick stayed for some while in Operations and then spoke to the assembled air crews in the Ready Room. He had already been to most of the gun sponsons and had apparently visited the hangar deck. There, his reception had been cool, almost hostile, as if the riggers and mechanics held him personally responsible for the losses to the Swordfish crews.

As he made his way to the upper bridge his expression gave no hint of anxiety or resentment.

He saw Buchan's shadowy outline against the glass screen and said, 'It's getting colder. Be winter soon up here. Poor bastards.'

Buchan watched him. 'It may make our return run easier, sir.'

There were some far off explosions, several patterns, one after the other.

Then the signalman by a voicepipe reported, 'Escorts have engaged a suspected U-boat, sir. Two miles south-west of the screen.'

Chadwick considered it. 'Still a few of the buggers about. They'll not get near us if we keep up this pace.' He looked at the luminous clock. 'Signal *Hustler* to begin her Swordfish patrols right away. No point in waiting.'

Buchan thought of Turpin and wondered what he would have done if *Growler* and not *Hustler* had stayed with the convoy. Would he have obeyed the last order to remain as convoy escort, or would he have flown-off his Swordfish to try and help the destroyers? And if the admiral had not been aboard, would he have ordered the death-or-glory attack which Chadwick had instituted?

'*Hustler*'s acknowledged, sir. First patrol in ten minutes.'

'Good.' Chadwick watched the nearest sloop, gauging the pull of the wind and sea as she rolled awkwardly in a procession of broken waves.

Most of the officers and men throughout *Growler*'s stubby hull were thinking of what might happen, how it would affect each one of them personally.

From William Laird, the Commander (E), standing on his shining, quivering catwalk in his engineroom, to his lowliest stoker, each was unwilling to talk or meet another man's eye. Laird often thought of what would happen if a torpedo exploded right here amidst his roaring world of machinery, demanding dials and all the complex mass of boilers, condensers and turbines. They never heard anything of the other world above. Rarely saw the sea but on their way back and forth from duty. Laird was good at his job, and had once been chief engineer aboard a Union Castle liner in balmier times. He had not seen much of that either.

A light winked above his little desk, and Johns, the second engineer, snatched up the telephone, covering his exposed ear with a grease-blackened hand.

He replaced the telephone and shouted, 'Balloon's gone up, Chief! Aircraft sighted!'

The Chief nodded. 'Tell the boiler room and the Chief E.R.A.' He watched the great, glistening shaft. The core of the ship and their lives. 'What wouldn't I give for a pint at the Nag's Head.' But nobody heard him.

In his immaculate operating theatre Minchin and the junior doctor, Surgeon Lieutenant Barstow, were checking their instruments when the alarm shattered the stillness. Minchin was very tired, and had swallowed several pills to give him some extra energy. He knew he was going to need it. He had been working all night on the wounded survivors, and thankfully, most of them were fast asleep, too dazed or drugged to know what was happening. He had amputated the young seaman's leg, but he had died just the same.

He looked at Barstow and smiled wearily. 'My father wanted me to be an accountant. I think he had the right idea.'

Up on his special part of the island Lieutenant Commander Eric Villiers, Distinguished Service Cross and Bar, trained his binoculars on the *Hustler* as her first patrol of three Swordfish bumbled along the flight deck and climbed slowly away on the opposite beam. The other carrier altered course again to steer parallel with *Growler*, her upperworks and tattered ensign showing with brief clarity in a shaft of dirty light between the clouds.

He glanced at his little team, the ratings at the telephones, balaclava-helmeted and muffled against the wind which was coming almost head-on across the blunt bows. *All the way from bleeding Russia*, he had heard his leading hand remark.

Above him the wind moaned through the lattice mast and radar lantern, and he imagined Buchan there with the admiral breathing down his neck.

Villiers rubbed his forehead with the back of his glove. He felt sick just thinking about it. He had had to pass the order to the air crews, knowing he was sending them to certain death. If Chadwick's patrol had failed to discover the cruiser, every one of those men would have been alive. It was no use talking about the balance of values, or what would have happened to the convoy. War was about friends, not about strategy and grand designs.

One rating reported, 'Red Flight standing-by, sir.' He waited, watching Villiers' strained face, his eyes white in the gloom.

'Very well, Pass the word to the Ops Room.'

He tried to ease his aching mind. But he kept seeing the nightmare. *Again, again, again.*

Being taken prisoner of war in the Mediterranean had been almost a relief to Villiers. Like most of his friends, he had been in the worst part of the Middle East campaign from the beginning. It had seemed as if nothing could or would halt the enemy. Every day he had flown-off to cover a battered convoy, or in support of some beleaguered army position ashore.

He had been in a carrier at first, and when she had been torpedoed he had joined a mixed squadron in the desert. They had flown anything and everything. There had been naval pilots and R.A.F. mixed up together. South Africans and Australians, New Zealanders and Canadians, with methods and ideas as varied as their machines. But they had all been veterans, if only by staying alive.

He had seen the awe on the faces of new, fledgling pilots fresh out of England. The same look he had observed on Rowan's face when he had served with him so long ago.

Then one day it had ended. He had been shot down and immediately rescued from the sea by an Italian destroyer.

One prison camp to another, and finally handed over to the Germans and thence to a place outside Minden.

For some reason or other a lot of them had been moved yet again, to Denmark. To his companions it had meant more than a pleasant change from German hostility. It had brought England nearer. If not in miles, then in one overriding fact. They were amongst friendly, downtrodden people who had reason to hate the occupying power and who would do anything to aid an escape via the North Sea.

Villiers had listened to the others planning and dreaming about the day when it might be possible. Some had tried it, a few had actually reached home.

He had pretended to be as eager as the rest, hating himself for the deception, his outward willingness to join any such attempt. For deep down he was more afraid of facing the war than of remaining a prisoner. Equally, he was afraid of showing the truth to anyone but himself.

The camp had only been ten miles from the sea, and separated from it mainly by farms. When the word was passed to the senior British officer that the local Resistance was prepared to aid a limited escape, things moved quickly. The camp commandant was no tyrant, and had until recently served with distinction on the Russian front. He had had one arm and one eye and had wandered around the camp more like an inmate than its commander.

They had had a whole night to get clear, having made their escape with some civilian workers who had been called in to attend to the drains.

It had been so stupidly easy that some of them had laughed about it as they had hurried in two separate parties through fields and lanes, being guided all the time by their Danish rescuers.

There was to be a two-day wait in safe houses, small farms, where they were immediately hidden, willingly supplied with food and drink by the Danes.

Something had gone wrong. He still did not know if a traitor had informed on them, or if the German intelligence service was better than it was supposed to be. On the second day the Resistance men had arrived to take Villiers' group away to other hiding places. But it had been broad daylight and they had been forced to leave singly. Villiers had been the last. He had lain in a hayloft above the barn watching the empty sky, feeling as if at last the war had passed him by. The sudden screech of tyres the harsh bark of commands made him think differently.

There was never a day when he did not think about it. The farmer, his wife and their attractive daughter, and one old man who worked around the yard. Surrounded by shouting Germans, threatened and pushed.

Villiers had known enough about the enemy to recognise that those soldiers were not old veterans who were retained to guard prisoners, nor had they been ordinary garrison troops. They had been from a local S.S. unit, called in to assist the search for the escaped prisoners.

He had known that the young German lieutenant had been asking over and over again for information about the escapees. He had taken out his pistol and had shot the old man dead before their eyes. Then he had shot the farmer. The two women had been dragged screaming and weeping into a truck and the soldiers had departed.

The Danes' silence had convinced the Germans. But their

164

inability to draw either information or a confession had ended in their brutal murder.

When the Resistance men had come for Villiers they had looked at the two corpses, and then at him, without a word.

All he had had to do was to walk down that ladder and surrender. It might have saved their lives, and he would have certainly have been returned to the prison camp.

The fact he had not haunted him and was daily destroying him.

He almost cried out as the alarm bells jangled violently and his leading hand shouted, *'Sir! Enemy aircraft reported to the south-west of the convoy! Thirty-plus of them!'*

The screen door grated open and the man turned quickly to see Rowan struggling around the damp steel, muffled in a leather flying jacket, with his cap jammed over his eyes. He had one arm round a stoker of the damage control party, and explained, 'Doc says I can come up . . .' He swallowed salt air. 'If I can help in any way rather than . . .' The sudden realisation that no one was moving or answering drove away the pain like an icy shower.

Then the leading hand said desperately to Villiers, 'Did you *hear*, sir? Thirty-plus bandits closing the convoy from the south-west!'

Rowan lurched to the screen and saw Villiers' face. It was like a wax mask. Stiff and uncomprehending.

He snatched up the red handset, asking the communications rating, 'Readiness?'

'R-Red Flight, sir.'

Rowan watched Villiers' shoulders. He had not moved. 'Red Flight? *Scramble!*'

Loud-hailers around the bridge joined in the noise.

'Short-range weapon crews prepare to repel aircraft!'

It was a little lighter, and as Rowan trained his glasses abeam he saw the activity aboard the other carrier, the mounting wash from the nearest sloop as she began to work up speed to her defensive position.

A few signal lamps shuttered demands up and down the lines of merchantmen, and below *Growler*'s bridge Rowan saw the first Seafires being manhandled into position for take-off.

The leading hand gave him the thumbs-up and he picked up his handset.

'Hello, *Red Leader*, do you read me?' He imagined Kitto's surprise at hearing his voice. Rowan had understudied Villiers many times, as had most of the senior pilots, but never in a real emergency.

'I read you. Loud and clear. Over.' Then, 'What the hell's going on?'

A small speaker below the screen intoned, 'Stand by.'

The leading hand muttered, 'Bridge, for you, sir.'

He held out a telephone, but Villiers blocked his way, his voice brittle as he snapped. 'Give it to *me*, man. What's the matter with you?'

He said more calmly, 'Commander (Flying), sir. Yes. Red Flight. Yes.' His head nodded, his eyes watching the Affirmative jerking up to the yard. 'Lieutenant Rowan is assisting me, sir.' He added with sudden anger, 'I just said so, didn't I?' He slammed down the telephone.

'Make the signal. The captain is holding this course and speed. The wind is in our favour.'

The light stabbed across the screen, and one by one the Seafires coughed and then snarled into movement.

Other fighters were preparing to take-off from *Hustler*. It would give the enemy something to chew on, Rowan thought.

Far away, ahead of the convoy and slightly to starboard, he heard the *crump crump crump* of gunfire as the destroyers and smaller escorts tested the range.

'All Red Flight airborne, sir.' The rating studied Villiers as a man would watch a dangerous dog.

'Very well. Inform Operations.' Villiers removed his cap and let the wind blow through his hair. 'Range a new strike of three Seafires on the flight deck immediately.'

He jammed his cap back on his head, his faced screwed up with the effort of thinking. 'Lieutenant Ellis will lead.' He looked at Rowan. 'G for George, right?'

Rowan watched him. 'Right.' Villiers was losing his

memory. Breaking up like an aircraft in heavy flak.

Villiers said suddenly, 'Much easier to do a dangerous job yourself, you know, than to order someone else to do it.'

Nobody said any more until the next aircraft had been hurried from the lift and arranged at the after end of the flight deck.

'Hello, G for George?'

Rowan wanted to take the handset from Villiers, to speak with Bill.

'Yes. Thirty-plus. Climb up and over them.'

The rating called above the mounting din of engines, 'Clear for take-off, sir!'

Rowan saw Bats, his body swaying precariously above the sea as he signalled to the advancing leader. *Bill*. He pictured him sitting there, filling the cockpit. Would he still be able to sing? *Thirty-plus bandits*. But they would be after the ships. They had probably been waiting for days for a crack at this convoy, and now having flown all the way from their field in Norway would have eyes for little else.

The gunnery load-hailers came alive again. 'Aircraft! Green four-five! Angle of sight two-oh!'

'All airborne, sir.'

Rowan watched Bill's trio rising away like hawks, making a fast climb towards the clouds. Lord Algy and Nick Rolston, the latter no doubt cursing all and sundry with his usual ferocity.

'Hello, *Foxtrot*, this is *Red Leader*.' Kitto's voice faded and then crackled noisily on the repeater, 'Now at twelve thousand feet and taking position. Over and out.'

Then Bill's voice, very slow and concentrated. 'Ten thousand feet and in position. Over and out.'

The centre of the convoy seemed to explode upwards in a great cone of stabbing flames. The anti-aircraft cruiser had opened fire with everything she had. Medium and short-range weapons hurled a torrent of shells and tracer across the convoy's starboard bow, and as if waiting for the signal, all ships on that side of the formation joined in. Every merchantman carried guns of some sort, and as the destroyers and sloops weaved back and forth they too kept up a continuous barrage across the path of the oncoming attackers.

Rowan trained his binoculars, searching for the enemy. It was all so slow after the snap decisions of the air. Slow, but even more deadly on the nerves.

Then he saw them, even as the speakers barked, 'Torpedo attack!'

They were Heinkel 111 bombers, dropping down in great, swooping dives and fanning out in line abreast, half a cable or more between each aircraft. The sky beyond and above them was soon pock-marked with shellbursts, but still they flew on. Well-rehearsed, deadly.

The gunnery speakers shouted, 'Commence! Commence! Commence!' and for the first time *Growler* began to jerk and quiver to the mounting clatter of her own defences. Bofors and Oerlikons, their crews working like demons, fired long bursts across the *Hustler*'s bows, as a seaman yelled, 'Christ, here they come!'

Rowan watched, unable to move as the unwavering line of bombers came down to some thirty feet of the water. He could hear them now between the sporadic crash of gunfire and the ear-scraping rattle of automatic weapons.

Each one would be carrying two torpedoes. He tensed as the deck tilted steeply, and knew that Buchan was responding to the commodore's signal to alter course.

A Heinkel fell blazing into the sea, and as somebody started to cheer the others released their torpedoes in one great, simultaneous salvo. As they struck the water and gathered speed their tracks raced towards the convoy like some giant, terrifying comb.

The Heinkels were gaining height, swinging away, two trailing black smoke as more cannon fire ripped into them.

Three black dots burst through the clouds, and ignoring the tracer and drifting smoke bursts, charged down on the rear-most Heinkels.

Rowan wanted to watch as the Seafires swept across the retreating enemy planes, their guns clattering, but could only look at the lines of ponderous merchantmen as they altered course towards the torpedoes.

A sloop, one of their own, lit up with a vivid explosion and started to turn turtle, dropping astern in seconds. There was a second flash, right in the centre of the convoy, then a double detonation, and as he swung his glasses round Rowan imagined it was one of the ammunition ships. But it was another warship, the anti-aircraft cruiser, blasted apparently by two torpedoes.

Another torpedo hit a Canadian freighter just abaft her bridge, the shockwave of the explosion rolling through the convoy and against *Growler*'s hull like a hammer on an oil drum.

A man called, 'That's the *Bristol Lady*, sir.' Then he added with amazement, 'God, she still going!'

Rowan tasted smoke and charred paint on the air, and saw the big freighter thrusting through falling spray like a steel pier.

Voices echoed through pipes and telephones, and he saw men hurrying along *Growler*'s port walkway, a fire-fighting party running from the forward lift to join them.

Then he saw the anti-aircraft cruiser looming through the dull light, her hull almost diagonally across the carrier's line of advance, smoke and flames gushing from her side and bridge. Out of control, steerage way gone, she was listing badly, displaying the great double crater which linked her maindeck to the water alongside. Several of her guns were still firing after the retreating Heinkels, but even they fell silent as the order to abandon was passed.

She was now almost abeam of the carrier, lying right over, the wash from the convoy rippling and surging over her broken side like waves across a reef.

Men, small and unreal, were dropping into the sea. Others were casting off the floats and rafts, while some were dragging wounded comrades towards the tilting stern. Rowan bit his lip. It was terrible to watch. The way men so often searched for the highest point in a sinking ship, prolonging the agony.

A light stabbed from the signal platform, and Rowan knew Buchan was ordering the tug *Cornelian* to do what she could.

One of the communications ratings said harshly, '*Hawfinch* has gone, sir. Poor bastards.'

That was the sloop, *Growler*'s faithful companion since the group had been formed.

'Hello, *Foxtrot*, this is *Red Leader*. Have sighted twenty-plus bandits directly south of you.'

The air quivered as more explosions shook the listing cruiser, bringing down a mast and a great tangle of rigging.

Kitto was shouting, 'Ju 88s! Going down! *Tallyho!*'

Villiers said dully, 'Above the clouds. They'll try and bomb the ships through the gaps.'

The intercom was muzzy with voices, and Rowan knew someone had left his set switched to 'send'. He heard Kitto, and in the background someone else shouting like a madman. Bill must have joined the others. He could see it as if it were right here in front of him.

A column of spray shot up from the starboard rank in the convoy, and the nearest lookout reported, 'Ship torpedoed, sir.'

They watched as another freighter started to fall out of the line, streaming smoke and steam, while the next astern altered course violently to avoid a collision.

Gunfire, depth charges, it was continuous. A submarine had sneaked under the screen and had surfaced between it and the convoy. It had scored a direct hit on the freighter, but before her commander could take her down she too was bracketed with shellfire and the depth charges of two circling Swordfish from *Hustler*.

A twin-engined Ju 88, flaming like a torch, burst through the low cloud and passed directly above one of the destroyers. She tracked it round with a long burst of cannon fire, and then it hit the sea and exploded.

The torpedoed freighter was drifting past, and Rowan saw that the fires had got a firm hold. It was strange how two separate torpedoes could have such different results. The Canadian ship had survived her explosion and was still keeping position in the line. This one, her decks loaded with crated aircraft and trucks, would not last another hour. Great gouts of fire punched up through her hold covers and decks,

170

isolating little groups of stampeding men, licking them aside without effort or pity.

Another alteration of course brought the ships wheeling round with blind obedience, their masters trying to close the gaps, to keep their proper distances.

A second bomber plunged through the clouds, struck the sea and threw fragments over the reflected glare. Two parachutes drifted above *Growler*, but were forgotten as another Ju 88 streaked down towards the port side, guns clattering, and a stick of bombs catapulting from its belly into the teeth of the flashing tracers.

Bullets ripped across the flight deck, gouging tall splinters, and then hammered like a bandsaw into the steel bridge. A bomb exploded right alongside, and Rowan saw another pass in front of his eyes in a black blur. It burst between *Growler* and the sinking freighter, and he felt the splinters crack into the hull, and heard others whine above his head like demented demons.

The bomber was swinging round, zigzagging violently as *Growler*'s starboard side guns took up the challenge. A sloop too was firing at almost point-blank range, until the bomber's belly was torn open, spilling out a trail of fire like blood.

'Cease firing!' The gongs along the gun sponsons slowly took effect on the dazed seaman. *'Cease firing!'*

The enemy aircraft had vanished, leaving only the drifting smoke above the water to mark those which had been destroyed. The A.A. cruiser was on her side now and half submerged, the rescue tug standing as close as she dared, her single funnel streaming smoke like a banner. The freighter was lifting her stern higher and higher, and as the guns fell quiet Rowan heard the tearing crash of those massive crates falling from their lashings, or machinery thundering through the darkened hull to complete the destruction.

Then Kitto's voice, very near. 'This is *Red Leader*. Bandits driven off. Six destroyed. Have sighted heavy units to the east of you.' The merest hesitation, as if he was steadying his voice. '*Makesafe*. Repeat, *Makesafe* is joining you.'

Rowan removed his cap and pushed his fingers through his

hair. *Makesafe* was the codename of the Home Fleet's heavy screen.

Villiers was speaking on another handset, his voice strange. Then he said to Rowan, 'Tell them. Return to base. *Hustler* will resume anti-submarine patrols immediately.'

Rowan passed the order and then said, 'We did it. I think they've had enough.'

A dull explosion echoed across the water, and he knew the freighter had dived and her boilers had burst apart.

The leading hand said, 'Message from the bridge, sir.' He waited, watching Villiers, who was leaning against the screen, apparently studying the merchant ships.

Rowan limped across the gratings. 'You all right, sir?'

Villiers made as if to turn, and then fell awkwardly beside the man by the telephones.

Rowan could not bend his leg, and shouted urgently, 'Help him, for God's sake!'

A seaman thrust his arm under Villiers' shoulders and then lowered him again. When he withdrew his hand it was covered with blood. It looked black in the dull light.

He stared incredulously at Rowan. ' 'E's *dead*, sir!'

Rowan took the telephone. When those last bomb splinters had hit the ship one small, red-hot fragment must have struck Villiers. He had not cried out, but had just stood there, willing it to kill him. The agony must have been terrible, minutes of unbearable torture for him. But as Rowan looked down at his face he thought he had never seen him look so peaceful. So content.

'This is Lieutenant Rowan, sir. I have to report that Lieutenant Commander Villiers was killed in that last attack.'

Buchan's voice. 'I see.' He must have put his palm across the mouthpiece. Then he said, 'Get those fighters flown-on. Then report to the sickbay. I'll send someone else to take over.'

Rowan asked, 'Did you wish to say something, sir? I mean, before I reported his death?'

Buchan said heavily, 'It doesn't matter now. It's closed and done with.'

Rowan walked back to the screen, remembering the shriek

of splinters, wondering what it had been which had really destroyed Villiers.

Chadwick must have been about to summon him to the upper bridge. If that had happened Villiers would have been unable to control his anger and his despair.

He watched a seaman cover Villiers' face with a piece of canvas.

Now, nothing could hurt him, and he would be thought of only as Rowan remembered him.

A lamp clattered from the platform, and a signalman called, 'First Seafire in sight to starboard, sir!'

Rowan nodded. They were all returning. That was something.

A shaft of brighter light filtered across the lines of merchantmen. Only one missing. Chadwick had done as he had intended. No matter what the enemy did now, those ships would get to Russia. With the Home Fleet screen joining forces and the big German units driven off, nothing could stop them. He tried not to think of the cost. Escorts and aircraft. And ordinary men like himself.

'Hello, *Foxtrot*, this is G for George. Permission to land-on.'

Rowan saw the Seafire making a steep turn around the ship, wheels and flaps down, the light glittering across the cockpit.

He took the handset. 'Hello, Bill.' He hesitated. 'This is *Jonah*. Affirmative.'

The next day they buried their dead at sea, and the following morning the ships steamed past a line of outward-bound Russian destroyers and entered the Kola Inlet.

The long haul was over.

II

Away from Everything

It was not until mid-November that *Growler* and her weatherbeaten consorts arrived home, or to be more exact, Loch Ewe in Scotland.

The return convoy from Murmansk to a rendezvous with fresh escorts off Iceland had been a quite different affair from the outward voyage.

They saw little of the enemy, and although they were shadowed and attacked at long range by a pack of submarines, only one ship, a tramp steamer which looked too old to be afloat, had been torpedoed. Even then, the ancient vessel, a Greek-crewed ship, refused to give in voluntarily, and had to be put down by an escorting destroyer.

The real menace was from the sea itself. Bitterly cold, it harried and buffeted the empty ships through every wearying day and night. Strong winds built up the waves into great terrifying crests, which had at times lifted one ship higher than the next, and then dropped it so deep in a trough that only a mast or funnel cap was visible. Station-keeping was a nightmare, and tempers became harsher and more dangerous with each change of watch.

It was only when the group anchored in Iceland to refuel, to land the more badly wounded at the hospitals there, to put right some of the many defects to equipment and machinery, that anyone found time to stop and consider what they had achieved.

An engineer from the base in Reykjavik had asked Bray, the navigating officer, what he had thought about Russia.

Bray had replied without hesitation, 'All sulks and bloody-mindedness. I know they're having a hard time, and compared with the losses on the Eastern Front our lads who were

175

killed on that convoy must seem small stuff. I wasn't expecting a brass band and garlands of roses, but I did think we might have been made welcome.'

Apart from a few visits to the heavily guarded jetties, and to a hut which had been laughingly called the Officers' Club, Rowan had seen as little of Murmansk as the rest of the company.

There had been an air-raid every night and morning, which had not been surprising, as the Germans were still very near. None of the convoyed ships had been hit, and the work of unloading their precious cargoes had gone on without a break, twenty-four hours a day, even in the dead of a bitter night when the massive barrage of anti-aircraft fire from around the port and from the many anchored ships lit up the heavens like some fantastic Brock's Benefit.

The Russians had used anyone and everyone for the work. German prisoners, others from civilian penal settlements, their own troops, men and women of all ages.

They had seen them resting between shifts, sustained only by soup and coarse bread, their faces so worn by the hard work and poor food that many of the sailors had tried to give them their own rations.

Before the brief contact had been broken by a local Russian official and a few threatening gestures from the armed guards, Rowan had seen quite a few packets of chocolate being hidden away, held with all the awe of somebody handling precious stones.

The Russian official had had a fiery interview with Captain Buchan. It had not been helped by the ship's interpreter, whose knowledge of Russian was almost nil.

Buchan had ended the discussion in his own way. A bottle of Scotch to the Russian, who in return handed him one of vodka.

But as Bray had said, it had been something of a let down, an anti-climax after what they had seen and endured along all those bitter miles.

Of Chadwick he had seen little. He had gone ashore in Iceland within minutes of mooring, and only returned an hour or so before they cast-off for the final run south.

Some had suggested he was to be replaced, that his head was on the block because of the flaws in the convoy plan. But when the rear admiral hurried up the brow, saluting in response to the trill of calls, his collar upturned against the first flurries of snow, Rowan could see from his shining face that he was well pleased with himself.

Rowan had been more than a little worried about his own future. He had done a lot of extra duty, mostly replacing the dead Villiers, and his wounded leg had been playing him up. The damp and the chill air, the ship's violent motion had had much to do with it, but his own stubbornness, his determination to avoid the sickbay as much as possible had kept him going.

The nearer they got to Scotland the more frayed his nerves became. Passes and travel warrants were being made out for leave. *Growler* would be out of service for weeks while additional detecting gear was fitted and some more automatic weapons installed.

There was the need to work-up a new Swordfish squadron, and to replace men killed and injured, or merely drafted elsewhere.

But to the bulk of *Growler*'s officers and men the reasons were unimportant compared with the end result. *Leave*.

In Iceland they had read very little of their convoy. But the Russians were launching another attack right along the front, and the Germans had suffered heavy losses.

One unexpected piece of news had been that of a midget submarine attack on the mighty German battleship *Tirpitz*. The tiny X-craft had penetrated the deep fjord where she lay, and had exploded their charges right underneath her hull. The enemy had clamped a tight web of security around the ship, and the Norwegian Resistance had been able to discover nothing of the extent of the damage. But the fact was they had managed to do it, and several of the officers from H.Q. at Reykjavik had hinted that Chadwick's attack and destruction of the big oil tanker had deprived the German battleship of fuel. And if she had sailed amongst the convoy, nobody had much doubt about what the gruesome result would have been.

In a steady drizzle, Rowan stood on a walkway with Bill

Ellis, watching the dull hump on the Isle of Lewis, gaining shape against a low sky.

Four rust-streaked corvettes went puffing abeam, exchanging signals and greetings, their dented hulls glistening in the grey light.

Many, many times since he had come this way before, Rowan had thought he would be killed, or broken in mind and body like some of those poor devils they had landed in Reykjavik.

But now they were almost home. *Home?* Where was that?

Bill asked abruptly, 'What are you going to do, Tim? Don't bite my head off, but I'd like to share it with you.'

Rowan glanced at his strong profile, recalling his relief at seeing him return from some patrol or another.

'Sorry, Bill. I've been a bastard. I didn't mean to get at you, of all people.'

Gulls swooped down and glided parallel with the slow-moving carrier, their eyes hard and unwinking as they examined the two figures standing in the icy drizzle.

Bill grinned. 'I know. Otherwise I'd have knocked your bloody head off.'

'The doc told me I'd have to wait a while before I can go on leave. The leg is playing up a bit.' It was always easy to confide in Bill. 'He swears there's nothing badly wrong. He was muttering in his beard about one of these country houses where they send blokes like me.'

Bill nodded. 'I know the sort of place. Kidneys and kedgeree for brekkers under silver lids. Then being chased round the grounds by her ladyship with a riding crop. All very recuperative.'

The mood changed and he added, 'But when you *do* get away, Tim. Come to London and spend some time with me, eh?'

'Yes.' He thought of the house by Oxshott Woods. With any luck it might be hidden under snow before he reached there. 'I'd like that.'

'Frank Creswell's in the same boat as you, Tim. He told me the doc's sending him to a convalescent establishment.

Probably the one you'll be staying at.'

Rowan turned to watch the gulls diving and screaming below one of the gun sponsons. Somebody must have hurled some gash over the side.

Frank Creswell had certainly changed, and could even be said to be enjoying his new role as the wounded hero. At least it appeared to have taken his dead friend off his mind. He would have had to accept it sooner or later. Otherwise he would never survive the next encounter.

'Let's go below and have some tea. Or shall we wait until the bar opens? It'll be nice to see somebody getting drunk again.'

Before Bill could reply a muffled bosun's mate peered at them and said, 'The captain sends his compliments, sir, and would you report to his cabin.'

'Thanks.' Rowan glanced at his friend. 'In his cabin? We *must* be safe if Buchan's left the bridge!'

Bill walked with him to a screen door and said, 'It's probably about your leave.'

Rowan tapped on the door marked Captain and was invited to enter. Buchan was sitting at his desk writing busily in a large file, a pipe jutting from his jaw like an extension.

'Ah, Rowan.' He looked up. He had obviously showered and rested, and the change was amazing. 'I've got your papers here. Thought I'd like to give them to you myself. We're getting in tonight, and I'll probably be busy for a day or so, until I've got my ideas across to the base staff, if you see my meaning.' He smiled gravely. 'You're to report to a place in Hampshire. Just to rest up for a bit. I'm sorry about it, but a lot of people have been less fortunate.' He glanced at a metal box on the deck beside his chair. 'Commander Villiers' personal effects. I'm sending them to his widow. She can do what she likes with them.'

He said it so brutally that Rowan stared at him. 'I didn't know he was married, sir.'

'She left him.' Buchan laced his fingers across his stomach and regarded him curiously. 'It's probably what finished him.'

So Buchan, who had not left his place on the bridge from

one emergency to the next, had even guessed about Villiers' death.

The captain said slowly, 'When you find a good girl, marry her. Never mind what the clever-dicks say. You hang on to her like grim death. They're not that easy to come by.'

'Was that all, sir?'

Buchan stood up and impulsively thrust out his hand. 'I don't know when we'll meet again, Tim, but then you know the Service. Take good care of yourself, and my thanks for everything you've done, and tried to do, for my command.' He gripped his hand very hard. 'I hope you come back to us.'

Buchan sat down and pushed a bulky envelope across the desk. It was all he could do to hold back a grin.

'These are your travel warrants, ration cards and all that stuff.'

Rowan turned the envelope over in his hands and then stared at the neatly typed label.

For the attention of Lieutenant Commander T. Rowan. D.S.C., R.N.V.R.

He looked at Buchan. 'I don't know what to say, sir.'

Buchan sounded pleased. 'Nothing to do with me, my lad. Had it been left to me I'd probably have promoted you to rear admiral!'

He re-opened his file. 'Now be off, and try to find yourself.' His voice pursued Rowan as he walked dazedly into the busy passageway. 'And see the tailor before you leave my ship!'

Rowan made his way to the wardroom, expecting to find Bill. Instead he discovered Frank Creswell sitting on the arm of a chair, his face split in a great smile.

He exclaimed, 'They've given me another stripe, Tim! I just heard!'

Rowan glanced past him towards the white cloth covered tables where several officers were eating bread and butter and jam with their tea. At the table where most of the Swordfish officers usually gathered there was only van Roijen and one other. He recalled what Buchan had just said. *A lot of people have been less fortunate.*

'Good. I'm glad for you.'

He walked over and sat down, automatically adjusting his leg under the table where it could not be kicked.

Van Roijen turned and nodded to him, the deep lines on his face giving way to his warm smile.

'Ah, Tim, my friend. We will be in soon, then maybe I get news from my family, eh? That will be fine, will it not?'

Rowan looked away. *We are all pretending still. Hiding from each other*.

'Just fine, Peter. I hope you're right.'

James, the Operations Officer, sat down opposite him and watched the steward pouring tea from a giant pot.

He looked across and said quietly, 'Congratulations, Tim. I knew about it this morning.' He glanced at his own faded stripes on his seagoing reefer. 'I hope it brings you luck.'

Rowan smiled. 'Thanks.'

He couldn't help wondering what James and some of the other regulars really thought. Now Rowan had a half stripe like him. If the war went on and on as many predicted, they would be seeing an overwhelming weight of temporary officers in senior appointments. Perhaps they dreamed of peacetime, when such matters were slow and drawn out. But then, few people died in peacetime, and had their entire lives collected in a metal box like Villiers.

He said, 'It'll take some getting used to.'

James sounded far away. 'Shan't be sorry to get on leave, I can tell you.'

Rowan glanced at van Roijen's hand on the table. Very still, as if it and not its owner was listening. Thinking of the unfairness of it. James had a German wife who was alive. Whereas his own family . . .

He replied, 'I'd just as soon stop aboard.' He did not know why he had said it. He was even more surprised to discover that he meant it.

The small naval bus with red crosses painted on roof and sides lurched through a narrow lane, the windscreen wipers barely coping with the sleety rain which would soon change to snow.

It was bitterly cold, and Rowan and Creswell, the only

passengers, sat huddled together, hands in greatcoat pockets, collars turned up over their ears as they watched the driver manoeuvering the bus with elaborate care. It was early evening and very dark, and with the headlights covered by slitted hoods to prevent their showing any sort of glare towards the sky, it was a wonder he had not driven them into a ditch long ago.

Rowan felt sick. Of the uncomfortable, jolting ride, of the fact it had been two days since they had left Scotland for the 'place in the country'. At night they had been admitted to local army hospitals, and then on again, the weather worsening all the way.

Creswell groaned. 'God, if this doesn't stop soon, I'll damn well get out and die!'

'You shouldn't have had so much to drink.'

Rowan smiled unfeelingly, remembering their small attempt to put some gaiety into their strange isolation. They had stopped at a small pub, which had been empty but for two farm workers, the landlord and an air-raid warden. The occupants had watched the two young naval officers without saying a word, as if they had just landed from the moon. It had not been a satisfactory celebration, and the beer had been stale, too.

On the bus again Creswell had become suddenly serious. He had said, 'I haven't really had a chance to speak to you properly.' His eyes had looked very dark, as if he had been feeling the pain. 'I'll never forget what you did. How you guided me down into the drink. Your voice in my ear, I can hear it now. So calm. So very near.' He had shaken his head. 'No, I'll never forget.'

Rowan had felt awkward. 'Just remember the important bit in future. Look and think before you start celebrating. Enemy fliers want to stay alive too, you know.'

He had certainly learned more about Creswell on their uncomfortable journey south than he had discovered the whole time in *Growler*.

He was an only child, and because his father had spent much of his life travelling abroad for his company, buying timber from Scandinavia and Burma, he had grown even

182

closer to his mother. Quite suddenly, his mother had been taken ill and had died while Creswell was still at school.

He had said flatly, 'My old man was married again before you could say knife. She's years younger than he is. I'm not sorry I'm going to this country house, or whatever it is. My last leave was a disaster. She seemed to delight in pawing him about all the time I'm there. And he just sits and grins like a great idiot.'

Rowan had suggested, 'Maybe she's a bit jealous of *you*? Did you ever think of that?'

But Creswell had replied vehemently, 'Not on your life. She's like a bloody barmaid.'

Rowan leaned back and closed his eyes, thinking of the drive south. Once they had stood for ages at a level-crossing, waiting while an endless train of flat trucks had rumbled slowly past. Each truck carried a powerful tank, brand-new and en route for some regiment or other. For the much talked about Second Front? This year, next year, sometime, never.

Otherwise he had seen little change. The houses looked even shabbier, denied their usual paint-work, denied in too many cases the care of their owners who were away in uniform.

The thin newspapers were full of vague reports. *The Secretary of the Admiralty regrets to announce the loss of H.M.S. So and so. Last night our bombers raided Hamburg, or the U-boat pens at Lorient.*

Times of blackout, notices of scarcer clothing or eggs, seemed to make up the rest of the news.

Perhaps if you were a civilian, anchored to a job or a way of life you could do nothing to defend, you saw what gave you comfort in the papers and discarded the rest.

He had dreaded the actual moment of leaving *Growler*. And when the time had come for him to board his transport with some of the walking wounded, as Minchin chose to describe them, the sense of loss and isolation had been complete.

The ship, normally so noisy and bustling, had been still. Just a few of the duty part of the watch remained aboard, and they had been sensible enough to remain invisible. Buchan had been there, and Rowan had seen his wife being greeted at the brow and swallowed up with the others.

To every corner of the British Isles, to their wives and families, to girlfriends and mistresses, to broken homes and to no homes at all, *Growler*'s company had scattered.

The bus gave a savage jerk, and Creswell gasped, 'That's either broken the axle or my bloody back!'

The driver muttered angrily and then said, 'We're 'ere anyway, gentlemen.' He threw open a door, letting the sleet patter across the floor. 'I'll get somebody.'

Rowan stood up gingerly and supported himself between two seats.

The building ahead of the bus was large and quite old. Although every window was blacked out, he could sense the elegance of the place, could imagine beautifully dressed visitors arriving at the high, pillared entrance. His heart sank. There would be no carpets or carefree chatter now. Steel pipe-cots, severe nursing sisters from another war, the smells of soap and pusser's blankets.

He said vaguely, 'I wonder where the nearest village is? I could do with a tot right now.'

A torch bobbed down the steps, probing through the sleet like an eye. 'This way, if you please.' It was a man's voice and somehow familiar. 'Need any help, sir?'

Creswell exclaimed, 'Chief Petty Officer Dundas, isn't it?'

The steward replied in his mournful voice, 'Yessir. Got 'ere this mornin'.' He gave what might have been a smile. 'We're very comfortable.'

Rowan felt a second man helping him up the steps. 'Are we?' He was as stiff as a board. What was Dundas doing here anyway?

Through two sets of doors and then into an entrance hall which left both of them breathless and half blinded by the glare of light from a glittering chandelier.

A lady with short gunmetal curls and a beautifully cut tweed costume was standing at the foot of a staircase. She said nothing as Dundas and an elderly manservant took the officers' caps and greatcoats, but stood with one hand resting on the heavy oak banister rail. Quite motionless, as if she had been there for hours.

Rowan straightened his tie and wished he had had time to do something about his untidy hair. As he glanced down he saw his newly-sewn rank on his sleeve with something like shock. He had forgotten all about it.

The lady said, 'You must be Lieutenant Commander Rowan.' She moved towards him and held out her hand. 'I hope the journey was not too tiring.'

Her hand was small but surprisingly strong. She was more than a head shorter than Rowan, and yet he had the feeling he was looking up to her.

He said, 'It was fine. Thank you. All this is a bit of a surprise.'

She smiled for the first time, it made her look like a young girl.

'We have to cut down in wartime of course.' She did not release his hand. 'But we do what we can for some of the wounded officers who need a complete break from routine, and other things.'

She did not elaborate, but removed her hand and looked at Creswell.

'You look terribly young, Lieutenant. But healthy enough.'

She smiled again. 'Your rooms are ready. We are not on the bombers' route for anywhere important. This corner of Hampshire has been lucky.'

A door banged nearby, and Rowan got his next surprise as Rear Admiral Chadwick, dressed in a grey fisherman's jersey and heavy gumboots, stamped into the hallway.

He saw Rowan and nodded. 'Got here then. Fine.'

The lady grimaced. 'Really, Lionel, must you go around the house like a tramp?' She saw Rowan's expression. 'You *know* my husband, of course.'

Chadwick rubbed his hands. 'I've just been in the cellar with Ford. He really is getting senile or something. The place is a bloody shambles.' He tapped the side of his nose. 'But I have discovered some suitable vintage for dinner. You'll dine with us, won't you, Rowan?'

185

Rowan flushed. 'Yes, sir. Of course.' He looked at Creswell. 'If it's convenient.'

Chadwick waited while Dundas pierced and lit a cigar for him.

'Good to get away from ships for a bit. Away from everything. I'll show you some of the estate tomorrow, if the weather lets up. We've a lot of people digging for victory, and my agent has collared twenty Italian P.O.Ws to work on the home farm. Quite useful fellows.'

A telephone tinkled discreetly in another room, and a very elderly man in a black jacket, whom Rowan guessed was the senile Ford, walked slowly into the entrance hall.

'It is the *Admiralty*, sir.'

Chadwick moved his cigar to the opposite side of his mouth.

'Who?'

'Who?'

Ford's hooded eyes were partly closed in concentration. 'Admiral Caistor, sir.'

Chadwick shrugged. 'Oh, old Tommy, is it. Well, tell him I'm busy and to ring at a more civilised hour.' He said to Rowan, 'Go and relax before dinner. If there's anything you need, tell Dundas. Don't bother Ford, or you'll have to wait till Christmas!'

He strode away, humming to himself, and vanished into the back of the house.

His wife said quietly, 'I'll show you the way.' She moved to the staircase. 'He's like a whirlwind when he comes on leave.' There was neither warmth nor surprise in her tone. She was merely stating a fact.

Rowan watched her easy movements up the broad stairs. She was in her thirties at a guess, a good bit younger than Chadwick, and very composed, very sure of herself.

She said, 'The medical officer from the artillery camp nearby deals with our visitors.' She turned on the stairs, holding his gaze with her own. 'But for changing dressings and so forth, we can manage pretty well on our own.'

Rowan was confused. 'It's very good of you, Mrs Chadwick, to open your house like this.'

She was studying him impassively. 'Is it? I hadn't thought about it. It seemed the thing to do.' She shrugged. 'Anyway, I understand that you have nowhere to go at present.'

'That's true.'

She reached out and laid one hand on his. 'Don't look so hurt. I didn't mean it to sound like it did. I, that is, we both want you here.' She tossed her head and started to climb the stairs again. 'So that's settled.'

Later, as Rowan sat in a deep armchair in his spacious bedroom, he almost had to pinch himself to reassure his confused mind that he was not still in the rickety bus, or that this was not a dream.

It was an entirely new existence. Beyond the tastefully decorated room with its adjoining dressing and shower rooms the house was noiseless. The war, the memories of blinding tracer and explosions, or the nerve-stretching hours trying to sleep, expecting a torpedo to turn your ship into an inferno, all had become remote. Like Chadwick's casual dismissal of the admiral who had telephoned. *Old Tommy*.

Like his wife, so distant and aloof, yet so warm, so feminine.

There was a tap at the door and Creswell peered in at him.

He said, 'Gosh, your quarters are even grander than mine!'

Rowan smiled. 'Proper thing, too. Rank has its privileges.'

Creswell sat down on the bed and looked round.

'What do you think of all this?'

Rowan caught sight of a bottle of whisky and some ice just inside the dressing room. 1943 was almost over, another year of war. But Chadwick could still get real Scotch for his guests.

He replied, '*I think*, that I could get to enjoy this life.'

Creswell seemed relieved. 'In that case.' He grinned like a conspirator. 'What about an enormous drink?'

12

And Back Again

DESPITE the excitement of his arrival at Chadwick's country house, the sheer luxury of his quarters, especially when compared with the vibrating biscuit tin he shared in *Growler*, Rowan felt that within a few days time was beginning to drag.

The weather had not let up for a moment, and it was impossible to leave the house without getting drenched. It tried to snow several times, but changed to heavy sleet or rain, and its constant pelting against the windows was depressing.

Chadwick had gone to London. He had mentioned it breezily to Rowan on the morning after his arrival, and the dinner which had lasted almost until midnight.

That too had been an enlightening experience after sea duty and flying patrols in all weathers. The glass and the fine china, the courses of the meal, each had somehow surpassed the one before. Rowan had become happily drowsy, listening to Chadwick's endless reminiscences of naval life before the war, the regattas and parties, the occasional excitement when dealing with riots or civil strife in strange, forgotten places halfway round the world.

There had been just the four of them at dinner. Chadwick and his wife. Creswell and Rowan. They had dined well, and Rowan had slept better than he could remember.

But that was over. Without Chadwick the house seemed larger, emptier. Two days after his departure Creswell had received permission to leave, and albeit unwillingly, had been driven to the station for the London train. He was being met by his father and his new mother. *The bloody barmaid*, as he called her.

He had seen little of the other visitors. They consisted of

about ten soldiers, as far as he could discover, but they stayed in another wing of the big house, and he was discouraged from visiting them by a fierce-eyed army nursing sister. It seemed as if the soldiers were to be permanent residents for the duration of the war.

Rowan had met one of them on the only fine morning of his stay. He had been walking down a sheltered stone path, stepping carefully around deep puddles, when he had come face to face with a major of the artillery. He had looked normal enough; with a bushy moustache, and the insignia of the Desert Rats on his uniform, he was like one of the caricatures in the Eighth Army magazine.

Rowan had made some remark to open a conversation, but the major had stood back and shouted violently, 'Don't you talk to me about those bloody Egyptians!' Then he had marched away, his heels clicking as if on parade.

Rowan had learned from Mrs Chadwick it was all the major ever said.

Perhaps he was another victim of 'combat fatigue', as the experts labelled it. Or trying to work his ticket, Rowan thought.

He had also asked Mrs Chadwick about her husband's hurried departure for London. Being left to his own devices, feeling entirely cut off from the war and the only life he understood. Rowan imagined that some new campaign was being planned, a more important carrier force already assembling to await Chadwick's leadership.

She had been in one of her glasshouses, examining some little pots, which to Rowan could have been almost anything.

'Something important, I expect. He's never here for long.' She had looked at him with her calm, level eyes. 'You miss your friend, I imagine. You must be bored to death.'

Rowan had replied, 'Frank Creswell is probably hating every minute of his leave.' He had hesitated, yet had been unable to prevent himself from blurting out his anxiety. 'But he'll be returning to the ship when his leave is finished. I'm not at all sure what I'm doing.'

'So that's it.' She had taken off her gardening gloves and

brushed a drop of rain from her sleeve as it had found its way through a cracked pane of glass. 'I knew it was something. I thought it might be a girl somewhere.'

She had said it with such abruptness that Rowan had been caught off balance.

When she had spoken again she had been as before. 'I expect you'll have to *see somebody*. My husband will put in a word. He seems to like you.'

'Does that surprise you, Mrs Chadwick?'

She had given a small smile. 'A little.' A quick glance at her watch. 'Must be off. I've got to speak to the Red Cross in an hour.'

It was always like that. Only Rowan seemed to be a permanent resident in that part of the house.

The army doctor came regularly and examined his injured leg. The wounds had healed very well, although the scars were livid, tender to the touch.

The doctor had remarked on his last visit, 'Nothing more we can do, old son. Up to you now. Walk about a bit.' He had chuckled unfeelingly. 'It's only four miles to the village. Do you good.'

If only the rain would stop. Rowan found himself fretting and becoming more tense with each passing day. After a full week, Bill telephoned from London, his voice carefully non-committal as he asked, 'Everything going all right, Tim?'

'I'm waiting to get out of the place.' He lowered his voice, even though he knew poor old Ford was the only other soul in the main building.

Bill sounded worried. 'I think they've got a bloody cheek! I'd have spoken to Rear Admiral Chadwick if I'd known, Tim, and damn the consequences.'

Bill's anger cheered him up a bit. 'You saw him, did you?'

'Sure thing. I was with my little Czech. Took her out on the town, no expense spared. I saw our illustrious admiral dining with his wife. A real smasher she is, too.' He must have sensed something. 'You still there?'

Yes.' He recalled the edge in Mrs Chadwick's voice. *I*

191

thought it might be a girl somewhere. She must have known or guessed about her husband. Maybe it had been going on for months. Years.

He said, 'I expect I'll hear from their lordships soon. If not, I'll damn well go and gatecrash the Admiralty myself!'

'Don't forget the phone number. I've another ten days of leave due. Try and get to London, Tim. We'll take good care of you!'

We. The word hurt in some stupid way.

'I'll remember, Bill. Take care.' The line died.

A door opened and Mrs Chadwick came in shaking her raincoat and kicking off a pair of rubber boots.

'Really, this weather is impossible!' She saw him holding a message pad. 'A call for me?'

'For me. I hope it was all right to use your telephone.'

She shook back her curls. 'You *are* a funny one sometimes. *All right to use the telephone*. I think you must be a Victorian at heart!'

Her smile, the impatient shake of the short gunmetal curls, made her suddenly vulnerable. Rowan tried not to think about Chadwick in the restaurant.

'I suppose I am. Sorry.'

She brushed past him. 'And don't keep apologising. I've just heard all about you.' She reached for the bell push. 'From an old school friend who has a nice job in Whitehall. Or rather in Bath until the war's over.'

Ford came through the door. 'Yes, ma'am?' He looked as if he had been dozing.

She studied Rowan thoughtfully. 'You're getting another medal. I think we should have a drink to celebrate.' She did not wait for a reply. 'Bring a tray, Ford. We'll decide what we'll have later.' She waited for the door to shut. 'Poor dear. If I asked for anything definite he would get it wrong. This way we do at least get a choice.'

Rowan stood by a window watching the rain teeming across the bare trees. The crazy major was marching purposefully along a path, his stick tucked under one arm, his cap and shoulders black with rain. *Don't you talk to me about those bloody Egyptians*. Poor, unhinged bastard. What had done it to him, he wondered?

And his own parents were dead, and Bill's girl, his little Czech, had lost her husband. And Chadwick was in London having a ball with his mistress, or whatever she was. He dug his hands into his pockets, hating the war. What it was doing. No wonder the news of another medal had left him completely untouched.

'What's wrong?' She was beside him.

'I'm sorry.' He smiled at her awkwardly. 'There I go again.'

She said quietly, 'I heard what you did. I knew you were different. I had no idea just what you had endured. No wonder you're bored half to death. I'll telephone somebody tomorrow. Have you moved to an hotel, somewhere where there's a bit of life left.' She looked at him gravely. 'It might help.'

Ford came in with a tray. Gin, whisky, water, ice, but only one glass.

Rowan replied, 'No. I'd like to stay here until I get my orders, if it's still all right.'

She poured a large measure of whisky. 'We'll share the glass.' She watched him. 'Yes, it will be fine.'

Somewhere a clock chimed. She became brisk again. 'I must go to the W.V.S. in the village this afternoon. Got to keep things moving.' She turned towards him, her eyes bright. 'I don't suppose you'd care to come, would you? Lot of ladies knitting balaclava helmets and seaboot stockings, that sort of thing.' She added quickly, 'Do sailors ever wear those ghastly creations?'

Rowan watched her. The last question was merely to cover something else. For once, *she* was unsure. Nervous.

'All the time, Mrs Chadwick.' He grinned. 'I'd love to come. *Really.*'

She bobbed her head and looked at herself in the mirror. 'Good. It's not often they see a real hero. No saying what it might do to some of them!'

Rowan said, 'I'll fetch my greatcoat.'

'Ten minutes then.' Before the door closed she added, 'Please call me Honor, if you feel like it.'

Rowan walked to the stairs. He would have to watch out or he would be making a fool of himself.

The nightmare grew and expanded with the wildness of a forest fire. It was just one great revolving pattern of flames, with inhuman sounds and shrieks coming at Rowan from every angle. A giant mirror dominated the fantasy, and in it he watched the stark silhouette of another aircraft, gaining ground, overhauling. The flames continued to gyrate around the mirror, and when he tried to use his limbs nothing happened. He looked down at his legs and saw that the left one was hanging like a piece of bloody sacking. He could do nothing but watch the other plane, the sudden ripple of stabbing fires along its wing. He felt the searing crash of metal into his body. Heard himself screaming and pleading as the blaze engulfed him.

There was another voice now. He sat up violently in pitch darkness, fighting the sheets, his pyjamas wringing wet, his mind cringing from the nightmare.

Then he realised the bedroom door was partly open, and he could see a pale figure against a small glow from further down the passage.

'Are you all right?' She entered the room, and he saw her etched against the dark wall and curtained windows. 'I—I'm sorry, but you were calling out.'

He nodded, trying to steady his breathing, to control the frantic heartbeat.

'Bit of a bad dream.' He ran one hand over his face. 'God, I didn't mean to wake the whole house.'

She sat down on the bed, her eyes like shadows on her face.

'I couldn't sleep. I was getting a glass of water. Anyway, the *whole house* is just about empty.' She reached out and touched his shoulder. 'Lie back now. Try and relax. I'll go and let you sleep. You should be better now.'

He looked up at her. 'Don't go. Not yet. It was good of you to bother.'

194

She said, 'It's four o'clock.'

He could tell from her voice that she was shivering. He took her hand. It was like ice.

'I feel a proper idiot.' He struggled to his elbows. 'It must be freezing.'

'No.' She was watching him. He could feel it. 'I'm fine. I might have a hot drink in a minute. When you're settled.'

Rowan took her hand again. She did not resist or flinch in any way. It was like holding a small, terrified animal, he thought. One move and the spell would be smashed.

'I find this very unsettling.' He felt the hand start to pull away and gripped it tightly. '*Please*. I didn't meant it to come out like that. To spoil it.'

She touched his hair with her other hand.

'Poor Tim.' She was speaking huskily. 'You couldn't spoil anything.'

Rowan was almost afraid to speak or breathe. He could feel the want, the ache churning inside him like fire. He could not help it.

He released her hand and laid his own on her hip. She was rigid, yet inwardly trembling. All this he could feel as if it were part of himself.

In a second he would awake. It would be over. Lost.

He moved his hand and touched her skin. It was very cold. As smooth as silk.

She said quietly, 'Oh God, Tim. You'd better stop now.'

He pulled her gently beside him, feeling the yearning like a physical pain. He stroked her, feeling her breast under his fingers, the nipple hard against his hand. She was moaning very softly, turning towards him, her mouth partly open as he leaned over her.

Then all at once she was helping him, throwing the nightdress to the floor, then pulling his pyjamas away, kissing him, murmuring small, secret words which he could not hear or understand.

He explored her body, feeling her excitement and need rising to match his own, until neither could stand any more.

'*Tim!*' She reached out and held him, prolonging the agony a moment longer. 'Now.'

They made love with the tenderness of youth, and with the passion of wanton experience. Then they fell exhausted, their limbs entangled, their bodies still joined.

The feel of her, the hot scent of her lithe body, their need for each other gave them little rest, and when the first grey light showed around the heavy curtains it was like an enemy.

She swung her legs over the side of the bed, but he held her, his hands about her waist, his lips touching her skin.

'I must go.' She ruffled his hair with her fingers, watching him. 'We'll not be alone much longer.'

As if to bear out her words, Rowan heard someone walking on the path below the window. The major perhaps, lost in his own world, separated from the darkened room above him, and all else.

She groped for her gown, her limbs white in the gloom.

He said, 'Please, Honor, I don't want—'

She came back to the bed and laid her hand on his mouth. 'Don't say it. *I* have no regrets.' She let him touch her again. 'No. I *must* go.' She was part laughing, but in another second would be unable to leave.

He stood up and held her against his body, her tousled curls pressing into his throat.

'God, I wanted you, Honor. I didn't know how much.'

She stepped away from him. 'Nor I.'

Long after she had left the room Rowan sat on the bed, staring at the door's polished rectangle.

What had he done? What did she really think about it?

He strode to the windows and threw open the curtains. It was raining again.

He stretched out his arms and yawned hugely. The rain no longer mattered. And as he made his way to his dressing room, and his scarred leg scraped against a stool in the half light, he did not notice that either.

Captain Bruce Buchan sat in his big leather chair and watched his wife pouring tea.

The refit was over, and with his company returned from leave, Buchan had brought his ship around the north of Scotland to Rosyth. There was still some work going on, and he could hear the occasional stammer of a rivet gun from the hangar deck.

His wife had never been far away, and they had put up in a small hotel for some of the time, and then moved to Edinburgh, where she would have shops to explore to take her mind off the ship when he had gone.

He looked at the new chintz curtains which she had insisted on doing herself. Through a sealed scuttle he could see the hurrying clouds above the dockyard. January in Rosyth.

His eyes moved to a newspaper on the table.

SEA BATTLE IN SNOW BLIZZARD. SCHARNHORST *SUNK*.

He thought of the Arctic as he had seen it. As it must have been just last week off North Cape when the German battle-cruiser had been destroyed by Admiral Fraser's *Duke of York*.

It was like a jigsaw coming together. A picture forming at last. *Bismarck* and *Scharnhorst* gone. *Tirpitz* out of action. It was a strange feeling to be winning instead of barely holding your own.

Buchan tried not to mull over all that he had to do before his ship was as he wanted. Trials to complete, new hands to be sorted into their best positions. Damage control, fuel, ammunition, perishable stores, medical supplies. Each and every one had a team, and someone to supervise it. But all lines led to the captain. As ever. Perhaps he was just being extra cautious.

His wife sat back in the chair and laid her hands in her lap.

'Well, dear.'

He smiled. 'Aye. Another day.'

Feet clattered overhead, and he imagined the Air Engineer Officer checking all the landing gear. The aircraft would fly-on once the ship was at sea. Seafires, and an entirely new bunch of Swordfish torpedo bombers. Fresh faces to greet, to penetrate.

She said suddenly, 'No news from London, I suppose?'

Buchan stirred uneasily. It was the first time she had mentioned it.

Throughout his leave he had visited the ship at irregular intervals. To watch over work progress. To catch out anyone who was slacking or abusing the ship's equipment. On one particular visit he had been surprised to find a man waiting with Commander Jolly to see him.

From the Admiralty. A severe looking little man in a crumpled blue suit. A senior clerk perhaps. Someone checking on a stores return which had gone adrift?

In fact, it had been a vice-admiral, a very important gentleman indeed from Operational Planning.

He had gone over the reports of that convoy to Russia. Had anything been left out? Glossed over?

It had been after the little admiral had departed, and Buchan had gone over it all in the quiet of his cabin, that he realised something he had not dreamed of before. Somebody, somebody very high up, did not like Chadwick. The slant of the questions, the casual references to positions and distances of the Air Support Group and the convoy escorts, *Hustler*'s part in the final battle against the heavy cruiser, what *Growler* was trying to do. Whoever was investigating Chadwick's much-publicised victory must have known of the rift between him and Buchan. Would guess that little would leak out about the informal interview. He thought of Jolly and felt worried. He might have spoken with Chadwick.

Buchan looked at his wife and forced a smile. 'No. Nor will there be. Storm in a teacup.'

She poured the tea. 'That man cannot be trusted, Bruce. He's so full of his importance. So devious. If he discovered you had been going behind his back . . .'

'But I was doing no such thing, Ellen!'

'I know. I'm only saying what *he'll* make of it.'

Buchan frowned. 'Anyway, it's right that he should get a rollicking. He took a stupid risk. He had no real intelligence that the Jerries were putting in that cruiser, or that the oil tanker was so damn vital!'

'Don't swear, dear.'

He grinned. 'Sorry. But it's true. He very nearly blew out this ship's boilers. As it was, we had to stop. Could have been tin-fished there and then.' He was getting angry as he relived the tension, the anxiety. 'No, I'm not sorry I spoke to the admiral from Operations.'

She nodded. 'Well, be on your guard. That man never gives up.'

Buchan watched her with sudden warmth. *Neither do you*.

It had been sickening to read the scant news in the papers about their convoy, of how Chadwick's skill and dash had been compared with Drake and Nelson.

He had been plain, down-to-earth lucky, and somebody high up knew it.

'Anyway, we'll not be carrying *him* when we weigh anchor, dear. Give us time to shake down as a going concern again.'

She did not look at him. 'I'll miss you terribly, Bruce.' He tried to reassure her. 'Ceylon. It'll be safer there. No ice, no U-boats milling around like killer whales.'

She nodded briskly. 'Drink your tea, and I'll pour you another cup.'

He smiled. *Bless you*. 'You just take care of the garden. I'll take care of me.'

Later, as she made to leave, she said, 'I'll think of you every day, Bruce.'

Buchan looked away, stunned. *She thinks I'm not coming back this time*.

At the head of the brow he watched her growing smaller as she walked between the towering gantrys and dockside sheds. Then he looked up at *Growler*'s boxlike bridge, at the crisp new ensign which floated from the gaff.

'Well, I am,' he said aloud.

They stood in front of a small fire which a railway porter had lit specially for them in the tiny waiting room. Side by side, their hands outstretched towards the little flames.

Rowan said quietly, 'It was good of you to come.'

'I'm glad you let me.' She glanced at his profile. 'But I hate losing you.'

They had just come from the house, from the churchyard where Rowan had found the grave in which one of his uncles had had his parents buried.

He had signed papers, spoken to a local policeman he had known for years. The man had said, 'I was first in the house, sir. They was all dead under the stairs.' As if to help he had added, 'Not a mark on 'em. Killed by shock. Best way.' By 'all', he had meant the dog, Old Simon had been with them when the stick of bombs had come down. He would have been.

Afterwards he had said, 'Let's go to a pub and have a drink. I'll have to get the train after that.'

'Are you sure you want me, Tim? Some of your friends may think you picked up some—'

He had squeezed her hand. 'What about *your* friends? What would they say if we met some of them, eh?'

She had refused to be drawn. 'I'm older than you. That's all I care about.'

Now they were in the waiting room. Remembering. The great house. Each day a rediscovery. Every night their love.

Suppose Chadwick had caught them? Just thinking about it made him sick for her. Chadwick had been back to the house three times, just for a few hours, and never at night.

If she knew what her husband was up to in London she never once mentioned it. But after each of his brief visits she had made love to Rowan more wantonly, more desperately than ever.

Now it was finished. Back to *Growler*. Off to some challenge or other. He should have felt something. He was not just another pilot. He was taking over the squadron. Just like that. They must be short of men.

The door opened a few inches. 'Train's comin', sir. Stops most of the way to Waterloo, I'm afraid. I'll get yer cases ready.'

He withdrew, and she put her arms up and around Rowan's neck.

'Thank you for making me so happy, darling Tim. I will never forget you. *Never*. You'll find someone else of course, and I expect I shall end up as the wife of our new First Sea Lord one day.' She was speaking quickly, as if to stop the tears.

He kissed her hard, tasting the salt.

He said, 'I'll be back. You see, I'll not be a nuisance, but

200

I'll be there if and when you need me. Always remember that.'

The train rumbled into the small station and doors started to slam.

'Stay here.'

He kissed her again and walked quickly to the train where the man was holding a door for him. He jammed a pound note in the surprised porter's hand.

When he wrenched open the window the train was moving, and he saw her watching him through the waiting room's doorway. She did not move or wave, but held one hand in the air until the train was out of sight.

Then she turned up the collar of her fur coat and walked out towards the waiting car.

13

Wives and Lovers

ROWAN hesitated outside the office labelled *Commander (Flying)* and then rapped on the freshly painted steel. It would be strange not seeing Villiers with his strained features and haunted expression.

'Come!'

Rowan sighed. The whole ship felt strange for that matter. The same yet different. Perhaps it was just him. He had only recently come aboard and had not met any of his friends. The quartermaster had explained that he was wanted right away. Up here.

He walked into the office and stared.

Kitto was watching him across the metal desk, his face set in a mask of mock severity.

'Well?'

Rowan said, 'I didn't know. I'd heard you'd been sent off somewhere. It seemed a bit odd that you didn't leave any messages.' He leaned over the desk. 'Congratulations. I can't think of anyone who could do the job better.'

Kitto grimaced. 'That's what they keep telling me. Christ, look at me. A desk-wallah. I was a flier just a month or so back. Now I have to tell others what to do. Just as well I used to understudy Eric Villiers. They only gave me a couple of weeks at the local air station to buff up on procedure.'

Rowan moved a pile of dog-eared files from a chair and sat down.

Kitto watched him curiously. 'Leg all right?'

'Fine. Stings a bit when I take a bath.'

'Then stay dirty like me. Help cut fuel costs.' He grinned, his blue chin shining in the January glare from a scuttle.

Rowan thought quickly of all the months he had known this

man. Other places and ships. Dymock Kitto. The old pro. The ace.

He glanced down at his gleaming new stripes on his reefer jacket. They had come a long way in a hurry. She had got that done for him. Through a tailor she knew. How did she trust the man to say nothing to her husband? Maybe she didn't care any more.

Kitto seemed to read his thoughts. 'I know. Dead men's shoes. You'll have your work cut out with your bunch, I can tell you. That's why I wanted to see you first.' He prodded some papers. 'You've lost two of your Seafire pilots. Drafted to other carriers. Things are a bit tight, I gather. You've still got Bill and Nick Rolston, Frank Creswell, and of course Lord Algy.' He grinned. 'The new boys are so green they make Frank look like Richthofen!' He became serious again. 'They've done all the usual stuff. Simulated landings and take-offs. And that's about *all* they know. You'll have to keep a tight hold on them. But I don't have to tell you. We've both had some good teachers. And Andy Miller was the best, bless him.'

'What about the Swordfish people?'

'Usual mixture, I believe. Their new boss is off a fleet carrier. A two-and-a-half called Dexter. A regular officer. Twice decorated for something or other. Said to be a bit of a goer.'

Rowan smiled. 'Like us. Pity they didn't give it to van Roijen.'

Kitto rolled his eyes. 'He's a bloody foreigner! How can you suggest such things?' Then he sighed. 'You're right of course. Especially as he's the only one left aboard from the old bunch.'

They listened to thumps and bangs on the flight deck, the whirr of cables as a dockside gantry rumbled along its tracks.

'We're loading crated aircraft, Tim. Convoy defence and freight humpers, that's us.'

Rowan considered it. Kitto, as a member of the bridge team, would know exactly where *Growler* was going next. He would not divulge this information outright, but the mention of crated aircraft suggested a fair distance.

No more Russian convoys. No more Western Ocean either.

He said, 'I'll go and unpack.'

'Yes. You're going ashore this afternoon to the local air station to meet your chaps.' Kitto kept his gaze steady. 'And pick up your new kite.' He waited. 'How d'you feel about it?'

Rowan shrugged. 'Fair enough. I'll be okay once I've been up again.'

He could see Jonah falling, the smoke trailing behind, until she hit the angry water. The parachute searing his shoulders. The blood seeping through his boot. Oblivion.

'Good. I've already been over to look at her. She's brand-new. Folding wings, so you'll be able to carry her on leave next time.' He asked casually, 'Was it a good leave, by the way?'

'Yes.' He felt guilty. 'Very.'

Kitto grinned. 'Thought so. Especially as you're so talkative about it.' He opened another folder. 'You push off. The Old Man will probably want a word with you.'

Rowan turned by the door. 'No rear admiral's flag this time then?'

Kitto's face was expressionless. 'No. Not yet anyway. Does it bother you?'

Rowan forced a smile. 'Of course not. Why should it?'

Kitto watched him go. *It bothers you all right.*

That afternoon Rowan was picked up by a staff car, and along with Lieutenant Commander James, the Operations Officer, was driven at high speed by an uncommunicative Wren who had apparently never heard of the Highway Code.

James said he had a few bits and pieces to clear up at the Fleet Air Arm station, but Rowan thought he was coming just for the ride. He looked very tired and worried, as if his leave had been something of a disappointment.

Rowan had asked him briefly about it. James had replied curtly, 'It was splendid. Grand to be home.'

Rowan settled down in the rattling Humber car and thought about Honor Chadwick. She would forget him in days. Her life as the wife of a senior officer, her position in her local community, its war effort of W.V.S. and Red Cross meetings, bundles of clothing for bombed-out families, endless work which probably helped her to stay sane. She could not afford to get involved. He looked at himself in the mud-splashed window. A young, temporary officer without prospects, even if he lived through the war. She would do well to forget him.

It depressed him to think of her pushing their time together out of her mind. He certainly could not forget. Even if he wanted to. Her moments of quiet composure. Her passion and ability to tantalise him until he was almost mad for her.

'Identity cards, please, gentlemen!'

A policeman was peering in the window, backed up by a petty officer with a pistol on his hip. They had arrived at the field without Rowan seeing more than a mile of the way.

James snapped, 'Identity cards! That's what's wrong with this bloody country!' He leaned across Rowan and thrust his card at the astonished policeman. 'Do you good to go out and fight. You might just realise then that there's a hell of a lot more to war than nosing into people's lives!'

The regulating petty officer said hastily, 'Orders, sir. Security has to be kept up—' He got no further.

'Don't make excuses! Bloody bureaucracy, that's all it is, man! If I was a German spy, do you imagine I'd be sitting here?'

'No, sir.' The P.O. sounded weary.

The Wren driver said unhelpfully, 'We're blocking the gates, sir.' She was watching Rowan in her mirror.

Rowan said, 'Easy. They're only doing their job. What's got into you?'

The car jolted forward, and Rowan saw the P.O. breathe out very slowly as he saluted. The hurt look on the police-man's face.

'Don't you start!' James's voice was a fierce whisper. 'I've had a gut full. Just because you've got another medal and—' He broke off. 'Sorry. That was a bloody awful thing to say.'

They drew up beside a line of wooden buildings where a White Ensign stood out from a mast like a sheet of metal in the wind.

Rowan replied calmly, 'Yes it was. But forget it.'

The Wren said, 'I'll have to take the car back to the motor pool. Get the gate to phone through when you're ready.' She hesitated, revving the big car. 'You're Commander Rowan, aren't you, sir? The one who was in the papers.'

'Yes.' Strange it should embarrass him.

She reached out and touched his sleeve impetuously. 'Nice to meet you, sir. My brother was shot down over Germany last year.' She let in the clutch and the car lurched away towards the gates.

Rowan watched it. 'Poor kid.'

He heard Bill's voice as a door was flung open. 'On your feet, all of you.'

They were standing around a big pot-bellied stove, dressed in their flying gear, crumpled and looking tired.

Rowan gripped his friend's hand. 'At ease. Good to see you. Sorry about . . .'

Bill guided him to a corner as the voices started again. They were quieter now, discussing their new leader, no doubt.

'*I'm* the one to be sorry, Tim.' Bill lowered his voice. 'I didn't realise you were in Chadwick's house. I arranged to meet Frank Creswell in London. He told me all about it. Sounded a bit remote from what he said. That's why I was surprised you didn't come up too when your discharge and orders came through.'

'Yes.'

He remembered the bulky envelope being handed to him by the rain-soaked postman. His orders for *Growler* again. His new role. The doctor's certificate to say he was fit to return to duty or to go on normal leave elsewhere. It had been the moment when they could have decided to finish it. Kill it stone-dead there and then.

She had watched him, her eyes filling her face. He could not make her ask him. He had said simply, 'I'd like to stay on here, if you'll have me.'

He said, 'It was what I needed. But I *did* go home. To the house. It's all boarded up, what's left. I don't know what to do about it.' He looked at Bill. 'What about Chadwick anyway? What was he doing?'

Bill sounded relieved to be on safe ground. 'He was with this woman. A real smasher. Saw them again when I was taking my girl to the Ritz for a drink.'

'You certainly live it up.' Rowan kept his voice level. 'Did he see you?'

'We left after a quick gin. But, yes, I think he did. He doesn't give a tinker's damn for anyone. It sticks out a mile. Still, nothing to do with us, is it? I expect his wife is pretty grim, eh?'

'Wrong.' Rowan met his gaze. 'She's anything but that.' He turned on his heel and said loudly, 'Just pay attention a moment.'

They pushed closer, their faces glowing in the fire from the stove. *God, they are young.* All the replacements were sub-lieutenants. He doubted if one of them was yet twenty. But Lord Algy was there, staring at his feet as if in deep thought. Nick Rolston, tall and gangling, hands in pockets, face set in a petulant frown.

Rowan began, 'You've been through all the training, and you've had a million lectures to endure, and probably more facts jammed down your throats than you can digest. In peacetime I expect you'd have had ten times the flying hours before you were trusted in a squadron. We don't have that sort of luxury, as I'm sure your instructors have *also* told you a thousand times.' He saw a few grins. 'Remember this. You are not just pilots. You are naval officers, and you belong to your ship as much as any stoker or able seaman. Don't go showing off to the ship's company just because you've managed to land without losing your undercarriage and pranging your plane. They take as many risks as you, and don't forget it. Also, they are a far bigger target.'

He realised there was complete stillness in the hut, that Lord Algy was studying him with surprise, and Rolston too had stopped frowning to listen.

He continued quietly, 'When *Growler* puts to sea we will have a short while to exercise together. To land and fly-off, to get the *feel* of her.' It was like speaking about a person. 'You've not a lot of room, but it's enough. Watch the senior pilots. The fact they're still here to be watched is proof enough of their ability.' His voice had become harder. 'In the air, do exactly as you're told. Cover your leader and watch your back at the same time.' Nobody laughed. 'You'll make mistakes. We all do. But you rarely get a second chance.' He saw Creswell staring at him beyond the stove. 'That's true, isn't it, Frank?'

Creswell grinned. 'Only too true, I'm afraid, sir.'

Sir. Even that made him start.

'You may think I'm being over-dramatic, pulling rank on you because you're new. If so, you're wrong. I just want you to learn the job, to do it well. To do that you have to stay alive.'

He nodded. 'Carry on. We'll make a start tomorrow.'

Outside the hut Bill fell in step beside him as they walked into the wind. Beyond the sandbagged anti-aircraft gun positions, the fuel tenders and hangars, aircraft were lined up on the runways or throbbing impatiently for permission to take-off.

They looked up as a flight of Barracuda torpedo bombers roared over the field, wingtips almost touching as they followed their instructor's orders.

Rowan shivered, remembering the great fan of torpedoes racing towards the convoy, the ship which had refused to sink, and the one which had become an inferno in seconds.

'I suppose you think I was coming it a bit strong,' he said.

Bill replied, 'No. It was just that you sounded like somebody else.' He chuckled. 'It suits you.'

'Good.' Rowan added dryly, 'Not what you've said in the past about other would-be senior officers.'

'Ah well, some of it rubs off on me, y'see.' He turned into a big hangar and stood aside, watching Rowan. 'Here she is, Tim.'

Rowan approached the solitary Seafire very slowly. Brand-new, Kitto had said, and looked it. He studied the tilt of her nose, the shining four-bladed prop. He stiffened as he saw the name freshly painted on the fuselage below the cockpit. Jonah Too.

He heard Bill say awkwardly, 'The lads thought it was

better, Tim. I hope you like it.'

Rowan nodded. Taking time to answer. 'That was a nice thought.' He nodded again. 'She looks fine.'

James was waiting in the guardhouse by the main gate. 'I've phoned for the car. Ten minutes, they said.'

Bill said, 'I'll take them up for another run round with the station instructor. It'll be too dark for much after that. We'll get a bus back to the ship, and I'll tell you how they've been getting on.'

'Yes.' Rowan was thinking of the Seafire. Jonah Too. Only Bill would have thought of that. 'Then I'll have a go tomorrow bright and early.'

It had started to rain again.

Bill said, 'Well, *early* anyway.'

Rowan sat on the edge of his bunk looking at nothing. He no longer shared a cabin, and with promotion had gained more privacy than he had known since he had joined the Navy. It was freshly painted, like much of the ship, and had no mark at all of its new owner's personality.

He listened to the muted throb of generators and fans, the occasional rumble of winches as last-minute stores were swayed aboard the carrier.

It had been a very long day. Outside the cabin it was all but dark, and he could sense the unrest of a ship preparing to discard the land.

They would sail tomorrow afternoon, and with their escorts go through the business of testing guns, flying-on the two sets of aircraft, fighters and torpedo bombers, putting ship and men through their paces to meet the captain's approval.

He thought about the day, his own apprehension at flying his new machine giving way to despair as he had watched his little squadron obeying their orders, making mock attacks, changing formation.

After lunch he had let Bill and Lord Algy take over. Nerves, or mere lack of real training, it was hard to tell. But the performance as a whole had been pitiful.

While he had waited with the station armourer and

210

watched him adjust Jonah Too's guns to his satisfaction, he had wondered what might happen if his pilots met with some crack enemy fighters on their first patrol. He did not think too much about it. He *knew* what would happen.

Like a lot of pilots who had gained their skill in close combat, Rowan liked to have his guns adjusted to converge at two hundred and fifty yards. It was a good range, and with luck and timing could deluge an enemy cockpit or reargunner with hundreds of rounds per second. Less experienced fliers had their weapons trained to give a wide but thin spread of fire.

He had flown his new aircraft over the field and thrown it about with every trick he knew. Across the gunnery ranges, climbing and diving like a mad thing, it did much to calm him before he saw the pilots again in the hut.

He had begun, 'It was a bloody awful day. You stray about, you do not listen to instructions, and at least six times you've left your Number One unprotected. In future we will fly in pairs. One hundred yards between each plane, two hundred between each pair. This will give more time to watch behind. Number Two in each pair will watch behind and will tell his leader which way to turn if and when a bandit is after him. He can then slip in behind the enemy. His leader could do the same for him. This way you're both covered for a stern attack.' He had paused, seeing stubbornness, resentment.

Creswell had said, 'Some of it was my fault, sir. I drifted too far in that last run-in.'

Rowan could hear his own reply, even now in this cabin.

'I thought it was *all* your fault. You of all people should know better. So don't *show off*.'

Creswell had looked as if he had been punched in the face.

One of the new pilots, Sub-Lieutenant Archer, had said, 'It's all different from what we've had to learn, sir. We've always kept to a V formation.'

'I know. So if there are three or four tight Vs, everyone is too busy avoiding collision to look behind. And *that* is where the shells come from.'

Nobody said much after that.

The curtain across the door moved aside and Bill stepped

into the cabin. 'You've not changed, Tim.'

Rowan stood up. Remembering. 'Five minutes. Stay and talk if you like.'

He dragged open a drawer and pulled out a clean shirt. Perhaps he had thought Bill had suggested a run ashore into Edinburgh merely to snap the tension after the training session. That he had forgotten about it.

Bill said, 'They'll be okay. They just need a bit of experience.'

'You mean, I was too tough with them?' He knotted his tie, watching his friend in the mirror. 'Is that it?'

'I know *why* you did it, Tim. And your reasons were good ones. But see it their way. They've just got their wings. To them, as it was to us, that is almost as close to heaven as any man can come. They'll get shocked out of it soon enough.'

Rowan slipped into his new reefer, seeing his medal ribbon and recalling James's sudden burst of anger. Now Bill was at it, too.

He said slowly, 'I suppose you're right.'

'But it won't do any harm to let them think they've got a hard-case for a boss.' Bill nodded approvingly as Rowan turned towards him. 'We'll have to fight off the girls when they see you.'

He had even wangled transport, a N.A.A.F.I. manager with a car half filled with fruit pies.

It was raining steadily when they reached Edinburgh, and Princes Street was as black as the inside of a boot. But the N.A.A.F.I. manager dropped them on the pavement outside the North British Hotel and they decided to make a start there.

It was surprisingly deserted, and as they sat quietly drinking their first gins Rowan was reminded of the house in Hampshire. The mad major taking his endless walks in the rain.

Bill said, 'I keep thinking about Magda.' He grinned. 'That's her name. I wish you could have met her. She's a beautiful girl. Very easy to talk to. Good company. You'd never guess what she's gone through.'

Rowan signalled to a waiter. It was not like Bill to get serious about any girl for long.

Bill added, 'I must admit I felt pretty rotten when I thought about her old man. He might be dead. Nobody knows. We just seemed to pretend he was dead, without actually mentioning it.' He sounded embarrassed. 'I'm in love with the girl, Tim. I think she feels like that about me, too.' He bunched his hand into a massive fist. 'God, what a bloody mess.'

Rowan smiled. 'Just as well I didn't come to London, or so it sounds. You probably got to know each other far better without someone else playing gooseberry all the time.'

Bill watched him, his eyes distant. 'Maybe. But still . . .' He banged his hand down. 'Oh hell! Here comes James and the new Swordfish chap.'

Rowan did not turn but said, 'Maybe they've not seen us.'

Bill groaned. 'No such luck.'

The two other officers came to the table and looked at them.

The Swordfish squadron's C.O., Lieutenant Commander Ralph Dexter, was straight-backed and very erect. He had finely cut features, and a permanent conspiratorial smile which was caused by a splinter wound in the corner of his mouth and some on-the-spot makeshift surgery.

James looked well away, jacket half buttoned, his eyes barely in focus.

Dexter said briskly, 'All right if we take a pew? Friend Cyril here is feeling a bit awash. I'm thinking of ferrying him back to the ship in a minute.'

Bill said a bit too loudly, 'Oh, bad luck.' His eyes suggested the opposite.

More gins appeared, and Dexter said, 'Glad to be off. Can't bear shore jobs. I've got a right bunch of oafs in my lot. Except for the Dutchman that is, he's *mustard*.'

Rowan warmed to this strange, erratic man. He had been through it, and it showed to anyone who knew the signs. Now he was off for another round.

Bill remarked, 'I hope it's somewhere hot. Where I can swim in the sea without getting frozen stiff.'

'Bound to be. My stewards saw fur jackets coming

213

aboard.' Dexter winked. 'You know how they get things wrong all the time!'

James let the conversation wash over him as he tried to pull his thoughts and wits together. His stomach felt raw from drinking, and he was sweating badly. He would throw up if he didn't concentrate.

The leave had been terrible. His home was on the outskirts of Gosport. There had been a lot of bombing in the past, but now the Germans were using single planes for hit and run attacks during daylight as well.

His wife had taken it badly. Most of the people she had got to know in the road had either moved away or preferred not to speak with her any more. Almost the worst part had been when someone had chalked *Bloody Kraut!* on the garden wall after one of the sneak air-raids.

He heard Dexter laugh about something, saw Bill Ellis leaning back comfortably, his hands behind his blond head. What did they know about it? James had nearly broken down at the air station when he had been asked for his identity card. His wife had gone on and on about it. About the new regulations for Germans who were married to British citizens. Must not change address without informing the authorities. Could not enter a service establishment or naval vessel. It was downright humilitating. Wrong. When *Growler* was alongside, and other wives were allowed aboard, she had to stay outside.

The Air Support Group was going to Ceylon. After that, nobody knew, or was saying.

He had wanted to tell her, to explain that she would have to manage on her own for a bit longer this time. But he had said nothing.

And he would have to share many of his duties with Kitto, who had taken Eric Villiers' place. Poor Eric had been bad enough, going on about German atrocities all the time. Kitto was a real fighter and would probably make things worse. Helga was German, and she was his wife. He loved her. Or he had once. He trained his eyes on a tall pillar, trying to stop the room from revolving. *He must have loved her!* The

214

sudden uncertainty was like panic, and brought sickness closer.

Rowan watched him doubtfully. Not long now. Poor bastard. Something had gone wrong for him.

Bill exclaimed, 'God Almighty, I thought he was still in London!'

'Who?'

Rowan swivelled round and saw her across the room, standing just behind her husband as he gave instructions to a waiter.

Chadwick turned and saw them, his face breaking into a wide grin.

He nodded to them in turn. 'This is my wife, gentlemen.'

To Rowan he added cheerfully, 'You enjoyed your stay, I hear. Good show.'

He snapped his fingers at the waiter. 'Scotch. Large ones for these gentlemen.'

The waiter made as if to deny the presence of whisky but changed his mind.

Chadwick said, 'Came up to see the F.O.I.C. Chum of mine. Bit of business to settle.'

Rowan barely heard. He was watching her across the table. She looked lovely, her skin very pale under the overhead lights, her hair shining as he remembered it. But there were shadows beneath her eyes. He wanted to touch her. Hold her. Desperately.

He asked, 'How is everything in Hampshire, Mrs Chadwick?'

'The same.' One hand moved slightly. 'Raining.' A pulse jumped in her throat. 'You must come again and see us.'

Chadwick had lit a cigar and was smiling through the smoke.

'They're off for quite a while, I shouldn't wonder. And I'll lay a level bet they're ready to go.' He nudged Bill's arm. 'Young tearaways, eh? Have no strength left for fighting if you stay ashore much longer!' It seemed to amuse him.

Bill smiled uncomfortably, thinking of Magda, how she had cried the first time they had made love in her flat. What did she think, he wondered? Did she imagine it was her husband who was enjoying her body, putting his arms where Bill's were, his mouth on hers in her desperate imagination? Perhaps he would never know.

He watched James swaying in his chair. *It just needs him to spew up in front of the admiral's wife and that will be his lot.*

He shifted his gaze to her and tensed. What a blind, stupid idiot he'd been. He glanced at Rowan, seeing the pain in his eyes. So that was it. Christ Almighty. *The admiral's wife.*

Chadwick turned his attention to James. 'You look a bit dicky.'

James half rose and slumped down again. 'I'm pissed,' he said vaguely.

Chadwick flushed. 'By God, how dare you speak like that in front of—'

She interjected, 'Leave him alone. He's ill.'

Dexter tugged James to his feet. 'I'll ask the porter to find a taxi.'

Chadwick eyed him grimly. 'In this rain? You'll be lucky.' He looked at his watch. 'I'll get my driver to run you to the ship. I shall be staying here tonight anyway.' He glared at James, who was almost unconscious. 'A *regular* officer, too.' He sounded outraged.

Bill said quickly, 'Here, I'll give you a hand.'

Some of the other people at nearby tables smiled as they lurched towards the door. An army lieutenant called, 'Up the Navy!'

Chadwick strode to the door, leading the ill-mixed trio like a centurion with his captives.

Rowan changed chairs and sat beside her. They looked at each other, the room, the guests and visitors invisible.

She said, 'I must see you again.' She reached out as if to seize his hand but withdrew hers again. 'I keep thinking, remembering.'

She was near to tears, and it was impossible to recall her as he had first seen her on the staircase. Calm and aloof. But this was the real one. The one he knew.

He said, 'Why did he bring you to Scotland?'

216

She shook her head. Even the movement of her hair brought back the pain.

'I insisted. Said I wanted a change. I knew I'd see you somehow.' She lowered her face, and he saw a tear run down on to her skirt. 'I can't bear it.'

He darted a quick glance at the door. There was no sign of a naval uniform.

'How long will you be here?' He chilled, remembering that he had nearly called her Honor in front of the others.

'A week, I think. He's seeing some important people about a new appointment.' She tried to smile. 'You look fine, Tim. Wonderful. I expect you thought you'd got rid of me for good.'

He touched her knee with his. 'You know I didn't think that. You're the one who should be careful. If he found out . . .'

She did not seem to hear. 'I don't care. I must see you. Just once.' Her eyes were very bright. *Try.*

He saw movement in the doorway. 'Of course I will. Somehow. I've been miserable without you, too. I wasn't going to tell you. It's not fair of me.'

She touched his arm with her fingers. 'Tim, my darling.'

Chadwick's voice boomed above the other sounds. 'That's that little mess cleared up.' He glanced from one to the other. 'We'll have dinner now, I think.' He smiled at Rowan. 'Care to join us? May be the last chance you get of some good food for a bit, eh?'

He saw her give just the smallest shake of her head.

'Thank you, sir, but no. I've got a lot to do before sailing.' He looked at her, seeing the relief, and what it was costing her. But she knew they would never get through a long evening without giving themselves away.

He turned to Chadwick, trying to discover any sort of suspicion or doubt.

But Chadwick said, 'Good show. What I like to hear. Get the new hands jumping about, eh? And God help 'em if they foul it up!'

A waiter hovered by the restaurant door, the moment was almost past.

She held out her hand. 'Good-bye, Commander Rowan.' She kept her eyes and chin lifted. 'I hope we meet again.'

'Thank you, Mrs Chadwick.' From a corner of his eye he saw that the admiral was already walking towards the waiter. He squeezed her fingers and added softly, 'I'll call you. Take care.'

He stood aside and watched the waiter opening the doors, the heads turning to watch the admiral and his lady.

Bill crossed the room. 'So that was Mrs Chadwick.' He looked at Rowan. 'And I thought *I* had troubles!'

14

New Year

By the end of January the Air Support Group was ready to
move. *Growler* and her escorts made a rendezvous with a
large southbound convoy at Liverpool, and without further
delay prepared to point her bows at the open sea once more.

Captain Buchan's orders left him in no doubt that he and
his ship were to work their passage and supply air cover and
patrols over what was largely a military convoy. Two big
troopships, some oil tankers, an ammunition freighter and
several smaller supply vessels, all deeply laden, they were
earmarked for the Far East via Simonstown and Colombo.
After that, the Air Support Group would receive fresh orders
and proceed to Trincomalee in the northern part of Ceylon.

Buchan was satisfied with the arrangement, for he better
than most knew of the low state of training amongst some of
his air crews. Also, he had to admit to some small pleasure at
seeing their sister-ship, *Hustler*, transformed almost overnight into a floating warehouse. Captain Turpin was senior to
Buchan, and as there was no admiral's flag on either carrier,
he was in overall control of the group. Buchan's earlier
resentment was soon overcome when he saw crate upon crate
of aircraft being hoisted aboard *Hustler* for transit to Ceylon
and points east.

There was barely an inch of space left on her flight deck,
and when the wind caught the strongly lashed crates in open
water, Buchan could imagine the problems of her watchkeeping officers and Turpin's displeasure. He did not like Turpin.
And Turpin was well aware of the fact.

As soon as the convoy was formed up and harried by its
strong destroyer escort the signals started to come from
Turpin thick and fast. Dawn to dusk patrols, target practice,

repelling mock air attacks, he thought of everything.

Buchan had another reason for wanting to keep his people busy. The long leave for most of the ship's company had left the usual scars. Men who had discovered unfaithful wives. Others who had arrived home to find only a gutted street where they had once lived or grown up as children.

James, the Operations Officer, had returned morose and snappy, and his department was too important to be upset by personal problems. Buchan would get the commander to take James on one side. If that failed, he would drop on him himself like a ton of bricks.

Some of the newly joined air crews would have to be watched, too. This was their first chance to fly on real patrols. Some of the landings and take-offs during their work-up in Scotland had shown some hair-raising results. But Rowan and Dexter, an unmatched pair if you like, appeared able to deal with that side of things. And from his fretting, ship-bound perch, Kitto would do the rest.

Out into the grey Atlantic again, with the bitter cold and blustery gales making each take-off a risk to aircraft and deck crew alike. The sickbay was kept busy with sprains and cuts, and a few poorly explained injuries which Minchin, the P.M.O., suspected were caused by more violent contacts with fists after somebody or other had had a near escape from being knocked down a lift or flattened by a runaway Swordfish.

But by and large, Buchan was pleased with his ship. She had shown what she could do, had made a name for herself, instead of just one more number.

The convoy stood well out from the land and the menace of the Bay of Biscay with all its German airfields and submarine pens. There were U-boats about, but most seemed to be concentrated well astern of the convoy, probably being homed to another, less well protected one from the States or Canada.

As they drove further and further south, dropping some escorts and receiving replacements from Gibraltar on the way, the weather improved, and the daily round of flying and exercising took on a more leisurely atmosphere.

Rowan was worried by the lack of real opportunity to keep his Seafire pilots on their toes. Just as he had been apprehensive that they might meet with some crack German planes within hours of leaving Liverpool, he was equally troubled by the new carefree attitude around him. The slow-moving Swordfish were doing much better, improving their daily patrols over and around the convoy, gathering experience, discovering all the problems which never happened in a training squadron.

Rowan guessed that some of the new pilots were amused by his constant demands for more and more practice. He found himself becoming isolated from them, his only contact through Bill or Lord Algy, and it was unfair to shed responsibility on them.

He did not spare himself, and suspected it was as much to keep his own mind occupied as to weld his squadron into a manageable force.

Whenever he was in the air, or alone in his cabin, he often found himself remembering his days and hours with Honor Chadwick. Distance from her only seemed to sharpen the memories, some events stood out more strongly than others to make him sweat, to impress on him the risks they had both taken.

Like that last time in Edinburgh. Sitting side by side while an elderly waiter had served tea.

She had whispered, 'I may not see you for months. Years. I can't take it. I want you so badly, Tim.'

He repeatedly thought of that particular moment. Standing to face each other, the tea untasted. Then up to her room. The reserve giving way to a desperate passion which had excluded all fear of discovery, or someone finding them together. It had been pure madness. As it had turned out, Chadwick had not stayed away as he had expected, but had returned to the hotel just as Rowan had left. He was still not certain if the admiral had seen him or even then would guess that moments earlier he had been holding her naked in his arms.

What would they have said or done? *Let me explain, sir*. It only added to his sense of loss and hopelessness.

Then fourteen days outward bound from Liverpool, as he

was sitting in his cabin trying to keep cool beneath the air vent, the telephone on the bulkhead called him to the Operations Room. He was stripped to the waist, and hastily donned a shirt, wondering what they wanted him for. As he buttoned his shirt he saw, reflected in the mirror, the small silver medallion which hung around his neck alongside his identity disc.

It too brought back a stabbing memory. As if it were merely hours ago. A night or so before he had left Chadwick's Hampshire house she had given it to him while they had sat on a rug in front of a roaring fire, listening to music on the gramophone.

She had apparently bought it from a small antique shop in Winchester where she had been visiting the tailor for him.

'I hear they call you Jonah. And I wanted to give you something for your birthday.'

The little medallion was fashioned like a spouting whale.

Some nights before that they had been lying in bed, listening to the rain lashing the windows.

She had said, 'I wish I was younger than you.'

He had turned towards her, feeling her softness. 'It's my birthday next week.' He had seen her smile in the darkness. 'I'm catching up.'

He sighed and tucked the silver whale inside his shirt. She had even remembered that.

Rowan found James and Kitto in a huddle with Dexter and van Roijen.

James said testily, 'You're taking your time.'

Rowan replied, 'I'm here now.' He did not understand James's nagging irritation. It made him sound like Turpin.

Kitto cleared his throat noisily. 'Look at the chart, Tim.' He jabbed the table with his finger. Like the quietly humming plot nearby, it showed the convoy steering south, with the Cape Verde Islands some hundred miles to port.

He said, 'Signal from Admiralty. It seems there's a U-boat about eighty miles south-east of us. Surfaced and damaged. How badly, we don't know. Intelligence think she was bashed by two South African destroyers three days back. She'd been hanging around the coast waiting for unescorted

222

ships and easy pickings. They blew her to the surface, but she got away in the darkness. Now the Admiralty say the German commander is heading north, trying to reach a base in Biscay. God knows where the information comes from. Probably a neutral.' He relaxed slightly. 'I thought we should fly-off a strike right away. If we can show Jerry we mean business, we might be able to keep the U-boat intact for the escorting destroyers to capture.'

Rowan leaned over the chart, remembering all the other times, the stabbing flak, the Swordfish exploding in a fiery ball.

He said, 'That'd be something. I heard we captured one a couple of years back. It'd be quite a feather for the ship.'

James said testily, 'Probably not there at all. These Admiralty Intelligence people read too many thrillers, if you ask me.'

Van Roijen looked at Kitto. 'How many will go?'

Kitto rubbed his blue chin vigorously. 'The U-boat might play up.' He too was probably thinking of that last time when the multiple cannon fire had blasted the Swordfish out of the sky. 'We'll fly-off three Seafires, and one Swordfish with depth charges. The Swordfish will be relieved at regular intervals until the U-boat's surrendered or we've put her down for good.'

James came out of his depression. 'I'll tell the captain. I've already made a signal to the escort commander. He's keen to have a go.'

'I'll bet.' Dexter nodded grimly. 'A captured U-boat. That's pretty rare.'

Kitto looked at Rowan. 'You happy about it?'

Rowan glanced at the clock. 'Fine. Nick Rolston is on stand-by. I'll go with him and take one of the new blokes. Nichols. He could do with a bit more experience.'

'Off you go.' Kitto picked up a telephone. 'I'll get it started.'

Twenty minutes later Rowan was in the air, the two Sea-fires swimming across his mirror like sharks to take station on either quarter. There was no point in adopting the pairs system. There were no hostile aircraft as far south as this, and the usual formation would give better vision. The U-boat might have carried out repairs and dived. But just to be flying, free of the canned air in the hull, the smells of diesel and dope, the dull monotony of convoy, it was worth it.

He opened his shirt front under his Mae West and felt the sweat run down his chest. Through the perspex the sun was very hot, and below the sea was spread away endlessly, like glittering blue silk.

A few minute wavelets and even a tiny sailing craft were the only flaws on the surface.

He looked back at Rolston's aircraft, seeing his helmeted head hunched forward as if he were praying. He always flew like that.

Back over the port quarter he saw the new pilot, John Nichols, keeping good station, the glare very bright on his own insignia, a girl with black stockings and nothing else. Nichols was the youngest so far, and had already become very friendly with Creswell. To start with he had followed Creswell's lead as a new boy will seek a perfect's compliments. In the short time they had been at sea he had started to copy Creswell's recklessness, and twice Rowan had been forced to give him a strong 'bottle'.

Even Kitto had said, 'That lad will either win a Victoria Cross or get himself killed in his first scrap!'

'Hello, *Jonah*, this is Nick.' Rowan came out of his thoughts and turned to see Rolston gesturing with his thumb. 'Submarine at Green four-five.'

'Got her. Thanks.'

He shaded his eyes with his hand. A thin, dark stick, making hardly any wash. How easy it would be to miss the U-boat altogether.

'I see her, *Jonah*.' That was Nichols. 'She's not diving yet.'

Rowan watched the submarine's tiny shape. From here it lacked menace and intelligence. Just a drowsy fish. *A pike in the reeds*.

He tightened his stomach muscles, letting the sweat run down over his groin as he tried to think.

Then he saw a faint glitter, almost lost against the shining water.

A shell exploded well clear to port, leaving the tell-tale stain hanging in the sky.

Rowan snapped, *'Echelon starboard!'*

He waited, counting seconds, as Rolston and Nichols vanished and then reappeared to the right of his cockpit, like part of a fan.

Another shell exploded above and astern of the three fighters, the sound lost in the throaty roar of engines, but making itself felt like a violent gust of wind.

Rowan wondered what the German commander thought he was doing. He would know the Seafires were not carrying depth charges, so maybe he was making a stand. On the other hand, he should realise they must be from a carrier, and that meant big trouble. He peered at his wrist watch. The Swordfish would be trundling along astern. Another ten minutes . . . He swore silently as a third shell burst directly ahead.

He said, 'Going down!'

He put Jonah Too into a power dive, knowing the others were peeling off after him. He blinked away the moisture behind his goggles, concentrating on the approach. Gun button to 'Fire'. He watched the tracer spluttering from the U-boat's bandstand.

Straighten up. Three hundred yards. The conning tower was across the sights, growing out of the blue backcloth like a solid rock.

He pressed the button, feeling the plane jerk and quiver as the tracers pounded down in long, smoky lines, knitting and bursting across the submarine in a whirl of flames and splinters.

He felt the pressure in his spine as he pulled out of the dive, throwing the fighter over and around as Rolston's shadow tore across the water like a black cross. He could hear his cannon and machine guns quite clearly. Brrrrrrrrrrrrr! Brrrrrrrrrrrrr!

'Hello, *Jonah*!' Nick sounded out of breath. 'The bugger's stopped shooting!'

Rowan did not reply, he was watching Nichols as he pulled away, his guns still unfired.

He said, 'We'll keep circling. At the first sign of a rubber dinghy we'll have another go. They might try to bale out if they think a rescue is on the cards.'

Lazily, keeping well apart, the three Seafires flew round and round the slow-moving U-boat. Maybe they had already had enough. Some other battle, or too many of them. Rowan could see the German sailors crowding in the bows, peering up at the aircraft. Most of them were dressed only in shorts, their skins dull like their boat. They must have been at sea for weeks, and how long before that? Now they were making their gesture, keeping up in the bows and away from the guns.

'Stringbag coming up like the Flying Scot!' Rolston gave a rare chuckle.

Rowan smiled tightly. He could see the Swordfish now, cruising at about five hundred feet, and miles away astern he could make out two other shapes hardening in a heat haze. Destroyers bustling from the convoy to complete the capture.

The Swordfish was already flashing its signal lamp towards the submarine. Telling the German commander not to abandon. To await boarding.

Rowan heard Nichols yell. 'Somebody's manning the bridge gun!' Nichols' Seafire was the nearest one to the U-boat at that moment, and before Rowan could reply he added wildly, 'Tallyho!' and put his plane into a sweeping dive.

A light flickered from the U-boat's bridge, and Rowan realised that one of the Germans was acknowledging the signal, and certainly not attempting to use a gun.

Then everything seemed to happen at once. Nichols levelled out and flew straight in across the U-boat's port beam, his guns hammering against and over the midships section and hurling up a pattern of white feathers some twenty yards on either side of the ballast tanks.

'Break off, you fool!'

Rowan pulled round in a tight arc, seeing the Swordfish, the U-boat and Nichols all pivoting before him as if on rails.

Rolston was flying parallel with the U-boat, barely thirty

feet above the surface, his wings tilting as he tried to see what was happening. A bright cone of tracer spurted from the U-boat's multi-barrelled A.A. gun and seemed to pass right through the fighter without harming it.

Then the Seafire seemed to fall awkwardly and roll right over on to its back, ploughing up a great furrow of bursting spray as it hit the sea.

Rowan circled the U-boat, ignoring the sailors who were dragging one man away from the motionless guns, and just staring at the Seafire's pale, upended belly as it grew fainter and mistier in the clear water, until it was gone altogether.

Confused, caught off guard, or enraged by what they had seen, the Swordfish crew released their depth charges. They were so close to the hull when they exploded that the boat appeared to rise right up in the sea like a wounded dolphin.

The crew, those who had avoided Nichols' torrent of bullets and were still on their feet after the charges had exploded, were already abandoning. Life-jackets bobbed around the hull, and spray was bursting up from the saddle-tanks like steam as the U-boat started to settle down.

Rowan said, 'This is *Jonah*. Return to base.' He did not recognise his own voice.

He saw the two destroyers charging towards the sinking U-boat with its widening circle of froth and oil.

He heard Nichols say thickly, 'They were going to fire!'
'Get off the air!'

Rowan turned to see where Rolston had gone down. There was always a chance that a man could fight his way out of the cockpit after it was under water. But the sea's face was smooth again, as he had known it would be.

He checked his course and speed, and waited for the Swordfish to complete another circle before tagging on astern.

There was the convoy trailing over the misty horizon. Larger humps here and there to denote the carriers and the troopships.

'Hello, *Foxtrot*, this is *Jonah*.' They would already have every glass trained on the returning aircraft. 'Cancel the relief. U-boat destroyed.'

There was a long pause, then, 'Hello, *Jonah*. This is *Foxtrot*. Report casualties.'

'One fighter down.'

What was the point of broadcasting a name? That Lieutenant Nicholas Rolston, R.N.V.R., a gangling, hot-tempered pilot, had just died because of another's blind stupidity. He felt the silver whale sticking to his chest and stared directly through the racing prop. And it might have been me. Just like that.

'Permission to land-on.'

'Affirmative.'

He flew round *Growler*'s square shape and landed on the flight deck with barely a shudder.

He thrust himself out of the cockpit, feeling the sun pushing down through the breeze from the bows.

Lord Algy was one of those who helped him away from the aircraft, his face very strained.

'Nick?'

Rowan pulled off his helmet and took a tankard of lemonade from a mechanic. He nodded and then tilted the tankard until it was empty.

Nichols' Seafire hit the deck with a screech, missed the first arrester wires and then came to rest on the last one, slewing awkwardly as the engine coughed and died. He came across the deck, half running, half staggering, oblivious to the men on the walkways and those who were already moving the aircraft to the parking area.

'I thought they were going to open fire, sir!'

Rowan handed the tankard back to the mechanic. He felt very tired. Crushed.

'You didn't wait. You didn't think. Now we've lost the sub, and Nick's dead. All because of you.'

He turned away, sickened, as Lord Algy lashed out and hit the other pilot in the mouth.

'That will do.'

He walked past the handling party who were staring at Nichols and the blood which splashed unheeded down his chest and Mae West.

Nichols pleaded, 'It was *an accident*!'

Lord Algy picked up his cap from the deck. 'Fly across my bows and there'll be another *accident*!' Then he too walked away.

Later, when dusk closed over the convoy and the last air patrol had landed safely, Rowan was requested to report to Buchan's quarters. When he arrived he found Kitto and Commander Jolly already there.

Buchan said, 'I saw what happened on deck today, Lieutenant Cameron will be reprimanded for behaving as he did. And he's damn lucky it didn't go further. The fact that I'm leaving it right there is because Commander (Flying) explained the circumstances. But I'll not have my officers acting like bar-room oafs in front of the ship's company.' He poured four glasses of sherry. 'Nichols will not make that mistake again. And punching him in the face won't help either him or Lieutenant Rolston now.'

Rowan nodded. 'I'm sorry, sir. I should have stopped it myself.'

He looked at the sherry, vibrating gently in the glass as *Growler* took up night station in the convoy. A destroyer had returned to the screen with some three dozen survivors from the U-boat on board. He found himself wondering if one of them was the man so stunned by Nichols' attack that he had run unaided to the A.A. guns and poured that deadly volley into Rolston's plane as it flew past. It was more likely that he was far astern with the others.

'And anyway,' Buchan was looking at his glass, too, 'there are other things to worry about. I've had a signal. At Trincomalee we will finish working-up and then head for the Pacific.'

Rowan glanced at the others. It was obvious they already knew.

Buchan added slowly, '*Growler* will be senior ship of the group. Under the flag of Rear Admiral Chadwick once more.'

Rowan asked quietly, 'Wasn't the admiral going to a more important appointment, sir?'

Buchan eyed him for several seconds, the sherry glass tiny in his fist.

'So I understand. It would now appear differently.' He glanced at his watch. 'I must get up to the bridge.'

Kitto walked down with Rowan to the cabins in silence. Then he said, 'Something odd about all this, Tim.'

'Yes.' He thought of her face. How she had looked whenever her husband had come back from one of his trips. Knowing he had been with other women. Now Chadwick was coming to *Growler* again. Why? Was it because of some old connection with Buchan? Turpin would certainly take it as a slight that his ship was not being given a chance of wearing the admiral's flag. Or had something worse happened which bound all these people and events together? 'But there's nothing we can do about it. I'd better see to Rolston's gear. Tell his steward to pack it up.' Another box. A letter from the captain to Rolston's family.

Bill met them in the passageway, filling it like a great bear.

Rowan said, 'I'm putting Nichols in your flight, Bill. A change will be good for him.'

Behind him Kitto nodded approvingly. A leader had emerged from the pilot and fighter whom he had known for far longer in Rowan.

Bill said, 'Fair enough. I'll use him as a punch-bag if he argues with me!'

Kitto walked away towards the showers, and Rowan added quietly, 'Chadwick's coming back.'

Bill stared at him. 'Phew! That could be nasty.'

'How d'you mean?'

Bill laid a large hand on his arm. 'For God's sake, Tim, I'm not bloody well blind! I just hope his lordship is, for your sake!'

Rowan opened his mouth, and then let the denial drop. 'Obvious, was it?'

Bill grinned. 'Just a bit.' He followed him into the cabin, adding, 'Lucky old James chose that moment to be sick!' He turned his back to the door, lowering his voice to a whisper. 'You didn't see her again after that, did you?' He shook his head. 'I see that you did.'

He sat down on Rowan's bunk and scratched himself noisily. 'I think I'd rather take on the Jap Navy than Chadwick.'

Rowan smiled. Glad he had told Bill, although it changed nothing.

15

Night before Sailing

BUCHAN sat with his arms folded watching Rear Admiral Chadwick as he read swiftly through a folder of recent signals.

Despite the fans and the spacious size of Chadwick's quarters, the air was humid and oppressive. Curtains were drawn across the scuttles, and outside the motionless carrier Buchan knew the sun was blinding and ten times as hot.

Buchan had been to Ceylon several times in his naval career, but he knew that after convoy work and the grey hardships of the Atlantic most of his company were seeing their new surroundings as some sort of paradise.

They had arrived in Colombo without losing a single ship or man, apart from Rolston that is. Buchan did not believe in relying on luck. It surely meant that at long last the combined Allied assaults on U-boats, the day and night bombing of enemy harbours and industrial targets were having visible effect.

It had been a proud moment for Buchan, who like so many had become conditioned to expecting a convoy to arrive at its destination with many of its numbers missing.

Three days in Colombo and then off again, to this thriving port and naval base of Trincomalee. And here, once more there was a sign of the 'turning tide', as Churchill had termed it, a change in their fortune.

For the first time since the bitter defeats in Malaya and Singapore, the Japanese domination of so many islands in the East Indies and at the gates of Australia itself, the Navy was gathering its strength again. A new British Pacific Fleet was being planned, and ships of all kinds being brought from other areas where they were no longer needed.

The Americans were used to the great expanse of the

Pacific, and had been involved and hitting back since Pearl Harbour. The daily arrival of ships and men from around the world showed that the pace was quickening, and Chadwick's appearance on board *Growler* this forenoon implied that their support group was to play a part.

Chadwick had changed in some way. Buchan tried to remember him as he had last seen him in Scotland after the Russian convoy. Maybe the refit, the replenishment of new aircraft and men, and the long haul around the Cape and across the Bay of Bengal had blunted his proper image of the man.

Now, dressed in impeccable white drill, Chadwick looked heavier. Older.

'This business of the pilot who was killed?' Chadwick looked up. 'Seems a bit of a foul-up?' When Buchan merely shrugged he added tartly, 'Lost the damned U-boat too, eh?'

The door opened and Chadwick's new flag lieutenant padded into the cabin and laid a small envelope on the desk and withdrew just as silently.

Lieutenant de Courcy was quite a different type from Godsal. When Buchan had mentioned the change, Chadwick had replied indifferently, 'Marcus Godsal? Went home on leave and got blown up in an air-raid. He wasn't much good anyway.'

Chadwick sat back in the chair and stared absently at a bulkhead chart of the Pacific.

'God, there's a hell of a lot of work to be done. While you were dragging your keels round the Cape of Good Hope, I was flying out to Australia. Had to see some of the American top brass.' He sounded vague, which was not like him. 'Get the feel of things.'

'Will we be joining with the U.S. Navy soon, sir?'

'Early days.' Chadwick took a cigarette and lit it irritably. 'I must decide where we can do the most good. Too much stagnant thinking out here. They've been out of the fighting, don't know what it's about.'

Buchan had no idea who 'they' were, but when Chadwick had come aboard he had arrived direct from the F.O.I.C.'s office. A cold reception perhaps? A rap on the knuckles for taking so much on himself? He thought of the admiral who had come to question him about that convoy. His searching enquiries about the group's part, and Chadwick's behaviour.

Chadwick continued, 'I want plenty of flying instruction while we're here. Keep 'em on their toes. Don't much like what I've seen and read so far.' He asked abruptly, 'How's Rowan getting along?'

Buchan smiled. 'Very well. He's only young but—'

Chadwick interrupted. 'I was *much* younger when I had his responsibility.' His own words seemed to unsettle him. 'I'm glad to hear it anyway. Picked him myself. We'll need as many skilled officers as we can beg and steal from every damned direction, I can tell you!'

He picked up the small envelope and turned it over and over in his fingers. Buchan noticed it was pink and had a handwritten address on it. It looked like a woman's writing.

Chadwick said. 'I'll be living ashore, of course.'

Of course. Buchan kept his face immobile. He had heard about Chadwick. It hadn't taken him long to get organised in Ceylon. Or maybe he kept one handy in every port, like the sailor in the song.

'It will give you a free hand, and I shall be able to keep a close eye on things where it counts.'

But as days ran into weeks and nothing more spectacular than extra training came the way of the ships under Chadwick's command, many who still cared about such matters began to wonder.

Kitto had been across to visit a giant American carrier which was on her way to join the fleet in the Pacific. He had a friend aboard who he had known before the war.

One evening in *Growler*'s wardroom, after a particularly frustrating day at sea, when they had exercised taking on fuel from a naval tanker, and had flown several practice sorties with the Swordfish torpedo bombers, he said forcefully, 'The Yanks don't want us out there.'

'What the hell are you talking about?' Dexter watched him with his twisted smile. 'They're on our side, aren't they?'

'It's not that.' Kitto sounded vaguely disappointed. 'You want to see their planes and equipment. We're so used to the short-range, hard-punching war, we've not got the experience of their operations. Thousands and thousands of miles, and they've got the ships and the aircraft with the endurance for the job.' He shook his head. 'I don't believe Admiral Chadwick had been sent out to form a master-plan with the Americans. I think somebody at home wants him to get lost. Trouble is, what effects him may rub off on the rest of us.'

Few present at the time really believed him, but as weeks dragged on and other ships arrived and then vanished to various theatres of war, Rowan for one had cause to remember his words.

The training programme was maddeningly monotonous. The ships spent several days at a time steaming up and down the Palk Straight which separated Ceylon from India, until everyone from bridge staff to the lowliest stoker was heartily sick of it. Each programme was followed by a short stay in port, and for a while many said, 'Ah, now we're off at last.' They were wrong.

And with the arrival of June came the news of the great Allied invasion of Normandy. The vital step for which everyone had waited, and dreaded at the same time. The announcement only pushed the Air Support Group further to the fringe of things.

Then at long last Chadwick came aboard, and shortly afterwards, with *Hustler*, her escorts and the loyal rescue tug *Cornelian* in company, *Growler* put out to sea.

Chadwick issued a short but rousing bulletin to his ships' companies. They were going to Sydney, and under new orders would then proceed to the real Pacific war. It was up to every officer and man in the group to use his extra training to best advantage.

At the thriving Australian naval base in Sydney they were made very welcome. Ceylon had been a colourful change for most of the seamen who had not been far from home waters before. But Sydney, with people who looked and spoke as they did, free of bombing and dull, wartime food, was something really special.

The newspapers were full of stories about the Allied advances in France and the U.S. Marines' progress in the

Pacific. There was plenty of speculation about the American hopes of returning to the Phillipines with a full-scale invasion. Luzon, as it was pointed out, was the real stepping-stone into Japan.

Dances and parties were arranged for *Growler*'s company, picnics and swimming at Bondi became as natural as fish and chips, and many of the unattached sailors soon had Australian girlfriends. Quite a few of the married ones did, too.

It sounded as if the support group would be operating from Sydney when the orders were eventually received.

Of Chadwick they saw little, which suited almost everyone. He was said to be visiting the various chiefs of staff, and in contact with London about the group's eventual role.

Growler put to sea only once during these weeks, and flew-off all her aircraft to a local Australian field. There they could be serviced and used at regular intervals to keep them and their pilots from getting rusty. To Rowan it looked as if *Growler* and the other ships were taking root at their moorings.

After one such session at the airfield, Rowan and Bill returned to the naval base in a small bus kept for the purpose. It was a blazing hot afternoon, and it seemed a long long way from Britain. The streets were crowded with tanned Australian girls, and servicemen of every shape and size, mostly Americans from the warships and troopers in the harbour.

Bill said, 'I'm thinking about asking for a transfer. What d'you say? This is useless being here.'

Rowan thought about it. He knew what Bill meant.

'We might have a word with the Old Man. He could have heard something by now.'

Bill grinned ruefully. 'Where were you, Daddy, when the war ended? In Sydney with all the lovely sheilas, son, that's where!' He sighed. 'Trouble is, I don't feel like it any more.'

Aboard *Growler* they discovered Lieutenant de Courcy in a rare state of excitement.

He said, 'A ship was torpedoed some weeks back. She had mail aboard. Some of it was for *us*.'

Bill chuckled. 'I don't suppose the torpedo knew that at the time, Flags!'

'You don't understand.' De Courcy eyed him severely. 'There was a letter for the admiral. Apparently his wife is coming out here. She must have pulled a few strings through the Red Cross or something.'

'Well, what about it?' Bill darted a quick glance at Rowan. 'That's good news surely?'

De Courcy picked up his cap. 'The ship arrived *today* with the new convoy.'

Rowan swallowed hard. 'I saw her docking when I was in the air.' He tried to think clearly, to discover his immediate reactions. 'Has anyone gone to meet the admiral's wife?'

'You've not been listening.' De Courcy looked near to tears. 'I've only just been told. Mrs Chadwick will probably go straight to the hotel where her husband has a suite.' He peered at his watch. 'He'll never forgive me for this.'

Rowan snapped, 'Has he got a woman with him?' He seized his arm and shook him. 'Is that it?'

'Well, I'm not supposed to say, but . . .'

Bill said quickly, 'I know what hotel he's at. The best. I'll go and tell the O.O.D. to get us a car.'

But it took time to get off the ship and away from the island base. As they sped through the busy streets again Rowan tried not to look at his watch. Wondered what she would say. How they would be together.

'*Stop!*'

The car screeched to a halt and the driver exclaimed, 'Jesus, lootenant, you sure know what you want!'

Rowan hurried through the glass doors and paused to accustom his eyes to the cool shadow of the hotel foyer.

Then he saw her. She had her back to him, but he recognised her instantly. She was wearing a plain green dress, and there were some suitcases beside her. She was speaking to a desk clerk, who was obviously confused.

Rowan hurried towards her, just in time to hear the man say helpfully, 'I am very sorry, ma'am. Rear Admiral Chadwick is out of the hotel at the moment. But his wife is in the suite, if you'd like to speak to her?'

Rowan said quietly, 'Hello. I thought you might be here.' His heart bounded as she turned to face him. If anything, she looked lovelier than he remembered her. 'The ship with your letter was sunk. I just heard.' He dropped his eyes and added, 'I wanted to stop all this happening.'

She took his hands in hers and waited for him to look at her.

'I'm all right, Tim. I've known for a long while. But until I met you, I think I wanted to sweep it under the carpet. Not see it.'

Rowan replied, 'You can't stay here, Honor. But when he comes back he'll know. That *you* know. You can't keep a secret like that out here.'

She looked suddenly helpless, and he wanted to hold her in his arms, as were some people greeting friends nearby.

She said, 'I don't want you to get into trouble, Tim. If he found out about us . . .'

Rowan made up his mind. 'Welcome to Sydney, Honor.' He lowered his head and kissed her lightly on the cheek. 'Let's make the most of it.'

He saw Bill and beckoned him across. 'This is Bill, my friend.'

She took his hand. 'Hello, Tim's friend. I met you in Edinburgh.'

Bill grinned, towering over her. 'We'd better arrange another hotel for you. I'll fetch the luggage.'

She slipped her hand through Rowan's arm. He could feel her bunching her knuckles and knew she was only just able to put a brave face on it.

She said, 'Take me away from here. I keep thinking of that woman up in his room. I suppose I'm no better than she is, but he doesn't care. *Any* woman will do.'

Fortunately, Bill had discovered a taxi, and he said quickly, 'I've told him where to take you. You'll be fine there, Mrs Chadwick, until you've decided what to do.'

He slammed the door and stood to watch them drive off.

She said, 'He's nice.'

Rowan squeezed her arm, still unable to believe she was with him.

'He's been here before. Playing rugby of all things. If he

says it's a good hotel, it will be.'

As soon as he had seen her booked into a comfortable room which overlooked the harbour he said, 'I'd better get back to the ship. We don't want to upset the applecart.' He saw her sudden anxiety, the way one hand moved to her breast, and added gently, 'I *mean*, I'm not having your name damaged because of my clumsiness.' He held her against him, smelling her hair, the fresh warmth of her skin. 'I love you. I want you for myself. I'm selfish like that.'

She twisted in his arms, looking at him, laughing and part-crying.

'It's better you go, Tim. We both know why.'

Aboard *Growler* he found Bill waiting anxiously in the wardroom.

Rowan asked, 'Did the admiral come aboard?'

'Yes. He's seen his bloody flag lieutenant, too. I'll bet he's gone back to the hotel like a mad bull.'

Rowan signalled to a steward. 'I need a drink.'

Bill watched him gravely. 'You will when I tell you. We've got sailing orders. The day after tomorrow. I know, because Kitto told me to telephone the airfield about getting our planes back.'

Rowan sat down and stared at the bulkhead. *The day after tomorrow.*

Maybe, deep down, he had been like the others. Thinking that for *Growler* the war was almost over. That she had outlived the role for which she had been thrown together in an American shipyard.

Bill asked, 'How does she feel?' He watched his friend's face. 'I know how *you* feel. But she's got a lot to give up.'

Rowan looked at him. 'I know. You should have seen the house and the estate it stands on, Bill.'

Bill nodded. 'Would you give up so much for her?'

'You know I would.' There was never any doubt. Nor could there be.

'Right. Then it's full ahead both engines, Tim. It'll be rough on you and her, I expect. But, by God, I envy you.'

Rowan stood up and walked to the bulkhead and straightened a framed picture of *Growler*'s first air crews. In the few seconds it took him he saw the dead faces looking at him from the past.

He said despairingly, 'But I don't know what to do. If I go for a Burton on this next tour of operation, what then? She'll be left with nothing.'

Bill shot him a warning glance as James and de Courcy entered the wardroom.

'It's my guess she'll make up her mind, and yours too, Tim.'

Rowan sighed. 'If I let her.'

Rear Admiral Lionel Chadwick opened the bedroom window and allowed the night air to cool his body. He was naked but for a towel round his waist, and he had a glass of Scotch in his hand. It was the middle of the night, but with the window open he could hear the steady hum of traffic and see the occasional activity of Sydney's restaurants and clubs. The sky was very clear, and there was the brightest, fullest moon he had ever seen.

He could see the great, single-arch Harbour Bridge, nicknamed the coathanger, the span shining in the silver glare like ice.

He swirled the drink round his glass and tried to think methodically.

Behind him, sprawled with arms and legs outstretched like a fallen statue, the girl was still asleep, her breathing regular and untroubled.

Chadwick swore under his breath, recalling the shock and momentary anxiety which de Courcy's news had given him aboard the carrier.

He had had so much on his mind lately, otherwise he might have suspected his wife would do something unusual. He should have guessed that even in wartime she might fix a passage on some pretext connected with her work for the Red Cross, or one of the other organisations she took an interest in.

The glass almost fractured in his powerful grip. It was so bloody unfair. Especially on top of everything else.

But why had she come? Not for his sake certainly.

He walked through the darkness and slopped another drink into the glass.

If she had heard about London, things could get really difficult.

He sat in a chair and tried to reason. Again, if he had not become so involved with the Admiralty department which was trying to formulate a plan for a new British Pacific Fleet, he might have been more careful. He thought of the girl in London. He had known her on and off for two years. Tall and blonde, it had been a pleasure to tame her. He had never grown tired of her demands, her uninhibited sexual appetites. Somehow or other she had become pregnant. In itself it could have been managed. But she was the daughter of a very senior civil servant in Whitehall, a man who had the ear of many a cabinet minister. When something as personal as this leaked out, it needed more than rank and friends in Admiralty to stay safe.

It had required all his old skill to start a salvage operation, which with luck and a few chums in high places might still have kept his name clean.

Chadwick had become deeply involved in the Pacific planning. He had been to Pearl Harbour and to Sydney to meet the new British Commander-in-Chief, and several of his American counterparts.

It was obvious that the Americans were not keen on having their operations altered to include a new fleet. They had suggested the British would be better employed hitting at Japanese oil supplies in the East Indies. Or if they came to the Pacific, acting as part of the Fleet Train, as it was called, which included small carriers, oilers and ammunition ships, the logistic tail of the larger, active fleet which would eventually be backing General MacArthur's assault on the islands where distances between bases were not so great.

The British authorities were eager to play their part, and soon the bigger fleet carriers and battleships would be freed from home waters and would then fight alongside the Americans.

Until then . . . Chadwick knew he should have seen it. That someone had purposefully steered him to what would surely be a naval backwater, well out of the main scheme of things.

Chadwick could remember the words of his best friend at the Admiralty. The one who had tried to persuade him not to take on the Air Support Group in the first place. He had said that Chadwick should make the best of it until a better appointment came along. There was a job on the horizon in Washington for an officer of Chadwick's standing. The war could not last more than a year or so, and even if it did, as the pessimists kept insisting, the real struggle would be in the Far East. When that happened, the power would be in Washington, at the doorstep of the President.

But, his friend had made it equally clear, Chadwick would have to be careful. His fondness for women was well known to many. But when others in high places became implicated, it was a different matter. Chadwick might find himself on the beach before the final notes of the bugle had died.

And Chadwick loved the life the Navy offered him. He had never allowed anything or anyone to damage his reputation in the Service, no matter whose name got hurt in the process.

Like Buchan, for instance. At the court of enquiry after the loss of life and the *Camilla*'s collision, Chadwick could have saved him, cleared his reputation with a word. Buchan was a dedicated seaman and an officer of the old school. But Chadwick's careful, non-commital evidence had finished him.

But to Chadwick it was right and proper. He had a useful life to offer. Whereas Buchan was a day-to-day man, who lived for this ship or that, with the solid dependability of an old sailing master. *Old*, that was the point. Not in years, but in attitudes. Out of the goodness of his heart Chadwick had got him appointed to command *Growler*. He would never admit that he enjoyed watching people like possessions.

He stood up and massaged his stomach vigorously. He kept in trim. People often told him he looked younger than his years. The flattery did not console him as it usually did.

He thought of Honor. De Courcy would find out which hotel she was at. Then he would have to go and 'explain' to her. He had done it before. She would have to accept that this matter was vital to his position and future, and therefore to her as well.

It was strange what his stupid flag lieutenant had told him about Rowan. Had he tried to shield his admiral from shame? Was it as well known in the fleet and around Sydney that he was living with Grace? He looked at the nude girl on the bed. Gracie, as she liked him to call her. Tall and strong, with a power which sapped even his demanding appetite. He could see her large breasts, still feel her urgent passion for him. Any other time and he would have awakened her in his usual way, enjoying her gasp of pain and then enjoyment.

Rowan had been all that time in the house with Honor. He shook his head, smiling in the darkness. *He* might, but not Honor. He recalled when he had first met her. It was shortly after his first wife had been killed in a car smash. Honor had been a friend of hers. She had hardly changed since then. Beautiful, obedient, completely devoted to the house and being the wife of a senior officer. He had already been a captain when he had married her. A yachtsman and pilot, squash champion, too. No wonder she had been willing to marry an older man. He frowned, the pleasure gone. *But not Honor*. She was too quiet. Too content at being the admiral's wife.

What had that fool Buchan said? Something about age and Rowan's ability?

The girl stirred on the bed and moaned, 'Come back to bye-byes, baby. Stop worrying, for God's sake.'

He walked to the window again. He would have to get rid of Grace, double-quick.

He took a deep swallow from the glass and felt some of the old confidence returning. It was more than likely that Honor had come all this way, despite the risk of being torpedoed, merely to stand by him. She must have heard about the girl in London.

Chadwick felt his face flushing with righteous indignation. By God, it was at times like these you discovered who your friends were. He pictured Honor in an hotel somewhere. Probably quite near.

Small and demure Honor. There must be more to her than

he had thought. He would go and see her first thing in the morning. The fact he was under sailing orders would help. A few soft words, a hint of behaving himself in the future. He nodded in the darkness. That was the ticket.

He walked back to the drinks table and struck his shin on a chair.

'Sod it!'

'What was that, baby?' She rolled over on the bed, her legs moving sensuously. 'What the hell have you got there?'

Chadwick felt much better. Get to sea. Show the Yanks how to run a support group. By that time everything would be calm again.

He let his towel fall to the floor.

'Come and see, Gracie.' He waited for her to reach out and hold him. If she were a cat she'd purr, he thought.

Dropping the glass he threw himself on top of her. He would show them. God help anyone who tried to stop him now.

They sat side by side in a small booth watching the last couple dancing in the darkened restaurant.

Rowan kept his knee against hers and wished they could be alone somewhere.

He asked, 'What did he say?'

She ran a finger round the top of a wine glass, remembering, fighting back the disgust.

'I told him *why* I had come to Sydney.' She turned and looked at him. 'That was why I didn't want to write to you. Until I had seen him. There's been quite a lot of gossip about him at home, you know. Him and his women. And some people are beginning to disagree with his actions on the Russian convoy. So many lives were lost.' She dropped her eyes. 'He kept on trying to make me change my mind. He said that by leaving him his career might be damaged.' She shuddered. 'Then he came up to my room and tried to force himself on me.' She tossed her head. 'But I managed.'

She did not tell Rowan about his pleading giving way to sudden, frightening violence. He had torn her dress and struck her on the face. He had been out of control, like a stranger, a madman, until he had calmed again just as quickly.

'So, Tim. It's over and done with. I'll never return to him.' She faced him gravely. 'But I'm not offering a bargain. I love you terribly, but I'd never use that to trap you.'

He gripped her arm on the table. *'I love you.'*

She smiled at him sadly. 'Strange thing was, he never once asked if I wanted anyone else.' She shivered, despite the humid atmosphere. 'You see, Tim, he's never *lost* anything in his whole life. I think that was why I married him. I thought I needed someone strong. But underneath all that confidence he's weak. And dangerous.' She looked away. 'So take care, Tim. I know you're leaving tomorrow. He told me how I'll be sorry when I see what he makes of his new appointment.'

'Poor darling.' He touched her skin with his fingers. 'If only . . .'

She nodded. 'Pay the bill, Tim. I'll not let him spoil our evening together. Not for anything.'

In a dark corner of the restaurant Lieutenant Commander James was already half-drunk, and one of the waiters was watching him apprehensively. It always looked bad to bounce a man in uniform, especially an officer.

James saw Rowan and the girl and jerked erect. Chadwick's wife. He could remember her, despite the fog in his brain.

So that was the way of it. The next time Rear Admiral bloody Chadwick made one of his sneering remarks about his German wife, he would tell *him* a few home truths. He stood up and knocked over a jug of water.

The night before sailing and he was here alone. James peered round the room. He would go out and find a woman. The waiter took his money and walked with him to the door.

He had been a waiter in Sydney for a long time. He knew a lot about sailors, no matter what uniform they wore. He thrust a card into James's pocket and said, 'She'll fix you up, mate. Just the job.'

He watched James stagger out on to the street and then shut the door after him.

16

Attack

WHILE the Americans maintained their pressure of attacks on the Japanese-held islands throughout the Pacific, their main fleet and its vast resources prepared for even more ambitious moves.

Like most of his companions, Rowan had not expected their little Air Support Group to be in the front line of every major action, but he had anticipated playing a part on the fringe of things. It did not take long, however, to realise that being part of the Fleet Train for the Allied build-up in the Pacific and Indian Oceans meant just that and nothing more.

As the time dragged on the group covered many hundreds of sea miles, but whenever they anchored or moored alongside a jetty they were barely ashore before they were off again with another convoy. The American base in the Admiralty Islands, up to Hawaii or across to the U.S. mainland and San Diego, wherever the supplies of war were required to be collected or delivered, they obediently went.

Dawn to dusk air patrols with unfailing and boring regularity, the convoys only varying in size to make one day different from the last. The group had been reinforced by the arrival of a Free French cruiser, the 10,000 tons *Spartiate*. Retaken during the Normandy invasion, she was manned by French sailors who had until then been serving in Britain. She was commanded by a spade-bearded dynamo, *Capitaine de Vaisseau* Tristan Perrotto, who was openly discontented with his role of nursing clapped-out supply ships, when in his opinion he should have been hitting at Germany.

Apart from the powerful French newcomer, the group had altered little. The sloops had been reclassified as frigates, and they and the two carriers displayed more rust through their dazzle-paint than when they had arrived in Ceylon.

Hustler spent most of her days ferrying replacement aircraft for the Americans, and her own planes spent more time ashore than afloat. It all made for tension and low morale, and Chadwick's varying moods of impatience did little to ease matters.

The news of the savage fighting in many of the tiny islands, hand-to-hand between Japanese and American marines, where no quarter was given or expected, seemed a world away from the lines of tired ships.

They had seen nothing of the Japanese at all. Russian convoys, U-boats and a dozen other perils they had faced and matched in the past were like history, and to those who had not even experienced them, this unbelievable existence was nothing but torment.

At the end of August the Americans launched the first of their massive carrier strikes against the Phillipines and the islands of Chichi Jima and Iwo Jima, the first of which was only five hundred miles from Tokyo.

When the news of the early successes broke, *Growler* and her consorts were just preparing to leave Brisbane and take another convoy all the two thousand odd miles to the American base at Manus Island in the Admiralty Group. Ammunition and fuel, food and crated Grumman fighter-bombers, which would then be forwarded to the big fleet carriers for immediate use.

The last item was almost the worst part. Every time the group touched land or was within safe signalling distance of high authority Chadwick had asked for the replacement of some of his Seafires with Grumman Martlets. They were more durable and of a match for the Japanese, if and when they met.

Rowan guessed the admiral's desire was to bring his group to the forefront of things and not allow it to be forgotten, himself with it.

But none came, and the normal orders for convoy escort were pinned up in wardroom and messdecks alike prior to sailing.

In Brisbane he found two letters waiting for him from

Honor. They had both been written in Sydney, and the last had explained that she would soon have to return to England.

Rowan was partly glad she was leaving, partly disappointed. Because of the long periods at sea, the uncertainties of which ports they would enter for re-storing, he had never known when he might see her again. But there had always been a slight hope.

But with her husband officially in a sea command, and her own excuse for being in Australia gone, she would have to leave.

He read and re-read her letters, discovering something fresh and different each time. He hoped she would find comfort in his letters too, after the censor had finished with them.

He was in his cabin writing another one to her when he was called to the Operations Room.

The convoy was smaller than usual, and as he paused on the flight deck, squinting, even through his dark glasses, he saw them forming into three lines, the French cruiser's craggy shape taking up her station in the centre lead.

The land was almost gone beyond the horizon, and the parts of the Queensland shore still visible were mere shadows in a thick haze.

He stepped into the Operations Room and found a chair as close to a deckhead fan as he could manage. He nodded to Kitto and James, to Dexter and Broderick, the Air Staff Officer. Even Syms, the globe-headed Met. Officer, was present. 'The old firm', as it was known. They had become so used, or bored with each other that few words were necessary.

But there was a difference, he thought. James looked as gloomy and tensed-up as ever, but Kitto seemed quietly excited, something rare these days. Any sort of hope of a break in monotony was usually dashed before it was properly explored.

Kitto announced, 'The admiral's coming here in a moment. The skipper, too.'

He shot Rowan the briefest glance. *The skipper, too.* Then it was important if Buchan was leaving his bridge before the

249

convoy was properly sorted out.

Muffled, like an angry beast, a Swordfish rattled into life.
The first patrol getting ready. So Commander Jolly would
have to take care of that, too. But the Swordfish crews, unlike
the fighter pilots, had had plenty of exercise, singly and as a
team. They flew-off. They landed-on. Check out local shipping and drifting flotsam. Come home again.

Some of their work had been taken over by the French
Spartiate. She carried three catapult-operated seaplanes, and
used them apparently quite independently of Chadwick's
standing orders on the matter.

The two men were either poles apart or so much alike that it
was hard to imagine them getting on.

Rowan had hardly seen Chadwick, apart from an occasional appearance in the distance. On the flying bridge, his
features expressionless behind dark glasses, or his head and
shoulders above the compass platform. He usually stayed in
his quarters and sent for anyone he wanted to see personally.

He was probably wondering what to do about Honor. If he
suspected Rowan of anything he had given no sign.

At that moment the door opened and Chadwick, Buchan
and the flag lieutenant came in.

Chadwick nodded. 'Sit, gentlemen.'

In crisp shirt and shorts, white stockings and spotless
shoes, he was every inch the senior naval officer.

They sat.

'You may not have noticed,' he swayed slightly as
Growler dug her bulk into the first big roller, 'that *Hustler*
sailed without her usual deck cargo of new planes.'

Rowan had noticed, but his mind had discarded it.

Chadwick continued, 'Because this time we shall have a
proper job of work to do. I said from the start we would show
what we could achieve. The Fleet Train is essential, but lacks
glamour. This job will lack both qualities, but will be a foot in
the door.'

He snapped his fingers. 'Wall chart!'

His flag lieutenant, who seemed to have aged considerably, ran to the bulkhead and uncovered the big coloured
map.

It showed the northern shores of Australia, New Guinea and north-west to the Japanese-occupied territories of Indonesia and Sumatra.

He said calmly, 'The Americans have got their hands full with the Phillipines operation. Our new British Pacific Fleet will not be properly operational until another couple of months, longer, if I know the Admiralty.'

That brought a few smiles.

'So we have been offered the task of leaving our visiting card at certain targets in Sumatra.'

In the following seconds Rowan saw the mixed expressions of the others. Those who would stay and plan. Those who would be flying.

Chadwick nodded gravely. 'The Swordfish torpedo bombers will not of course be suitable.'

Rowan thought he saw Dexter's hands relax across his knees. He must have been thinking of the slow approach through land-based flak.

'But when we get better information I will use the Stringbags for a diversion on local shipping, or something like that.'

It was then he looked directly at Rowan.

'The Seafires from both carriers will be in their separate role of fighter-bombers. Each will carry the full load of one five-hundred-pound bomb. In and out.' He slammed his fists together. 'Bonfire night!'

He nodded to James. 'Anything yet?'

James stood awkwardly and fiddled with his papers.

'The enemy have some fighter cover near their Sumatran ports and refineries, sir. But much of it has been ferried elsewhere to help against the Americans.'

Chadwick gave his old grin. 'You see, gentlemen, it's a game. You wait your chance, and have to eat dirt while you do it, and then . . .'

Rowan saw in those few moments the original Chadwick, the one who had come aboard at Liverpool, so full of confidence and optimism. *The game*.

He found he was touching the little medallion under his shirt.

It was no more a game than the oil tanker in Norway had been.

And this was a different war entirely. In Europe people always had the strange feeling they could get home. Somehow. If the worst happened. And when it did, if you went into the bag, the Germans would abide by some vague rules of an outdated etiquette.

But the Japs. There had been plenty of terrifying stories of what had happened in Malaya and Burma, and anywhere else where their victorious army had hauled down the flags of the colonies powers. Britain, Holland and France. Europeans captured by the enemy, men and women alike, had suffered terribly.

He tore his mind from the sudden apprehension and made himself stare at the big chart.

The sea distances around each overcrowded group of islands were vast, supply lines so stretched, it was no wonder the Americans had found it a hard fight to regain lost ground. It was a war of aircraft carriers, submarines and supply convoys, and then the mad dash from landing craft under the protection of bombardment from sea and sky.

He pictured their two escort carriers, the French cruiser and a handful of frigates. Hardly an armada.

'So, gentlemen, I want a massive effort from everyone. I intend to fly over to *Hustler* today and say my piece to them also.' He raised an eyebrow at Dexter. 'Fix that, will you?'

He picked up his cap from the deck and stared at it thoughtfully.

'If we pull this off successfully, I think we shall carry more weight when our new fleet arrives. That cannot be a bad thing.' He looked at the small group of officers. 'So let's not foul it up, eh?'

They delivered the convoy to the Americans at Manus without incident, and after a long and maddening delay weighed and proceeded.

South and then west into the Indian Ocean. Although the supply ships were convoyed without loss, there had been news of several attacks in the same vicinity from Japanese submarines. Some supply vessels and a destroyer had been sunk and others damaged. It made the war seem real again. And closer.

The ships of the group exercised as much as they could during daylight hours, but even after his visits to the American admiral at the island base Chadwick had said nothing further about his proposed assault on Sumatran targets.

The pilots had discussed it at great length, which was hardly surprising. Views ranged from unlikely to absurd. Bill Ellis had said that even if the Americans and the growing strength of the British naval forces were stretched to the limit it was highly improbable that two hard-worked escort carriers would be used against dangerous objectives on land.

But then, Kitto had argued, paddle-steamers were not designed to be used as minesweepers, nor had millionaires' yachts been thought of as anti-submarine vessels. After five years of war, he was quite prepared to believe anything.

It certainly began to look as if Chadwick had got his way. As the little force steamed on a north-westerly course, leaving the nearest piece of Australia some fifteen hundred miles astern, the idea of a real operation started to take on new dimensions.

Sitting on his steel chair, or pacing in the confines of the bridge, Captain Buchan thought of little else but the pencilled lines and bearings on his charts, which daily showed him how near they were getting to danger. Like the other commanding officers in the group, he knew exactly what had happened when Chadwick had visited the American admiral.

A light fleet carrier under the American admiral's command had been badly damaged by torpedo bombers and would be out of action for some while. She had been part of the group used to draw Japanese ships and aircraft from the really important theatre of war, the Phillipines and Leyte Gulf in particular, which was now obviously the vital hinge in the whole campaign. It was a war of great fleets and capital ships, one which had to be won totally, and which had already shown the superiority of the carrier over the line of battle.

While Chadwick's Air Support Group had languished in

Manus, and had watched the daily bulletins about the mounting battle being fought two thousand miles away, it became equally clear that the Japanese were hitting back with fanatical determination.

And so as reports of heavier fighting and greater losses came in, Chadwick received his orders and his clearance to move.

His group would make a feint attack towards the southern tip of Sumatra, just above the Sunda Strait. It would engage nothing, but any enemy patrols would think differently. Long enough for an American carrier group to launch a real attack on the big oil refinery at Palembang.

Viewed from a distance it was a good plan, Buchan thought. To divide the enemy's resources and then strike a real and damaging blow from the air would have two effects. The Japanese would lose a valuable fuel supply, and the people they were dominating with barbaric force would see that the war was going against their oppressors.

But Buchan was worried about Chadwick. Perhaps the Americans did not understand people like him. The fact was nobody really knew what to do with the Air Support Group. Without a real British Pacific Fleet they had no proper purpose. When that fleet finally arrived the group's usefulness would dissolve entirely. Maybe the U.S. Navy thought it was a good way to keep Chadwick out of their hair. If so, they did not know him at all.

No doubt, thousands of miles away, in a bomb-proof bunker under Whitehall, a staff officer had stuck a little pin on a map to show the group had moved again. Somebody else might remark that it was good to see a bit of Anglo-American co-operation at this stage of the Far East campaign.

Buchan thought it more likely that nobody cared there either.

He was troubled too by the weather. It had worsened in the past twenty-four hours, with several bouts of violent tropical rains which had made such a drumming on the wooden flight deck they had even had to shout to each other on the bridge.

It was now October, usually a safe time for weather. The fierce storms of typhoon force were more prevalent in the

254

early part of the year, but freak upheavals were not unknown. It was hard to accept that the fate of aircraft and men rested on flimsy information and the knowledge of an ex-school-master. Syms, the Met. Officer, was competent enough, but he was no Greenwich expert.

He walked to the flying bridge and looked down at the deck. The rear part was full of fighters, and around them mechanics and members of the handling party moved like worshippers with lifeless idols. It was time Chadwick told them it would be called off, he thought. He had even allowed the gunnery people and armourers to prepare the massive five-hundred-pounders which the Seafires would carry to their prescribed target.

He lifted his glasses and moved them slowly across the ships ahead and around him. They had been joined by four destroyers of the Royal Australian Navy, and with a total absence of helpless merchantmen the group had taken on the appearance of a proper naval task force. But only the *appearance* of one.

A bosun's mate said, 'Call from the Operations Room, sir.' He kept his hand over the telephone. 'It's the admiral, sir.'

'Captain speaking, sir.' He watched the nearest destroyer through the salt-smeared glass. Lifting and plunging. A thoroughbred.

'I've just received a signal from the C. in C.' Chadwick's tone was clipped, unemotional. 'The Americans have had a bit of bother. They underwent a bad battering off Mindanao, a full-scale air attack. Severe losses. It will take them time to regroup.'

Buchan waited, and thought he heard him breathing.

Chadwick said, 'So our operation is on. It's no mock attack. I will inform the group.'

'I see, sir.' Buchan tried to think. 'I'd like to discuss it with you.'

Chadwick sounded impatient. 'This is our real chance. Perhaps the only one we'll get.' He slammed down the telephone.

Buchan walked out into the hot wind again and watched the

activity around the tethered aircraft. From the Americans to the British naval staff in Sydney. Information and confirmation. *Availability*. That was the word they always used at staff college or on a command course. It meant you used what you had. He looked along his ship, at the dip and roll of her flight deck. And they were right here, ready to be used. He felt light-headed, as if he was going to be sick.

Another telephone buzzed. This time it was the Commander (Flying).

Kitto said, 'I've just been told, sir. It sounds like a tall order.'

Buchan looked beyond the bridge. His domain. Kitto had nothing really to tell him. He merely wanted to be reassured.

Buchan replied, 'We'll do what we can.' He hesitated, afraid of showing doubt. 'Have you spoken to the met. officer?'

'There's a chance of more heavy rain squalls ahead of this south-easterly, sir. If it gets bad we'll have to call it off.'

Buchan tightened his jaw. He had said too much already.

'Get your people together. The attack is timed for dawn. Four days from now. You know the rest.'

At the other end of the line Kitto replaced the handset very gently and looked at Rowan.

'It's on, Tim. I know the target. A Jap oil dump. Only recently completed.' He rubbed his chin. 'I was beginning to think it was a mock attack to draw the enemy. It seems I was wrong after all.' He became brisk and businesslike. 'As of now we will have to fly extra patrols. If a Jap recce plane appears it must be clobbered fast.' He banged his hand on the table. 'God, if only we had more fighters and fewer Swordfish, just this once.'

A communications rating looked up from a telephone. 'Signal, sir. More enemy attacks on American shipping south-east of the Phillipines.'

'Thank you.' Kitto looked at Rowan. 'Do you really believe that our little effort can make any difference? To another battle two thousand miles away?' He nodded, answering his own question. 'Out here, things seem to move fast. I suppose it just might.'

A messenger approached Rowan. 'The admiral wants you on the bridge, sir.'

Rowan shrugged. 'Advice, I expect.'

He left the Ops Room and started towards the bridge ladder. This was the first contact. It had to be.

He found Chadwick in the chart house, smoking a cigarette and drinking coffee.

'Sir?'

'Ah, Rowan. How's the leg?'

It took him off guard, as it was intended.

'Fine now, sir.'

'Good.' Chadwick picked a shred of tobacco from his tongue and looked at it thoughtfully. 'Are you happy about the raid?'

Happy? What a question.

'I've been looking at the maps and sketches, sir.'

'That's not what I asked.'

Rowan watched him gravely. 'I think it's risky to send escort carriers to do a job like this one, sir. If you want honesty, I believe that whoever thought of the idea has no notion of what war is about.'

Chadwick smiled. 'When I first flew it was off a platform affair on a battleship. Yet a week back I flew a Swordfish, carrier to carrier, no bother.'

Rowan had heard from the Swordfish pilot how Chadwick had taken over the controls when he had visited *Hustler*. Chadwick had flown within feet of the ship's mast, and had been waved off by the batsman three times before making a landing which had almost shaken the teeth from his head. He had apparently been quite unruffled by the experience and had said breezily, 'Nothing to it.'

Chadwick was saying, 'This ship is a platform for a purpose. To carry bombs to that damned oil dump, or whatever else is decided. Just as Nelson's *Victory* was a platform for her broadsides, and a bloody uncomfortable one to all accounts. Except that the Jack Tars of his Navy didn't come back to coffee and ice cream after half an hour's work, eh?' He was smiling, but there was no mistaking the steel in his tone.

Rowan said, 'I didn't mean we couldn't do it, sir.' He felt angry at his own compliance, but at the same time knew it had to come some day.

'That's good news.'

Chadwick poured another cup of coffee. There were dark patches of sweat on his back and armpits. It did not seem right for Chadwick.

He said offhandedly, 'If we pull it off, I will make certain we all get something better. It will probably be your last operational job . . .' He turned slowly to watch Rowan's reaction. 'No, not in *that* way!'

Rowan said nothing, feeling his anger grow. That had been quite deliberate. To let him think he had already been written off.

The admiral said, 'Transfer to something larger, or a staff job maybe. We'll see.'

'And you, sir?' Rowan could not resist it. 'What will you do?'

Chadwick regarded him calmly. 'My duty.' He smiled. 'In the best way I know.'

Rowan moved slightly towards the door. He needed to be alone. To face and then discard the possibility of being killed.

Chadwick said, 'I understand you met my wife in Sydney?'

'Yes, sir.'

'It was not by chance.'

'If you asked the flag lieutenant—'

'I'm not asking anyone, Rowan. I'm telling *you* to mind your manners.'

'Yes, sir.'

Rowan felt the chart house closing in on him, so that Chadwick seemed to fill it.

'I don't care what she may have said to you, Rowan. And in any case, our private affairs are nothing to do with a junior officer who thinks he knows more than he should.' He was in control again. Entirely relaxed. 'I will decide what is to happen.'

Rowan looked at him impassively, feeling the anger being replaced by contempt.

'I am in love with her, sir. There is no point in pretending.'

Surprisingly, Chadwick remained very still. 'I suspected as much. It's nonsense of course. But if you insist in deluding yourself it will mean a rather sordid picture in the law courts. For her and for you. I don't feel there'll be much *love* left to crow about when it's over.'

Rowan turned away. He had fallen right into it. What she had tried to stave off. No matter what anyone said or suspected about Chadwick, he would appear as the blameless and wronged one when the news got out.

'Of course, if you act with some last fragment of common sense, we might still sort something out.'

'Is that all, sir?' It was unnerving to hear himself. So calm. Flat.

'Yes. Carry on.'

As the door closed behind him Chadwick added harshly, 'And go to bloody hell!'

Rowan walked through the bridge and saw Buchan speaking with Bray, the Navigating Officer.

Buchan said. 'Still no change in the met report. Everything all right?'

'Yes, sir.' He stood there, rocking with the hull, remembering that time when Buchan had sent for him to tell him about his parents.

'What is it?' Buchan shook his head and Bray moved away. 'Something you want to tell me?'

'It's a letter, sir. If anything goes wrong. There's someone I'd like to get it.'

Buchan did not scoff or argue. 'I see. Certainly.'

Rowan added, 'Thank you, sir.' He could not give it to Bill. It might unsettle him. Even if he survived. 'I appreciate it.'

Buchan watched him leave the bridge. He did not know Rowan had anyone to leave a letter for.

Bray's voice swept all else out of his thoughts.

'Signal from *Redshank*, sir! Aircraft in sight to the north-west!'

He nodded, reaching for his glasses. 'Sound off action stations and inform the Ops Room.'

259

He strode out into the harsh glare, searching for the small frigate, which like a pointer led the little fleet towards the horizon. Klaxons and bells echoed throughout the ship, while across the water he heard the blare of a bugle as the French cruiser went to quarters.

Below the island he saw the deck handling party sprinting to the stand-by flight of Seafires, the gun muzzles on the sponsons below the flight deck training outboard.

'The commander reports ship at action stations, sir.'

Crump—crump—crump. The distant thud of anti-aircraft fire rebounded against the bridge plating.

His eyes watered as he watched the tiny dots in the sky as the leading frigate and then some of the other escorts joined in.

It could not have happened at a worse time. The wind was fairly strong and following the ships from the south-east.

He waited as Bray hurried back from the compass.

'Ready, sir.'

'Make the signal, then bring her about.'

He ignored the clatter of the lamp, the replying stabs of light from two of the destroyers as they waited to follow *Growler*'s steep turn into the wind.

'Hard a-port!'

Buchan reached out to steady himself as the order was acknowledged by the wheelhouse.

The waiting game was over.

17

Odds on Survival

ROWAN held his back pressed against the steel bulkhead as he watched the intent figures around the Operations Room. Blue Flight had been airborne for ten minutes, and the reports were coming in about the enemy. A twin-engined reconnaissance bomber.

It had probably sent back a signal to its base already, although it was a long way out from land.

He heard the muted voices of the pilots in the Ready Room as they waited to see if there was to be a full 'Scramble'. He had done it often enough, and remembered those first times. Trying to appear relaxed. That you didn't care.

He also recognised Kitto's voice on the intercom. Curt, matter of fact.

The flight was at eighteen thousand feet and in sight of the recce plane. There was a rush of static across the speaker, and he heard Bill exclaim, 'Watch for the rear gunner!' Then the speaker went dead again.

Rowan watched James and Broderick with their communications ratings. They saw it from a different angle. Rowan was up there with the pilots. His stomach muscles ached, and he realised he was holding them in as if he was actually involved.

James remarked, 'That Jap pilot was too slow off the mark. He went after one of the Frenchman's seaplanes and shot it down. He should have buzzed-off when he had the chance.'

Rowan looked at him grimly, recalling the German seaplane plunging into the waves, the Walrus coming to rescue him, all the other times he had seen those maddening but essential amphibians.

The petty officer with the headphones snapped, 'They've

got it!' He leaned forward, his face lined as he added. 'One of ours has been hit, sir!'

Rowan asked sharply, 'Who is it?'

The P.O. looked at him. 'B for Baker, sir.'

Rowan turned and walked through the Ready Room. He made his way to the bridge and to Kitto's little platform. Together they peered astern, above the ships which were still steering on an opposite course.

There was a long stain across the sky where the recce plane had plummeted towards the sea. Much lower, balanced it appeared on the upperworks of the French cruiser, was another smoke trail. Then came a bright orange flash, but no sound reached the *Growler* from that range as the fighter hit the water. There was no parachute.

He watched the next patrol being ranged on the deck, and waited until the tannoy speaker announced the return of Bill's flight.

Later, at the de-briefing, as *Growler* put on the revolutions to catch up with her consorts, Bill said heavily, 'I fired a long burst into the Jap, and he started to dive. Lord Algy took a pass across his quarter. Like he always did. The rear gunner must have been sitting there waiting for him, despite the fact his own aircraft was on fire and going down.'

'Did he try to get out?'

Bill looked at him, his eyes red from strain. 'He sort of waved to me. Then his head went forward. The flames did the rest.'

That night as the darkened ships pushed through a sea lashed into white froth by another torrential downpour, Rowan prowled about the hangar deck and deserted flats. He could not sleep, he knew it without even trying.

The rain reminded him of the house in Hampshire. So far away, and yet so clear in his mind and thoughts. Perhaps she was already there. With other wounded or shocked officers to comfort. He rejected it, knowing theirs was something they could not break, just as it was a bond they had not expected or prepared against.

If only he had been able to stop himself from telling Chadwick. By defending her he had made it more likely he

262

would never see her again.

It had been arranged that *Hustler*'s fighter-bombers would go in first, then *Growler*'s as a second wave. If the enemy had heard nothing from their recce pilot, they would be ready enough by the time the last attack was started.

He looked at Jonah Too's smooth shape glinting beneath an inspection light, her wings folded at the tips, the other planes crowded around her as if for company.

Rowan had shot down several aircraft and strafed more enemy ships than he could remember. But always over the sea, or right alongside it. This target was inland, a low-level bombing attack. In and out. *Bonfire night*, Chadwick had said. He had never done anything like it before, except across the bombing ranges and on a grounded wreck near the Goodwin Sands.

He thought of those who would be with him. Apart from Bill, the rest were as green as grass. Creswell, despite his second stripe and his luck, was over-confident and lacked proper experience.

Rowan looked at Bill's plane, a rugby ball painted on it with a glass of beer balanced on the top.

He walked towards the next ladder. Football and beer. At least Bill had done something before the war.

Up in the Operations Room the duty watch was lolling with weariness in the imprisoned air. Around them the plots ticked and whirred, and from a voicepipe Rowan heard the faint stammer of morse from the W/T office.

He glanced at the illuminated chart, seeing the scimitar shape of Java curving up towards the strait which separated it from Sumatra. Over there, Japanese soldiers were guarding roads and gun-sites, or watching the skies. He knew it was so, but it was hard to accept that there was any real life beyond this ship and the men around him.

High above Rowan's head, on his steel chair, Buchan sat with his hands in his pockets and watched the black glass of the screen directly in front of him. He listened to the relentless rain, to it sluicing off the bridge and across the Oerlikon gunners below.

Tomorrow it might all be over. The enemy could launch an

air attack on the group and that would show they knew about it. There would be little point in pushing on after that. He reached out with one foot and touched the rough metal below the clearview screen. Get the old girl out of it. To a war she understood and had been built for.

He heard Commander Jolly come out of the chartroom and cross to his side. He would most likely get a ship of his own after this.

Jolly said, 'All quiet, sir. I passed the word to go to action stations at first light.'

'Good. Better to be safe.'

In his own quarters Rear Admiral Chadwick walked back and forth across the carpet, a glass of brandy in one hand. Uphill and down again as the deck lifted and dipped beneath him.

He thought of his wife, how she had looked at him when he had hit her and torn open her dress. He had never really wanted her like that before. But at that moment he had almost raped her. The thought of her being with Rowan, when he had never even imagined such a thing could occur, was still beyond his understanding.

But it was strange how events dropped into a pattern, he thought. At one time he had imagined that everything was coming apart. Now, he was about to put a stamp on his name that nobody, no matter how high up, could ignore. She would bloody well beg and crawl to him then.

He returned to the brandy.

It might prove interesting.

The enemy did not come and find them the next day, nor the ones which followed. In the rest of the world, and in the Pacific in particular, a naval war was reaching a new peak of ferocity. But on the fourth dawn, as the rain retreated from the slow-moving ships, and the wind dropped to a whisper, it was as if everything and everyone else had already died.

Buchan watched the long, blood-red smear along the eastern horizon, and then the nearest gun-mounting as the droplets of rain on the twin muzzles glinted very faintly to betray the first light. It was extremely quiet, and at slow speed he could barely feel the beat of Laird's great propeller.

Below, it would all be working smoothly. Pilots briefed, plans and maps examined in total silence.

On deck, still hidden in darkness, the aircraft had already been assembled and were waiting, their noses pointing at the sky. The armourers had done their work, and the big bombs were hung one to a plane. Like obscene fruit.

Across the water he saw the nearest ships as black shadows, although on the Frenchman's superstructure two scuttles had caught the dawn light and shone like a pair of angry red eyes.

Buchan touched his breast pocket to make sure it was tightly buttoned. His oilskin pouch was safe if he had to swim for it. He also had Rowan's letter there. Now he knew a lot more about him, and Chadwick, for he had read the woman's name on the envelope.

He had seen her a couple of times ashore. A very attractive girl. He wished now he had had time to speak to her. But his wife had kept him away because of Chadwick.

'Commander (Flying) reports he is ready, sir.'

'Very well.'

Buchan lifted his glasses and watched *Hustler*'s blunt silhouette. Any moment now and the first strike would be taking-off.

He heard Chadwick speaking to Bray as he came on to the bridge.

The admiral smelt of after-shave lotion and fresh coffee, and in the semi-darkness his shirt and shorts were like snow.

'Two minutes, sir.' Bray sounded hushed. Awed.

Chadwick's palms rasped together. 'Good show. We'll give those Nips something to squeak about!'

'*One* minute, sir!'

Buchan tried not to watch *Hustler*'s flight deck, and to concentrate on his own ship. On all the wires and pipes which connected him to every flat and compartment, each gun and piece of machinery throughout the fat hull.

'There they go, sir! First one is taking off *now*.'

Buchan said nothing, but watched the little spark of exhaust as the fighter climbed steeply away from the carrier, banking over and holding the dawn light like blood. Then the sound reached him, the high-pitched whine, rising to a throaty roar as the next and the next took off.

It seemed no time before the report came, 'Squadron airborne, sir.'

He held out his hand for the telephone. One of the wires which joined him to his command.

He heard Kitto's voice. As if he had been holding the handset already.

'Captain here. It's all yours. Tell them, good luck.'

Behind his back Chadwick smiled slightly in the gloom. At Buchan's ponderous sentimentality. His lack of words.

But at this particular moment, at their little pencilled cross on the chart, he was glad Buchan was here, in command. Men with flair and ideas were unreliable at such times. He smiled again. Buchan had neither, which made him an excellent subordinate. As he always had been, and would remain.

'*Ready*, sir!' Bray's voice made him start.

Buchan folded his arms. 'Affirmative.'

A few minutes later Jonah Too was in the air.

Rowan settled himself firmly in the cockpit and went through his checks again until he was satisfied. He felt like a machine as he watched the rest of *Growler*'s squadron working into position, into pairs, as he had made them practice again and again until they had become sick of it and of him.

He glanced at his compass and tried to prune all unnecessary details of the raid from his mind. In the briefing session with Kitto and James, with Broderick filling in gaps when they arose, the raid seemed an enormous operation. But then it was often like that. When it was all boiled down it was just you and what you recognised through the racing prop.

He saw the crimson glow moving across his hands as he brought the Seafire round to the north-east. He imagined Jonah Too felt heavier with her big bomb under her belly. That and the fuel tanks topped up to the limit were best not thought about. Rowan had always dreaded fire since being shot down that first time. The freezing water across his smouldering flying suit had been like a precious balm, even though it would have killed just as mercilessly given the chance.

Fifteen thousand feet already. He watched the sea spread away into darkness on one hand and a rising dawn on the other. Deep, deep blue with occasional flurries of white. The ships had vanished astern, and of the land there was no sign.

He pictured the Seafires as an onlooker might see them, if it were possible. Himself, Bill and Frank Creswell, each with a young Number Two to guard his tail and keep a wary eye open for enemy scouts.

He wondered if Bill was thinking about Nichols, his Number Two, the pilot whose hasty judgement had done for Nick Rolston.

One Seafire remained aboard the carrier, having developed mechanical trouble within an hour of take-off. He could well imagine the frustration and anger in the hangar deck. Some relief too on the new pilot's part, if he was honest enough to admit it.

It was much brighter now, and the sea's face looked fresh and inviting. He shifted against his parachute and harness, feeling the drag of his clothes, the touch of the silver medallion under his shirt. The thought of lying on his back in the water and just drifting made him itch all over.

'Hello, *Jonah*, this is *Katie*.'

Rowan craned his head round to the extreme right of the undulating line. That was Archer, another of the replacements.

He was speaking very excitedly over the intercom. 'Ship on the starboard bow!'

Rowan saw it even as he spoke. A small coaster by the look of her dim outline, but too far out for comfort. Probably an air observation vessel of sorts. There was no time to find out.

'Disregard. But keep a good lookout to starboard. They might come out of the sun.'

He heard Bill laugh. 'What sun?'

Then they fell silent again, concentrating more after sighting the lonely ship. Like gulls, ships meant land.

Rowan checked the time. Any second now.

He felt a bead of sweat run down behind his goggles. There

it was, a brown and green elbow of land. It was flashing towards them now, with the inshore currents as clearly etched as if they had been painted on the sea. Several boats, some anchored, others moving slowly and aimlessly. A faster, smaller one was cutting a sharp white line between them, a patrol probably, he thought.

The wires would be humming now. Enemy planes. How many? What bearing?

He tried to estimate if *Hustler*'s squadron had already finished their part. They had flown in further north, and would retrace their course without making contact at this stage. If they had survived.

Their orders were to regroup and circle at a good height where they could supply extra cover when *Growler*'s aircraft got out.

He blinked rapidly as the sea vanished beneath his wings. It was like steam heat below him, and it was difficult to see much more than a green blur.

'Smoke, dead ahead!' That was Bill, very calm and sure of himself.

Rowan acknowledged and squinted through the perspex, hating the glare on the cockpit as the sunlight gained strength and power.

He saw the smoke. It looked solid. Unmoving. A great brown mass standing out of the land. He licked his lips. Like a vast, inhuman brain.

'Line astern!'

He checked the bomb-release switch, wondering if it would fail at the last moment.

This was it. He recognised a thin silver thread. The small river used by barges for the fuel dump. James was usually right about the details. Pity he didn't have a better temper.

He clenched and unclenched his hands. They were slippery with sweat, and his heart was going like a trip-hammer.

It was like being entirely alone and flying headlong towards that great brown cloud. He could see that it was in fact much larger and rising all the time. As if it was unbreakable, that he would eventually shiver Jonah Too to fragments against it.

Control yourself, you maniac!

He glanced quickly in his mirror, seeing the others stretching out behind him in a ragged line. It was far worse for them.

He flinched and took a firm grip on the stick. Here was the flak, though God alone knew where it was coming from. Patches of shellbursts, a dozen or so in each group, drifted across the greenery, and he thought he heard the sharp crack of more explosions astern.

He recognised the hill. Slab-sided, as if the rest had been hacked away by a giant axe. The smoke was rising beyond it. That was where the dump had been built, almost mid-way between the big refinery in Palembang and Batavia in Java to the south-east.

The aircraft rocked violently and lifted her nose as more shells exploded directly ahead. It was time to begin. To get it over.

'Going down!'

He felt his harness drag at him and watched with fixed fascination the land taking shape and substance through the prop's glittering arc.

There was local flak from the hill. He held his breath as lines of bright tracer cut past to port, hosing from side to side as the invisible gunners tried to fix the angle of his dive.

Faster and faster, the wind rising to match the Merlin's roar as they zoomed towards the lopsided crest. He saw scattered buildings, huts, and then a blackened scar between some trees and a few blazing pieces of a crashed aircraft. One of *Hustler*'s. He could even see where its bomb had burst, making a savage scar to the edge of the crest itself.

He stiffened as the oil dump rose to meet him like a model on display. There were several big craters and a lot of fire. But most of the dome-shaped tanks were still intact. One even had a gun position right beside it, and he could see the tracer coming round, needle-sharp as it loomed above the cockpit in a clattering, jarring procession of searing lights.

He watched the target, shutting out everything but the central tank.

Rowan heard someone shout wildly, 'Fighters! Twelve o'clock!' But he shut even that outside himself. The enemy fighters were above somewhere. There was nothing but light flak between him and that tank. The heavier guns were on the hillside, or down by the little river, and could not be depressed on to the diving fighters. Even the impressive Japs could not think of everything.

He pressed the release and felt the cockpit lift violently as if blown by a current of hot air.

Bullets were hitting below the engine, but Rowan concentrated on pulling out of the dive. It was so hard he could feel the pressure on his eyes, as if they could be forced back into his skull.

Round, turning steeply away from that hill, hearing the dull roar of the bomb exploding into the smoke, and another following close behind as the next pilot released his load.

There was a pencil-shaped barge on the river, right against the bank, and all but hidden by trees and a tattered camoulage net.

Jonah Too steadied and went into a shallower, less demanding dive. Rowan was almost relaxed as he pressed the firing button and watched the shells and bullets ripping down branches and fronds until they crossed the barge and turned it and the river into a torrent of fire.

He heard Bill snap, 'Pull up, *pull up*, John!'

While Rowan climbed in a tight semi-circle towards the dump he saw a Seafire diving headlong towards the one open space. The Japs must have had it cleared for transport or future fuel tanks.

He watched, sickened, as the aircraft made an awkward belly-landing and ploughed across the bare earth like a crazy thing. It was John Nichol. He must have taken some tracer as he released his bomb. Rowan could see him staggering and then falling from the cockpit, getting out before the Seafire brewed-up.

Surprisingly, it did not burst into flames. Better if it had, Rowan thought, as he saw some tiny, khaki-clad figures running to encircle the dazed and no doubt terrified Nichols.

The whole dump area was burning fiercely, and even the surrounding trees were well alight. Upended vehicles, blasted buildings, it seemed incredible that such a small

270

attack could achieve so much. He tried not to think of what they would do to Nichols before they let him die.

He shouted over the intercom, 'Watch for those fighters! We're getting out!'

Creswell saw them first. He sounded strained beyond the limit.

'Three o'clock high!'

Rowan blinked in the glare. They were at about twenty thousand feet, flying round in a large, protective circle. It was a good tactic. If the A.A. guns could not catch them as they rose above the hillside, the fighters would be in the best position to cut them off. There were eight or nine of them.

The cockpit shuddered as small shell splinters fanned out on either beam. One cracked into the fuselage, and he felt his muscles tightening as he anticipated fire.

He opened the throttle, thinking of nothing but the glittering circle of midget fighters against the empty sky.

Why couldn't there be heavy rain and cloud now that they needed it?

'Echelon starboard!' He knew they were fanning out on his right without looking for them. 'We'll have to break up that bunch, Bill!'

'Yeh.' He pictured Bill, filling his cockpit. 'Otherwise they'll take us singly.'

Crump . . . crump . . . crump. The flak was getting nearer, more concentrated.

The Japanese fighter formation started to break up even before *Growler*'s aircraft were anywhere near enough.

The human element again. What Chadwick would describe as the 'game'.

It was hard to watch their fuel dump being blown up and do nothing.

Rowan picked out one machine and held it in his sights. He could see the pilot pulling round, his leather helmet very stark in the sunlight. He let the red sun on the fuselage drift across the sights and then poured a four-second burst into it.

The fighter, a stubby-nosed Zero, fell away on to its back, turning round and round as it corkscrewed towards the burning fuel dump. Rowan did not linger to watch it crash, but pulled away sharply to starboard, marking down another fighter which was twisting and turning across Creswell's quarter. Again, he felt totally nerveless. An automaton. Three hundred yards. Easy. *Fire*.

Tracers darted above the other fighter's cockpit, then dipped as Rowan pushed the stick forward and ripped the rear of it into a whirling mass of torn streamers. But the pilot was fighting to free himself from Rowan's attack, going into a steep climb, then plunging sharply to port while Rowan chased him round.

Another long burst, the tracers converging along the Zero's spine and exploding into the cockpit and the engine beyond. He saw the pilot's arm beating at the side, perhaps trying to free himself. Then the Zero exploded and threw smoking fragments, some human, into the path of two dog-fighting aircraft.

Rowan blinked again to clear his vision. He was icy-cold and baking hot all at once, and he felt despair crowding in as another fighter, with *Growler*'s markings on it, dived steeply past him, already alight, and a Zero following it down, speeding its end with machine gun and cannon fire.

Sub-Lieutenant Maple, nineteen years old, who had volunteered for submarines but had been rejected as unsuitable, managed to free himself from the shattered Seafire and was plucked from it by his parachute within seconds of it exploding in the air.

Rowan had not got to know Maple very well, but he seemed pleasant enough.

He watched him adjusting to the pull and drift of his parachute, and then kick frantically as the Zero flew past him, guns blazing, ripping the parachute into holes. Maple too was cut to ribbons before he dropped towards the trees like a stone.

'*Behind you, Tim!*'

Rowan gasped and glanced quickly at his mirror, seeing the Zero swimming through it, guns hammering. He pulled Jonah Too round savagely, hearing the engine falter before it recovered. He had felt some of the bullets hitting him, and when he looked in the mirror he saw the Zero rising above him once more. Something plucked at his right sleeve, like a hesitant hand, and he saw with horror that a bullet had opened up the leather with the precision of a scalpel.

Brrrrrrrrrrrrr! Brrrrrrrrrrrrr! That was a different sound, and he caught sight of Bill flashing across his front, his own Seafire punctured like a pepper-pot.

Jonah Too quivered to a dull explosion, and Rowan knew Bill had put down his pursuer. It had been a close thing.

'Tallyho!'

Rowan tugged away his goggles and wiped his streaming eyes as three more Seafires dived into the fight. Beyond them he could see writhing surf and dark blue ocean. *Hustler*'s fighters, the three which had survived, were joining the battle.

'Break off! Return to base!'

There was no point in prolonging it. The Zeros had a longer range and would soon be reinforced. Better to get away now while they were still confused by *Hustler*'s support.

Zigzagging through ground flak and isolated shellbursts, the oil-streaked and battered survivors headed out to sea. The fast patrol boat was still there, but not for long. Bill went into a dive and raked it from bow to stern, and before his shadow left the water the boat burst into flames, the small crew leaping overboard and swimming towards the fishermen they had been guarding.

And then the land was hidden by the wings, with the ocean shining and empty before them.

'Everyone okay?'

Rowan had seen that *Hustler*'s leader was not amongst the survivors. It was up to him to rouse their morale for the flight back. This was the worst part in some ways. You expected to be killed. Then later, when you were getting the hell out of it, everything came crowding in on you. Dead friends, memory of fear and real terror. Respect for the unknown enemy. Calm giving way to hatred as he tried to get you before you got him.

He listened to their acknowledgements, their voices brittle and hoarse.

Then Bill asked, 'How is your fuel?'

Rowan stared across at him and then at the gauge. *He had been hit badly.*

Without being actually wounded, you often imagined all was well. It was surprising how calm he felt. He had not escaped after all. It was just as he had expected, only delayed to prolong the shock.

Even his voice sounded unemotional. 'I'll not make it, Bill.' He looked across at Bill's blurred outline. 'Unless you've got a drop to pass over?' It was unbelievable that he could make such a stupid joke. He could guess what it was doing to Bill. How he would have felt.

He imagined the other pilots listening in. Feeling for him. But already writing him off. He felt for the revolver he had worn since coming to these waters. Japs or sharks, he would see that neither took him alive.

Bill said, 'Are you *sure*?' He was moving nearer. 'There's always a chance, Tim.' He was almost pleading.

'Keep your eyes open, Bill. The bastards have pulled away. It doesn't mean they'll not come popping out of the blue again.' In an unspoken answer he added, *I don't want to die, Bill. I really don't. Not now of all times.*

He remembered the nightmare, when he had cried out and she had come to him. He had been dreaming then of a plane on his tail. Had felt the slogging impact of steel. But for Bill it would actually have happened back there above the burning trees.

If she had not come to him, would anything further have happened? The question was already answered. They had been lost to each other from the beginning without knowing it.

Rowan felt the bitterness prick his eyes like wood-smoke. Now Chadwick would get everything. Congratulations and glory, and maybe her, too. And who could blame her? If Chadwick kept his threat, she would have lost even security.

Jonah Too coughed and roared brokenly, and her nose dropped before coming under command again. In those short seconds Rowan saw death. By rights he should be in the drink

274

already. The gauge showed 'empty'. *Done for*.

Without realising it he said aloud, 'Won't be long, Bill.'

Bill replied instantly, 'Hold on, old son. I'm no bloody good without you.'

Rowan listened to the engine's drone, waiting for it to stop altogether. He calculated the time needed to get clear. Whether it would be quicker to take her straight down and let the sea finish the job for him.

He wondered what Chadwick would say as the remaining aircraft returned to their carriers. He would feel bound to say something, if only for his own satisfaction.

If the group was nearer Rowan would have opened radio contact, but with enemy bases so close it would merely extend his own fate to the rest of them. The French cruiser had a seaplane. It could be flown-off to pick him out of the water before the sharks got him. *Could, might, if*.

The cockpit quivered and continued to shake. Perhaps the undercarriage was coming adrift. It didn't make any difference now.

It was how Honor would get the news that really made him ache. The letter written before he had flown-off would only add to the agony, and he wished he had not given it to Buchan. Better just a word from a good friend. He glanced over at Bill's machine and waved to him. The action was automatic. Probably the same as Lord Algy when he had bought it.

Bill exclaimed, 'Tim! I can see the group, for Christ's sake! Tell me you can, too!'

Rowan pulled against his harness and stared through the oil-smeared perspex. He could see bright gashes around the engine, and a piece of torn metal standing out and flapping in the airstream.

Then he saw the ships. Very tiny and balanced on the glittering horizon like beetles.

He looked at his altimeter and at the sun, then at his watch. It was impossible. They should be standing much further out. Chadwick had risked everything as it was to bring unarmoured carriers so close to danger.

Bill yelled, 'Can you *do* it, Tim?'

He said between his teeth, 'I don't know what I'm flying on, but I'll have a go.'

He eased back the stick very gently, feeling the cockpit shake and buck in protest. She was falling apart under him. But he might manage a shallow climb. Another two thousand feet. It would at least carry him within possible pick-up range.

Rowan realised he was humming into his oxygen mask and glanced over again at the other fighter.

He said, 'Don't look at *me*, Bill. Watch your tail.'

Bill sounded unsteady. Emotional. 'Don't give me orders. I'm bigger than you.'

Creswell chimed in. 'Uglier anyway.'

The trio climbed so slowly and painfully that it took an age for *Hustler*'s aircraft to vanish below them. And then all at once they were there. Real ships with individual shape and personality.

'This is *Jonah Too*. Permission to land-on.' He hesitated, remembering all those times when he had heard others say it. *'Emergency.'*

'Affirmative.' A pause. 'You've nothing to land with.'

Rowan looked at the landing gear release. He did not want to test it just yet, its drag might cost him those last precious miles. Now there was no point in bothering. He pictured the bustle, the preparations to receive him. It might take their minds off the shock of seeing so few aircraft returning.

He thought suddenly of the crashed Seafire, the pilot's angry stare, the undignified way his boots had stuck out as they had hauled his corpse away for disposal.

So perhaps *this* was the moment after all. Right at Chadwick's feet, like the dog in *Beau Geste*.

He felt for the medallion and pressed it tightly. *Here goes*.

18

Divine Wind

BUCHAN resisted the temptation to leave the bridge and go to the chart house again. So soon after the dawn had shown itself in the sky, and the fighters had flown-off on their mission, yet it was already hot and oppressive. Around him the bridge superstructure rattled and groaned as *Growler* maintained her maximum revolutions, regardless of Laird's reminders of what had happened in the Arctic when Chadwick had insisted on full speed for long duration.

Buchan had almost accepted that the raid on the oil dump had a chance of success, if only because of the lack of enemy aircraft in this area, when Chadwick had exploded his new bombshell on the bridge.

It had started with a signal decoded in the Operations Room, from the C. in C's office, with all the latest intelligence about known enemy shipping movements. A Japanese troop convoy was said to have left Singapore several days back, and would be passing through the Sunda Strait on passage to ports in Java the previous night.

Chadwick had shouted down all opposition immediately. 'We'll fly-off the Swordfish boys directly. The group will alter course to the nearest interception point at once.' He had looked at Buchan confidently. 'I'm doing Rowan and his squadron a favour at the same time. Less distance to fly home, eh?' It had apparently amused him.

A quick glance abeam told Buchan that all the ships were keeping station, the destroyers and frigates smashing through the endless procession of shallow troughs, the carriers and the French cruiser riding above it all like Goliaths.

He moved restlessly in his chair, thinking of the next signal which had been received from the American admiral.

The U.S. carrier attack on Palembang had been cancelled. Due to severe losses unexpectedly incurred at Leyte, all available warships, and many others which in fact could not be spared, would be sent to reinforce the embattled fleets around the Phillipines forthwith.

The reports gave just the bare facts, but it seemed that the Japanese were fighting back every inch of the way, and there was some mention of suicide attacks on the larger ships by fighter-bombers. It was more likely to be accidental, Buchan told himself. But as the little group steamed at full revolutions nearer and nearer to the enemy-controlled Sumatra and Java it was one more worry to cope with.

All Chadwick had commented was, 'Pity *I* wasn't allowed to have a crack at the main oil refinery!' He had scoffed, 'Honestly, they get in a proper flap about nothing!'

Buchan heard Chadwick re-entering the bridge and braced himself.

The admiral snapped, 'Any new reports from anyone?'

'None yet, sir.'

Buchan tried not to show his apprehension. As he had watched Rowan and the others vanish into the crimson sky, and then shortly afterwards the Swordfish torpedo-bombers, he had sensed disaster for them. Now, with the news of the Americans cancelling their raid, the realisation that the enemy might now be able to use ships and aircraft more freely in the Indian Ocean became more of a reality.

Chadwick must be out of his mind. But by flying-off the remainder of his serviceable aircraft he had played a trump card. Nobody could even suggest that he had ordered the group out of the area and to abandon the aircraft to crash in the sea.

A rating said in a hushed tone, 'From the Ops Room, sir.' He was looking at the admiral.

Chadwick snatched the telephone, his eyes on the nearest destroyer. 'Yes. Is that you, James? I see.' He bit his lip. 'It's confirmed, you say?'

Buchan watched him. Wondering.

The yeoman, who was holding another handset, said sharply, 'Aircraft returning, sir.'

As if to back up his announcement the tannoy blared, 'D'you hear there! D'you hear there! Stand by to receive aircraft!'

Buchan looked at the yeoman. Thank God for that. The first part was over.

'Make to escorts, Yeoman. Stand by to alter course.'

He realised Chadwick was beside him. 'The fighters are back, sir.'

'Yes, I heard.' He sounded dull. 'That fool James has decoded another signal from the Yanks. They say the Jap troop convoy was attacked last night by their submarines in the Java Sea. It turned back.' He looked at Buchan's grim face. 'So that's that. We'll just have to wait for Dexter to find out for himself and return to us with his Swordfish.' He glanced at the bridge clock. 'Not too long, I'd say.'

Buchan watched him, hating him. All because of his greed for glory. The fighter-bomber raid had been hare-brained enough. But to keep pushing, to go for that damned convoy even after the Americans had said they were not able to supply pressure against Palembang was sheer stupidity. A madness born out of conceit.

Bray called, 'Only three Seafires, sir. The remainder are circling *Hustler*.'

Buchan picked up Kitto's telephone. 'Captain here. What's the news?'

Kitto sounded tense. 'Just three for us, sir. And Rowan's lost most of his undercarriage. I've done all I can. He'll try a bellyflop.'

A klaxon squawked, and without looking Buchan could picture the fire-fighters and medical team watching the sky.

He said, 'Very well. I'm turning into the wind now.' He nodded to Bray. 'Execute, Pilot.'

Someone said, 'I can see it! Poor bastard!'

Buchan snapped, 'Enough of that!' To Chadwick he added, 'I hope it was all worthwhile, sir.'

For once Chadwick had no quick answer. He too was watching the Seafire's dark silhouette as it started to turn in a wide arc across the stern. He could hear the intermittent bang of its engine, and even without binoculars could see the

279

damage to fuselage and wings.

'*Sir!*' It was de Courcy, his flag lieutenant. '*Spartiate* had signalled that her seaplane has sighted hostile aircraft to the north of us, sir!' He stared at the admiral as if stunned by the enormity of his own announcement.

Buchan heard it all, the buzz of voices from the Operations Room voicepipes and telephones, the murmur of landing instructions over the bridge speaker.

He had known a captain of many years experience, who before the war had been suddenly confronted by a giant iceberg which had come out of the night like a cliff. All his years of experience and training, his responsibility to ship and men, had been locked in time. He had been unable to move or react, could do nothing to prevent disaster. In fact, a subordinate had jumped in to give the necessary orders and had saved the ship. The captain had been doomed from that instant.

It was how Buchan felt. His ship, all the various men throughout her vibrating hull, were being carried relentlessly into oblivion, and he could do nothing to prevent it.

'W/T report that the Swordfish squadron are in contact, sir. Operation cancelled. No enemy convoy discovered.' The man looked uncomfortable at having to tell what everyone in earshot already knew, and which the only ones still in ignorance were the returning Swordfish crews.

'Order them to stand off while we get the fighters aboard.' Buchan was amazed at his own unruffled voice. 'Tell the gunnery officer to prepare to repel aircraft at all levels. As soon as the damaged fighter is aboard I want every aircraft refuelled and ammunitioned at once.'

'Swordfish too, sir?'

Buchan looked at Chadwick, expecting him to answer. When he said nothing, he added, 'Yes. We're so far from help that we'll have to fight with every damn thing we've got.'

The tannoy rattled, 'Stand by to receive one damaged aircraft. Fire and stretcher parties at the ready!'

He thought of the letter in his oilskin pouch and then he looked at Chadwick again.

He slid off the chair and said harshly, 'I'll take over the con, Pilot. This one's important.'

Rowan watched the carrier sliding across his port wingtip as he made a wide arc towards *Growler*'s frothing wake. Everyone was waiting for him, but he could still find time to notice that the guns were all at immediate readiness along the sponsons, and on the escorting ships nearby. That meant trouble. He squinted in the reflected glare from the water and concentrated everything on the carrier's bulky shape.

If the engine cut now he might still get out, and be picked up by an escort. He bit his lip, seeing the ship levelling off, becoming real again. Flaps were down, as far as he could tell, but most of the switches and gauges appeared to be broken or unreliable.

'God Almighty!' He clung to the stick, watching the ship shooting up to meet him at an incredible speed. 'Down, *down*, old girl!' He groped for the throttle and was almost knocked senseless as the fighter smashed on to the deck, grinding across the lowered arrester wires and careering on towards the island. He was gasping with each violent shock, with each wild swerve and lurch. The engine was silent, the prop twisted like a giant whisk.

He saw the island loom over him, and found time to notice a seaman running from the point of impact waving his arms in the air.

Jonah Too still would not stop. The starboard wing was ripped off, and as the propeller boss smashed into steel plate with the force of a battering ram, Rowan thought his head would go straight through the gunsight.

The next moments were confused and frightening. His vision was shut off by foam from the extinguishers, and he could hear feet scraping above him, then feel hands clawing at his harness and shoulders as if at any second the Seafire was going to explode.

He was halfway between blackout and shock, and allowed himself to be carried like a corpse into the gloom of the bridge structure.

As his nerves recovered from the impact and accepted the

realisation he was still alive, other sounds crowded in on him. The bark of orders and clatter of ammunition hoists, the urgent roar of an engine as another fighter landed-on, regardless of Jonah Too's scattered entrails.

The P.M.O. was ripping open his flying suit and snapped, 'Busy day, Tim. The Japs are coming our way. The sky's full of them apparently. We're still getting our aircraft back.' He looked at Rowan impassively. 'I'm afraid you've broken your leg. Still, it could have been worse.'

Rowan laid back and stared at the deckhead. He thought of the smashed fighter on the hillside, and the one in the clearing, the hurrying Japanese soldiers. Both carriers had lost half their aircraft. *It could have been worse.*

Bill stooped over him, his face blotchy with sweat and heat. 'That was *fine*, Tim.' He glanced at Minchin. 'Just the leg?' He stood up and looked round. 'Got to be off, Tim. We're going up again.'

'What?' Rowan tried to struggle but felt the pain for the first time. He said, 'Strap the leg, for God's sake.'

Minchin was preparing to leave the job to his S.B.A. 'Anything else?'

'Yes. Have me carried to the bridge, Doc. I'll give Dymock a hand.'

He felt his mouth go dry as the first guns in the group began to fire. The *Spartiate*'s heavy armament. Then the destroyers joined in with a sharper, more vicious chorus.

He nearly fainted again as he was bundled roughly up the several ladders to the bridge.

Kitto regarded him thoughtfully. 'I thought you might arrive.' He smiled. 'The Swordfish are landing-on now. We'll talk later.'

He returned to his intercom, and Rowan had time to see the attackers as they approached the rear of the group in two separate waves. Medium bombers and fighter-bombers. He stared at the growing pattern of shellbursts. There must be eighty-plus aircraft. They meant business all right.

He saw another Swordfish land gracelessly on the flight deck, to be manhandled immediately to the parking area beyond the safety net. Some of the mechanics were looking over their shoulders at the shellbursts as they ran to refuel the returning aircraft, and each was probably thinking of the proximity of all that high-octane.

Growler's own Bofors guns were shooting now, blowing smoke-rings above the walkways and lowered aerials, while their crews watched the oncoming attack. The enemy was well out of range of the automatic weapons, but *Growler*'s gunnery officer was taking no chances of misfires when the time came.

A petty officer called to Rowan, 'The cap'n for you, sir.'

Rowan took the handset, following a thin smoke trail down and down until an aircraft hit the sea with a flash.

The other rating reported, 'That was *Spartiate*'s seaplane, sir.'

Kitto nodded. 'Hard luck. The pilot at least gave us some time to prepare.'

Rowan listened to the captain's voice in his ear. Unhurried but sparing in words.

'You know the score, Tim. I've got two fighters fuelling up now, and the A.E.O. reports that the unserviceable one is about ready to fly again. If we're to have any chance at all, I need experienced pilots up there. I want Kitto to take that fighter. Can you do his job?'

'Yes.' Just like that. With half the fighters gone already and the sky full of Jap aircraft, he would not have much to do for long. 'I can manage, sir.'

'Good. Tell him for me.' Buchan paused. 'Damn glad you got back. I hear the raid was a success.'

Kitto received the news with what could have been mistaken for relief. 'Thank Christ for that.' He handed Rowan the microphone and glanced at his petty officer. 'He'll see you all right if you feel like passing out.'

They all jumped as the barrage opened up in earnest. Heavy armament, Bofors and Oerlikons, and then the clattering bridge machine guns. It was ear-shattering.

'*Leader* to *Control*. Permission to take-off.' Bill's voice.

'Affirmative. Watch it, Bill.'

Then the fighter was streaking along the deck and lifting away like a comet.

Creswell followed in minutes, his fighter still smoking from some earlier damage.

Kitto went last, his Seafire strangely clean and bright after its rest in the hangar.

'Come on, *Hustler*!' The petty officer was steadying his glasses on the other carrier. 'Let's get moving, shall we?'

Rowan felt his skin cringing as if under a cold shower. Shock was setting in, and it was all he could do to stop his teeth from chattering.

A stick of bombs fell between a destroyer and the frigate *Woodlark*. The last in the line hit the *Woodlark* a glancing blow on the quarterdeck and exploded in her wake. The frigate went out of control, one screw gone, and the other almost torn from its shaft.

More bombs were falling ahead and around the French cruiser, but there was no let-up in her reply, even when one bomb made a direct hit just abaft her bridge. Smoke and wreckage were hurled everywhere, and Rowan saw a man lifted from a gun and flung fifty feet into the wash.

The gunnery speakers kept up their constant instructions. Aircraft were attacking from ahead and from either quarter, some flying with total disregard of the barrage and the danger of collision with their own comrades as they dropped their bombs and raked the ships with machine-gun fire.

A twin-engined bomber hit the sea and planed along the bow wave of a destroyer before lifting its tail and sinking from view. Two more fell to the criss-crossing tracer and cannon shells, and another lunged out of the sky like a burning torch.

A destroyer on the wing of the group had two hits in minutes and began to settle down, her people cutting free the rafts and floats and cowering in the bombardment.

Rowan listened to Bill's voice and those of the pilots who were at last joining him from *Hustler*.

'Watch it, Frank!'

Brrrrrrrrrrrrrr. Brrrrrrrrrrrrrr.

Their voices faded and boomed through the barrage like lost souls in bedlam.

'Here comes another!' A lookout trained his glasses and

snapped on his intercom. 'Single aircraft at Green four-five!'

A small fighter-bomber was flying on a straight course diagonally to the ships' line of advance. Gun crews, realising the aircraft was unsupported, concentrated their defences, and soon the air around the Zero was black with shellbursts and tracer.

'Got him!'

Rowan watched the Zero stagger and a large portion of wing spiral away to the sea. But the pilot did not bale out, nor did he alter course by one degree, despite the growing cone of fire being directed into him.

Rowan followed him round with his glasses, propping himself against the screen to take the weight off his strapped leg.

The Japanese pilot was passing astern now, would he soon hit the—?

Something solid moved into his lens. It was *Hustler*'s flight deck, and he could see the parked Swordfish by her round-down preparing to take-off, though God alone knew what they could do.

He shouted harshly, *'Tell the bridge!* That Zero is going to crash-land on *Hustler*!'

The detonation, when it came, was muffled. The Zero hit the wooden flight deck and exploded as it tore through like a rocket. The impact rolled across the water and hit *Growler* with the force of a typhoon.

Everyone was yelling at once, and horrified. Rowan saw a wall of flame bursting up through *Hustler*'s deck, the smoke being forced from her hull and gun sponsons by more internal explosions.

'Aircraft bearing Green nine-oh! Angle of sight four-five!'

Rowan snapped, 'Hello, Bill, this is Jonah. Bandit attacking us from starboard beam. See if you can get him.'

He saw the familiar Seafire plunging through smoke from a sinking destroyer and gunfire as Bill went into a power dive.

There was no mistaking the newcomer's intention. He was going to crash on *Growler. A human bomb.*

The gunnery officer was well aware of the danger, and every weapon which would bear, plus those from the two nearest escorts, were hosing the air between plane and ship with rapid fire.

Rowan licked his lips, seeing his friend come hurtling towards the ships. He had seen him do it so often, with the ease of a lifelong professional.

He watched the guns glitter along the Seafire's wings, the fragments ripping from the brightly painted Zero before it exploded with a tremendous bang, making tiny feathers of spray over a quarter of a mile apart.

Bill pulled out of his dive and thundered over Chadwick's flag, shouting, 'There's another bastard coming for you, Tim!'

The other Zero had plunged through the smoke between two frigates as if it were crashing, then with engine whining in protest pulled round the French cruiser's stern almost at sea-level, and even now was lifting up and towards *Growler*'s port bow.

Creswell was yelling on the intercom, *'Got you, mate!'* Then he screamed, and seconds later his fighter hit the water and broke up.

Rowan could feel the helm going over, the great effort of screw and rudder as Buchan tried to work his ship out of danger.

The Japanese pilot was either wounded or had lost control, for at the last second he pulled out of the dive, staggered in mid-air through a burst of machine-gun fire and fell within yards of Jonah Too's remains.

The explosion was more feeling than sound. There was no daylight, and Rowan's lungs were too scorched for him to breathe. He rubbed his streaming eyes and stared dazedly at the forward flight deck. *He should not be able to see it*. He was lying on his chest, his ears ringing, but he *could* see it.

Understanding returned reluctantly with his hearing. The front of his steel platform had been blasted away. How he had survived was nothing less than a miracle. The P.O., the communications team and even the lookout had vanished, sucked or blown outboard by the blast. Their deaths were marked only by dangling and severed wires and blood over everything.

Voices were shouting and screaming from every angle, and when he dragged himself to the shattered screen he saw the tail of the Zero at the opposite end of the flight deck, and three Swordfish, either completely wrecked or upended in the walkway. Below the bridge was a crater big enough for a bus.

But there were men already struggling through the belching smoke with hoses and extinguishers, and more stooping figures were running towards the wrecked aircraft where an officer was trying to pull himself from his cockpit, one arm ripped from his body.

Rowan wanted to vomit. He knew it was the big Dutchman, van Roijen, could almost hear him talking about his family, proudly showing his photographs.

He felt a seaman dragging at his shoulders.

'Easy! I'm not dead yet!'

Then he realised the man was almost crazy with terror and pain. It was a bosun's mate from the bridge staff.

'They're all dead up top, sir!' He cringed down as a great explosion shook the hull. 'I can't find anyone!'

'Help me!' Rowan saw the wretched uncertainty on the man's face. *'Now!'*

Together, while splinters clanged against hull and bridge, and the air was blasted by shells and bombs alike, they struggled to the upper bridge. Handrails were twisted like coils, and an Oerlikon gunner hung in his harness, his face contorted at the moment of impact.

The bridge was a scene of horror. Dead bodies, pieces of men were scattered amongst buckled voicepipes and shattered equipment.

Rowan dragged his leg through glass and torn clothing, clinging to the bosun's mate, guiding him towards the forepart of the bridge, which was hanging open like a jagged door.

He saw Lieutenant Bray staring at him, his eyes very bright in the smoky sunlight. But he was dead, as were the men around him, and the admiral's steward, Dundas, who had been hurled against the unyielding steel, his head stove in like an eggshell.

Rowan reached the captain's chair and held on to it. It was solidly made, but now leaned sideways like reeds in a wind. Underneath it, Buchan was regarding him with glazed eyes. But he was breathing.

Rowan gasped, 'Let's get him up!'

But Buchan said in an almost normal voice. 'No. Back's broken. That bloody chair.' The pain was coming now, making his eyes mist over. 'Get Jolly up here. Watch for *Hustler*!'

Rowan held on to the buckled chair as an explosion echoed through the lower hull. *The ship was out of control.*

He looked at the bosun's mate. 'Call the commander.' He gestured to the telephone rack. 'Do what you can!' If he let the terrified seaman off the bridge he'd not see him again.

A figure lurched upright between an upended flag locker and a gaping corpse. It was Chadwick. Rowan had imagined him to be in the Operations Room. Nobody down there could have survived, he thought. The Zero must have exploded right amongst them. James, Broderick, even Syms, the Met. Officer, would have been at his action station there.

Chadwick wheezed, 'Never mind Jolly. He'll have his hands full below, if he's still alive.' He stared at his steward's corpse and said, 'He'll never get that job now.'

Then his arm shot out and pointed through the shattered screen.

'God! Look at *Hustler*!'

The other carrier was heeling right over, her aircraft falling alongside like broken toys, while the flames explored the hull and lit each loading port and gun sponson with sparks and fire. Ammunition was exploding, and burning fuel ran down her side like molten lava.

Rowan exclaimed tightly, 'We'll be into her in a moment!'

Chadwick nodded. 'Take the con. You always said you were once a watchkeeper in a destroyer!' He grinned, the effort bringing agony to his face like a mask.

Rowan almost fell on the voicepipes as another bomb exploded on the opposite beam and hurled pieces of metal and aircraft high over the bridge. He should have realised. Chadwick had been badly hit. There was blood on his legs and

288

spreading on the deck by his feet. It was taking all his strength to appear in control.

'Bridge—wheelhouse!' Rowan ducked as more oddments from the radar position rolled over the chart house and down to the deck below.

'Wheelhouse, sir!'

It was the coxswain's voice, which was reassuring.

'*Starboard ten!*' He crouched over the gyro repeater and wiped the face free of blood and dust. He tried to avoid Bray's unwinking stare as he watched the quietly ticking compass.

'Midships. Steer one-five-zero.' Thank God, the helm was still responding.

Chadwick groped for his glasses and let them fall to his chest again. He was staring at the other carrier, at the crackling flames which were consuming her insides from bow to stern.

'Course one-five-zero.'

A sick berth attendant and men with stretchers clattered through the smoke and stood appalled by the entrance.

Rowan said, 'See to the captain. He's by the chair.'

To Chadwick he added, 'What about you, sir?'

The S.B.A. stood up. 'He's dead, sir.'

Rowan looked down at Buchan's face. 'I didn't know.'

'Well then.' Chadwick pulled out a silver hip flask. 'That answers your question, Mr Rowan. *I'll stay here.*'

He lurched against the voicepipes again as a new pattern of bombs came thundering across the zigzagging ships. Some had obviously hit their targets, the bomb-aimers taking full advantage of the suicide attacks earlier.

Then he said thickly, '*Kamikaze* they call themselves. The Divine Wind. According to that fool James they've already done for two American carriers the other day.' He groaned, but took a long swallow from the flask. 'Now. Get the bosun's mate to find Jolly. Tell him I want to fly-on all the group's aircraft while there's still a deck left.'

Two more ratings had arrived and were huddled by the rearmost telephones.

Rowan looked at them. 'Get the most senior pilot you can find. Lieutenant Commander Dexter is still on board.'

But Dexter was dead too, and the task of guiding the surviving aircraft from *Hustler* and *Growler* to the remaining length of flight deck fell to Bats making hand signals, assisted by a youthful telegraphist using an Aldis lamp.

Chadwick watched in silence as his command continued to fight back. If he was dying on his feet he showed no sign of leaving the bridge until the attack was finished. One way or the other.

'Only one Seafire has survived from our squadron, sir.'

Rowan looked at the messenger, afraid to ask, and unable to see for himself which one had managed to land-on.

Chadwick was nearer the side, and said vaguely, 'It's your ball-kicking friend.' He shook his head wearily, 'Kitto must have bought it. Very good. For an amateur.'

The Japanese bombers made three more attacks, losing two of their number and sinking another Australian destroyer which had already been damaged.

Down the embattled ships the barrage eased, and men stood back amidst empty shell cases and dead comrades.

Chadwick said very slowly, 'I'll not give her a divorce, you know.'

Rowan pulled himself round, unable to grasp that Chadwick could speak like this when the enemy might attack again at any moment.

He answered quietly, 'This group could have been wiped off the face of the sea. We've lost so many good men in the past two hours that victory or defeat will never come into it. Do what you like. Say what you will. But I'd never let her come back to a man like you. You'd destroy her just like everyone else.'

'Aircraft bearing Red three-oh!' One of the bridge speakers had come back to life.

Then with a break in his voice the unknown man said, 'Disregard! These are friendly aircraft!'

Feet scraped through the broken glass, and Commander Jolly, as neat as ever in spite of the filth on his arms and legs, entered the bridge.

'Fire out. Bulkheads shored up. Wounded taken below. Communications in process of being restored.' He saw the captain's body and looked at Rowan with astonishment. 'I was told it was bad, but I thought he was still driving *Growler*.' He covered Buchan with a bridge coat. 'I could never imagine him dying.'

Chadwick turned his head as Bill appeared with some more spare seamen.

Rowan tried to smile, but was shaking so badly he had to hold on to the gyro with both hands.

'Hello, Bill.'

Bill grinned, and then froze as he saw the carnage around him.

They all looked up as aircraft roared low overhead. When somebody could find a receiver which still worked they would no doubt be told who had come to the rescue. Not that they cared.

Jolly said, 'You'd better help Tim below. I'll take over now.'

Chadwick rasped, 'You'll take over *nothing*!' He stepped away from the side and the silver flask fell unheeded by his blood. 'I made this group what it is. *I* and nobody else had the imagination and the know-how—' He gave a terrible cry and fell heavily on to his side.

Bill said, 'I'll get Minchin.'

Jolly shook his head. 'No. I've seen enough dead men today. This is just one more.'

'Signal from *Spartiate*, sir.' The rating kept his eyes half closed as if to protect himself from the sights which awaited his entry. 'Repeated from the new air escort.' He held the pad to a bright shaft of sunlight which came through a fist-sized hole in the plating. Probably the one which had brought Chadwick's last moments. 'Can supply limited air cover until arrival of inshore squadron tonight. Have you ability to fly-off any aircraft yourself?'

Jolly looked from Rowan to Bill. 'Well? That's what I shall have to ask you two. There's nobody else *to* ask.'

Rowan felt some of the tension and shock smoothing away. Like a ripple on water left by low-flying aircraft.

'Affirmative.' He looked down at Buchan's body. 'It's what he would have said.'

Jolly nodded, studying Rowan's face as if expecting to find the answer to something.

In his clipped, precise tone he said, 'Make to *Spartiate*, repeated to air escort. We are pleased to have you with us. But normal service will be resumed as soon as possible.'

Bill put his arm round Rowan's shoulders and helped him out on to what was left of the flying bridge.

Bill's Seafire and a solitary Swordfish were already ranged on the flight deck.

Bill said softly, 'Normal service indeed!'

Rowan did not answer, and was looking at the other ships, what there were of them. The cruiser, still smoking from her bomb damage. A destroyer towing a frigate, another frigate so low in the sea she looked more like a surfacing submarine. The rest, though few in numbers now, seemed untouched. But *Hustler* was gone, and *Growler*, from the look of her damage, would not be at sea again for a long, long while.

He touched the bent steel, recalling all the faces, and Buchan's pride. Even his last words had been a warning to Rowan to protect his ship from collision with the sinking carrier.

Overhead, the long-range aircraft which had come to look for them maintained a watchful patrol. Rowan thought of his own last flight. Back to base. To *Growler*. He ran his palm over the torn metal again.

Growler had been good to him when he had most needed her. As he looked at all the damage and extinguished fires along her stocky hull he was suddenly grateful that he had been aboard when she had needed him.

Epilogue

It was halfway through the forenoon on a cold March day in 1945 when H.M. Escort Carrier *Growler* entered Rosyth with a small group of watchful tugs and made fast to her pier.

For many of her company it was a very moving moment, as lined on the scarred flight deck, or standing at their allotted stations throughout the ship, they watched the buildings and ships gliding past, the crisp stillness only broken by the occasional trill of calls as the ships made their salutes and returned them.

And for others it was something of a mystery. Unknown to themselves, they were not merely replacements for the many who had died or been badly wounded five months earlier just south of Sumatra. They were standing-in for those same men as *Growler* came home.

To the dockyard men and tug skippers she was just one more responsibility in a port and dockyard which had become conditioned to such matters. But the tugs gave her a hoot or two, and from the jetty a small crowd of onlookers who waited to meet the ship waved and called, their voices still lost in distance.

Rowan stood on the bridge, his glasses scanning the upturned faces as the first heaving lines went ashore. Mostly officials and a few privileged relatives. He saw a pilot he had first met aboard when he had joined *Growler*. That was two years ago. It did not seem so long now. The pilot had been promoted and sent to another ship. But he had heard *Growler* was coming back and had been waiting with the others to see her dock.

Rowan glanced at the crude welding and fresh paint which scarcely hid the damage she had received in the last battle. Poor, beat-up old girl, yet she had meant that much to the pilot on the jetty, whose name he could not remember.

He saw Bill standing at the head of the air crews and handling parties on the flight deck, his hand to the peak of his cap. How different they all looked. The seamen and stokers, the mechanics. No longer in greasy overalls or scuffed flying jackets. They stood in swaying lines, a blue collar ruffling here and there along each rank, and further down the deck, their much-used aircraft, although there were few of them.

'Ring off main engine.'

Rowan looked at the captain. He was quite a different man from Buchan. Jolly had been flown off to another ship of his own. There were not many faces up here who had seen the bombers and the blazing carrier.

He lifted the glasses again. There were others on the jetty who had no cause to be here today. A frail little woman in a black coat with a glittering naval crown on the collar. Mrs Buchan. Trying perhaps to share all she had left. A tall, plain-looking girl who turned away even as he picked her up in the lens. James's widow. She had been allowed in the dockyard at last.

Rowan had not expected to see Honor here. He had told himself over and over again. He had written to her from Australia, where *Growler* had been bustled from dock to dock, and nobody seemed to have an inclination to complete the repairs. Honor had replied while the ship had been in Sydney. Thanking him for writing, and for describing as simply as he could her husband's death.

After that, the ship had been moved again and again. The war was hotting up, and victory was no longer a mere bit of fantasy. The Allies were through Germany, and total surrender there was anticipated in weeks. It did not seem real. And in the Pacific, where *Growler* and her consorts had played their small part in the whole, events were also moving fast, and most of the Japanese-held areas had been taken.

It was no wonder that *Growler*'s problems excited little interest in dockyard superintendents.

Rowan had got two other letters from her, forwarded on to the South African base at Simonstown where they had been forced to stop with major engine failure. But she had told him little. The letters had been warm, but lacking the promise he had been hoping for.

He lowered the binoculars as the ship's company fell out and the work of securing brows and fenders got under way.

The captain was speaking with the harbour master and the pilot. The signalmen were rolling up flags, the new navigation officer was rubbing pencilled lines off a chart.

Rowan had not expected to see her. But the disappointment was real enough. As raw as a wound.

He left the bridge and went down the ladders to watch the busy jetty alongside. They would all be ashore soon. Then new ships, new faces, while they waited for the Pacific War to end. Even Bill would be off within an hour. He had heard from Magda. She was free to marry him.

He felt Bill's heavy tread on the rough metal and heard him ask bluntly, 'Why don't you ring her?'

Rowan looked at him, trying to hide his feelings. 'She's probably only just getting over it. Trying to pick up the threads again.'

Bill took his arm and turned him round towards the pier. 'Are you more afraid of being snubbed than of losing her?' He added gently, 'She's probably thinking the same about you. That if she tries to make contact, you'll feel an obligation, love or no love.'

Rowan did not look at his friend. 'You're right, of course.' He walked towards the quartermaster's lobby. 'I'll see if there's a shore line yet.'

There was, but it took an age before the call was cleared and switched through several different exchanges.

When she spoke, it was as if she was here. In the ship. 'Hello? Who is that?'

'Tim. You remember when I last wrote I said—' He broke off, hearing her quick intake of breath and what sounded like a sob.

'Oh, Tim! My *darling Tim!* I was afraid. I thought . . .'

Rowan gripped the telephone, wanting to hold her, to stop her crying. He knew Bill, the quartermaster and several seamen were watching him, but he did not care.

'I want you. I'm coming for you. I shall be with you tonight if I have to steal the transport!'

She was very quiet now, and he could hear her breathing.

He continued, 'After that I just want to be happy. Together.'

She said, 'I'll meet you at the station. I don't care what time you get here. I'll be waiting. Oh, Tim, I'm so happy.'

Bill watched his face and smiled thankfully. They were so right for each other, and yet had been held apart by their selfsame sense of consideration.

He watched him replace the telephone and asked, 'All fixed, old son?'

Rowan nodded, and looked up at the empty island. 'Better than that. I'm going to her right away. *Now.*'

Bill breathed out slowly. 'I'll see you over the side myself.'

Later they stood at the top of the brow, beneath which a taxi waited with its engine ticking over.

Rowan hesitated, his eyes moving over *Growler*'s scarred hull. Then he raised his hand in salute and walked down towards the land. To a future.